My Bloody Valentine

ALASTAIR GUNN

PENGUIN BOOKS

PENGUIN BOOKS

UK | USA | Canada | Ireland | Australia
India | New Zealand | South Africa

Penguin Books is part of the Penguin Random House group of companies
whose addresses can be found at global.penguinrandomhouse.com.

First published 2015
001

Set in 12.5/14.75 pt Garamond MT Std
Typeset by Jouve (UK), Milton Keynes
Printed in Great Britain by Clays Ltd, St Ives plc

A CIP catalogue record for this book is available from the British Library

ISBN: 978-1-405-91446-8

www.greenpenguin.co.uk

MIX
Paper from
responsible sources
FSC® C018179

Penguin Random House is committed to a
sustainable future for our business, our readers
and our planet. This book is made from Forest
Stewardship Council® certified paper.

For Anna

Acknowledgements

As somebody still overwhelmed to be writing the acknowledgements for his second published title, I must thank the following people. Eternal gratitude to Rowland White and his team at Penguin, and to my agents, Caroline and Joanna at Hardman & Swainson, for working collectively behind the scenes to make this incredible experience a reality. Heartfelt thanks also to my family, friends and colleagues for their continued encouragement, feedback and support. And, of course, to Anna, who still amazes me every day with her insight and strength. Writing a novel requires an innate compulsion to commit thought to page, but every writer needs a reason do what they do, and you are my reason. Here's to the next story.

True devotion is deadly

Prologue

They taught you stealth; that was one good thing about them.

Maybe the only *good thing*.

Bull didn't have to think about it as he reached the end of the alley and stopped in deep shadow, looking at the Tandoori restaurant out on the main street. His feet didn't make any noise, because they'd trained him to move silently, no matter what sort of terrain he was on, or what kind of shoes he wore.

He sniffed the black air. It was dry and cold, but he couldn't tell whether the smell of burning was real or just a memory. The permanent ringing in his ears confused everything, blurring the differences between now and back then.

He checked his watch.

Almost time.

Footsteps, left, two people, ten yards. Bull reacted, reaching into his jacket. By the time the couple passed he'd lit up and was facing the wall, smoking, swaying, taking a leak. Nothing to see.

He waited for them to pass and gave it a few more seconds before he turned back, glancing up at the camera above him; it was pointing down the road to his right. There was no way it could see him; it couldn't look straight down, and the next two cameras were in the wrong places to zero him, too. Motors whirred as the camera turned, and he imagined some unwashed civvy operator in a poky control room, chomping a burger and zooming in on drunk teenage girls as they fell out of the pubs.

He sank further into the darkness as the door across the road opened, right on schedule.

And there she was.

Rosa stepped on to the pavement; timid, alone, her fragile neck wrapped in a scarf, her bag clamped tight to her side. He watched her face in the darkness, seeing the usual signs. The bowed shoulders; the empty eyes . . .

Part of him strained towards her, nearly making him step into view, but it was a distant part, buried by years of torture and pain. He held back. Showing himself now wouldn't help either of them; it was way too late for any of that. There was no room for compassion.

Or sympathy.

Rosa zipped her jacket and crossed the road in front of him, heading north towards the junction, not even glancing his way. Bull didn't follow; there was no need. He knew exactly where she would go.

She'd followed the same pattern every week since coming here, to this new town; her new life. Finish work at eleven, tidy up and leave the restaurant by quarter to twelve. Wander along the high street, turn at the bank on the corner and take the short route home, behind the Palace Exchange, through the dark, deserted paths.

Where Bull would strike.

He watched her trudge away up the high street. Was she walking even more slowly than normal? Pity flared again, but he forced it down. It was nothing, just nerves, caused by what he was about to do. But that didn't make it wrong.

He approached the shadow's edge, seeking a better view. Thirty yards ahead, Rosa had reached the bus stop at the end of the road. But just as Bull expected her to disappear around the next corner, she did something unexpected.

She stopped and looked back.

Bull shot sideways, losing sight of her as he slid behind the wall. *Had she seen him?* He wanted to look again, but what if she was watching, waiting for him?

A bus thundered past, the noise and fumes making him jump. His hands flew to his face, clawing at the dust blown into his eyes. He heard someone shout in the distance.

It isn't real.

Bull lowered his hands, annoyed; renewed his concentration. He leaned around the corner and looked up the street. Rosa was still there, standing right where she'd been, not looking down the street towards him any more. But then he realized why she was there: she was waiting for the bus that had just passed him and was now pulling into the stop.

She was going off plan.

He almost started forwards, only just remembering the cameras and stopping himself in time. The police weren't looking for him yet, but they would be soon.

He couldn't follow.

Rosa got on the bus, its doors closing behind her, and Bull swore as it pulled away, realizing this would cost him another week. She only worked here Fridays, on top of her day job in a sports outlet in the nearby retail park. *This* was his chance, and she was getting away.

But as the bus turned right at the end of the street, he noticed the number on its rear display.

121.

Straight off, Bull knew what to do. He turned and headed back along the alleyway, into the dark. Rosa had caught that bus once before, a couple of weeks ago. She'd been lugging some heavy baggage, and had probably caught it to save her skinny legs. Bull hadn't pursued her directly – it was always best to keep some distance – but he had waited for the next 121. He'd soon found out where she'd gone, because the bus followed the one-way system until two stops later, when it pulled up on Cecil Road, opposite Sydney Road.

Where she now lived.

Tonight she was tired or unwell, so she'd caught the bus straight home. It fucked up Bull's plan, but he could deal with that. He just had to adapt before he lost focus.

Because he needed to get this done.

If he was quick, he could cut through the paths and head her off. It was risky: hitting her between rows of houses rather than in a quiet alleyway. But the first hundred feet of Sydney Road were unlit, and mostly deserted at this time of night.

Bull picked up his pace, careful not to let himself sprint. His bad leg was already giving him shit, and there was no point getting there in time only to give his position away by breathing too hard.

He reached the corner and turned left, leaving behind the last traces of yellow light from the street, glad of the half-moon's glow. The alley was narrow, wire fences either side holding back thick bushes and trees that hung above his head. He ran surrounded by darkness, so caught up in planning his first strike that he forgot all about the shopping trolley.

The mesh obstacle leapt out of the shadows just inches in front. He'd passed it earlier on, had shoved it against the fence. But it still filled half the path.

Bull jumped mid-stride, trying to avoid it. But his foot caught the metal edge and he fell, tumbling sideways. Wet leaves exploded around his face, and the heels of his hands ground painfully across the concrete as he slid to a halt.

He scrambled back up and kept moving, brushing the gravel off his palms, ignoring his clothes. The fall would have put him behind, and he still couldn't see the far end of the path. Pain ripped at his bad leg: stress on bones that were meant to be supported by muscle. He blocked it out and ran faster, clenching his teeth, feeling something grind between them. He raised a hand to his face. It was on his lips, in his mouth. From the fall.

Grit.

He coughed and spat. That shit was everywhere, carried in the air by the wind. He pulled up his collar and held it across his face. If that stuff got into your teeth, you were chewing it for days.

You're losing focus.

He banged a hand against the side of his head.

Suddenly, he saw the end of the alley. The patch of light grew as he ran, pushing the memories away. He reached the street and stopped, just inside the entrance to the pathway, trying to bring his heart rate down. Opposite him, the shop fronts flanking the bus stop.

The *empty* bus stop.

Bull stepped forward just enough to see the end of Sydney Road. No sign of her. Either the bus had already gone and she was now too far ahead, or –

He turned as the sound of the engine reached him. The bus was approaching, the number 121 clearly lit above the driver. Bull waited while it pulled in, watching Rosa step out on to the pavement on the far side. The bus pulled away, leaving her at the stop, fiddling with her music player. After a moment, she found a track and set off.

6

Bull gave her a small head start then followed, crossing the now quiet street to where he could trail her from straight behind. They turned left into Sydney Road, and Bull started closing the gap as they reached the unlit sector. The street was run-down, covered in graffiti and lined with busted cars, but he still had to make the most of the dark. A hundred yards in, brick walls and windowless buildings were replaced by a pay-and-display car park, where the light was much better. And just beyond that was the scruffy house his target shared with a few other girls.

It had to be now.

Bull closed in, glancing around for other people, reaching into his jacket for the weapon. He pulled out the hammer and raised it. Rosa didn't look round, and he wondered what sort of music she'd chosen to listen to in her final moments.

He caught her up.

And the hammer swung.

PART ONE

I

Samantha Philips entered the room, ushered in by a stern-looking older woman who poked her head in to make sure her consignment wasn't alone before retreating.

'Hello, Samantha,' he said as she stopped just inside. 'My name is Pierce Reid. I'm a counsellor.'

Philips didn't respond. Instead, she scanned the space around her, moving just her eyes, but not in the nervous manner often demonstrated by others. Her expression was more of cold assessment. Distant recall.

It wasn't surprising; she probably hadn't seen anything *approaching* luxury for the last six years, and this would certainly be the first time she'd visited the boardroom, with its scented dried flowers and carpet.

In truth, he'd expected a little more reverence. Visitors to parole prep sessions like this were never warned. An early alarm call preceded the ominous march to this comparatively opulent room, accompanied by an unfamiliar guard. Usually that combination helped to lower the subject's defences, briefly at least. A seasoned inmate's reaction to the room often revealed more about her desire to re-join society than anything she might say afterwards. The reason he used it.

He motioned to one of the soft leather chairs. 'Would you like to sit down?'

Philips looked at him for the first time, a fleeting, emotionless flick, then away. But still no reply. He could see the unnecessarily heavy-duty cuffs digging into her wrists, but she hadn't attempted to adjust them. Instead she continued scrutinizing the room, obviously aware of the camera lens trained on her from above.

'Stand if you prefer, but we may be here for a while if you're going to insist on communicating telepathically.'

Another flick. No smile.

He waited, studying the slim woman in prison-issue overalls. Sam was twenty-four, and feisty – according to her record, both before and since she'd earned herself twelve years inside, six of which she'd served. Remnants of a pretty girl peeked out from behind the scragged-back hair and jail-hardened façade, but their traces were further subdued by an emptiness in the eyes that he'd seen too many times.

The void left by rape.

'I heard about you.'

Reid only just caught her quiet, monotone words. He'd been expecting to play the one-way game for a while yet.

She was looking at him.

He cleared his throat, revising his position in the chair. 'Go on.'

'Few of the girls spoke to you before they left. Said you were all right.'

'That's interesting. Do you believe them?'

'Maybe.' Still no emotion, but with that Philips stepped around one of the chairs and sat, apparently unimpressed by its comfort. Reid watched her settle, cuffed hands coming to rest on her knees. He picked up the notepad and pen from the low table between them and positioned the pad on his crossed leg, turned up so that only he could see the page. He wrote 'Samantha Philips' on the top line.

'So, Samantha.' He looked up at her. 'The board has decided that, based on your behaviour and their psychological assessments, you pose no continuing danger to others. There will be conditions, of course, but having now served a reasonable term, you are eligible for immediate parole, which represents a substantial cut in your sentence. That is, of course, if I agree.'

It was barely perceptible, but he was experienced enough to see the question cross Philips' mind as realization broke.

Are you my way out of here?

He nodded, answering her unspoken query. 'My job is to make sure you want to return to normal life. That you're ready for, and capable of, reintegration.'

She looked away, to where a window might have been if they weren't in the bowels of Holloway Prison. Her first emotional response.

Then, softly:

'What do you want to know?'

2

'Please, Mrs Antonio,' the Indian doctor flapped as DCI Hawkins tried for a second time to slide off the hospital bed, 'it is *so* important that you take things just one step at a time.'

'It's Antoni*a*, and yes, you said. But I'm telling you; I can walk.'

'Oh dear.' Dr Badal backed away as Hawkins' feet made contact with the freezing floor and she rocked into an upright position. Then he shot forwards again as she almost doubled over.

'You see, Mrs Toni*a*, the upper abdominal muscles have not yet recuperated.'

She steadied herself on the mattress. 'Then get me some crutches.'

'I don't think that's a good –'

'*Now, please.*'

'Right.' The doctor retreated, palpably brimming with fear of malpractice.

Hawkins waited for him to leave before she sagged against the bed. The intense burning sensation in her chest and stomach said he was probably right: she hadn't recovered sufficiently from the near-fatal knife attack just six weeks ago to be standing up, let alone walking. Apparently, the network of muscles in her torso had been torn to shreds by the eleven stab wounds. And her subsequent fall – leading to several mashed ribs – hadn't helped.

But this place was driving her mad.

Projected recovery time from injuries like hers was more like a month. But, thanks to extra layers of complication provided by Sod's Law – in her case an MRSA infection contracted ten days after her operation – Hawkins had spent an extra two weeks in a private room, returning only once purged to the general ward. She was improving steadily, but whereas bacteria had failed to finish her off, psychosis brought on by this riling confinement still might.

Dr Badal buzzed back into the room holding a set of crutches, followed by a young nurse pushing an empty wheelchair. He just about stopped himself placing a hand on Hawkins' shoulder. 'I . . . understand your will to leave, really I do, but I must stress that a wheelchair would be a much better –'

'Thank you.' Hawkins took the crutches and began wrestling their supports around her forearms.

'Err . . .' The doctor squirmed. 'You have to appreciate your anatomy, Mrs . . . please. Your axilla will be extremely sensit–'. But his words were drowned out by Hawkins' scream as she rested her weight on the crutches and pain erupted in her armpits.

The nurse, obviously having been primed, appeared beside her as Hawkins dropped like an anvil into the wheelchair, crutches clattering to the floor.

'I did tell you, Mrs Antonio.' The doctor sounded genuinely sorry. 'But you are strongly willed.'

Hawkins glared at him, breathing hard. 'How long till I can leave?'

'You must try to understand that your injuries are severe. You nearly died. You're lucky.'

'How long?'

'You are making good progress. I think that, given –'

He stopped as the glare intensified, his shoulders sagging. 'You can self-discharge at any time; I can't prevent you. Sign a waiver and you can leave. But I highly recommend you remain here in hospital for at least one more week, giving your body time to recover.'

Dr Badal visibly shrank as Hawkins' expression developed into the full Anne Robinson. Even the nurse leaned back.

'Fine,' she said at last. 'I'll stay.'

'I think you are making the right choice, Mrs . . . really. I will come back later to check on you. Or . . . it may actually be my colleague.'

He withdrew, leaving the nurse to assist Hawkins out of the wheelchair and back into bed. She began untangling the catheter.

'You're not putting that godforsaken thing back in,' Hawkins growled. 'Leave the chair.'

3

Half an hour after Hawkins' aborted attempt to use crutches, her armpits stopped ringing. She'd spent the intervening time watching the cup of tea provided by the nurse go cold, regretting her acquiescence. She pictured her office gathering dust. And her inbox, which would already be arranging emails into creaking monthly folders.

And what of the criminal backlog? Surely there were illegal acts going unpunished because she was in here. Or worse, if her team were able to maintain operations without her, there'd be no point in her going back at all. She groaned and looked out of the window.

The house would be spotless, of course. Her mum had always been a clean freak. MRSA hadn't taken off until the nineties, probably not because of increasing resistance to antibiotics but because that was when Christine Hawkins retired from the NHS.

Hospital was a maddening experience, especially after two weeks of bedridden near-solitude. Her arse was permanently numb, and for someone who usually curtailed family contact after thirty minutes, visiting hour was purgatory. Her dad; fine. Mike or her friends;

great. But her mother and sister, *together*, for three thousand six hundred seconds? Never again.

She needed to speak to Maguire.

Hawkins leaned across, trying to block out shrieking abdominal muscles, and retrieved her mobile from the bedside drawer.

She selected his number, which rang. And rang.

She ended her call and checked the time: 9 a.m. Her detective inspector, and sporadic boyfriend, was probably still in the morning briefing. Their on–off relationship had started two years ago as an illicit affair behind the back of Hawkins' then fiancé, bounced along between amorous and torrid extremes, and ended when Hawkins had confessed everything to the man who then quickly became her ex. Meanwhile, Maguire was redeployed to Manchester, leading to a six-month hiatus. His return, less than two months ago, had precipitated similarly intense events. Together they had tracked down a dangerous psychopath, fallen in, out, and back in love again, and almost simultaneously saved each other's lives.

She imagined him in the briefing, a tall, black American smiling atop a sea of pasty-faced Brits never short of something to criticize. Mike said the session had overrun every week since the new chief super's introduction of his One-force Ambition Talk, or the 'One-stop Bitching Shop', as it had immediately become known: a 'clarification and efficiency chat' nailed on to the end of the daily meeting. Maybe hospital wasn't that bad after all.

Her phone rang.

She answered, happy to hear Mike's US accent. 'Toni. My cell was on mute. What's up?'

'I wanted to hear your voice,' she lied. 'How's work?'

He snorted. 'Just got out of *the shop*. Geez, you Brits complain. Look, sorry I didn't drop by last night, but I got a great excuse. We were in Craven Park, looking for the gang members who killed that student last month, when who should turn up but your favourite paedophile?'

'You got *Clarke*? What happened?'

'Long story, tell you later. How're you feeling?'

'Shocking. Distract me. What else is going on?'

'Err, not much. Ran into your mom today at the house. Have you guys still not found her sense of humour?'

Something was wrong; he knew to exhaust work news before family got a look in.

'Don't lie to me, Maguire. What's up?'

'It's nothing, just a rumour. Not even worth –'

'Tell me.'

'Ah, hell Toni, it's just talk.' He sighed. 'Whatever. I heard they're bringing in some hot-shit graduate to cover your role . . .'

Hawkins didn't speak.

'Just till you're back.'

'Jesus.' She eyed the crutches, taunting her from beside the door. 'It won't be just *till I'm back*, though, will it? You know how these things work. He'll be the chief's protégé; the guy Vaughn's had his eye on for a top job; the one he's been waiting to promote. And I just vacated the perfect rung, didn't I? Once graduate boy's feet are up on my desk, I'll be moved out quicker than the last Mrs Cruise.'

'It won't happen. That job's yours.'

'Bollocks. Come and get me.'

'You're still sick.'

'I'm coming back to work, it's the only way.'

'Not on this train.' He hung up.

'You're joking.' She stared at the phone, then at the wheelchair. Then she scrolled down and selected another number, waiting for the answer before she spoke.

'Dad? It's me.'

4

The two men passed through the deepest patch of darkness on Chambord Street. A bony cat crossed the road in front of them, darting through the railings into the small park area beyond, when one of the men launched an empty beer can at it.

'Fuckin' pussy!' he shouted as the cat fled, the can clanking along the pavement where it had been, and both of them burst out laughing. The cat shot under the nearest park bench and stopped, watching the men as they continued along the pavement, eventually disappearing from view.

Confident it was now safe to move on, the cat slid from its hiding place and started crossing the tatty grass towards the swings, stopping briefly to look back before rounding the corner. It seemed completely unaware of the homeless drunk huddled in the darkness under a damp cardboard duvet on the next bench.

Except there was no homeless drunk.

Bull sat under the broken streetlight, invisible.

Hunting.

From his covert position, he had a perfect view of the flats. The entire block was a toilet, that much was obvious, but there was something else, something weird about the whole area. There were no kids hanging out on the corners, no hookers, no dealers with dogs. But it went deeper than that. There was no buzzing sense of danger, like you usually got in this kind of low-grade shithole. Maybe that was it: the place had nothing left worth fighting over?

It had given up.

He scanned the buildings for signs of life. Nothing. But that was no surprise. People here didn't want to see or be seen. Every window was either shielded by thick curtains or unlit. Bull had seen no more than a few locals since arriving an hour ago and those he *had* seen slunk away fast.

Suddenly there was movement, next to the battered Toyota parked across the road.

The man was back.

Bull hunkered low on the bench, careful not to draw attention. There was no panic, though; the guy was a prune, a scruffy-haired thumbsucker with suede shoes and a cheap coat. He was slim, maybe younger than Bull, but no threat.

The man heaved another box from the car boot, balancing it between his leg and the bumper while he reached up to shut the tailgate. He pulled it down sharply, yelping as it wrenched his fingers, swearing when he dropped his keys. He bent awkwardly, groping for them.

Then he locked the car and trudged back towards the flats, into the central staircase and up to the second

floor of the seven-storey bughouse, where the authorities probably dumped all their scum. It was his third
journey, so there couldn't be many more boxes left. The
Toyota's boot wasn't that big.

The guy reached the door of number twenty-eight,
shoved it open with his foot, and went inside.

Ten minutes later he reappeared, but this time with
company. The two people trudged to the pavement and
stood talking by the car, although they were too far
away for Bull to hear what was being said.

He watched, straining to make out detail in the dim
light. She looked older, obviously, but there was no
question.

It was her.

Even from a distance he could tell she looked tired,
the face he knew so well lined with emotion and fatigue,
creases etched ever deeper by the passing years. But he
knew those feelings, too; shared every one with her.

That's why she needed to die.

It looked as though the guy was trying to cheer her
up, but he wasn't having much luck. She stared into the
distance as he rubbed her shoulders, and her arms hung
limp when he gave her a hug. Then he got into the Toyota and drove away, leaving her alone on the kerb. Bull
watched her standing under the streetlight. Was she
crying again?

He wouldn't have blamed her. Just being here was
excuse enough. The council might have paid for this
place, but now she was trapped by their rules, having to

wander down two flights of stairs in the middle of the night just for a fag. He'd seen the NO SMOKING sign on her front door. *How sick was that?*

A moment later she moved across to lean against the wall, lighting up.

He waited, recognizing her routine. The only times she'd left the flat since he'd begun watching her were to buy food or to smoke, and all her pre-midnight cigarettes had been doused where she now stood.

But things changed after that. Once the temperature dropped she'd appeared less often: once every few hours through the night, wearing a coat and scarf, shuffling round several circuits of the small park area while she smoked.

But this time he'd be ready. Not on the bench like the first night, when she'd surprised him by coming into the park and walking straight past. With no choice then, he'd ignored her. Luckily, she hadn't even glanced his way. And tonight he'd be further round the path, in the deeper shadows near the monument.

Twenty yards away she scratched out her cigarette against the wall, before dragging herself back up the stairs and along the balcony.

Then Bull watched as Samantha Philips opened her front door and slipped inside.

5

Hawkins jerked into consciousness, heart pounding. Blurred faces hung above her in the half-light, and immediately she was fighting the hands pinning her down, feeling the hot chill of sweat on her skin. Someone was talking.

'*All right, Antonia, just try to relax. You're okay. You're safe.*'

Suddenly, her right hand was free. It flew to her chest, frantically searching for the raw puncture marks.

Where the knife had gone in.

'*Miss Hawkins.*' Another voice. '*Try to calm down. You were dreaming. You've pulled out your drip.*'

Hawkins stopped searching and swallowed, senses thumping, looking from face to face at the nurses standing over her bed. Slowly, her dream began to fade, the dimly lit hospital ward coming back into focus around them, her heart beat beginning to slow. She took a few deep breaths, rubbing her left hand, where the drip had torn the skin on its way out.

'Better?' one of the nurses asked.

Hawkins nodded, sitting patiently while they moved the cannula to her forearm and put a plaster on her hand, reassuring them again that she was fine, accepting the offer of tea just to get rid of them. They retreated, leaving her exhausted but in peace, aside from her aching body and the pejorative stare of the old lady across the ward. She checked the time, sighing when she read 02:15.

Morning couldn't come fast enough.

6

He struck.

The hammer dug in, punching straight through her temple. Perfect aim. There was a dull pop but no scream, and for a second they both froze.

Then she dropped like her brain had switched off.

Bull stepped back, watching her crumple on the path. He glanced around to check if anyone had seen, but the gloomy park was empty; the road outside clear. He could disappear in the shadows and let the freezing rain begin washing her mistakes away.

But there was a noise.

Panic flared as Bull looked down. Somehow she'd survived, and was trying to drag herself away.

Had he made a mistake?

He went after her, noting the extensive blood loss and the way her legs hung limp. Death was certain now.

He caught up in a few strides and hit her again. She dropped face down, twitching, but he didn't stop, driving the hammer in time after time. Doing it right.

At last he stopped, shaking, his breathing ragged. She lay at his feet. Not moving.

Gone.

Bull steadied himself, tucked the hammer into his coat, and walked away.

7

'Whoops a daisy!' The old man lost hold of his daughter's wrist and she slumped into the passenger seat of his ice-gold Rover 75 estate. But his expression of mild amusement became one of admonition when he saw the resulting discomfort on her face.

'Antonia . . . are you *sure* the doctor said you're ready to go home?'

Hawkins looked out through the windscreen at Ealing Hospital and shuddered. 'Yes, Dad. Would the nurse have wheeled me to the door otherwise? Now, please get us out of here.'

She'd neglected to mention the self-discharge form she had signed before her father arrived, the one that said something like 'I understand I should stay in hospital, and I accept full responsibility for my own health, or lack thereof, as a result of my decision to leave.'

Her father made the short humming noise that meant he didn't agree, but neither could he see any point in arguing. He stepped back, allowing her to shut the door.

She watched in the wing mirror as he pushed the wheelchair around to the back of the car and raised the tailgate. Her dad had entered that stage of life where some people entirely stopped caring how they looked and settled into a pattern of wearing whatever the hell they liked, regardless of whether they were collecting their daughter from hospital or having tea with the queen. His mustard cords and psychedelically patterned jumper might have passed for Christmas irony if it hadn't been mid-February. The tragedy was that satire had nothing to do with it.

Behind her, Alan Hawkins placed the distended crutches on to the cardboard that protected the plastic that protected the boot carpet, and then spent a while pulling at every bolt and protrusion on the chair, in search of the release catch shown blatantly to him by the nurse not five minutes ago.

Eventually, the law of averages won and he managed to concertina the wheelchair before hauling it on its side into the boot. Then he eased the tailgate back into place and shuffled round to the driver's side.

It was only when he sat down that Hawkins nearly insisted, despite her injuries, on driving. This was why she resorted to asking her father for help only in the most dire of situations. Almost seven billion people on the planet, and who did *she* get in a crisis?

Alan Hawkins was wearing slippers.

8

'Why don't you come and stay with us?' Alan Hawkins turned off the main road into his daughter's estate. 'Just for a few days.'

'It's nothing personal, Dad; I just don't get on with your wife.'

He smiled. 'I know you and your mum clash sometimes, but she'd love to help. She did use to be a nurse.'

'Really? Why doesn't she ram *that* fact down everybody's throat whenever the opportunity arises?'

'Antonia.' He frowned at her. 'She'd be upset if she heard you.'

'And that's why I can't stay with you guys.' Not to mention the fact that, if she stayed with them, her mum would try to stop Hawkins from returning to work.

Tomorrow.

Her dad made his short humming noise.

They rounded the final corner and the knot in Hawkins' stomach pulled itself tighter as the house came into view. She dragged in a long breath.

You have to face it at some point.

'Here we are, then,' her father announced, before embarking on a five-minute parking ballet that ended only when he involuntarily mounted the kerb at low revs and stalled the car.

The subsequent build-up to entering the house, which involved him retrieving the wheelchair from the boot, wrestling it back into shape, loading his daughter into it and edging her up the path, did nothing for Hawkins' growing anxiety. But it wasn't until she had to stand, in order to negotiate the step over the threshold, that the nausea really kicked in. She swayed.

'You don't look too well.' Her dad left the wheelchair halfway through the door and caught her arm. 'Do you need a bowl?'

'No, I'm good.' Hawkins propped herself against the wall while he dragged the chair inside and shut the front door. Then she sank into it and allowed him to push her slowly along the hall, willing the colour back into her cheeks as they passed the mirror.

She swallowed hard when they entered the front room, watching the kitchen slide into view.

The room where she'd been attacked.

'Blimey.' Her dad, oblivious, interrupted her anxiety. 'Brass monkeys in here, isn't it?'

He adjusted the thermostat, waiting for the sound of the boiler kicking in. 'That's better. Now, I'm under instructions from you-know-who. The deal is that if you're having difficulties getting about, which you are, then I'm either to insist that you come and stay with us, or I have to stay here with you. So which is it?'

Hawkins groaned. She'd noticed her dad's weekend

bag in the back of the car, which meant her mum already knew which way this would go. They all understood that, once her mother decreed an either–or ruling, you were getting either–or whether you liked it or not. Proposing that Mike, a man her parents had met just a couple of times, look after her, especially when he was on shift for the next couple of days, wouldn't cut it. And if she refused both recommended options, things would only get worse. Because that would compel her mother to intervene personally.

'You win.' She shook her head and pointed at the ceiling. 'You'll need to make up the spare room.'

'It's not about winn–' He stopped in response to the frown. 'Where are the sheets?'

'Airing cupboard.'

'Right, I'll pop up and do that. You get the kettle on.' He headed for the stairs, apparently unaware of the irony that his slippers were appropriate footwear once more.

Hawkins watched him go, mildly hurt that he hadn't asked if she was okay first. Then it occurred to her that he probably didn't know much about the attack. She hadn't been exactly forthcoming, and what little he *had* known he'd probably forgotten. He thought her difficulties entering the house had been purely physical, and last time he'd asked about that she'd bitten him. As far as he was concerned, she was back in the chair, so she was fine.

And, actually, aside from some residual demons, why shouldn't she be?

Fine.

Hawkins assured herself that the clunking noises emanating from upstairs meant her father wasn't far away, and that it was impossible for the man who'd attacked her six weeks ago to repeat his actions now. She took hold of the grip rings either side of the chair and rolled herself forwards; ignoring the discomfort this caused her armpits and chest.

She crossed the threshold into the kitchen, thankful for once that her mother's obsession with cleanliness meant there were no obvious traces of her blood on the dark floor tiles. But that didn't stop her feeling sick.

The room was exactly as she remembered, just tidier. Every surface was clean, and she knew without looking that the cupboards and drawers would be organized enough for use in TV advertising. She was safe.

So why was her heart racing? And her cheeks wet?

She blinked the tears away, trying to steady her breathing as she rolled herself towards the bench. Just like everything else, the kettle shone. Hawkins stared at her reflection in its mirror-finish. But even her mother's elbow grease couldn't shift memories. And the room was infused.

She closed her eyes, immediately opening them again for fear of inviting back the trauma lurking behind her eyelids. Her attacker's face, his hateful stare, the knife, the *pain*. She'd lost count of the times she'd relived those final moments. Maybe it *was* too soon.

She realized she was scratching and pulled her hand

away from her chest. The stab wounds were healing, but nowhere near as fast as she'd have liked, and her nervous system was in tatters. Although that, ironically, was probably the main reason she was still here.

Get a grip.

She shifted forwards in the chair and reached out for the kettle. Her fingers made contact.

You can do this.

For an instant she was back there, standing, flicking open the lid, thrusting the boiling liquid at her assailant. Hearing him hiss.

'I can't find any sheets.'

Hawkins nearly dropped the kettle as she jerked round to see her father standing in the doorway.

'Jesus, Dad.'

'Sorry, love . . .'

Concern entered his expression. 'Have you been crying?'

9

Bull renewed his grip on the scalpel, keen to maintain precision.

Where to cut next?

He glanced up at the laptop. Aside from the high-intensity lamp lighting his work, the computer screen was the only thing breaking the darkness in this small upstairs room. The image on its display was large and detailed. But it was only a guide.

He had to translate.

Bull lined up his blade and pushed the point in behind the ear, running it carefully down and along the jaw line. Over and over, each stroke lighter and more exact, reshaping his silent subject.

Satisfied, Bull put the knife down and flexed his fingers. He'd been at this all evening. His hand would probably pack up soon, but he was nearly done. Just another half-hour.

He switched his attention to the eyes, using the razor point of the knife to strip away one fragile layer at a time. Digging out the pupils with delicate care.

Then he picked away the offcuts and cleared the mess that had built up on the table beneath. Without debris in the way, it was obvious his creation was nearly finished. Just the mouth needed work.

He ran a fingertip lightly across the scalpel's edge.

Blunt.

Bull eased the worn blade off the handle and dropped it in the bin. He took a new one from the pack, seated it and spent another ten minutes shaving the lips and chin. Finally, he sat back, assessing his work. His skill was improving; the likeness to the photograph on the computer screen not bad at all.

He picked up the carving and placed it with the others before stepping back to survey his collection of lime wood figures – one for every life cut short.

His memorial.

Their numbers were growing.

But there were many more to come.

'Twelve–four!' Slater shouted, watching the Ping-Pong ball skip off the scruffy table and bounce erratically into the corner. 'You fuckers see that?'

She began punching the air with both scrawny, tattooed arms, the type of celebration that might have been justified had she just won Olympic gold. There were mutters of support from the women sitting nearby, as Timpson, Slater's younger, dumpier opponent, retrieved the ball like a weary child whose competitive parent never tired of humiliating her.

To their left, Miller and Burnett were playing a loose approximation of darts, arguing over the scores whenever one of the Velcro-ended projectiles refused to attach itself to the worn-out board. At a couple of the smaller tables, groups were hunched over games of draughts or cards. A few others sat around, chatting among themselves, or just watching their mates.

And on the periphery, Amanda Cain sat, her stare returning to the middle distance.

There was nothing new to see here. She knew the scars on every wall, every patch of dirt extending slowly outwards from the tiled corners where the cleaners' mops didn't quite reach. But, of her poor and limited choices, this was still the best place to be. In fact, she spent as much time as possible in the busy recreation area, not because she had any desire for the lurid company of her fellow inmates; precisely because she *didn't*.

Following her arrival at Holloway nearly nine months earlier, Cain had realized quickly that, in prison, the more you tried to hide, the more visible you became. Everyone went for the vagrant. If she hid in her cell, as at first she had, to repel the suffocating proximity of those crammed in around her, it was perceived either as weakness, which drew in the resident bullies, or as sensitivity: a magnet for desperados craving sympathy, affection, or both. And if it wasn't other inmates, it would be the screws, rounding up their herd, as if they didn't understand why someone starved of company would choose solitude in the rare intervals when they were offered a choice.

So now, whenever the opportunity arose, Cain came here: the games room on the ground floor of B Unit. She'd been around long enough now that the others knew she'd decline any offer of competition, not to mention attempts at conversation. But most of them valued an audience, too, so her idle company was endured. And while the guards were constantly in place, backed up by those passing through on journeys between various strays, they seldom intervened. In this room, Cain's presence was obscured by its blatancy. In familiarity, she became no more significant than the paint on the walls.

Across the room, Slater was coaxing Timpson into another game, and a moment later the tic-tac sound of a plastic ball passing from one end of a table to the other resumed. But only when the clamour suddenly died did Cain's attention return fully to the present.

Her head didn't move, but her eyes picked up the two new arrivals as they entered through the door in the far wall and moved purposefully across the room. Tor was first in, six feet of muscle and scar tissue, the appalling V-shaped dent in her forehead reputedly the result of being hit with a flail made from a lantern battery in a sock. Her attacker hadn't benefited, though. That murder was the reason behind Tor's third life sentence.

Behind her came Reedy, the sidekick: also tall, but contrastingly thin. Reedy wasn't exactly bright, but she was as violent and cruel as Tor, with an on–off temper that nobody in possession of any sense tampered with. Cain watched a couple of cons who happened to be near the exit slide carefully out of the room.

There was a shift in the screws' demeanour as Tor strode towards Slater, but nobody moved. If the guards jumped at every early sign of aggression, they'd never be done.

Tor reached Slater, who visibly leaned away, although her feet stayed planted. There was nowhere to go in this place, so running only made things worse.

'Commission, bitch,' Tor demanded. 'Now.'

Slater frowned. 'Sorry, boss, don't know what you mea–'

'Don't give me that shit.' Tor grabbed Slater's jersey, almost lifting her off the floor. 'You sell your shitty fags on my wing, you pay for my permission. So where is it?'

Slater squirmed. 'I ain't . . .'

But she had wasted her only chance.

Without further warning, Tor's free hand flew at Slater's jaw. There was a dull crunch as it made contact and Slater's legs gave way. But Tor didn't let her drop, hauling the skinny woman on to the table, landing a second blow in the centre of her face, bursting Slater's nose.

At the far end of the table, Timpson took a step towards the fight, an instinctive attempt to assist her friend. But Reedy saw her and blocked her path, body language alone enough to halt Timpson in her tracks.

Tor landed another crushing blow to Slater's face.

Cain looked around for the screws, expecting them to rush in and haul Tor off her already pulped opponent. But the three guards in the corner of the games room, and another up on the first level gantry, hadn't moved. All had their batons drawn, but their expressions suggested they were enjoying the show too much to intervene. Cain realized that survival of the fittest was being allowed to play out in front of them.

The guards were going to let them fight.

She turned back to see Tor drop an elbow in Slater's gut, but her victim had already stopped reacting and just lay bleeding on the Ping-Pong table. Someone would have to intervene soon, or Slater might not survive. Reedy and Timpson were mere observers now, and still the guards hadn't moved.

Cain studied the larger woman, with her damaged skull and triple life sentence, still raining blows on her fellow inmate. If she ever got out, Tor wouldn't stay free for long: a true boomerang prisoner.

With nothing left to lose.

Suddenly Cain was on her feet, striding between the other cons, faces around her turning in awe that anyone other than a screw would voluntarily enter the fray. Reedy saw Cain as she got within feet of the table. Her eyebrows rose, but she didn't interfere. Behind her, Timpson looked about ready to cry. Then Tor noticed Cain standing over her.

She looked up, fist raised, her victim lolling. 'Fuck do you want?'

Cain didn't answer.

'Come to save your mate? She your bitch or something?'

Still no response.

'Fuck off.' Tor dumped her victim and straightened, wiping the blood off her hand on to her jeans. 'Or you're next.'

Cain looked down at Slater. One eye was full of blood and a couple of teeth hung from her mouth by bloody threads.

Tor followed her gaze. 'She won't be going down on no one for a while. You sure this is worth it?'

Cain looked at the guards. They still hadn't moved.

'Fuck you, then.' Tor dropped her shoulder.

The first strike was an upper cut. It smashed into Cain's stomach, doubling her over. She dropped to her knees, fighting for breath, just as a second heavy punch connected with her right cheek, sending a white flash across her vision. She hit the floor, head ringing, as a kick landed square in her gut, driving the oxygen from her.

She coughed, opening her eyes just enough to see Slater's legs hanging over the edge of the table.

Still alive.

She waited for another hit, hearing nothing but the air wheezing in and out of her lungs, wondering whether it would be a head shot.

But the next blow never came.

Cain rolled on to her back, hearing loud voices, trying to focus on the blurred shapes merging above her. She realized why the attack had stopped. The screws had intervened.

She waited, swallowing blood, watching the group of guard-coloured distortions dragging the two prisoner-coloured ones away.

Then she was hauled to her feet.

11

'Cuppa for you, love.' Alan Hawkins pointed to the mug on the bedside cabinet as his daughter emerged, yawning, from the sheets.

Hawkins lifted her head, blinking, and peered at the steaming liquid. 'I thought I showed you where to find the unused teabags.'

'Cheeky madam.' He perched on the edge of the bed. 'How did you sleep?'

'I'm getting there.' She hefted herself on to an elbow, opting not to mention the cold sweats that had woken her at least three times in the night. She also resisted the urge to stretch, wincing as now familiar pain shot through her torso.

Her father half stood, visibly alarmed. 'Blimey, that looks painful. Want your pills?'

'No more drugs.' Hawkins eased herself into a sitting position against the headboard. 'You could let some light in, though.'

'Seeing as you ask so nicely.' He shuffled over to the window, his dodgy knee obviously playing up. 'Isn't a bad day out there, as it goes.'

He opened the curtains, flooding the room with bright winter sunshine. Hawkins picked up her tea and sipped, before pulling a face that he caught, turning back.

'Oh, love. At least take some paracetamol or something.'

'It doesn't hurt, Dad.' She raised the cup. 'This is disgusting.'

'You're full of gratitude this morning.'

'Sorry, it's early. What time did Mike leave?'

'Oh, sevenish. He didn't want to wake you.'

'Quite right, too.' She glanced at the clock. It was nine thirty on Saturday morning, which meant that Maguire, thanks to shift work's inherent lack of compassion for normality, would be with the rest of their team, in the operations room at Hendon.

Where she should be.

'Anyway' – she put the cup down and began edging her legs off the bed – 'I can't lounge around here all day.'

Her dad smiled. 'That's my girl.'

Hawkins' feet made contact with the floor. 'So what's on your agenda for today?'

'I was going to pop out for a paper, but I can't find my bloody shoes.'

She suppressed a grin. 'Well if they don't turn up, I think there's a pair of Mike's trainers under the stairs that'll fit you.'

'They must be here somewhere.' He headed for the door. 'Shout if you need me.'

'Cheers,' she called after him as he descended the stairs. 'I do appreciate you being here, Dad.'

'Just remember that this afternoon, when your mum arrives.'

Under normal circumstances, his words would have filled her with dread. What he didn't know was that today, if things went to plan, by the time Christine Hawkins got anywhere near the house, her daughter wouldn't be there.

Joking aside, her mother wasn't so bad. On a good day they got on like matches and gunpowder; it was just that the results were equally explosive. Neither of them liked to admit it, but in truth they were quite alike. Both were intelligent, capable women to whom others naturally apportioned authority. They were also similarly dissatisfied with the human race, although Hawkins preferred to keep the wider public at arm's length, reserving warmth for those closer to home, while her mother's greatest affection was for people she hardly knew. And while the daughter typically did her grousing outside of the subject's company, her mother's immediates were regularly sprayed with disdain face to face; opposing views that had probably triggered mother and daughter's respective careers. While Antonia was out arresting society's unsavoury types, Christine's job often involved patching up their prey. Perhaps the similarities between mother and younger daughter – none of which seemed to apply to Hawkins' sibling, Siobhan – were what forced them apart like two magnets with the same pole. Siobhan had obediently fulfilled their mother's every tedious aspiration, the job in social care, the kids, the dull-as-dishwater husband. But a young Antonia had refused to conform. Instead, her career had taken off, the vocation which, after just six weeks without, she craved.

Yet somehow Hawkins had enjoyed the last twenty-four hours. It was the first extended period of time she'd spent with her father in years, but it had been surprisingly cathartic for them both. Since returning home, she'd been an honorary septuagenarian, piggybacking on her dad's routines. They'd slipped back into the old father–daughter routine more easily than she'd been expecting. It was great to hear his stories again, even if they were a lot tamer thirty years on, while the occasional mischievous wink told Hawkins he still enjoyed her acidic wit. Even when it was directed at him or the woman he had married.

The previous evening, Mike had joined them for takeaway and matchstick poker. He'd been fantastic while she was in hospital and since her return home, although she wasn't the sort to stoke his male ego by telling him so. Of course, Mike's work commitments meant that Dad had been the one who was always there, but only Mike understood her compulsion for not letting jobs build. Where he found the energy to keep on top of everything astounded her.

Obviously, he had a surplus due to the enforced vacation their physical relationship was on, but her dad's presence, not to mention snoring capable of dampening a Shakespearian romance, had precluded anything more, although that wasn't the reason Mike had spent the night on the sofa. The two of them had shared precious little intimacy since his return from Manchester just over two months ago, which was likely to remain the case for a while yet. Hawkins wasn't physically up to anything remotely energetic, and that wasn't even the worst of it.

Not only did she find it hard to sleep because of discomfort and nightmares, her spirit still sank whenever she dared to face a mirror unclothed. She simply wasn't ready for anyone else, even Mike, to see the scars. Although she could probably get away with ignoring the situation for a while longer. At least till she was out of the chair.

She shuddered, then tried to reassure herself that today would mark another milestone in her emancipation from the attack that had scarred her body almost as badly as it had scarred her mind.

Eager for progress, she heaved herself off the bed and fought her way into a somewhat crooked but now almost upright position, surprised to find that, despite the lack of painkillers, her stomach and torso weren't as painful as expected.

She'd fought to enforce it, but Mike and her dad had eventually accepted her desire to be as independent as possible. Perhaps the message that she wasn't going to play the obedient recuperation game had reached her body, too. Encouraged, she edged towards the corner and retrieved the crutches, gingerly placing her weight on them, ignoring muscles that protested against even this mild abuse. Several seconds of dogged endurance later, most of Hawkins' weight was off her feet, but the burning sensation was already cascading through her upper body. She relented, placing the metal supports back in the corner.

Walking short distances unaided was possible, but also painfully slow. She creaked her way across the landing, hearing strains of Capital Gold from downstairs, pleased to discover that, for the first time since returning home, she reached the bathroom without having to pause halfway.

She closed the door, leaving it unlocked in case of emergency. Then she plugged the bath and cranked on the taps before inspecting her make-up-free appearance in the mirror, resisting the urge to strip and inspect the laceration marks. She brushed her teeth, watching the bath slowly fill, feeling a hint of unease. Today was a big deal.

Now six weeks old, her wounds would at last be watertight. The external sutures had been removed by a doctor a week ago, leaving only the internal binds, with butterfly stitches outside, just in case. But now she was allowed to soak and thereby dissolve those. Then she'd get her first proper look at the repair job carried out by the surgeons.

Fortunately, Hawkins had always done a reasonable job of looking after herself. Okay, so she enjoyed the occasional cigarette or bottle of wine, and chocolate was a weakness, too, but none was indulged to extremes, and she countered their effects with regular running and healthyish food. She liked to think her size ten figure was due more to this effort than to random biological or metabolic good fortune. Stress was part of life, especially of her job, and she had yet to find any grey hairs. But she worried about the long-term effects of her scars because, as anyone approaching their thirty-sixth birthday would testify, things didn't heal as fast as they once had.

Beside her, the bathwater was getting deep. Hawkins turned off the taps and positioned a towel within reach, in case she needed to call on her dad. There was no point embarrassing them both in the midst of an emergency. Then she slipped out of her pyjamas, glad that the mirror had steamed up, and grimaced her way over the edge to immerse herself in the hot liquid.

Forty minutes later, Hawkins drained the tepid water and showered. She carefully dried herself and manoeuvred back on to the bathmat, catching sight of her towel-covered reflection.

She turned to face the mirror, standing up as straight as possible, aware that her last line of defence had gone. Previously, stitches and dried blood had provided visual noise, behind which the scars could credibly have ranged between extremes. Obviously, she'd been able to view her stab wounds obliquely, once the stitches had dissolved or been picked away, in the bath. But there was something scarier about confronting them from a distance, as others would. She took a deep breath and dropped the towel.

After a moment's pleasantly surprised assessment, however, Hawkins edged forwards, risking closer inspection. Yes, every wound was obvious, but they all seemed to have knitted evenly, free from the potential puckering of which she'd been so afraid. The skin around each mark was pink rather than pale, too, which the doctors said was a good sign.

Her torso bore a strange pattern of eleven at-angle entry wounds, where the blade had been pushed in, retracted, turned, and then reinserted somewhere else. Fortunately, thanks to the same warped logic that precipitated his actions, her attacker hadn't been trying to kill her directly. His aim had been exsanguination, a method of knifing around the vital organs to induce bloodletting, thereby allowing the victim time before their inevitable demise to rue whatever actions had led to their fate. It had been well on the way to working, too. Except she'd been found just in time.

Hawkins rewrapped herself in the towel and turned away. She shuffled back to the bedroom, confirming with her dad on the way that she had survived solo ablutions.

Difficulties in holding her arms above her head for long meant she needed help with the hairdryer, but at midday Hawkins stood, smartly dressed, at the top of the stairs. She listened to the sounds of her father preparing lunch in the kitchen, planning the conversation they'd have as they ate. She needed the outcome to go her way, but she wasn't looking forward to it.

Because she hated lying to her dad.

I 2

The sturdy door swung open and she was manhandled through it. For a second, the low winter sun filled the window in the rear wall, blinding her, but as she limped beyond its glare, Amanda Cain had to remind herself that she was still inside Holloway Prison.

In contrast to everywhere else inside the complex, the air in this room was perceptibly fresh, as if it had been filtered somehow. A large glass-topped desk dominated the centre of the floor; around it, several plush chairs. And, in the largest of them, directly behind the desk, Graham Fitch. The prison governor.

Fitch didn't look up, choosing instead to complete whatever he was doing on the laptop in front of him. Intentional or otherwise, his action told Cain she was of minor import.

She stopped a few yards in front of the desk, watching as one of the female screws who had escorted her through the labyrinth of Holloway's main building moved around beside her boss. Cain still didn't recognize her, but the fact she took precedence over the more familiar guard, Jones, who remained near the door, meant she had probably come with the PM from his former post at Thameside, a few weeks ago.

Cain's gaze drifted to the window, not to the depressing grey and red buildings immediately below them but to the residential streets of Islington beyond: to the trees, and the gridlocked cars crawling along beside empty bus lanes.

To *freedom*.

'Dr Cain.'

Her eyes flicked back to the man behind the desk. The PM's voice itself hadn't startled her, but his use of her professional title had.

'I read my officers' intervention reports regarding your latest altercation.' Fitch stood and moved around the desk in front of her, lifting her chin with a gentle hand. He assessed her swollen right eye. 'That's going to be a shiner.'

Cain nodded, uncertain whether he wanted a response. Her jaw throbbed, despite the lightness of his touch and the drugs administered by the infirmary shortly before her stumbling journey to this office.

Fitch wasn't tall, so their eyes were almost level. The top of his head was bald, but he wore a neatly trimmed beard and moustache, too uniform in colour for a man in his fifties not to be dyed. Intelligent eyes studied her through the tinted lenses in his dark-framed glasses, but the facet most evident to Cain as he released her chin was how clean he smelled – somewhere between talcum powder and fresh linen.

He leaned claustrophobically close, peering at the butterfly stitches above her right eye, his odourless breath skimming her lips. 'I have to say, Dr Cain, I find your behaviour perplexing.

'Apparently,' he continued, retreating to perch casually against the desk, 'you spend most of your time in solitude, disinterested in your fellow inmates, something I might anticipate from someone of your intelligence. Except that, according to your record, you've been involved in three fights in as many weeks, when the original disturbances had nothing to do with you.'

Cain regarded him, wordless.

'Multiple injuries,' he went on, 'ranging from a fractured cheekbone and concussion to this morning's stitched temple and cracked ribs. Do you see yourself as some kind of guardian angel?'

His brow fell when she didn't reply. 'I see. We have a trust deficit. Understandable, but I promise your insecurities are misplaced. Given more time to build a relationship, I think we'd get on.' He left the desk and wandered over to stare out of the window.

Cain glanced at the unfamiliar screw, whose gaze was fixed on the far wall, so she took the opportunity to scan the space around her. It was then she realized what was bothering her. Despite its relative opulence, the office had the same sterility as the rest of the prison, even though Fitch would have unbounded latitude to make it his own. There were no photographs, no art, not even an executive toy, which jarred in an environment where the first thing *anybody* did was attempt to make the place feel just a bit like home. But her thoughts were disturbed as Fitch, still facing the city, addressed her again. 'You're due to leave us this coming week, aren't you?'

The lack of eye contact forced her to reply. 'Yes.'

'I'm glad.' He turned back. 'After all, part of my remit is to facilitate the reintegration of prisoners into society. What are you planning to do when you get out?'

She hesitated. 'I'm not sure yet.'

'Well, I hope you do.' Fitch retook his seat, 'I like to think that the skills of our more capable inmates are not wasted as a result of their detention, especially in cases such as your own. Your error was a costly one, but an error nonetheless.'

Cain swallowed discreetly, determined not to let this man see the tidal wave of emotion building in her gut as memories flared, vivid repercussions of the day she made that pivotal, deadly mistake.

'Anyway' – Fitch waved the one-sided conversation away as if they'd been discussing the weather – 'whatever your reasons, I'm not prepared to have you leave us looking like we run some sort of human cockfighting ring. I could prolong your stay, of course, but I'm reliably informed that neither carrots nor sticks are particularly effective where you're concerned.'

He sat forwards. 'So you'll spend your final few days here in solitary confinement.'

13

He was shoved. 'Up, now.'

Bull's eyes opened. His mouth tasted foul.

'What?' He looked around for whoever had woken him, but it was dark and he could hear movement everywhere. Quiet noises, though; nobody talked. The only light came through an open doorway at the far end of the room, black shapes moving back and forth across the patch of brightness.

'What's going on?' he asked the nearest shadow.

'Shut up, man. Get dressed.'

It sounded like Trey.

Bull rolled up on to an elbow, feeling the start of a headache beginning to bang in his head. He'd always hated being woken before he was ready; sometimes it made him throw up. Not that it was unusual for sleep to be interrupted here. And there was no choice; if they said get up, you got up.

Bull heaved his legs off the bed, straight away feeling the chill. He fumbled under the bed for his clothes, dragging the pile free and finding his trousers by touch. He needed to speed up; others were already filing out. He shrugged on the rest of his clothes and followed, blinking as he passed under the spotlight outside the door. The others were ahead and to the right, lined up behind two trucks waiting in the dark.

He joined the nearest queue, checking around him for the more experienced guys, anyone who might be able to explain. But they all looked confused.

Bull glanced around, suddenly scared. He didn't want to get in the truck without knowing where they'd end up. But others had joined the queue behind him, and it wasn't a good idea to show weakness.

He reached the truck and climbed in, back into darkness. Enough light leaked in from outside for him to make out around fifteen other guys, but he couldn't tell who was who. He joined the end of the right-hand bench. Still nobody spoke.

Chill.

His brain started scratching for clues. Last night they'd eaten at the usual time, everything had been normal, nobody seemed uptight. That meant one of two things. Either the others had known about this and weren't bothered, or he wasn't the only one caught by surprise.

The last few guys arrived, two more joining the end of the bench next to Bull. There were muffled voices from outside.

Suddenly, vibration shot through the bench and Bull's gut turned over as the truck pulled away. Was he supposed to know what was going on? Had he not been paying attention when they were told? The headache was getting worse. He pinched his nose.

They rode in silence as the truck turned left out of the gates. They must have been behind the other vehicle, because he could hear both engines. There were no windows, but the rear of the truck was open and Bull watched the scenery pass as they jolted and swayed along the pitted road. These crates weren't built for comfort, and he strained his ears over the crashing suspension, trying to pick out familiar sounds. It might have been his *imagination, but the night air seemed strangely peaceful, and for a moment he wondered if it was all over.*

Maybe they were being taken home.

He lost track of time as they jerked along, passing through a couple of small towns before a longer stint on a dual carriageway, then back on to local roads. Eventually, a few of the guys started talking quietly. Was it good that none of them seemed to know where this journey would end?

But everyone shut up as the truck slowed and began crawling through a built-up area.

Then it stopped.

They all sat in the blackness. Nobody moved, and Bull realized he was holding his breath. He inhaled, catching the first traces of a smell he hadn't known before two months ago, something like a mixture of fireworks and scorched wood. A smell that meant only one thing.

Trouble.

14

'Hold on a minute.' Alan Hawkins stopped the car and peered out through his partially steamed-up window. 'This isn't the doctor's surgery; this is your bloody work.'

Rumbled.

He scowled at his daughter but was forced to break eye contact and park when another car drew up behind them in the restricted space and sounded its horn. Silence endured throughout the typically protracted manoeuvre, but as soon as the car had stalled and the handbrake was engaged, he regained the attention of his passenger, who was staring the opposite way.

'What's going on?'

Hawkins turned to face him; there was no point trying to prolong the façade. Until now she'd forgotten that he'd been here a couple of times, once to drop her off for an interview, and another when she was lecturing at the Peel Centre and having car problems. She'd been convinced, right up to the moment he recognized the place, that her plan was going to work.

The previous day, she'd made the mistake of approaching Mike and her dad simultaneously to propose her immediate return to work. Their response had been annoyingly cohesive. Mike had dug his heels in so far that he could have anchored a wind farm, which compounded the problem by prompting her father, who was normally more malleable, to harden his line. Both men, and by proxy her mother, had insisted that Hawkins spend at least a week on the sofa. At the time, she'd been smart enough to concede, but only until their draconian ranks had been depleted by Mike's early-morning departure.

Over lunch she'd asked her father for a lift to a fictitious doctor's appointment for a check-up and then directed him on a deliberately circuitous route to her work. He hadn't twigged on the way where they were headed; she was sure of that. But it had obviously been too much to hope that her ageing chauffeur would fail to recognize Hendon's unsigned car park, which could have passed for any other to unfamiliar eyes.

'I'm not senile just yet, madam,' he persisted. 'Don't think you can get round me.'

'Look, I'm sorry, okay? I knew you wouldn't bring me in if I asked directly. But you can still tell Mum I was at the doctor's.'

'Women's problems, you said.'

'I was just trying to make things easier for everyone.'

'By lying?'

'Oh don't be so dramatic; you know what she's like. I lied for the same reason you always make the tea: so you can put whiskey in yours.'

His brow contracted. 'I didn't know you knew about that.'

'I'm a detective, Dad.'

'It's medicinal. I never drink and drive.' He held out his hands, retracting them quickly when he realized they wobbled these days whether he'd had a drink or not. 'Bad example.'

'So we understand each other?'

'I suppose. What's so urgent about coming back here, anyway? You're not being bullied into it, are you?'

She laughed. 'Dad, I'm not six.'

'So why the rush?'

She sighed. 'Okay. You know I'm on temporary promotion to Chief Inspector. Well, I bent a few rules before Christmas and got my wrists slapped. So I can't afford to be off any longer, in case they second someone else into my role and demote me. They've already got some graduate prodigy lined up.'

'Oh.'

'I promise I won't overdo it.'

He chewed a fingernail. 'We don't have to tell your mother?'

'Our secret.'

'I don't want you to be demoted.'

'And neither would Mum, really.'

'Right.' His eyes lit up. 'What's the plan?'

Moments later, with details of their conspiracy agreed, Hawkins watched her father exit the car. She almost laughed as he negotiated his way along the

Rover's flanks, probably picturing himself in a tuxedo, licensed to kill.

He was crouching.

After manhandling the wheelchair back into shape in remarkably un-spy-like fashion, Alan Hawkins loaded his daughter and pushed her across the car park to the building's entrance.

In the foyer of Becke House, she reiterated their cover story about his having delivered her to a girl-friend's house for afternoon tea, from where Mike would collect her on his way home. It was flawless. As long as she could convince Maguire to play along.

Hawkins pecked her dad on the cheek and, after he reassured them both that he'd find his way back to the house, she watched him walk away, feeling a renewed faith in the independence of this seventy-three-year-old man in navy-blue trousers, bottle-green jumper, grey flat cap.

And Mike's fluorescent orange trainers.

15

Hawkins bumped the wheelchair over the door runners and out of the lift. She turned left and propelled herself slowly along the wide, soberly decorated corridor. Fortunately, the tall glass door ahead on the right stood open and, after aligning herself with a mildly painful three-point turn, she rolled through the entrance.

In the centre of the room, four squat leather chairs surrounded a coffee table, occupying most of the space in the glass-fronted meeting-cum-waiting area. The tasteless wallpaper hadn't changed since her last visit, but at least somebody had dusted the artificial flowers.

'Good afternoon.'

Hawkins nearly cricked her neck as she turned to find the recess to her right; previously home to an oversized vase containing a tragic collection of dead sticks, it now housed a desk. And, behind it, a secretary.

'Hi.' Hawkins masked her surprise. 'Am I still in the right place to see the chief superintendent?'

'Oh yes.' The secretary smiled. 'Mr Vaughn is out on lunch at present, but he won't be long. May I take your name?'

Hawkins told her, wondering why she had pronounced 'Detective Chief Inspector' so specifically. Perhaps it was because the irritatingly attractive secretary was not only ten years younger than her but neither had she been repeatedly stabbed and ended up, albeit temporarily, in a wheelchair. As the assistant tapped her keyboard, Hawkins read the name plaque on the desk: Amy Park. She resisted asking if the younger woman needed help because all the words in her title contained more than four letters.

As if hearing her thoughts, the secretary looked up. 'Is there anyone with you?'

'*With me?*' Hawkins frowned. 'No. Why?'

'Oh.' Amy's composure faltered, but only for a second before the smile returned. 'No reason.'

Hawkins let it go, wondering whether it was her imagination or if the secretary was talking more loudly than the environment seemed to require.

Apparently keen to move on, Amy offered her a coffee, which she accepted. The slender aide stood, before sweeping elegantly past her and out of the room.

Unsure whether to be impressed by or annoyed at the woman for ignoring the fact she was in a wheelchair, Hawkins zigzagged herself into line with one of the armchairs, rotating back to face the hall. Opposite, visible through the floor-to-ceiling glass, was the handsome wooden door of the Detective Chief Superintendent's office, beyond which her last visit had ended in suspension from the force. Technically, that abeyance still stood. But, since then, Antonia Hawkins had personally bagged the most notorious serial killer in recent history and spent six weeks in hospital recovering from the near-fatal wounds she had sustained in the process.

Surely that made them even.

She glanced at the wall-mounted clock, 1.50 p.m. She'd arrived at the perfect time. According to Mike, the current DCS was a true believer in mucking in. Vaughn operated an open-door drop-in half-hour daily, from two o'clock, even on a Saturday. So unless others arrived in the meantime, Hawkins would have the full thirty-minute session to herself. Which gave her ten minutes to figure out how she was going to convince her boss she was ready and, more crucially, that she deserved, to return.

Mere weeks ago she'd been summoned here to explain a missing detective, a faltering investigation and her own flagrant disregard for authority. Had she been about to face the same man who suspended her, Hawkins' hopes of success would have been low. However, the past six weeks had seen one of the fastest leadership transitions she could recall. Lawrence Kirby-Jones, her previous commanding officer, had obviously been lining himself up for the exit well in advance of their collective triumph, because, thanks to some typically sensational media headlines, he'd handed over command within weeks and ridden out on a crest of public and political acclaim. Rumour said he was due to receive an official commendation for his management of the case, in addition to an honorary non-executive post at the top of Special Branch.

Narrowly averted disaster, it seemed, worked out for some.

His younger replacement, Tristan Vaughn, had come straight from Special Enquiries, the media-centric unit set up to deal with people on either side of high-profile criminal cases. He'd become involved towards the end of Hawkins' most recent investigation, although it hadn't been clear at the time that his feet would end up quite so far under the table. Yet his attitude throughout had been reasonable, and Hawkins was counting on his experience with the type of extreme media pressure she'd been under to curb his ire. The outcome of this meeting had profound implications for her future career, because she was in competition with an unidentified rival, unproven but also unmarked, while demotion would mangle her chances of returning to DCI status anytime soon. So she was counting on her previous record, plus the positive outcome of her and Vaughn's recent collaboration, to save her now.

Plus, there had to be at least a *tacit* sympathy vote for the chair.

But as two figures appeared in the corridor beyond the glass, thinking time was up. The slender Amy led, carrying Hawkins' coffee, followed by the even taller but equally fluid Tristan Vaughn. Like his predecessor, Vaughn's height and stature lent him an imposing air, but Vaughn's modern dress sense and a less brooding nature set the two men apart. There was something altogether more approachable about the new Chief Superintendent. Or so Hawkins hoped.

Amy opened his office door and disappeared inside, while the DCS arrived in the entrance to the waiting area.

'Antonia.' He was smiling. 'Good to see you. Please come through.'

He moved to let Hawkins pass, and followed her into his office. Amy stood obediently by as her superiors settled, before departing gracefully. Hawkins watched the Met-liveried mug of coffee steaming away on the near side of his desk, and waited for the secretary to close the door.

They sat in silence for a few seconds, the hiatus allowing Hawkins to spot further differences in otherwise recognizable surroundings. Pictures of the previous DCS' family had gone from the walls, replaced with tasteful art, and the whole room seemed brighter somehow. The walls could even have received a coat of lighter paint. *Had she really missed just six weeks?*

She also realized that, in their few case-specific meetings over the final days leading up to the attack, she and Vaughn hadn't had anything you could call an informal chat. For a few moments they both fished for non-weather-related dialogue, as Hawkins sipped her drink. She congratulated Vaughn on his appointment, and he praised her composure in peril. But the atmosphere soon demanded focus.

68

Vaughn led the way. 'So, how's the recovery going?'

'Faster than expected, sir. The chair's just a precaution; I'm pretty much back on my feet.'

'That's good, although I have to say I wasn't expecting to see you this soon.'

She smiled. 'I'm healing well.'

The DCS drew breath. 'What about the psychological side of things?'

Hawkins felt herself hesitate. Several times, hospital doctors had mentioned her risk of developing psychological issues as a result of recent harrowing events but, repeatedly, she'd rushed to assure them that the Met provided excellent private support where such complications were concerned.

She spurred herself just before the pause became incriminating. 'Trust me, sir, it's in hand.'

'Good.' Vaughn nodded at her upright tone. 'Anyway, what can I do for you?'

Hawkins paused, rephrasing the statement in her head three times before the direct approach came out. 'Well, I'd like to resume my duties.' She watched his brow knit. 'Today.'

Suddenly the room provided familiarity, albeit in the form of a moment's permeating soundlessness.

At last Vaughn answered, with visibly tapered demeanour. 'I'm afraid it isn't that simple.'

'Why not?'

As the words left her mouth, Hawkins realized that she was testing untried mettle. Lawrence Kirby-Jones had handed her a suspension for not much more, and then hijacked her subsequent success in order to catapult his own career skywards, leaving her with physical stab wounds to the chest and metaphorical equivalents in her back. But at least he'd been a known quantity. She had no idea what to expect from a riled Tristan Vaughn, who might be about to make his predecessor's wrath look benign.

She held her breath as he responded.

'Without wishing to state the obvious, Antonia, because you're suspended.'

'But,' she ploughed on, 'you agreed with my approach. We *got* him. Surely that still counts for something around here.'

'He came to *you*, though, didn't he, if we're honest?'

'Only thanks to tactics you and I implemented together.' Hawkins felt herself redden, aware that she was making things worse. 'Technically, it was *your* idea.'

'True, but irrelevant. You were suspended for ignoring the chain of command.'

'I didn't ignore it . . .' She shot for a more successful end to the sentence than she achieved. ' . . . entirely.'

Vaughn's eyebrows lifted. 'Is that like being *a bit pregnant*?'

'No . . . I.' Hawkins broke eye contact, realizing he wasn't going to budge.

She sighed. 'So what's the procedure?'

After a few seconds of silence, she looked up to find him smiling. 'Sir?'

'Sorry.' He almost laughed. 'I can't keep it going any longer.'

She stared at him. 'You're . . . winding me up?'

'Lawrence was right; you go off like a rocket.'

'You *are* winding me up.'

'Of course. Look, Antonia, I like the way you handled the investigation. I'd have done much the same thing; I told you that. And he might not have said so at the time, but Lawrence agreed.'

'So . . . why suspend me?'

'I probably shouldn't tell you this, but he was trying to protect you.'

'*What?*'

'It was clear you thought you had nothing to lose. You'd mislaid all sense of perspective, and you needed reining in. So he called me: an intermediary you could level with. But when you bypassed that command structure as well, he had no choice but to remove you, for everyone's sake, mostly your own. Unfortunately, no one realized quite how critical your involvement was.'

Hawkins just sat, reassessing events. It all seemed so long ago.

'Still,' Vaughn continued, 'you came through, and Lawrence put in a very good word for you with the commissioner before he went. Without that, I might have had a hard time convincing everyone you should retain acting DCI status, but not now. Your suspension's been lifted.'

Hawkins didn't respond. She'd misjudged the

situation, especially Lawrence Kirby-Jones' position within it.

'Anyway,' Vaughn continued, 'I'm sure you'll have an opportunity to thank him at some point. Welcome back.'

She mumbled confused thanks.

'There are conditions, of course.' Vaughn opened a drawer and produced a printed document, sliding it across the desk towards her. 'I'm sure you're familiar with the Met's "Code of Conduct", but it's probably a while since any of us saw a copy. Please reacquaint yourself, especially with the sections on command and disclosure.'

'Sure.' She took it, understanding the implication. 'Anything else?'

'Actually, there is. I don't think you'd be in that chair if you had a choice, which means you aren't quite as fixed as you'd like to be. So come back today by all means, but stay away from anything stressful. Find some paperwork or something to catch up on, until you're properly back on your feet.'

Relieved, Hawkins excused herself and trundled back into the corridor. She could hear Amy typing away at her desk in the meeting room alcove, out of sight around the corner. Other than that, the hallway was empty in both directions. She sat for a moment, staring at the 'Code of Conduct' in her lap.

She was well aware that, upon her return to active duty, she'd be completely unable to resist getting involved in the meatiest case on offer. Vaughn was right, too, about her not being fit; her armpits and torso were already singing from even today's moderate exertion. Really, she should call her father and go home, thankful that her position was intact, and concentrate on getting out of the chair.

But the word 'home' meant different things depending on who you asked, and as she rolled into the lift and selected the top floor, for the first time in six weeks Hawkins felt a sense of worth.

Moments later she reached the doors of the serious incident suite, beyond which lay her office, her team, and Maguire. She was already locked in battle with the side of her brain that said it was a bad idea to tell Mike and the others about Vaughn's instructions to take it easy. Her position was safe for now, but she also had a reputation to fix. If she turned up at a performance review in two months with nothing more exciting than alphabetized arrest reports, they'd probably demote her anyway. She needed a personal result in a big case, and the chances of that would only reduce if she lumbered herself with everyone else's paperwork. She needed to get back on the front line. Did that constitute ignoring the chain of command?

Perhaps.

But as she entered the SIS, Hawkins remembered the Grace Hopper quote she first heard from her favourite secondary-school teacher.

'It's always easier to ask forgiveness than it is to get permission.'

16

'Done?' Jones asked, as Amanda Cain tucked the last medical journal into her plastic crate.

Cain turned back to stare at the room. 'Yes.' She lifted the box, wincing as its weight pressed against damaged ribs.

She certainly wouldn't miss her cell. It might have been single occupancy, and the lightly padded mattress was more comfortable than it looked, but there was a reason people with a choice avoided sleeping four feet from their toilet.

The guard reached out, offering to take the crate.

'I'm fine,' Cain said.

Jones assumed her default expression, one that blended disapproval and concern, but she didn't argue. She hadn't been around earlier when things kicked off with Tor, although she'd arrived soon afterwards, to help carry Slater to the infirmary. She was one of the longest-serving screws on the wing. Quiet, but no shirker. No leader, but humane.

Yet, in contrast to most of the other guards, her reputation among the inmates wasn't bad. She made occasional eye contact, for a start. And, beneath all the hardened layers of experience, it was clear that this lithe woman in her late forties was here for more than a wage. Something behind those stoic eyes said she enjoyed her work.

Cain adjusted her grip, resting the container against her less painful side, and joined her escort beside the low doorway, nodding to indicate she was ready to go. The screw backed out on to the gantry.

The two women walked slowly along the first floor, skirting the tall atrium of B wing. Cain felt a dozen pairs of eyes burning into her back, but she stared ahead and moved on. Having solicited neither friendship nor affiliation during her time inside Holloway's walls, she had no use for goodbyes.

They descended to ground level at the first intersection, turning right at the end of the block, and within a couple of minutes they had left the wing.

The corridors grew increasingly quiet, until nobody passed in the opposite direction and a lack of post guards meant Jones was opening security doors for herself. They moved on into the oldest part of the prison. The air grew colder. Dust sheets hung here and there from the battered gantries, denoting renovation work underway on the shabby fixtures. But there was no workforce to be seen.

Jones walked a pace or two behind, steering Cain with occasional grunts of 'Left' or 'Right', her directions the only dialogue to pass between them. There was something spooky about the way two pairs of prison-issue boots echoed off unfinished walls.

At last they stopped beside a row of renovated cells at the far end of the wing. Three doors stood ajar. Jones glanced up and down the deserted annexe before turning back. She nodded at the rooms. 'Take your pick.'

Cain hesitated. After months of incarceration, being offered a choice of any kind was unfamiliar. She moved along the line, eventually choosing the corner cell, which seemed to let the most light in through its lattice-barred windowpane.

Jones stepped aside as Cain limped in to find a familiar six-by-eight space. Stark white walls, pine laminate fixtures, plus a combined steel basin and loo. Except this room smelled of plywood and sawdust, which definitely beat stagnant water and damp.

She'd heard about the newer Ofsted-approved layouts; the other cons had been anticipating their arrival for months.

Cain placed her box of possessions on the shallow desk, hearing the door close behind her. She straightened and looked round, waiting for the sound of a lock being turned.

Suddenly she was shoved backwards on to the bed and pinned down, an elbow digging painfully into her neck. Jones' face was in hers, their foreheads almost touching. Tears burst in Cain's eyes.

Jones pressed harder. 'You're fucking lucky you kept your mouth shut in front of the old man.'

She meant the prison manager, and her concealing the fact that the guards stood by while Slater took a beating, when Cain had drawn Tor away, taking the fight beyond a reasonable amount of time for the screws not to intervene.

She tried to swallow.

'Don't go thinking you've saved your friend, though.' Jones didn't ease up, 'Slater's marked. That bitch is on her way to permanent damage, and next time there'll be no one to step in. Just count yourself lucky the old man put you in here, and keep your scummy trap closed for another week – got it?'

Cain didn't respond; she was starting to choke. Her vision began to blur.

Please.

Jones gave one final shove and released her hold, straightening to tidy her uniform as Cain stayed down, coughing between ragged breaths.

The screw paused at the door. 'And don't think we can't get to you on the outside. Blab about this and you'll end up making Slater look like a fucking beauty queen.'

17

The young sergeant leapt off his chair to help her with the door.

Hawkins thanked him and rolled through into the operations room, a decent-sized square area with offices along the left-hand side, two large desk clusters in the centre and windows across the back. Aside from laminated wood desks, everything from the walls to the light switches was grey or white. And, despite the area's three occupants, all of whose volition was to detect, Hawkins' arrival went completely unnoticed, amid a level of intensity that could mean only one thing.

A big case had just broken.

The majority of Hawkins' core team were engaged in the recognizable early stages of a murder investigation. Frank Todd, her most experienced DI, and DS Amala Yasir, a twenty-something fast-riser, hunched together over a monitor. They faced away from Hawkins, who could see the screen past Yasir's shoulder. They were trawling the HOLMES 2 database, probably looking for individuals previously convicted of crimes similar to the current case, and for historical links to the deceased.

Beyond them, Aaron Sharpe held a phone handset to his ear with one hand and scribbled in a notepad with the other, probably piecing together a timeline of the victim's last known movements. Since his recent arrival on the team, Hawkins had yet to find anything about him that made sense. His first name suggested a younger man; his second someone more intelligent. His poorly chosen clothes neither suited him nor fit. And, on the rare occasion he'd seemed to make a joke, nobody had understood sufficiently to know if it was funny or not.

In truth, she would much rather have hung on to Pete Walker, the six foot seven sergeant who had been seconded to her team just before Christmas. But Walker's imposing physicality and strong work ethic meant he was in demand elsewhere, too. According to Mike, Vaughn had been forced to let him go to another investigation soon after the case had been closed.

For a moment her mind drifted back to their most recent investigation. She glanced at the two empty desks and shuddered. She had never lost a team member, let alone two on one case. Heat ran up the back of her neck, and her scars burned as she remembered that she'd almost joined them.

Fortunately, her thoughts were interrupted.

'Antonia?'

She looked up, smiling. 'DI Maguire. I was just wondering where you were.'

Her cheer wasn't returned as Mike's expression clouded, but within seconds they were surrounded.

'Ma'am.' Yasir seemed relieved to see another woman. 'How are you?'

'Fixed, pretty much, after six weeks of intensive relaxation.' She glanced at Mike, who looked like he was already itching to get her out of here. 'Thanks to everyone for the chocolates, by the way.'

'So is this . . .' Yasir motioned at the wheelchair. '. . . permanent?'

'Oh no.' Hawkins patted the armrest. 'I'll be out of this thing in a few days.'

Sharpe leaned in. 'We couldn't believe it when we heard about –'

'You know what?' Mike cut him off, taking hold of the chair's handles. 'Internal guidelines say we don't discuss the case, not till the inquiry's tied up. Antonia, we need to talk in private.'

He began to push, but Hawkins flicked on the brake. 'Let me say hello first.'

'So are you back?' Todd asked. 'Or just visiting?'

'She's visiting,' Maguire said.

'No,' she retorted. 'I'm back.'

There was a moment's silence.

'Anyway,' Hawkins pointed at the sparsely adorned white boards, 'looks like I arrived at just the right moment. New case, is it?'

'Yes.' Sharpe began. 'Young wom–'

'Actually,' Maguire spoke over him again, 'mine's

urgent. I'll brief you in your office, then maybe after we'll play catch-up on the case.'

He leaned over and released the brake, staring at the others until they cleared a path in the direction of Hawkins' office. As she was propelled forwards, Hawkins realized the argument was going to happen whether it took place in private or not.

Mike rolled her into the office and launched her towards the desk before closing the door behind them. Hawkins grabbed one wheel, rotating herself to face him as he reached up to twist the blinds shut. Through the shrinking gaps she caught a glimpse of her team returning to their desks, and realized just how badly she wanted to be involved.

Mike turned on her. 'What the hell are you doing here?'

'What the hell are you doing here, *ma'am*?'

'Screw your rank-pulling; you shouldn't be here.'

His voice rang in her ears. The words hadn't been spoken loudly, but an ongoing inability to sleep, combined with whatever fog still clouded her thoughts, ensured they were loud enough to cause Hawkins discomfort. She ignored it, assuring herself that half the issue was boredom; that once she was back at work her psychological discord would ease. She also chose not to mention the detour she'd almost taken towards Occupational Health on the way over from Vaughn's office. She'd visit the duty counsellor at some point, deal with the ongoing flashbacks for good, but right now she needed work more, and the two requirements didn't mix.

So her personal problems could wait.

She regarded Maguire. 'You know your accent really comes through when you're annoyed.'

'We agreed, Toni, no work till you're out of the chair. I won't let you play fast and loose with your recovery, and neither will Vaughn.'

'Actually, he will. I just left his office. I'm back in charge.'

Mike paused; she waited for his reaction. It would be highly irregular for a DI to stomp off to the chief super's office, demanding an explanation for why his immediate boss had been allowed back to work against *his* better judgement. Of course, that was assuming he believed she'd seen the DCS at all; Mike wasn't the gullible type. And, if he called her bluff, she'd be back in trouble five minutes through the door.

At last his expression softened. 'Vaughn okayed it?'

'Yep.'

'No restrictions?'

'None.'

Mike stared at her for a moment, as she felt the weight of untruth settle in her lap.

'Geez, I coached Alan on this. He was supposed to be my wingman. Said he wouldn't bring you here, no matter what.'

'Don't blame Dad, he's losing his edge. And, technically, I may not have told him where we were going.'

'You lied to him.'

'Slightly, but he came round once we got here. Come on, Mike, I'm approaching insanity after six weeks out. My dad and Vaughn understand, and you do, too, underneath all that asphyxiating protectiveness.'

For a moment he just breathed. 'Samantha Philips.'

'What?'

'The victim.' He waved towards the main office, at the investigation going on out of sight beyond the blinds. 'Twenty-four-year-old Londoner. Sam to her friends. Repeat hammer blows to the head.'

Hawkins raised her eyebrows. '*Very* Sutcliffe. Where?'

'Found before dawn yesterday in a park near Bethnal Green, right out front of the housing block she just moved into. And that ain't all. The apartment was state-funded, 'cause Sam just got out of the joint; she served six years in Holloway for killing some guy called Brendan Marsh, who she accused of raping her straight after she turned eighteen. Verdict was murder. This attack may not be linked, but we're checking out Marsh's family and friends, in case it was payback.'

'Did they know each other before?'

'He was one of her college lecturers. There were rumours about them being into each other beforehand, but nothing solid. And the whole campus was blown away when she attacked him. Details are weird, though. First, Sam didn't even report the rape, leave alone point the finger at Marsh in the six months between the alleged assault and his death. Which means there was no proof he raped her in the first place. Then, out of nowhere, she starts sending him texts like a loaded groupie, begging for them to meet up. Then she turns up at his house, and he lets her in, but as soon as he relaxes she cuts his throat with a knife from his own kitchen. Afterwards she doesn't even bother to run, just calls 999 and hands herself in. Cops arrive and there she is, covered in blood, just staring at him. She confessed to the whole thing in court.

'One thing in her favour, she wasn't his first. Trial heard that Marsh had a thing for students. He'd already been convicted of one rape, a few years back, and accused a stack of times before that. But no one checked his record when the college took him on.'

'What about her? Any other previous?'

'So far we found nothing in her past that's even *near* what she did to Marsh, but she was no saint, either. Drug use, violence, shoplifting; she had the whole set.'

'Sounds interesting.'

'Oh yeah,' Mike replied. 'But that ain't the worst of it. You didn't catch the news today, did you?'

Hawkins thought for a second. Her father had imposed John Denver at volume all the way to Hendon, probably in retaliation for her continued – and bad-tempered – imposition, while Hawkins herself had been so focused on her pending conversation with

Vaughn that checking on current events hadn't entered her head. 'No. Why?'

'Think about it. What was yesterday?'

She checked her phone. 'The fourteenth.'

'Of . . .'

'February.' As she spoke, Hawkins realized what he was talking about. 'Shit . . . Valentine's Day.'

'There she goes. And the papers ain't gonna pass up a gold-plated opportunity like that, now, are they?' Mike walked to the door. 'Wait, I've got some of the tabloids here someplace.'

He disappeared into the main office, as the implications blighted Hawkins' mind. She had just spent six weeks in hospital, watching the after-effects of an apparently Christmas-related murder spree being callously wrung out for every second of airtime they were worth. And it had stayed on the agenda throughout, thanks to high levels of interest from an increasingly panicked London population.

But now, just as mass paranoia had begun to subside, if a new murder could be linked to an entirely different seasonal event, especially the next most widely recognized one on the calendar, no doubt the whole media spectrum would happily re-tap such a fresh and lucrative vein.

Mike returned, handing her copies of the *Mail* and the *Express*. She looked down at exactly the types of headline she'd just foreseen: THE VALENTINE KILLER; BLOODY VALENTINE.

It took her a moment to excavate a comforting thought.

'Ah' – she held up a pensive digit – 'but Valentine's Day is a yearly event, and even the tabloids can't string a single murder out till next year, on the off chance he'll do it again.'

'I'll go with that.' Maguire nodded. 'But what if this is a regular thing for him, and they find a whole string of bodies, going back years? Or what if he killed more than one ex yesterday, and we've only found one of them so far? That's gonna plant a big old smile on your average editor's pan.'

Hawkins' short-lived positivity shrank as she accepted the possibility. He was right; of course, the papers were full of stars newly disgraced for decades-old indiscretions, so why should murderers be any different, especially given fresh notoriety by their latest gruesome act?

At least it was the sort of case that, successfully resolved, could revive a tattered reputation.

In this instance, hers.

She looked up at Mike, suddenly energized. 'Is the scene still ours?'

'Yeah, why?'

'Come on, then.' Hawkins rolled herself forwards, poker-faced as her muscles protested. If Mike knew she was in pain, he'd take her straight home.

'Come on, then, *what*?'

'Well, in my experience' – she stopped beside

him – 'it's generally best if the officer leading the investigation gets to visit the murder scene. Don't you think?'

Mike didn't reply, just shook his head and opened the door.

18

Doors banged up front, and footsteps moved along either side of the truck before the two men appeared. Bull recognized the taller one, but the second guy was new.

They let down the tailgate. 'Out.'

Everyone stood, crouching inside the truck. Bull's heart pounded.

They shuffled in twos to the edge and dropped on to the road. Bull was out early, scanning the scene.

The lights on the trucks were off, but the sky was clear and the moon was high, allowing him to see the derelict buildings surrounding them and the piles of random crap dotted here and there.

They were told to line up.

Bull joined the queue behind Liam, one of the older kids who was normally up for everything. But, tonight, Bull could see Liam's legs shaking. Which was good, because his were, too.

They moved off, entering a narrow alleyway that ran between two buildings, leading down a slope to their right. The alley swallowed them one by one, blackness closing in all around. It went on and on, falling away more steeply the further they went, but at last they came out on a second, even narrower street.

Bull joined the crowd forming ahead of him. There was a stronger smell of burning now, and an eeriness to the silence that made him feel sick. Quiet chatter broke out in the crowd, but Bull didn't join in.

They were told to shut up.

Everyone stopped talking as the voice at the front told them to get into groups; that the trucks would be brought down now the area was confirmed clear, that their job was to clean the place up.

Confused, Bull worked his way around a few of the taller guys for a better view. At first he couldn't see anything through the steam venting from a burst pipe. He moved forwards, peering deeper into the dark.

And saw bodies all over the ground.

19

'Of course I'm worried,' the caller urged. 'Every time I look there's another attack; some new girl getting killed. I have two daughters, Peter. I'm barely sleeping at night.'

'So what should be done?' the radio presenter asked.

'I think the police should be out on the streets; taking control.'

'You mean martial law?'

'No, no, Peter, I'm talking about community policing, like we had in the sixties.'

'You think that would help?'

'It certainly wouldn't hurt. Otherwise, things are only going to get worse, you mark my words. We'll be under curfew by spring if they don't sort this out.'

'Okay, Maggie, thanks for your call, but we need to move on. There are plenty of people waiting to tell us how the recent spate of murders in London has affected them. Let's move on to Shaun. Hi, Shaun . . .'

Hawkins turned the radio down, tensing as another shockwave shot through her torso, just about managing to keep the signs of agony from registering on her face. She didn't want to show Maguire that, despite having been back at work only a few hours, her still-recovering body had already given up for the day.

'Sorry.' Mike steered the Volvo around the next pothole. 'I know you Brits like a challenge, but I've seen smoother ranch tracks. You okay?'

'Fine,' she lied. 'But if you keep it out of the deeper gorges, my internal stitches might hold till dinner time.'

Mike smiled thinly, reinforcing Hawkins' suspicion that he'd been upset by her not even mentioning Valentine's Day. They'd only been back together for a few weeks, and so far their peak amorous encounter had been the previous evening, a five-minute fumble when her father had gone for a walk, which Hawkins had curtailed when Mike's hand brushed one of her scars. She hadn't told him that, of course, replacing honesty with a lame excuse about not wanting to be interrupted by her dad, tangling like a couple of teenage amateurs. For the rest of the evening, she'd gently avoided opportunities for affection, despite Maguire's best efforts to engage. So perhaps he'd been hoping for some kind of amorous gesture, to reassure him she hadn't lost interest for good.

Whether that was the case or not, Hawkins had spent most of Valentine's Day planning her return to work, utterly blinkered to the date's significance, and to Mike's potential need for her to show commitment to their relationship by marking it.

She spooled back in her mind. Had he been quieter than normal, maybe waiting for some small sign she'd remembered before he would reveal his undoubtedly thoughtful gift? It was difficult to say. American society had always placed greater emphasis on seasonal celebration, although even school proms and baby showers were invading British culture these days. But he also knew Hawkins tended to draw the line at birthday and Christmas presents, so it was just as likely he'd disregarded the event, too.

In fact, now she thought about it, he seemed more concerned about her health.

So far, the journey from Becke House had been dominated by a quick-fire round of delving questions about her capabilities, followed by a lecture on recognizing and respecting her constraints.

As if to emphasize the point, they crashed through another pothole.

Mike glanced across. 'Oops, that one leapt out on me.'

Hawkins renewed her contented face, keen not to blow her fragile credibility on day one. Clearly, Mike knew she was uncomfortable; they'd chosen their Volvo S60 from the car pool simply because it offered the most cosseting ride, but for now at least he was happy to have her along. The fact she knew *Deal or No Deal* was just starting on Channel Four meant Hawkins really needed to be at work today. And she was determined not to regret her decision to resume duties because of a few divots in the local tarmac.

But she was still glad when they emerged from a row

of seedy bookmakers and charity shops to see the park, surrounded by police incident screens, opposite one of the most tragic-looking housing projects she'd seen in a while.

Maguire pulled up next to the perimeter. Immediately, Hawkins released her seat belt and reached for the door handle. She got one foot over the sill before there was a tap on her shoulder. She turned.

'Don't even think about it.' Mike wagged a finger. 'Invalids are not to exit the car till personal transport arrives.'

'Oh.' Hawkins realized she still hadn't become accustomed to dependency. She'd been so eager to get inside the cordon that thoughts of self-preservation had completely left her head. She sat back, accepting that she'd probably only have made it halfway to vertical before collapsing in a heap.

'Fair enough.' She closed the door. 'Get the stupid chair, then.'

Her comment earned a look somewhere between amusement and rebuke, but Maguire didn't fire anything back. Hawkins waited until he got out before searching her bag for the painkillers, hurriedly washing down two of the industrial-strength tablets with swigs from the bottle of water she'd brought along for the purpose.

The car rocked gently as Mike heaved her chair out of the boot.

Hawkins sat impatiently, consoling herself with the

thought that at least she had his support. Whether it was due to recent traumatic events bringing them closer together, she couldn't say, but she and Mike had been tighter than ever these past weeks. They still bitched at each other like a pair of cantankerous pensioners, but since the attack there was something else underpinning their relationship, something below the surface; a deeper bond.

Granted, the greater level of complication that would accompany the resumption of their physical relationship was still to be introduced. They'd never had issues in the bedroom before; in fact, that side of things had always been fantastic, which was probably why, in its absence, they were sniping at each other more than usual. But even though her rational side said Mike wouldn't care about the ugly scars covering her chest, the stab victim's view was that his libido might run a fucking mile.

She'd considered a strategically positioned T-shirt to obscure the ugly marks. But surely that was akin to wearing a paper bag over your head.

Thankfully, the doctors said modern cosmetic surgery could almost erase the scars. The only problem was that she'd have to wait until the healing process was more advanced before they could carry out such a procedure. Which either meant weeks of frustration, or a bullet-biting moment that could lead to permanent dysfunction on, and of, Mike's part. Or paper-bag sex.

For the moment, abstinence won.

She sighed and turned back to the paper in her lap. Mike hadn't been exaggerating about the renewed level of public panic in response to the latest homicide, both reflected in and stoked by the press. The *Sun*'s entire front page was dedicated to the Valentine's Day murder: a large background image of the pressure groups already camped outside Westminster, overlaid with headlines about rampaging killers and impotent cops. And the national rags were more than happy to hearten terror by playing to the poorly informed risk-averse, constantly revisiting the one-man killing spree before Christmas; highlighting the prospect of another one now.

Nobody seemed to care that you were a hundred times more likely to die from heart disease or cancer than you were at the hands of an indiscriminate maniac with a penchant for fame. Never mind common or garden murder, which happened on a daily basis in the capital; honour killings, gang violence, contract hits. The fact you had more chance of dying in a fight with your spouse barely registered in such a propaganda war. It wasn't sexy news. So the media kept hammering the same paranoia home.

YOU, DEAR READER, COULD BE NEXT.

Even some of the broadsheets had gone straight for the sensationalist touch paper. Several publications were digging up Valentine's Day murders from years past, looking for even *tenuous* connections that allowed them to pronounce this latest perpetrator of serial-killer grade. Not that Hawkins blamed them for that. Since Mike had suggested the possibility, she'd had people doing the same thing.

But there was still a decent chance the Valentine's Day angle would burn itself out. Collective memory was short where these events were concerned, and the furore would cool fast if no concrete links to other murders were found, and if no more occurred.

Or so she hoped.

A tap on her window roused Hawkins from introspection. She opened the door to see Maguire standing next to a half-constructed wheelchair.

'Thing's impossible.' He kicked one of the footplates. 'Frame won't lock. Cut my finger.'

'Poor baby.' Hawkins fished a tissue out of her handbag and handed it to him, retrospectively giving her dad credit for being able to assemble the thing without help or injury. 'Turn it round so I can see the mechanism.'

Moments later, Maguire and his tattered ego pushed Hawkins towards the park entrance. They still couldn't see inside, due to the plastic sheeting erected around the area's extremities, outside the railings to avert prying eyes, albeit too late to have thrown the media off. The ramparts seemed to run straight into the sky, whose similarly grey colour hadn't lifted since earlier rain. Fortunately, the showers had stopped, but the bitter wind and sub-zero temperatures remained. And, already, daylight was starting to fade.

They arrived at the makeshift entrance cut into the

surrounding plastic sheet. When they'd been introduced the previous year, the screens had borne 'Police Investigation Area' warnings, but these had quickly been removed when top brass realized they were simply creating forbidden fruit. Forensics had ended up working harder to fend off curious kids than sweeping the segregated area for clues. The updated grey covers were blank, ostensibly inviting observers to assume that a cash-strapped council had sold the space within to some faceless corporation or firm.

Maguire eased the sheeting aside and identified himself to the uniformed officer just inside. They moved through as Hawkins got her first look at the place where Samantha Philips had died.

The park's footprint was almost square, with edges of about thirty feet in length. It was odd seeing what should have been a public area turned into a secret garden by the barriers now enclosing the space. A small network of pathways criss-crossed the ground, intersecting patches of emaciated grass, on some of which sat wooden benches on thick metal supports. Weathered streetlamps followed the paths. And, to the left, a children's playground and a few trees flanked a large stone statue.

But it was the central area to which Hawkins' attention was drawn, where a group of crime scene operatives were busy deconstructing a white investigation tent. The privacy walls were effective at street level, but the news channels had recently invested in airborne drone cameras, so tents were still used to protect critical zones from prying eyes, as well as potential weather damage. This tent obviously marked the spot where Samantha Philips' body had been discovered by five barely teenage kids. That they'd been out, unsupervised, at four in the morning, didn't commend the area as somewhere to raise a family, but Hawkins shivered at what might have happened had the group arrived while the killer was still around.

The fact that the tent was being cleared away meant the body was long gone, the canvas structure being left in place simply to preserve any residual evidence. The corpse itself would have been studied *in situ*, swept for fibres and DNA, photographed, and only then taken for more detailed analysis and autopsy at a nearby morgue. Typically, that happened within twenty-four hours of discovery, and this particular scene was over thirty hours old. But at least that meant there'd be no infuriating wait while Forensics carried out restricted personnel sweeps, and saved Hawkins the awkwardness of donning an anti-contamination suit while sitting down.

Mike stayed silent behind her, aware that she preferred to survey this type of scene for herself, initially at least, rather than inheriting someone else's hypotheses.

After a moment she looked up at him, pointing towards the group of suited men occupying the far corner. 'Let's interrupt.'

Maguire wheeled her across.

As usual, Gerald Pritchard, the Home Office pathologist, was in attendance. Nicknamed Mr Bean on account of his nasal timbre and retirement-home dress sense, Pritchard wasn't her favourite colleague, although that owed more to his inclination to drool over any woman within perving range than anything else. Pritchard was flanked by the usual scenes of crime mob, along with a couple of photographers and some other guys who were probably with Scientific Support.

Hawkins waited for a break in the conversation. 'Gerald, how are you?'

Pritchard turned, raising eyebrows when he was forced to lower his gaze. 'Chief Inspector Hawkins, how nice to see you back. On the mend, are we?'

'Absolutely, just a few torn stomach muscles. Nothing permanent.'

'Glad to hear it.' He treated her and Mike to a seedy grin each. 'However, you're a bit late to the party; we're about to release the area. You should have come down yesterday with your DI here.'

'First day back,' she replied. 'But I'm eager to get started. Do you have photos of the body as it was found?'

'Naturally.' He turned to one of the younger men. 'Otis, a moment, if you please.'

The youngest and most sharply dressed member of the group, with an enormous camera hanging around his neck, turned and lolloped over, holding an iPad.

'This is our new crime scene analyst, Otis King.' Pritchard introduced everyone as handshakes were exchanged between the male members of the group. Hawkins managed to lid her temper at being treated only to a nod. *Did the guy think she'd break if he pulled too firmly on her pathetic female arm?*

Luckily, Pritchard was talking again, distracting her. 'Please show the detectives your work, Otis. I'll be along presently.'

King led them back to the central area, from which the tent had now completely disappeared. Three operatives were packing its components into sturdy bags on a nearby patch of grass.

They stopped where the gravel path began to sweep round in a gentle arc before splitting up ahead. One fork continued in line with the perimeter; the other covered the short distance to the memorial away to their right.

'If I can just shove you back a bit . . .' Otis ushered Maguire and his seated cargo to the edge of the path, lining them up so they faced the stone structure.

'Here's where she was.' He spread his arms, indicating a blood-stained section of path. 'Head towards you, feet over there.'

Hawkins watched as King wandered backwards, describing the victim's likely steps, persistently addressing Mike, without even a corresponding glance to her. Now that *certainly* wasn't down to concern for her health.

The guy was a dyed-in-the-wool sexist.

King re-joined them, firing up the iPad and handing it straight to Mike. 'These photos were taken from exactly where you're standing now. I'm no expert on trauma, but whoever left her looking like that really meant it. Just swipe to move on.'

Hawkins cleared her throat so loudly that not only did Maguire and the photographer look round but so did the operatives standing ten feet away.

'Thanks.' Without further preamble she took the tablet from Mike and studied the first image. Neither man spoke.

The photograph had been taken before dawn the previous day; probably just after the first response team had arrived on site. The quality, of the photography and of the screen itself, was excellent, allowing her to pick out individual blades of frosted grass, even in the picture's darker areas. As Otis had promised, they were correctly lined up. The photo showed the pathway and the cenotaph beyond, from the same angle she viewed it now. The only differences were that the scene in the picture was covered in a light frost, and that there was no longer a body sprawled across it, face down.

Hawkins maximized the victim's head on the display, picking out the right temple, where Samantha Philips' skull had been caved in. Unfortunately, shadow, and the angle at which the photo was taken, prevented much detail from being seen.

'Flip forwards,' Otis suggested quietly. 'There are better shots further in.'

Hawkins began swiping through the images, noting the gradual increase in light as time moved on. Some shots contained scenes of crimes officers in anti-contamination suits, crouching beside the body to lift fibres or take swabs, while various close-ups showed specific details on the clothing or hands. Hawkins noted cigarette stains on the right forefingers, and decent amounts of dirt under most of the victim's nails.

She pointed it out. 'Was this contamination –'

'Collected during the attack?' Pritchard's nasal tone cut in from behind them. 'No. Neither the composition nor age of that material matches anything here in the park. It's a mixture of domestic particles built up pro-gressively over recent days. It seems Ms Philips wasn't fastidious in her approach to personal grooming, a fact confirmed by the general state of her physical hygiene during autopsy.'

Hawkins turned her chair towards him. 'So what's your view?'

'May I?' Pritchard took the iPad from Otis and began skipping through the photographs, before holding the device out, pointing at the image on screen. It was a close-up of Philips' right temple, or at least the crum-pled mess it had become.

'Epidural haematoma,' he stated. 'Induced by a sharp, heavy blow to the pterion, a weak point in the skull between the frontal, parietal, temporal and sphe-noid bones, rupturing the middle meningeal artery and causing a fatal seizure. Surrounding strikes to the same area were simply to make sure. Combined with the demonstrable absence of other injuries, this damage appears to have been inflicted by design, to prevent the victim defending herself; to debilitate and kill. This assumption is backed up by the angle of the initial blow, consistent with a strike from behind and slightly to the victim's right. These details indicate that the killer – who's right-handed, by the way – took care to ensure the target didn't see it coming. In short, Detective, our perpetrator isn't interested in the process of killing, only in its result.'

'Seems reasonable.' Hawkins followed the gist, if not the terminology. 'What sort of implement are we talking about? Anything fancy?'

Pritchard shook his head. 'I'd suggest nothing more exotic than a domestic hammer, I'm afraid. We haven't found the murder weapon, but the victim's injuries are consistent with such a tool. The killer would have required nothing more complex.'

Hawkins resigned herself to the fact that chasing the weapon's origin would be no more than fruitless courtesy. Certain cases involving guns or unusual objects could sometimes be advanced by tracing their source. But a household tool that could have been brand new or years old, and was available from a thousand outlets in the capital alone?

No chance.

She looked over at where the attack had happened, assessing the memorial's position adjacent to the path as the perfect place to stage an ambush. The structure's plinth was tall enough to hide an adult so willing, while the overhanging trees and lack of proximate lighting would deepen the shadows further still. She pictured Samantha Philips wandering slowly past in the dead of night, and the killer's silhouette emerging unseen from behind the structure, shoes silent on the dampened grass.

She asked, 'Does this type of attack indicate any training on the killer's part?'

'A strike to the pterion? Only what you or I could pick up after ten minutes on the internet. Such information is easily found.'

Mike joined in. 'Any useful traces?'

'Unfortunately' – Pritchard nodded at the darkening horizon – 'winter has played its caustic role. Shortly after Ms Philips expired, a heavy shower fell and then frosted over, obliterating most of the material evidence we'd otherwise have been able to exploit. Sadly, Detective, until we find a way of getting our tents in place prior to al fresco murder, British weather will remain the greatest curb on forensic science.'

'Predictable.' She glanced at Mike. 'So what was our heroine doing out here alone at quarter past one in the morning?'

'No mystery there.' Maguire pointed up at the housing development poking out above the barricades. 'Like I said, Sam lived up in that apartment block, courtesy of the state. But she was a smoker, and these days you can't do that stuff in government-funded estates.

Department of Health have cracked down; so the place is shot through with detectors. Parolees like Sam have to be ten feet outside the boundary before lighting up. Who cares if every other mother in there is chain smoking on their DFS recliners? The locals who will talk to us say Philips was down here three or four times a night, every night since she moved in last weekend.'

'Good old CPS, winning hearts and minds,' Hawkins commented. 'What do we have character-wise?'

Maguire shrugged. 'Not much. Kept to herself, no real shots at making nice with the locals. We're working friends and family now. Both parents are dead, but there's a brother called Simon.'

Hawkins nodded, already constructing a mental list of anyone with a potential interest in Samantha Philips' death. It could have been a random act of violence, of course: an indiscriminate killer who picked his target purely due to circumstance, although, in Hawkins' experience, that was almost never the case. To hate someone sufficiently to kill, first you had to care.

The vast majority of murders were committed by those emotionally involved with their victims. Motivation for anyone to wait out an entire jail term and then settle the perceived debt as soon as the focus of their rage was released could come only from deeply impassioned roots. Anyone with strong emotional connections – and therefore prospective discontent with the deceased – had to be a suspect, at least. Potentials to exclude, therefore, began with boyfriends, husbands, or significant others present or past, which might reduce the likelihood that this murder was, as the media proposed, linked to Valentine's Day.

Then there was the brother. It seemed unlikely that a sibling's rage could spawn such a callous act, but you never knew. A potential lifetime of resentment would only deepen the roots of such hatred, for which a paid assassin would be the perfect shroud. However, Hawkins still wasn't convinced that emotionally imbued vendettas were ever settled in so calculated a style.

Still, the investigation would soon reveal its protagonist's past, along with any smoke that might belie fire. People rarely jumped straight from law-abiding behaviour to murder, so if the brother and any exes had no form, it was less likely to be one of them. All of which meant their strongest line of inquiry had to be Philips' criminal past. Revenge was one of the strongest incentives for murder, and not only did Sam have history of her own in that regard, she'd just spent six years locked up with hundreds of other people in exactly the same situation.

Typically, once a person has crossed the Rubicon of murder, life changed for good; the perpetrator's existence was permanently scarred by the irreversibility of their action. And, with that pillar of self-respect gone, a different mind-set often then prevailed.

Once condemned, a killer has little left to lose, a situation that generally transforms their approach to every interaction. Life becomes a series of trade-offs and threats, simple agreements that ease or prolong the survival of those involved.

Unless one crosses another.

And yet, according to the team's initial research, Samantha Philips had made it through her time inside without major incident. She'd kept her head down and done her stint, never showing up on the prison radar as a troublemaker or upsetting fellow cons. It was unusual, but Philips had left prison without any known grudges against her; a state colloquially known as 'clean'.

As a result, Hawkins decided the investigation should now prioritize anyone close to Brendan Marsh, the man who allegedly raped, and was then murdered by, Sam Philips.

Taking one last scan of the darkening green, she looked up at her second in command. 'Which flat was she in?'

'Twenty-eight.'

'Let's see it, then.' She banged the armrests of her chair, indicating that she was ready to leave.

'Sorry, no can do.' Mike jabbed a thumb at the estate. 'Flat's second floor, so unless you want a piggyback or you're up to climbing a bunch of stairs, it'll have to wait.'

Hawkins was about to fight her way out of the chair when Otis saved her.

'It's okay.' He retrieved the iPad from Pritchard. 'I've got pictures.'

He fiddled for a moment before handing her the tablet. The first image showed a small studio flat with plain walls and a dirty carpet, to one side of which was a makeshift bed. A few boxes were stacked against the rear wall, presumably clothes and possessions that had remained in storage during Samantha's jail time, possibly with the brother. Otherwise, the place was bare.

Subsequent photos depicted an equally clutter-free kitchen and bathroom, perhaps unsurprising when you considered that Philips had been in residence for no more than a week.

Hawkins passed the iPad back to King. 'Any observations about the places these pictures don't show?'

The photographer thought for a second. 'Only an overriding smell of damp.'

'Okay.' She turned to Mike. 'Had she been out and about much?'

'Sure doesn't look that way. Cupboards are full of canned goods, so I'd say she was holed up for a while. Only reason she came out here was to smoke.'

Hawkins nodded. 'So what was she doing for cash?'

'Unknown. The court set up some interviews for manual work – you know, reintegration stuff – but they weren't till later this week.'

She made a mental note to check the woman's financial history. 'What about the lack of any attempt to unpack?'

'Maybe she had nothing worth unpacking?' Pritchard offered.

'Could be,' Hawkins agreed. 'Or is it the behaviour of someone not planning to stick around?'

Someone who knew they were being hunted down.

20

Bull lay on his back, staring at the underside of the bed above.

'Nobby', 'Swish', 'Barker', and a hundred other names had been scratched into the shabby slats, filling every inch of space so there was nowhere for Bull to carve his own, even if he'd wanted to. How many of these guys were still around? It was probably best not to know.

He stretched in the tight space; there wasn't much room in the bunks, and this one smelled permanently of sweat. At least he had the lower level, with storage space underneath.

He could hear some of the others talking at the far end of the room. Normally, by now they'd all be out working, but after last night they'd been allowed to rest. He'd crawled into bed about four, but hadn't slept. His head was full of death.

He'd seen bodies before, but this time it was different. There had been women.

Kids.

They'd lifted the bodies by hand, working in groups to shift the bigger men, lugging the corpses across and passing them up to the guys in the backs of the trucks. Then they'd gone back to search for more, working in teams, but as the bodies became harder to find, the group had begun to spread out. Bull had seen his chance, and slowly drifted away, hoping the others wouldn't notice he wasn't making as many return trips.

Then he'd found the baby.

The small body lay crumpled in a corner. Bull had looked around, but no one else was nearby. Reluctantly, he had reached down and picked it up.

But the body broke in two.

Bull had fallen, retching. He'd knelt in the dirt, swallowing bile, then the urge to run hit him. He'd staggered to his feet. It didn't matter where he was going, or how far he was from home. He just wanted out.

Away from the baby boy with no legs.

The others had found him soon after that, curled in a corner, talking nonsense to himself. The ride back had been shit, too, although Bull was glad no one else had wanted to talk. He'd still been busy trying not to puke.

That feeling had passed, but the images of the previous night came back whenever he shut his eyes. He needed something to take his mind off it all.

Then he remembered the wood.

He rolled to the edge of the bunk and reached underneath, right into the corner. He found what he was looking for and pulled it free, holding the small block of wood up in front of his face. He'd found it there a couple of days ago. He had no idea what type of wood it was, but it was solid enough and, apart from a few rough areas, its surface felt nice.

He ran his fingers along the grain before digging in his pocket for his knife and picking open one of the tools. He tried rubbing down the splinters, but the file was too small, so he swapped to the large blade and began shaving off small chunks instead, pleased to find the wood soft but dense enough to leave a smooth edge.

As he carved, his mind wandered, and for the first time since the night before he began to relax. For a moment he was back in his room, listening to music when he should have been doing homework. It wasn't so long ago, but now it seemed like another life.

Footsteps interrupted his daydream as someone passed his bunk. He hid the piece of wood behind his leg until they faded. Then he held the carving up and studied it again.

What the fuck?

Maybe it was just the angle. He turned it over. But still the carving reminded him of the same thing.

He put the wood back under the bed and closed his eyes, wishing the thoughts would go away. Last night, destruction and death.

His part in it all.

But he couldn't forget; the carving looked just like the image now turning over and over behind his eyelids.

It looked like the baby boy with no legs.

The poorly nuanced British accent caught her up. 'Back in a jiffy.'

Hawkins turned, shaking her head as Mike's Range Rover pulled noisily away from the kerb. She turned the chair back towards her house and rolled on up the path.

Only when the deep thrum of the engine had faded did she let herself crumple in the seat, exhaling hard, attempting to relieve some of the singing discomfort in her stomach wall. Her heart thumped in her ears, reminding her it was working overtime to repair as well as to sustain. She stayed motionless for a long moment, glad that the February days were still short enough to shroud her in darkness, checking the windows for signs that her dad had heard them arrive. But the curtains remained undisturbed.

Her secret was safe for now.

However, just six hours of holding herself upright, heaving herself in and out of the chair and moving about had annihilated her feeble stamina. She was already a day ahead on her painkillers and, unless she could sleep it off, Hawkins had to accept the possibility that she might have pushed herself too far.

At least she'd managed to keep the pain from

showing on her face as Mike loaded her into the chair, and had sent him straight off to get a takeaway, saying that Dad would open the door and help her up the step. Her efforts had been rewarded with this moment of solitude, away from two people intent on placing her in mental traction until her damaged body caught up with her frustrated mind.

At last she was able to sit up, and resumed her slow journey towards the house. Approaching the scene of the attack still gave her a twisted feeling in her gut, but she kept going, determined not to let anxiety win. Otherwise, she'd be running for ever.

She reached the door, turning the chair sideways so she could reach the bell, and pressed, hearing the chime, aligning the chair so her dad could help her up.

But no answer came.

'Come on, Dad.' She tried again.

After another moment she decided he hadn't heard the bell and resorted to her phone, calling the home number. She sat back as it started to ring, watching for shadows in the light coming through the glass. Still nothing. Perhaps he was out.

Hawkins dug in her bag for the keys, edging her chair closer and fighting with the lock till it released. She pushed the door open.

'Dad?' she called into the empty hallway. 'You there?'

The lights were on in the front room.

Silence.

Then the smoke alarm went off.

'*Dad?*' Hawkins shouted, looking around for passers-by, seeing no one. Next door worked long hours and wouldn't be in, and she'd have to go the long way round on chair-friendly paths to reach the property after that, still with no guarantee they'd be there. She turned back to the house, straining her ears for any sign of a response. And still the alarm blared.

Suddenly she was fighting her way out of the chair, dropping to her knees inside the front door, looking back. There was no way she'd be able to pull the wheel-chair up the step without standing.

She had to leave it.

Hawkins crawled forwards, ignoring tortured stomach muscles, picturing her dad lying on the floor with smoke curling around him. She reached the lounge, battling the urge to crumple and curl, checking the room for occupants.

'*Dad?*' she shouted again, over the incessant beeping, which she could now tell was coming from the kitchen.

Hawkins renewed her efforts and struck out for the next doorway, trying to speed up. *What the fuck had he done?* Had he been smoking again? He had promised everyone before Christmas he'd quit.

She tried to work out how long Mike had been gone, realizing it could only have been minutes at most. If her father was in physical distress, she was the worst assistant he could have hoped for. It was one thing being found, quite another if your supposed saviour then buckled, too.

She made it to the kitchen, quickly checking the floor, relieved to find it was clear. But that lasted only for the brief second before she realized that her father might be upstairs, still in need of resuscitation. And, in her current state, Hawkins had no chance of making it up there without help.

Then her eye was drawn to the black smoke rising from the top oven, forcing her to make a snap choice. Even if she went for the stairs, by the time she reached the landing the whole house could be alight.

She had to stop this first.

Hawkins set off towards the far side of her kitchen, knees crunching against the tiles, seeing flames starting to lick the underside of the grill. She realized with dread that reaching it would require her to stand.

She came to a halt by the lower oven, hunching for a moment to relieve the worst of the pain, trying to block out the alarm. Picturing the flames getting worse.

She grabbed the nearest handle, dragging her right leg forwards until her foot was flat on the floor. Without pausing, she pushed upwards, bearing violent protest from her stomach wall. At first she made progress, but then her head went light and she dropped back, breathing hard. She stared at the floor, recharging for another attempt. And then she saw it: a tiny patch of discoloured grout between two of the tiles. At any other time, in any other kitchen, it would have meant nothing, but its significance rocked her. This was the spot where she'd been found just six weeks ago, near to death. Which meant the patch was probably blood.

Her blood.

Hawkins' head swam, a mixture of injury, confusion and drugs battering her senses.

She heard a sound and glanced up through bleary eyes at a facsimile of the moment that had changed her life – at the figure entering the kitchen through the back door.

It all came flooding back: the killer's expression, the attack, the pain. The night she almost died. Her arms clamped around her head and she screamed.

A second later the illusion shattered as a familiar voice reached her. 'Blimey, what's going on in here?'

Dad.

Hawkins looked again, her vision clearing. Her father leaned across, pulling the tray from the oven and dumping it in the sink. He turned the taps on full, dousing the flames, spinning to flap at the alarm with his hands before resorting to a towel. At last the din stopped, and Alan Hawkins crouched beside his daughter. 'Bloody hell, love, are you okay?'

A few minutes later, once he'd retrieved the wheelchair from outside the front door and helped her into it, Hawkins sat awkwardly in the lounge, incredulous. 'I've told you on at least two occasions about that bloody grill pan.'

'Sorry, love.' He stared at his feet.

'What were you doing, anyway?'

'Sausage and mash. I'm bored with all that takeaway rubbish, so I thought I'd make myself useful now you're back at work.' He risked a look up. 'Your mum normally cooks.'

'No, I mean . . . where *were* you?'

'Oh. Sorting the recycling in your garage. There are so many bloody bins, I didn't know what to put where.'

She rolled her eyes, hiding the fact that she felt sorry for him. 'Well, in future, no recycling while you're cooking, and don't put the sodding grill pan on the top runners, okay?'

'Okay.'

'Holy crap.' Mike walked in, holding a carrier bag. 'What's with the smoke?'

'I'm glad you've got curry,' Hawkins told him. 'Dad nearly cooked.'

22

Matt slumped in the chair.

He looked up, catching sight of himself coming in and out of focus in the dressing-table mirror across the room. The whiskey was kicking in now.

He took another swig and slid the chair sideways till it hit the bed, trying to avoid his own stare. But there wasn't enough space and, when he checked, there he was again. Matthew Hayes.

Murderer.

Without thinking, he launched the bottle across the room. It caught the edge of the mirror, cracking the corner, shaking the whole table. When everything settled, the mirror had moved, but his reflection was still there, staring back at him. The bottle lay on the carpet, leaking. And above it the clock ticked onwards, nearer and nearer to 11.40 p.m. The instant, just over a year ago, when his life had turned to shit.

He let his head drop back against the chair, willing himself to sleep or pass out.

Anything that would let him skip the fatal moment.

But he couldn't let go.

Amanda laughed, leaning in.

Matt relished the feel of her long, painted nails as they ran gently down his arm, watching her calves tense as she steadied herself on the bar stool. She had fucking great legs.

His joke wasn't even that good.

Next to them, Harry, their boss, paid for a round. And, across the bar, their colleagues Ian and Julian were setting up another frame of pool.

'Here you go, champ.' Harry handed Matt and Amanda a glass of champagne each. 'Bloody well earned.' He clapped Matt on the shoulder before heading towards the pool table with three more glasses.

'Here's to you, Mr Wonderful.' Amanda raised her glass, and they clinked before sipping their drinks.

The whole team had toasted him on the first round, of course, but Matt was still savouring his Lanson, thinking about the two huge property deals he'd pulled off right at the end of the month. The wonky barn conversion had been a pig to shift, but the country house right under the revised Heathrow flight path was the pièce de résistance. They'd all tried. Even Harry's experience and Amanda's charm had failed. But Matt had offloaded both.

Amanda slid off the stool and whispered in his ear that she'd be back soon. She floated away, glancing back. Sensual poetry; just for him.

But he knew her game.

Matt waited until she'd disappeared and drained his glass before heading towards the three other men at the pool table. He shook hands all round, overplaying the modesty as they cheered him all the way to the door. The car park was pretty much empty, and the road outside clear, unsurprising given the pitch winter blackness, and the Baltic temperatures to match. But none of that bothered Matt as he strode towards the C Class, confident that he wouldn't be over the limit, not after two glasses of champagne.

He hit the start button and pulled smoothly on to the high road, feeling the surge of the V6, savouring the way Harman Kardon speakers reproduced the first movement of Piano Concerto 21 as if Mozart were playing live in the back seat. He drove until he saw the sign for Oak Drive, a sweeping diversion that dived gracefully between crossroads. He took the turn. This route home was longer, but it allowed him to dream.

He ghosted down the hill, watching the houses retreat further from the road, heavier gates and taller foliage filling the gaps as the street grew darker beneath ever more elegant lights. He passed the dip and began to climb, slowing up, craning his neck for a glimpse of Treetops, a modern architectural masterpiece he'd sold not long after Harry took him on. He knew the current owner was looking to move. Another few months like this, and Matt might be doing a lot more than dreaming about the place . . .

The bang shook Matt from his fantasy. Something crunched against the front-left corner of the bonnet and ground along the wing.

'Fuck!' He gripped the wheel as it jerked in his hands, jamming the brakes on as he felt the rear of the car jump over something in the road.

The Mercedes pulled up sharply as Matt stared in his mirror, heart thumping, cursing his lack of awareness. Had he drifted into the kerb and glanced off one of the huge cornerstones some of *these properties used to mark their driveways? Or maybe some dickhead had left their recycling bin out on the wrong day.*

He couldn't see a thing in the inky blackness. Better check, though; the car might be damaged. He'd only had the thing a bloody week.

Matt flung open the door and climbed out, looking back down the road, failing to see what he'd hit. He strode round to the front, anticipating a dent in the bumper, a broken headlamp, at least. But when he got there the xenon light was fine, its sleek housing completely intact. Matt bent and stroked a hand along the Mercedes' flank. There was damage, but nowhere near as bad as he'd expected.

He straightened, now even more curious to see what he'd hit, moving along the car's flank, his vision still impaired by the glow from inside the cabin.

Matt reached the back of the car, squinting into the darkness as he moved past its glaring red LEDs. There was definitely something in the road. Then he saw the bike.

And the young boy lying in the road next to it. Dark clothing; no lights.

Oh fuck!

Matt's gut twisted as the chilling scene established itself as reality. Seconds passed. He saw himself running towards the boy, shouting for anyone who could hear to call an ambulance.

But he hadn't moved.

Something held him fast, just staring at the kid. And then he realized what it was.

He'd been drinking.

Suddenly the future was playing itself out in his mind; nightmare flashes of what would begin as soon as he dialled 999. His whole life ripping apart.

Then everything became a blur.

Headlights appeared, a quarter of a mile away on the crest of the hill. Another car had turned on to the road. Matt found himself walking back to his Merc, sliding into the seat, checking as the door closed and the interior lights faded that the street around him was still deserted.

Then he was driving away.

He watched the other car's lights in his rear-view mirror as it slowly descended the hill. Nearer and nearer the kid. Telling himself the other driver couldn't miss the crumpled form in the road. They'd find him, call an ambulance. He'd be okay.

And so would Matt.

There was no need to risk his life to save the kid's. He'd been drinking; a dozen witnesses would confirm that. But even if he was over the limit, it would have been by a gnat's whisker. It hadn't impaired his ability to drive. If he was guilty of anything, it was admiring a fucking nice house. The kid had been riding along a dark street with no lights.

And whose fault was that?

Certainly not Matt Hayes'.

Minutes later he was home, straight on to his drive, so the damaged wing was tight against the wall. He killed the engine and dug in the glove box for tissues. Then he got out and strategically wiped the dented panel, checking in the light from his phone that there was no blood on the tissue.

Then he calmly entered the house, walked straight into the downstairs loo.

And threw up.

His eyes opened.

He watched the ceiling orbiting him and relived the moment when two police officers had arrived on his doorstep the evening after the crash; the look on his wife's face when they'd told her why.

Your vehicle carries damage consistent with reports of a hit and run not far from here.

He hadn't bothered denying it. They'd already inspected the car; he hadn't had time to send it for repair. Jodie had been hysterical.

They'd taken Matt in. Questioned him.

Told him the kid had died.

The ambulance crew had been minutes too late . . . time Matt had wasted before driving away.

Fifteen years old.

Events he couldn't change.

He grabbed his mobile, fumbling with the electronic lock, selecting the number still stored under 'Home'.

'Hello?' Her voice was croaky. He'd woken her.

'Jodie. Get Tom and Rebecca.'

'Matt.' She was annoyed. 'You can't keep doing this.'

'Just . . . for a minute.'

'It's gone midnight. They're asleep.'

'They're my kids, too.'

He heard her telling someone else to leave it; to go

back to sleep. 'They stopped being your kids the day you left that boy lying in the road.'

Tears formed. 'Jodie . . .'

'What if it had been one of our children, Matt?'

'Please.'

The line went dead.

23

'Mrs Watts?' Hawkins held up her badge to the woman holding a small child in the doorway. 'I'm DCI Hawkins, and this is DI Maguire. Sorry to intrude on your weekend. We're here about Samantha.'

'Okay,' Nicola Watts responded slowly, as if she hadn't really understood. 'But I have to go soon. Collect my older one from his grandparents'. They're going away.'

'That's not a problem,' Hawkins told her. 'We don't need much of your time.'

She studied Watts, who must have been in her mid-twenties, the same as her recently deceased friend. Her dark hair was gathered in a ponytail and, although she wore no make-up, her skin was immaculate. But the woman's youthfulness was under attack, not just from the challenge of two young children but now from bereavement as well. She looked exhausted.

Mike reached for the chair's handles and began to rotate his boss.

'Don't worry about the step.' Watts' voice stayed flat. 'My partner's mum's in a chair. We have a ramp. Go round the side and I'll let you in through the kitchen.'

'Thanks.' Hawkins stopped herself from explaining

that the wheelchair was only temporary, acknowledging at last that nobody cared except her.

Watts disappeared inside, still holding the child, closing the door with her back.

As Mike pushed her towards the side gate, Hawkins marvelled at the Watts' front garden: rampant weeds strangling skeletal plants that looked as if they'd once been well tended, and a small pond full of sludge. Either Watts' family had bought the house from people who liked gardening a lot more than they did, or looking after two young kids had proved more difficult than they'd anticipated.

They reached the corner, negotiating the narrow gate and heading for the shallow concrete ramp grafted neatly on to the path. The back garden was unkempt, too, except for the recently mown grass area, housing an enclosed trampoline to one side, plethoric toys everywhere else.

Nicola Watts was at the door when Maguire rolled Hawkins level with the threshold. Behind her the kettle was just coming to the boil, while her infant had been deposited in a plastic high chair and was now banging a plastic spoon against the attached table.

Being fair, Watts looked remarkably composed for someone who'd only known about her best friend's murder for a couple of days. But the timing of their arrival wasn't coincidence. Family liaison officers would have been sent to inform next of kin, in this case Philips' brother, but friends generally found out on the grapevine or via media reports. Sam's death had been widely reported the previous day, so if Watts had known since then, it was actually good news, because grief did strange things to the bereaved. Usually, if it was someone close, the person being informed wouldn't be much use to anyone for a while immediately afterwards, at least until denial and anger had played themselves out. Conversely, if you left it too long, they were often too dejected to assist. Typically, however, there was a short window of clarity once the initial shock had passed, when the newly bereft were inclined to get things in order for the inevitable numbness they somehow knew was on its way. The window usually incorporated a desire to see justice done by helping the police with their inquiries. Hawkins was hoping she had accurately estimated when this would occur.

Watts helped manoeuvre Hawkins inside, and Mike parked her across the utility room doorway, next to a huge scribble made in black marker pen on otherwise elegant wallpaper. He settled on one of the leather-effect bar stools as drinks orders were taken.

'So' – Watts poured boiling water into the first mug, failing to hide the tremor in her voice – 'have you arrested someone?'

'Not yet.' Hawkins watched her mash the teabag. 'We're still investigating. That's why we're here; Sam's brother tells us you were her best friend.'

Watts looked round, with an expression half pleading for the subject to be left alone, but she found an answer. 'Yes. We'd known each other since primary school.'

Mike took over. 'We know it's hard, Nicola, but the more you can tell us about Sam, the more chance we'll catch whoever did this.'

'I realize that.' Watts added milk and passed a mug to Mike. 'I just want to understand *why*.'

'Hopefully, we'll know soon.' Mike took his mug, thanking her. 'What was Sam like?'

A smile flashed across Watts' face, as if memories of her friend momentarily eclipsed the fact that she'd been murdered only forty-eight hours ago. But it was replaced instantly by a look of despair, and sorrow contaminated her voice. 'Sam was just . . . such a laugh. Whatever she thought of someone they'd know, but if she liked you, she was the best mate you could –' She broke off, crossing her arms and staring out of the window for a moment, slowly shaking her head.

Hawkins and Maguire exchanged glances, giving her a moment. But they all responded to the clattering sound.

'Amelie, please.' Watts bent to retrieve her daughter's spoon from the corner into which it had been launched, wiped it and gave it back. Amelie looked at it for a second before she threw it into the same corner and burst into tears.

The two detectives sipped their drinks politely until their host had pacified her child.

At last she straightened. 'Sorry, she's teething.'

'No problem.' Hawkins was pleased that the woman had such an effective distraction from recent events. 'You were telling us about Samantha.'

Watts drew a long breath. 'Look, I loved Sam, but I won't try to tell you she was everyone's cup of tea, because she wasn't, especially since . . . you know, the whole thing with Brendan.'

'We know about Marsh,' Hawkins said. 'Did she come to you after the attack?'

'Yeah. I tried to help, but I can't . . . imagine what it must be like. Rape, I mean. Sam was just, destroyed.' Watts tilted her head up, blinking back tears. 'I told her to report him, but she wouldn't do it. She had a reputation for flirting with the male teachers – not just him – and sometimes she'd lie about stuff for no reason, so she was convinced they wouldn't believe her. But I knew her well enough to know she wasn't lying about this. The next few months were awful. She dropped out of school and started sleeping around, drinking and taking drugs; but none of it was her.'

She stopped, but Hawkins stayed silent, encouraging her to go on.

Watts took the hint. 'She started treating people badly, just so they'd leave her alone, but every time Sam upset someone she'd just end up more depressed. It didn't stop, though; she even came on to my husband, and when I forgave her she broke down. That was her lowest point, when she said she couldn't stand it any more. That's when she tried to kill herself.'

Hawkins nodded. Philips' suicide attempt was on record because she'd needed emergency medical attention at the local hospital, to repair the damage to her wrists.

Mike asked, 'Why do you think she failed?'

'I suppose she didn't really want to die.' Watts looked from Mike to Hawkins. 'Isn't that what they say?'

'You think it was a cry for help.'

'I suppose so. But whatever help she wanted never came. And after that she was just . . . different, sort of cold and emotionless. I guess that's what led her back to Brendan.'

Hawkins leaned forwards. '*Led her back?*'

'She started talking about him more and more. At first I thought she wanted to see him again, like some weird dependency thing. Infatuation – I guess that's how she framed it to him. But I never expected . . .' She paused. 'You have to understand, she was so messed up; otherwise, she'd never have been able . . .'

Hawkins finished her sentence. ' . . . to kill Marsh.'

Watts looked at her, nodding.

'I'm sorry to ask' – Hawkins knew they were testing Watts' composure – 'but can you think of anyone who might have wanted to hurt Sam?'

Watts thought for a moment. 'She fell out with people here and there, but just over petty stuff; nothing that could have led to this.'

'What about ex-partners? Was there anyone steady?'

Their host shook her head. 'No one serious. The

only guys she told me about were flings, and that was for a long time before she went down.'

'Were any of these flings . . . intense?' Hawkins phrased her question with care.

'I didn't think so at the time.' Watts' stare dropped towards the floor. 'She never mentioned any violence, if that's what you mean, but after this week I don't know *what* to believe any more.' She was clearly fighting distress.

Hawkins decided to move on. 'Did you ever meet any of Brendan Marsh's family or friends?'

'No. Why?' Watts regarded her briefly before answering her own question. 'You think it was one of *them*?' Her gaze floated away, as if the prospect genuinely hadn't occurred to her.

'It's possible,' Mike said. 'So is there anyone we should talk to?'

Watts thought for a moment. 'I really don't know. Like I said, I never met them.'

He pressed. 'Did Sam?'

'I don't think so.' She sighed as she looked at her daughter, who had started crying again. 'You don't mind if I feed her, do you?'

They waited while she buzzed around the kitchen, mixing various types of anaemic mush in a bowl, negotiating as much of the results as possible into Amelie. The majority of it didn't stay there long, and Hawkins watched the woman's frustration build, deciding to

pursue her second intuition quickly. Before they out-
stayed their welcome.

She asked gently, 'How did Sam deal with prison?'

Watts looked up, the spoon mid-approach. 'Better
than I expected. She always hated being confined, so I
thought she'd fall apart in there. But, like I said, she'd
changed; and prison just made her harder. I barely recognized her on my last couple of visits, but a while
after that they stopped her privileges and I couldn't go
any more.'

She shuddered. 'The worst part is that I hadn't seen
her for months. I'd heard she was due for release, but I
didn't even know she was out.'

Hawkins dug, aware that their window was closing.
'Why were her privileges stopped?'

'For fighting, I think.' Watts extended a trembling
hand to wipe her daughter's mouth. 'She was pretty
bashed up the final time I went, but all she'd say was
that someone had kicked off.'

Ten minutes later Mike loaded the wheelchair into the
boot of their unmarked Astra while Hawkins sat in the
passenger seat, using her mobile to find the number of
Holloway Prison.

They'd made their exit shortly after Watts' revelation
regarding her late friend. Hawkins' original plan for the
afternoon had been to focus on Sam's previous partners, followed by Marsh's family and friends, and to

assist the investigation team in tracing them and setting up interviews. Considering it had been six years since his death and Philips' subsequent incarceration, it wasn't surprising that some of them were proving hard to trace.

But her instincts, which said that greater progress would be made by talking to those who knew the victim personally first, had served her well. If there had been hostilities between Philips and her fellow inmates, as it now appeared there had, it became much more likely that one of them had contracted a hit on their adversary shortly after her release. Which also meant that the police needed to pursue this new line of inquiry before Philips' former fellow inmates had time to think about it and decided to clam up.

What worried Hawkins was that Amala Yasir, normally one of her most thorough investigators, had already spoken to various contacts at Holloway.

Yasir would have asked about any antipathy between Philips and her peers. Which meant either that the sergeant had forgotten to mention Philips' violent tendencies.

Or that Amala purposely hadn't been told.

24

Hawkins pushed herself up on the wheelchair's armrests to peer over the second-floor windowsill. She looked down at the tidy flowerbeds and manicured hedges intersected by raked gravel paths with wooden seats; there was even a conservatory. The gardens were certainly well tended, but really there was nothing remarkable about the medium-sized park except its location.

Slap bang in the centre of Holloway Prison.

Unfortunately, the same cathartic appearance didn't apply to the rest of the place. Its interior walls were all the same depressingly clinical off-white, and every face scowled. At least the recirculated air in this section smelled fresher than it had near the cells, where five hundred female bodies were crammed into a space that wouldn't have contained more than a fifth of that number outside.

And people wondered why violence was a way of life inside.

So it wasn't too much of a leap to suppose that one such incident might have led one of Sam's rivals to contract a hit on her once she'd been released.

And, if someone had threatened Sam, perhaps that explained why she hadn't been sleeping, and why she hadn't attempted to make her flat into any kind of home – because she'd been planning to run.

But who made the threat?

Most of London seemed to disagree with Hawkins' line of investigation; they had been convinced by mounting media assertions that the killer was a discarded ex, somehow sufficiently incensed to use Valentine's Day as symbolic backdrop to his impassioned revenge. For various reasons, Hawkins couldn't afford to ignore the possibility, so she still had a small team working to identify ex-lovers and intimate friends, but intuition told her not to ignore less obvious avenues. Hence this visit to the place where Philips had spent the last six years of her life.

Hawkins hadn't expected an easy time when she'd lined up interviews with several key inmates at Holloway, mainly because convicts generally weren't that keen on the police. But she'd been hoping to obtain slightly more information than she had so far. Her tactic had been simple: talk to potential perpetrators first. Of course, they'd admit to precisely bugger all as far as anything they were involved in, but Hawkins had hoped at least one of them might be prepared to burn a rival.

No such luck.

Then she'd moved on to the most notorious gossips in Holloway, the people who made it their business to know everything about everyone, and had no qualms about sharing the facts – for a price, of course, typically in the form of increased privileges, maybe even early release.

She'd been given three names: Sandra Martin, Tyra Shore, Dorothy Clarke.

Over the last three hours Hawkins had tried to persuade each woman to divulge anything they'd known about Sam and who she'd fallen out with during her time at Holloway. She wasn't proud of it, but she had ended up playing each one off against the next in a game of scandalmonger one-upmanship.

It hadn't helped.

Either some sort of criminals' honour was muting her subjects or they really didn't know. None would even *speculate* as to who had attacked Philips on at least one occasion inside.

Hawkins had just one more interview lined up, a final chance for Holloway to provide the answer. But she wasn't holding her breath.

The wall of innocence she'd hit so far only increased the chances that Sam's killer came from an entirely different pool of potential suspects. As Hawkins sat there at the window, the rest of her murder investigation team were tracing Brendan Marsh's family and friends.

It was important to remember that Samantha Philips herself had been a cold-blooded killer. Her premeditated actions had ended a life. Revenge, as Hawkins knew from personal experience, was a powerful incentive. But, regardless of whether Brendan Marsh was a rapist or not, there were people out there who cared about him. Others who might have wanted Philips dead.

Hawkins spun in response to the recently familiar sound of a heavy metal lock being disengaged, almost turning an ankle between the floor and the footrests on her chair for the second time that afternoon. She swore. Her joints, now thirty-five years old, didn't resist abuse as effectively as they once had. She really needed to break her habit of wearing heels for work.

Twenty yards along the corridor, Amala Yasir was being ushered through a gate by one of the female wardens, who then secured it behind her and trudged away.

Yasir's rubber-soled flats squeaked loudly on the polished floor as she approached; her charcoal suit and plain high-necked shirt accurately reflected her straight-laced character. In contrast, Hawkins' caramel above-the-knee skirt and white chiffon blouse had drawn wolf whistles from a group of women prisoners they'd passed on the way in. Despite the wheelchair.

Hawkins regarded her younger subordinate. Yasir's parents were from Malaysia and Pakistan, although many would have called her exotic appearance striking, rather than beautiful.

'Wow.' Yasir made an exasperated face as she re-joined her commanding officer. 'Remind me to hold it next time, will you, chief? It takes an age to get *anywhere* in this place. Nearest loo's seven locked gates away.'

Hawkins heard another door slam in the distance. 'No wonder the guards are so miserable.'

They both looked up as muted voices became audible along the corridor and, seconds later, four people rounded the corner to Hawkins' right. Up front was a huge female warden whose cropped hair perfectly depicted her as someone you didn't mess with. Flanking the group was another guard, smaller and less imposing but still stony-faced. And, between them, the two people for whom Hawkins and Yasir were waiting.

The first was a scrawny long-term inmate called Jean Coker, who Hawkins was hoping might reveal some insight into Philips' time inside. The second was a manicured white man in his late forties who had earlier introduced himself as Pierce Reid, Head of Prisoner Counselling and Reintegration for the London area. The expensive suit had retained its composure throughout the day, but after having sat in on all six interviews with prisoners, the counsellor himself appeared to be flagging. He broke off from the group as the two guards shepherded Coker into the interview room and closed the door.

Reid came over to them, checking his watch. 'Can we keep this one brief, Detective? It's the weekend.'

'We'll try,' Hawkins told him. 'Although I can't promise anything. Go if you want.'

He frowned. 'I'd love to, but it's procedure these days to have a counsellor present in all police-led interviews with inmates. I thought I mentioned that.'

'You did,' Hawkins said, not really interested. 'But if

you're shooting off right after this one, there are a couple of questions I need to ask you about Sam.'

Reid had appeared in the room with each inmate and disappeared with them directly afterwards. This was the first opportunity she'd had to talk to him alone.

He sighed. 'If you must.'

'How well did you know Samantha Philips?'

'I only met her once.' Reid slid his hands into his pockets. 'When I carried out her pre-release assessment. She never requested to see me, or any other members of the counselling team, during her sentence.'

'So who *did* she confide in?'

'Perhaps no one,' Reid said. 'As you requested, I did some preliminary checking prior to your arrival, but nothing came up. Obviously, not all the prisoners are keen to answer questions from *the establishment*.'

Hawkins nodded. 'Did she receive any hate mail?'

'I found no evidence of any,' the counsellor replied. 'The prison screens for that sort of thing, mainly to protect the inmates from harassment, but there's nothing on Miss Philips' record about any having arrived, even when she first came in. I suppose thirty-something rapists like her victim don't warrant public sympathy. Even the challenged individuals who become obsessed with dangerous men tend to prefer their idols with a pulse. It's often the subject of psychological debate, but I don't believe Brendan Marsh was sufficiently notorious to have inspired a so-called fan to murder in his name.'

'What about allies?' Hawkins fired in when he paused. 'Who did Sam get on with?'

'I could be wrong,' Reid continued, 'but it appears that Miss Philips spent most of her sentence in solitude, and I don't mean of the institutionally dispensed variety. Apparently, she made it through a six-year sentence without forging any of the standard alliances.'

Yasir's eyebrows dipped. '*Standard alliances?*'

'Yes.' Reid glanced around, as if he were about to reveal who had shot JFK. 'Any longer than a few months in here is difficult for *anyone*, but to do it without establishing certain ... loyalties ... is nigh on impossible. Yet all my sources – for example, guards with the confidence of certain inmates – say that Philips remained genuinely unaffiliated throughout her stay. And, before you ask, she certainly wasn't keen on the wardens either.'

Yasir still looked confused. Hawkins was about to explain when Reid obliged.

'Usually, prisoners go one of two ways. Some cling to the system at first, treating the wardens like police officers, often withdrawing everything the prison library has on penal law. They think that, if they abide by every rule, the system will protect them. But that delusion doesn't tend to last. The smarter ones recognize straight away that, when you're in Rome, it's better to be Caesar's friend, so they join one or other of the "families". That's my own term, but the rival factions I'm talking about are definitely real.'

'Do you think that's how she ended up fighting?' Hawkins asked.

Reid frowned. 'You assume there has to be a reason behind such violence. Disorder in prisons isn't a male-only phenomenon, Detective. In my experience, women are as bad, if not worse.' He motioned towards the interview room. 'Look, we aren't allowed to keep the inmates in session for longer than half an hour. You've already had five minutes, and Coker won't be getting any more compliant in there.'

'You're right,' Hawkins conceded, still determined to capitalize on her fleeting time with the counsellor. 'But surely you can give us *some* insight into Sam's character.'

Reid shrugged. 'Like I said, Detective, I spent just twenty minutes with the woman, shortly before she was released, and during that meeting I talked far more than she did. But, in my professional opinion, she was ready and wanted to leave. Whether that had anything to do with specific people or conditions here in Holloway Prison, I couldn't say. And, anyway, providing you can get her to talk, the lady in that interview room knew Samantha far better than I did.'

'Okay.' Hawkins reluctantly allowed the conversation to be curtailed. 'Let's see what Coker knows.'

The small, windowless room was still clogged with stagnant smoke when Hawkins, Yasir and Reid entered. Unlike in the allegedly free world, prisoners serving time in British prisons were still allowed to light up indoors; a liberty of which all of the afternoon's interviewees had made the most.

Yasir wheeled Hawkins' chair over so that she could face Coker across the table in the centre of the room, and retook her seat on the remaining edge, opposite Reid. A small tin ashtray sat between them, already overwhelmed by the twelve or so butts which had helped infuse the day's earlier conversations.

Their wiry subject sat in the fourth wooden chair, cuffed wrists on the table, hands clasped together as if protecting a good poker hand. Her arms bore the same dense tattoos as the rest of her body, heavily inked motifs that crept over her skin like marauding foliage. She was easily late fifties, although her emaciated frame suggested that most of those years had been sustained by prison food. And if her vest *had* ever been washed, there were likely few who could claim living memory of the day. But Hawkins recognized Coker's intelligence immediately. It wasn't just the depth behind the eyes that studied them, the message in her body language and expression was clear.

You're afraid of me.

The two guards stood against the wall behind Coker, opposite the door, making it six of them in what was best described as a generously sized cupboard, with dingy grey walls and a carpet harder than most of the inmates.

Hawkins took her time flicking the brake on her

chair, playing down the fact that they were already pressed for time. Her hope was that, having been brought straight out of solitary confinement, where she'd apparently spent the previous three days, at least Coker was unlikely to know anything about Philips' demise.

The inmate spoke first, in a rough London accent. 'Cough up, then.'

'Excuse me?' Hawkins kept her response neutral. There was no point antagonizing the woman. *Yet.*

'Let's not fuck about, love,' Coker said without humour. 'Make with the cigarettes so we can get started, yeah?'

'What makes you think –'

'That the other girls didn't bring their own?' The convict waved at the overworked ashtray. 'Because I taught them better than that. You get summoned for interview like this, it means someone needs your help, so go empty-handed and milk the opportunity. Chop chop.'

'Fair enough.' Hawkins produced the packet of Marlboros she'd purchased especially for the purpose, extracted one, and held it out.

'More like it.' Coker took the cigarette, and Yasir leaned over to light it for her. 'Leave the pack.'

Hawkins dropped the box on the table, watching the prisoner settle back and take a few quick drags, holding the filter to her lips with both hands, the cuffs heavy on her wrists like outsize jewellery.

'So' – Coker tipped her head back and blew out a long, thin trail of smoke – 'who are you?'

'Met Police. I'm Detective Chief Inspector Antonia Hawkins, and this is Detective Sergeant Amala Yasir.'

'Okay,' Coker smirked. 'Though you could have saved us all half an hour by just saying "Filth".'

Hawkins didn't rise. 'We understand you shared a cell with Samantha Philips for eighteen months prior to her release.'

The prisoner sniffed, watching the end of her cigarette burn for a moment before she looked back at Hawkins. 'Yeah, so what?'

'So you know each other pretty well.'

'Depends how you mean. We shared a crapper, so I know her bowel movements better than most, but I wouldn't say we were mates.'

Hawkins eyed her. 'Apparently, you were the nearest thing she had in here to a friend.'

'Probably.' Coker took another long drag. 'But that ain't a title you had to fight for.' She exhaled fresh smoke, which rose to join the opaque cloud hanging near the ceiling. The smaller guard suppressed a cough. In contrast, Hawkins savoured the fug, wondering why she hadn't missed cigarettes until now. She hadn't succumbed since before the attack. Obviously, that had nothing to do with putting an end to her previous sporadic guilty indulgence, but perhaps *any* brush with death was sufficient to make you reassess your daily conduct.

She checked her watch as Coker looked round at the

coughing guard, aware that they had just fifteen minutes of access time left and that this woman might be their final chance to glean some useful information about Sam. Compared to their earlier interviewees, Jean Coker was Reid's only suggestion of someone Philips might have trusted, to however small a degree.

Hawkins watched her flick ash in the tray. 'Sam was mixed up in some fighting a while back, and we'd like to know who was involved.'

Coker's brow contracted, and she was silent for a moment before she asked, 'Why?'

'We're investigating how she was treated during her time in Holloway.'

Mischief flickered in Coker's expression. 'Bollocks.'

Hawkins didn't reply.

'She's fucked off,' Coker said. 'Hasn't she? That's why you're here.' She jabbed her cigarette at them in turn. 'You, Miss Pakistan and the counsellor. Either she's cracked another skull or she's given your parole monkeys the slip, and you want to know where she's gone. So which is it?'

Hawkins sighed internally. The other convicts they'd spoken to already had all been intellectually limited enough to answer questions without firing any back, all more concerned about being in line for a reduced sentence than why they were being asked. But that tactic wouldn't work here.

'She hasn't disappeared.' Hawkins clung to her strategy. 'We know exactly where she is.'

Coker frowned. 'What is it, then?' She looked around from face to face. 'Come on. You lot ain't interested in that fair-treatment crap. You wouldn't be here unless something big had happened, and you think I know stuff about Sam that'll help you sort it out.'

Hawkins ignored her prompt. 'Apparently, she took a pasting not long before she was released. We want to know who did it and why. Forget about us; you'll be helping Sam.'

'Nice try, darling' – Coker leaned back in her chair and winked at Reid – 'but I don't feel like talking at the moment. And, by my calculations, you've had about nineteen of the thirty minutes you're allowed to keep me in here, so if you want some decent answers you better tell it straight.'

Hawkins conceded; they'd get nothing from this woman unless they levelled with her. And, she reasoned, Coker would learn of Philips' murder as soon as she was released from solitary confinement anyway. So there wasn't much to lose.

She left a long, thoughtful pause, catching Coker's eye before she spoke again, purposely composing her short, incendiary phrase.

'Sam's dead.'

The cigarette between Coker's lips dropped slightly at Hawkins' statement, and for the briefest moment her swagger faltered, revealing a mother hen who couldn't usually afford to show her softer side.

Coker stared at her. 'What?'

'Sam was murdered,' Hawkins said. 'Two days ago.'

'That's what I thought you said.' The convict's eyes dropped. 'Fuck.'

Hawkins continued. 'Now you know. So who had reason to hurt her?'

Coker slowly rested her hands back on the table, apparently no longer interested in the diminishing cigarette. 'How'd they do it?'

'Blow to the temple. A hammer, we think. She died instantly.'

The convict nodded.

'Help us out here, Jean.' Hawkins watched their subject closely. 'Who had a problem with Sam? It wouldn't have to be anyone obvious; maybe somebody she only mentioned in passing.'

Coker shrugged.

'Someone with contacts on the outside,' Hawkins pushed. 'Or cash.'

Silence.

'You'll be doing Sam a favour.'

Coker's head rose suddenly. 'You ain't listening to me, darling. I don't fucking know, okay? I liked her. Why would I lie?'

Hawkins leaned closer. 'What was she fighting about?'

'Your guess is as good as mine. Everyone fights in here, all the time; that's how it is.'

'Who else was involved?'

'For fuck's sake.' Coker rubbed the backs of her thumbs against her forehead in apparent frustration. 'She didn't tell me.'

'What about gangs? Was she a member?'

'This ain't a fucking library.' The convict stubbed out her cigarette. 'Far as I could tell, she stayed clear.'

'You must know why she didn't get involved with the gangs. I hear it's the best way to survive.'

'It is,' Coker said, 'but Sam had no time for all that. You know, properly didn't give a shit. I know it don't make sense to you people, but that can happen to the girls who've done the worst stuff; killing or abusing or whatever. Lights were on, but no one was home. Sam did what she was told, just about, but she never went out of her way to stay the right side of anyone.'

Hawkins nodded. Frustrating as it was, Coker's words only confirmed what other inmates had already said. Samantha Philips had been as reckless in prison as she had on the outside. Anyone capable of cold-blooded murder, regardless of their reasons for it, spent very little time worrying about what was best for them in the long run, which meant Sam wouldn't have cared about upsetting the undesirables she'd encountered on a daily basis here in Holloway. But reputation was often more important to the discerning criminal in jail than it was on the outside, and if Philips had upset the wrong person, she might have been marked at any point during her sentence. The list of potential contractors for the hit would be long.

If the fight in which Philips sustained her injuries had been a failed attempt on her life – and especially if she'd come off better than her assailant – that might explain why the instigator had waited for Sam to be released before exacting revenge via proxy.

Granted, the number of prisoners with opportunity and resources sufficient to contract out such a hit would be limited, but Hawkins would have to rebook with the prison and come back another day in order to speak with any of them. That type of operation was labour intensive and, considering that they had other lines of inquiry to pursue, it was probably best left for now.

Hawkins ended the session, resigned to the fact that they'd learned everything they were going to learn from this inmate about Sam, and also wary of breaching the allowed interview time. That sort of thing might lead to inconvenience later on, should certain convicts see potential for crying harassment in court.

Pierce Reid passed Hawkins a business card before exiting with the two guards and Coker, who collected her newly acquired cigarettes on the way out. The door closed, leaving the two detectives alone in the small room.

'Well,' Yasir said after a moment, 'that went pretty well.'

Hawkins ran a hand through her hair, fighting exasperation. Amala's boundless enthusiasm, not to mention her unshakeable faith in her chief inspector, was invaluable in some situations, woefully misplaced in others. ' "Pretty well" is stretching it.'

'You extracted vital information,' Yasir ploughed on, 'from a difficult source.'

Hawkins shot her a look. 'If that's the best we can do, Amala, we're in trouble.'

She nodded towards the door, indicating that it was time to go, ignoring the confounded expression on the sergeant's face. Despite an intense day of prising open her past, Samantha Philips remained a mystery.

25

The stranger approached in broken, disjointed jumps, the way something appears when it moves under thick ice. A flicker, then a jerk, then a second of smooth progress. The man was heading straight for Bull, but it was hard to judge his size and weight. Or his intent.

Don't get caught out.

Bull slowed; they were less than ten yards apart. He sniffed hard, trying to taste the freezing air as it entered his body.

He swallowed as the gap disappeared, telling himself not to reach for the wall that was right next to him, or a memory from eight years ago.

He's not your enemy.

And suddenly the stranger was there. Beside him. Bull flinched, but only inside. The stranger had stepped off the pavement to give him space, even appeared to nod as he passed. Bull didn't respond, and his guts stayed twisted for a long time afterwards.

He was outside, *in public*, and the glitch his eyes developed during daylight was worse than ever. Everything looked wrong. He would have been used to it by now, except it kept changing. Today, objects that should have been distant sprang out, while a hand held in front of his face seemed far away. Sounds were confusing, shapes messed up, his breathing loud in his ears.

But none of it was real.

That's why he kept on dragging himself out here, during the day. Stumbling around, confused.

Looking for normality.

Bull dug his hands in his pockets. The coat was heavy and warm. Too warm: but he wore it because it was three below zero. Otherwise, people stared.

Check out the guy in the T-shirt.

He hadn't felt anything as ordinary as temperature since the day he came home.

He turned a corner, seeing his destination. *Not far now.* But he noticed the truck as it entered the road up ahead. His pulse leapt, and sweat broke out on his skin. He focused hard, picking out the bright colours, the brushes underneath. It was sweeping the streets.

Nothing more.

But the noise triggered memories, their static ringing in his ears.

He gagged, sensing the hardness of the wall as he fell against it, just managing to right himself. His senses turned inside out, the flashbacks burning his mind, but he kept going, head down. There was the gate.

He reached out, relieved to feel the metal, distant under his palm, as he pushed through to safety, a rapid heartbeat filling his brain. He'd made it.

It took a minute longer for the panic to ease, but when he was calm enough to look around he saw empty paths both sides in the place he came to right his mind.

The park.

It was a short walk from his house, although recently even that distance felt like miles, thanks to his fucked-up mind. But that's why he kept coming back: to fight the damage done by his past. There was calm and beauty here; happy people, kids. He needed that stuff in his head. If he gave in, let himself turn towards home, terror won.

Bull read stories on the internet about others like him, who needed help even leaving the house once they were free. They didn't eat or sleep; they just wasted away. But he wouldn't end up like that. Every day he forced himself to eat, though it didn't matter what. His sense of taste, even for the hottest spices, had gone. Then he came to the park.

To think a nice thought.

That was the plan, and he had to stick to it. Holding on to the smallest shred of innocence would stop evil owning him.

Because, if that happened, he really was fucked.

He checked his breathing. It was almost back to normal, so he moved away, heading deeper into the park. Soon he reached the playground, his usual bench just outside. His timing was good. Two kids, maybe brother and sister, were playing together on the slide, while Mum watched them from a seat next to the swings. She was smoking, but that was okay. Not *evil*, just bad.

He focused on the kids.

The boy was about five, with lots of energy and hair. He wore a puffy red jacket and one glove. The girl was younger, maybe three, and she kept wiping her nose on the fluffy sleeve of her pink duffel coat. She had trouble keeping up with her brother on the steps, down the slide, and back around. The boy kept catching up and passing her on the way to the stairs, using the slide twice as often as her. But both kids were enjoying the game, shouting at Mum to watch when they got to the top, laughing as they slid down.

Bull shut his eyes and concentrated, letting the sounds echo in his head, build into a positive thought. Yesterday had been hard. It had rained. There had been no kids, and the time of year meant no flowers in the beds. But he'd managed a nice thought then, about the morning his parents had taken him to the zoo on his eighth birthday, and he could feel another good memory building now.

The girl screamed.

Bull's eyes flashed open and he saw her lying on the ground by the slide. Her brother was on the steps above, looking down. Then he laughed and began to climb, ignoring his mother's shouts as she rushed to her daughter.

He knew what had happened. The boy had caught her on the ladder, wanted her out of the way.

Bull buried his head in his hands, feeling the positive thought die. Evil took hold, even here, with *kids*. It tore people apart, causing pain that would stay with these children for ever.

He couldn't stand it.

He stood, rubbing his eyes, trying to clear his vision. Suddenly he was holding something inside his coat. The hammer. What was it doing here? He hadn't meant to bring it. No one in the park deserved to die. His mind was crashing, but he knew what to do.

He stumbled off along the path, hoping that he was going the right way. Still the girl's cries reached him. Then a familiar voice drowned them out.

'*What's wrong with you, boy?*' it screamed. '*Don't you see, this is how the world is? We're all evil. You, me, everyone. Man up.*'

Bull kept his head down; moved on. The voice wasn't there; *couldn't* be.

'*Don't ignore me!*' it shouted. '*I'll end you!*'

The voice was so clear, so real.

He brought his head up and looked around. No one was there, but he caught sight of another man approaching, his shape swimming in Bull's messed-up sight.

'*That man's a fucking rapist!*' The voice yelled. '*Take him out!*'

Bull veered away.

'*Drop him. Now!*'

Bull fought on, past the man, letting him go. He saw the toilets up ahead. Had to get there.

He reached the doorway, bursting through into the

cold, stone block. He scanned the room, shattered vision moving past open cubicle doors thick with graffiti. But no one was there.

'*What are you doing, chump?*'

Bull found an empty section of wall and lined himself up. His guard came up, fists clenching, and he drove a punch into the tiles. The ceramic cracked.

He drew back and struck again, feeling nothing as his knuckles smashed into the damaged surface. But he kept going, watching the patch of red building on the wall from his torn skin; straining to feel the jagged splinters from the tiles forcing their way into his flesh.

He stopped, breathing heavily, trying to experience the sensations that should have been attacking his senses. Pain was good; the only thing that had a chance of clearing his messed-up head. He closed his eyes.

'*Give it up, idiot!*' the voice shouted. '*You can't get rid of me.*'

But it was quieter this time.

Bull straightened, drew back his injured hand again.

'*Don't you fucking dare . . .*'

He put everything into the final blow, pounding his fist into the dented surface. The tiles gave way, shards falling towards the dirty floor. And at last the wound screamed, releasing waves of agony that made him cry out.

Bull withdrew his hand, pulling it in to his chest as it started to shake. He'd injured himself badly, but the tactic had worked.

The voice had gone.

He stood, breathing hard, aware of the world again. *There had been no voice.*

Which meant the evil was inside Bull, trying to convince him to kill. Today, he'd silenced it, but there was only one way to destroy it for good. And that was to stick to the plan.

Bull's eyes were still closed when he heard footsteps outside. He looked up just as the boy appeared at the door. He recognized the kid straight away, from out in the park; he was red-faced from running. The kid who pushed his sister off the slide.

The boy stood in the doorway, staring at him.

And Bull, cradling his damaged hand, stared back.

26

'Right.' Hawkins dumped her notepad on the desk. 'That's about all Amala and I can tell you about Sam Philips' former peers. There's a good chance this murder had nothing to do with anyone from Holloway, but let's keep open minds about the possibility for now.'

She glanced around at her murder investigation team. DI Frank Todd lounged on a wheeled office chair next to the standing DS Aaron Sharpe. Mike perched on the edge of a nearby desk, in front of which Amala Yasir occupied a third chair.

The team had been through several incarnations even during its most recent case, although such rapid change was hardly unusual. There was no such thing as a permanent crew; detectives were simply seconded to and off particular murder investigations as required. Similar mixtures of personnel were often repeated, of course, as management accepted that familiarity among colleagues sped up work rates, while different gaps between cases ending meant the same officers tended to be available at the same times.

But despite having been back at work for just over a day, Hawkins suspected the report she was about to receive from these officers wasn't going to lift her metaphorical skirt. She had called everyone back for an end-of-shift catch-up in the operations room at Becke House, in the hope that more headway than she'd achieved at Holloway had been made by others elsewhere.

'So' – Hawkins spread her hands, inviting contributions from the floor – 'who's going to make my afternoon?'

Nobody spoke.

She rephrased. 'Does anyone have anything that backs up this media fixation with Valentine's Day? Exes, rejected lovers, cuckold concubines?'

Still nothing.

'Good' – Hawkins crossed her arms – 'because the sooner that particular sideshow exhausts itself, the better. Obviously, the "Murderer with a Message" angle is a great hook for the papers, especially after what happened at Christmas. They're milking public concern about indiscriminate psychos at large, but I still say it's coincidence.' She looked from face to face. 'And even if I'm wrong, this Valentine's nonsense only happens once a year, so the longer we go without finding additional bodies from yesterday or previous years, the more likely it becomes that we're dealing with an isolated event, or at least that we have until this time next year to track the killer down.'

Nods went round the room, reassuring Hawkins that her views were shared.

'Okay.' She turned to her most experienced DI. 'Let's do progress instead. Frank, what do you have?'

Immediately, Todd's face contracted into an expression that said, 'Oh yeah, pick on the Geordie', making Hawkins wish she hadn't started with him. Her choice, to go straight to her most insightful researcher, had actually been a backhanded compliment.

'Well' – Todd motioned to DS Sharpe – 'as instructed, my esteemed colleague and I have been chatting to Brendan Marsh's friends: quite a challenge, as it turns out. It's been years since Marsh was murdered by our latest victim, so several had moved away, but we caught up with a few of them.' He looked at Sharpe.

'Oh. Right.' The DS stood up a little straighter on being handed the limelight. 'There's nothing revolutionary, but we managed to scrape together a few interesting bits.'

Hawkins smiled inwardly at his Todd-ism. The two bachelors were still living together after being involuntarily paired up for safety reasons during the team's last case, so, increasingly, they'd ended up working together, for convenience, according to Mike. She'd been quietly hoping Todd's fastidious nature would rub off on the so far underwhelming Sharpe, although she'd happily have left the cynicism. Time would tell if the older man's influence had moved things in the right direction overall.

Sharpe flattened his tie; an odd habit considering the usual state of his clothes suggested he slept in them. 'Looks like Marsh had a pretty tight core group of about four male friends, old mates from school and university, all now in their mid-thirties. Two of them, Mickey Borders and Dennis Sowden, are still local, both supervisors for Makro in Croydon. Number three, James Wallace, moved away last year when his accountancy firm relocated to Norfolk, and the last one, Richard Miller, is overseas with the RAF. We saw both the local lads, and spoke to the accountant on the phone, but we're still waiting on the MOD for an update on Miller.'

He looked around, the way people do when they're used to being ignored, before continuing in a more confident tone when no one jumped in. 'We've confirmed that Borders was on shift from Thursday night into Friday morning, and Miller is definitely out of the country, but the last two are each other's alibi. Both said independently that Sowden spent the week with Wallace in Swaffham, but that's rather convenient, considering they could have worked together to take out Samantha Philips, so tomorrow we'll dig into that claim.'

Sharpe finished up by detailing the group's physical attributes, although, considering that any of the men could be right-handed and the striking force a hammer allowed, any of the four could conceivably have inflicted the decisive blow.

Hawkins curtailed the subsequent discussion when it began to digress, and turned to Maguire. 'What else do we have?'

Mike stood. 'I spent some time today with Marsh's folks. His mom, Juliette, died four years ago of a heart attack, leaving just the father and two other kids. The brother, Aidan, is top suspect there, 'cause the dad, Paul, is too old, and the sister, Carla, is too small; we're talking five feet if she's an inch. Thing is, though, none of 'em seem too broke up over Brendan's murder. I know it was a while back, but clearly this ain't a close family we got here.'

Hawkins' spirit sank. 'What about more distant relatives?'

'We know about some cousins and stuff like that. Haven't caught up with them yet, but from what I heard today, most only saw Brendan for weddings and funerals. Eight of them or so, counting cousins and great-aunts, but there ain't a rap sheet between them worth mentioning, just a couple of County Court judgements from an uncle on the mom's side, so I don't think we're looking at prime suspects there, either.'

'Okay.' Hawkins brought the session to a close. 'Good work, everyone, but don't jack it in yet. Even if they didn't do it themselves, any of these people could have contracted a hit.' She was about to dismiss her team for the day when she caught sight of someone standing behind and to her right. She rotated the chair.

'Don't let us interrupt.' Tristan Vaughn stood just inside the door with a second, unfamiliar man. 'But I need a moment with everyone when you're finished.'

'It's fine.' Hawkins smiled, wondering how long he'd been there. 'We're just about done.'

The DCS nodded and stepped forward in front of the group. 'I'd like to introduce DI Steven Tanner.' He motioned to the other man, who moved in beside him. 'He's on the High Potential Development Scheme and he has some important information to share with you all.' He gestured for his colleague to take over.

Tanner moved further into collective view. He had dark hair, a strong jaw and, unusually for a serving Met detective, a tan. He was young, perhaps late twenties, six feet tall and athletic, with a demeanour right on the line between confidence and conceit.

Tanner made a self-assured opening comment in a deep, abrading tone, about some of the team probably having seen him around. He winked at Amala and made a joke that Hawkins knew was about football but didn't get. All the men laughed.

But his expression hardened as he produced an A4 envelope and laid it on the table in front of him. He turned to the investigation board and began reciting the events leading up to Samantha Philips' murder. Describing the team's own case to them.

Hawkins forced herself not to interrupt, looking over at Vaughn, but the DCS seemed more than at ease.

Tanner reached the photograph of Philips' body, outlined her injuries and described the weapon that caused them. He was obviously building towards something, and Hawkins watched his chest swell as he approached his big moment.

'Unfortunately' – Tanner glanced at Vaughn. *I'd like to thank my sponsor* – 'Samantha Philips wasn't the first. I have evidence that this killer has struck before.'

The floor seemed to fall from under Hawkins. She looked around the operations room as the shockwave of Tanner's revelation spread.

This killer has struck before.

She fought the panic rising out of her gut like air bubbles in water. Two multiple murderers in just over three months? Questions flooded her mind. She watched the rest of her team exchanging stunned glances as the new arrival stood coolly before them.

Mike caught her eye. *Did you know about this?*

She hadn't, of course, but neither was she going to let the DCS or his lapdog hijack proceedings so fast.

'Sir.' She addressed Vaughn. 'If there was fresh evidence in this case, shouldn't we have been made aware?'

The DCS nodded. 'That's why we're here. Steve made the discovery no more than half an hour ago, after reading your reports on the system. He informed me immediately, and we came straight here. I'm glad we caught you all.'

'Right,' Hawkins fumbled, lacking a riposte.

'Anyway,' Vaughn continued, 'I'm sure you'll be interested in what DI Tanner has to say.' He gestured to the man standing, proverbially, on her toes. 'Go ahead, Steve.'

'Thanks.' Tanner picked up the mystery envelope and reached inside. He spread the contents on the nearest desk. 'Take a look at these. The victim is Rosa Calano, a nineteen-year-old Portuguese immigrant.'

Everyone moved in to view the collection of photographs showing a young woman's corpse from various angles. The set of her limbs demonstrated that her prostration was due to death, even without head injuries disturbingly similar to those that had killed Samantha Philips.

Hawkins frowned at Tanner. 'Where did you get these?'

The DI gave her a sideways stare, as if trying to work out whether she was accusing him of something. 'An associate of mine in Forensics worked on this case a few months ago. He wrote a now esteemed paper on the assessment of manually inflicted cranial injuries relative to assailant height and weight. Have you read it?'

'It's on my list,' she feigned. 'What's the link?'

'I remembered these shots as soon as I saw your report.' Tanner reached into the envelope again. 'So I brought up the details we had on the murder weapon.' He held out several pieces of paper, stapled at the corner. 'The specifics should be familiar to you.'

Hawkins took the sheets, recognizing the standard forensic injury report.

She read the investigator's summary of the weapon used to kill Rosa Calano: 'Heavy, club-ended tool, head approximately two inches in diameter and of dense compound – probably metal, slightly tapered towards the peripheral contact surface, consistent with the attributes of a large domestic hammer. Weapon head weight likely to be in the region of 450g (16oz), to provide a convenient balance between lightness and feasible striking force sufficient to kill.'

She flipped to the second page, which showed a grainy printed image of a ball-peen hammer; the type with a wedge on the reverse of the head instead of a claw. It was clear from the report that the Calano murder weapon hadn't been found either. But the forensic investigator had noted that, if the assailant had any sense, he'd be more likely to use this type, as a claw's sharp edges would catch easily on clothing, making the weapon harder to handle and increasing the risk of stray fibres being left at the scene.

She looked at Tanner. 'When did this happen?'

'I know what you're thinking,' he said, 'but Miss Calano died in October last year, which debunks the whole Valentine's Day idea.'

'Hold up,' Mike interjected. 'What date was it?'

Tanner checked his notes. 'The fifth. Why?'

'Phew.' Maguire blew out his cheeks. 'In the States we celebrate Sweetest Day, basically a fall re-run of Valentine's. It's in October, but always the third Saturday of the month.'

Hawkins took over. 'So that kills the romantic occasion link, but given the choice I'm not sure I'd have traded confirmation of that for a second body.' She passed the report to Frank. 'Did we look at this case?'

'Well' – Todd squinted at the photos, immediately defensive – 'we might have, but *dozens* of people get murdered with hammers every bloody year. What makes *this* one so special?'

They all looked back at Tanner, whose face became suddenly more serious.

'Good question.' He used a magnet to clamp a photo of Calano to the investigation board. 'But one I think I can answer.'

He looked straight at Frank. 'There were thirty-six fatal attacks last year in London where a hammer was the main murder weapon, but Calano shared something else with Samantha Philips that none of the other victims did.'

There was silence.

Tanner paused, holding each of their stares in turn. 'Two weeks before she was murdered, Rosa Calano was released from jail.'

27

Hawkins watched the rest of her team file out of the operations room before she hauled the chair around and followed Mike into her office, banging the door closed.

Maguire watched her from across the room. 'All right, what's up?'

'Steve Tanner's *up*.' Hawkins propelled herself around behind the desk, symbolically reclaiming territory. 'Why didn't we find that link to Calano?'

'Beats me.' Mike sat down in Hawkins' office chair, which she'd reluctantly banished to the visitor's side of the room so she could roll her wheelchair up to the desk. 'Frank and Amala were looking at precedents, right?'

Hawkins nodded, still pissed off.

According to Tanner, Rosa Calano had served nearly three years in a young offenders' institution for manslaughter, convicted of shaking a baby to death while working as an au pair. The term had been short due to Calano's age – just sixteen at the time of her conviction; nineteen when she was released.

'Anyway,' Mike continued, 'didn't Steve just help us out?'

'Yeah, making the whole team look sloppy in the process.'

'Is this about the team, or about you?'

'Of course it's not about *me*.' Hawkins realized she'd reacted too fast. 'Apart from the fact he's obviously being lined up for my job.'

'*What?*'

'You heard Vaughn.' She recited the superintendent's words in a childish voice. '"Steve's on the High Potential Development Scheme." It's a coup.'

Mike rolled his eyes.

Hawkins scowled at him. Clearly, Steve Tanner was in with the right people, expediting his way to the top. A couple of tactical lunches here, some strategic golf there, and he'd be scrubbing the smell of cronyism off his hands in the executive washroom before he was thirty-five. He was the pretender Mike had heard about; the wonder-kid being lined up for big things. Maguire must have realized that, especially after Vaughn had delivered his final piece of bad news, just moments ago, when Hawkins had thanked Tanner for his assistance, saying that they could handle the investigation from there.

Tanner had looked straight at Vaughn.

'Actually there is something else . . .' Their commanding officer's tone had been far too breezy for comfort. 'As you can see, DI Tanner is already up to speed with the case, and I know his skills will be useful in apprehending this killer. So, for the foreseeable future, Steve is joining your team.'

Whether it was done on purpose or not, announcing this in front of everyone had given Hawkins no opportunity to object without looking threatened by what should have been positive news. It had been the spectre of competition, of course, that had brought her rushing back to work in the first place, but since then she'd been hoping that her return to active duty would have diverted reinforcements elsewhere.

No such luck.

Vaughn had even subjected them to some team-building drivel, with round-the-group introductions. Yasir had been typically intense; Sharpe habitually dull. Somehow, Mike had managed to sing her praises. Vaughn was already familiar to everyone, and Todd, who reviled any kind of corporate stroking, said he wished he were dead.

Then Tanner had described his career history, from the mandatory two years in uniform, through stints in organized-crime and commercial-fraud investigation, on to his time helping to develop the National Intelligence Model. An impressive cv for his age, which turned out to be twenty-nine.

Finally, Vaughn had managed to make matters worse by explaining that Tanner's remit was not to work under her but to *learn the ropes of murder investigation* directly from Hawkins. To shadow her. *Day to day.*

Which begged the question: had Tanner gone to Vaughn, peddling his new information with an agenda, thereby earning himself an instant place on the team? Or was it the other way around?

Jobs for the boys.

She dismissed the notion immediately. There was no way Tanner could have known they'd miss the link. But the similarities between the two cases were too strong to ignore. Two former inmates in the London area, both murdered within days of finishing their sentences for murder and manslaughter, with the same weapon and MO. At first, Hawkins had been hopeful of Sam Philips' murder turning out to be an isolated case. Now, with a second fatality attributed to the same killer, and both women having been released from prison just days before their respective deaths, she might have chosen the Valentine's Day angle, given the choice. It could still be coincidence, of course, but it looked for all the world as if the attacks on these two victims were connected directly to their crimes, a fact Hawkins' new competitor had obviously enjoyed being able to expose.

Tanner had handed out copies of the entire Calano file before leaving with Vaughn, probably for a gruelling game of squash followed by whiskey and highbrow conversation.

And she was sure about the coup.

A couple of months ago she'd suspected Lawrence Kirby-Jones of trying to undermine her, while Vaughn had looked like he was at least partially on her side. But that situation seemed to have been reversed. Kirby-Jones had used his influence to keep her in-post, while it now looked as if Vaughn wanted her out of the way. With his help, Tanner could be made to look like the obvious choice for Hawkins' role. And if he did it while she was still on secondment, she could be eased back to DI level without any fuss. And without grounds for complaint.

'Toni . . .' Maguire's voice punctured her thoughts. 'Stop it.'

She looked at him. 'Stop what?'

'I can see the conspiracy cogs turning.'

Hawkins shook her head.

'He ain't here to take your job.'

'Fine.' She grabbed her laptop and rolled herself away from the desk, feeling the familiar strain in her torso which meant her recuperating body was approaching exhaustion for the day. 'Let's get home and eat at a humane hour for once.' She hauled the door open. 'We can look at Calano's file later on.'

What she didn't say was that she also wanted a decent night's sleep because Tanner's arrival made one thing more urgent than ever.

She needed to get out of the chair.

Bull slammed his fist into his thigh.

Why couldn't they leave it alone?

He changed the channel and threw the remote away, sick of bullshit TV news. *Valentine's Day this, Valentine's Day that. Another screwed-up killer trying to scare the world.*

But they were wrong. There was no *message*.

And Valentine's Day had fuck all to do with it.

Okay, so he'd killed Sam on the fourteenth. *Hands up; his mistake.* But it hadn't been planned. If he'd even *thought* about the fucking date, he'd have waited a couple of days.

Then the media wouldn't be spouting this crap.

He got up and turned the television off, wandering into the kitchen to eat, reminding himself that it would all change soon. The press would have to park their drivel . . .

. . . As soon as his next target died.

29

'*Toni?*'

Hawkins started awake, inhaling hard, the Range Rover's cabin materializing around her.

'Whoa!' Maguire's hands were up in mock-surrender. 'Stand down, okay? I give up.'

'What?' she asked, only then noticing her hands, left braced against the dashboard, right pressed into Mike's chest. She retracted both, clearing her throat. 'Oh. Sorry.'

'What was it, a nightmare or something?'

'Yeah.' Hawkins forced a smile. 'I was just about to waste someone for interrupting my beauty sleep.' Her conscience grumbled, reminding her that Mike was the only reason she was here to worry about tiredness, or anything else, at all. But for some reason it still didn't feel right to discuss her ongoing flashbacks about the night she was stabbed, even with him.

She broke eye contact, glancing at the dark street outside the windscreen, noting that they were home. 'How long have I been out?'

'Only the whole way back, snoring like a two-ton walrus. Sure you don't need a few more days with your feet up?'

'You know me, I'll take Chinese water torture over daytime TV. I just need to get back in the routine.'

He didn't look convinced. 'Why don't you stay home tomorrow; get some extra zees? No one was expecting you back yet; the guys can handle things.'

'That bunch of headless chickens? They can't solve a Sudoku without me.'

'Seriously, we got more than a full team.'

'I told you I'm fine.' She snapped, immediately relenting. 'Sorry, it's these bloody painkillers, they give me a fuse like a gnat's manhood, and I drop off when I'm not even tired. I'll see the doctor about getting off them. Really, I'm okay.'

'Whatever you say.' Mike withdrew, obviously not in full accord. They sat for a moment, sharing silence, before he changed the subject. 'So if you're good to go, what say we let your dad get back to sleeping in his own bed?'

His implication was clear, and he was right. Fit for work or otherwise, she no longer needed her father's help day to day, while the grin said Mike was looking forward to them having some privacy. Under normal circumstances, she'd have agreed: he'd been fantastic since the attack, helpful and patient, almost to the point where it became annoying. Ultimately, she wanted their relationship back to normal, too, but having the place to themselves would also present opportunities for intimacy between her and Mike, and she simply wasn't ready for that. Purple scar tissue reared in her mind; something else she needed to broach.

But not now.

'We might have a job convincing him,' she countered. 'He's been free of my mother for two days.'

Mike touched her arm. 'I've missed you.'

She nodded, trying not to recoil. But when he leaned in for a kiss, she found herself pulling away.

He frowned. 'What is it?'

'Nothing.' She tried to make light. 'We walruses have terrible morning breath.'

Mike retreated with an expression that said he wasn't entirely convinced, but he didn't press the point. She moved on swiftly. 'Anyway, I'm starving. Let's get inside and see what dad's charred for dinner.'

'Sure.' Maguire opened his door and climbed out, wearing a kicked-puppy look that would have made any man proud. Hawkins watched him wander round to the boot to retrieve her chair, feeling guiltier than she'd expected to. Having her father around had inadvertently postponed the discussion about how soon she and Mike would resume horizontal relations. But now she'd underlined her recuperation by returning to work, he had every right to raise the subject again. Part of her was thankful, and keen to reciprocate, but until her remaining insecurities were in check, it was a conversation she'd rather not have.

Silently, she promised Mike she'd deal with her anxieties and have the two of them back to normal in the coming days.

Until then, her dad had to stay.

30

The mark appeared just after 2 a.m.

The door at the base of the tower block opened, and Matthew Hayes lurched out on to the street, the glow from inside lighting him from behind.

Hayes steadied himself on the rail beside the steps. Rat-arsed.

Same place Bull would have been by now.

If not for his work.

The guy was fortyish and heavily built, but prison had aged him.

Taking him out wouldn't be hard.

Bull knew the story. Fifteen-year-old kid from a good home, riding his bike after dark, ploughed down by a drunk driver who'd hardly looked back, leaving him face down with a fractured skull.

Across the road, Hayes turned and staggered away, quick trails of his breath disappearing into the blackened night air. But he moved fast for a pisshead, and Bull had to pick up his heels to stay close, watching his target's head loll as he walked. Luckily, the street was near straight, with a frost-covered car in every gap, so Bull could track his prey from the far side of the road.

He kept pace, glancing over from time to time, watching Hayes' head and shoulders floating above the line of car roofs.

It was the third night in a row they'd done this, and Hayes still hadn't given him a decent chance to strike. He'd appeared each night between midnight and two, already steaming, to stumble along the main road and back, no more than five or six minutes each way. Even at this time of night cars passed now and again and, while the pavements were empty, somebody could see them through a window or walk out of their front door at any time.

Bull needed some luck.

But he wasn't going to get it; not yet, anyway, as Hayes reached his destination and pushed open the door of the off-licence on Weybridge Road.

Bull watched him through the shop window, behind the chalkboards showing discounts and deals, a good two days' worth of stubble clear under the lights. Hayes' mouth moved as he talked to the man at the till. Then he came back out, winding the lid off the bottle as soon as he got outside. He took a long shot of the contents, threw the lid on the ground and turned towards home.

Bull gave him a head start and followed, trying not to let himself get wound up. But if this pattern didn't change soon, he'd have to find another way. It had to be done outside; striking indoors was too much of a risk. Out here, though, in winter, traces disappeared fast. All he needed was a chance to attack, and somewhere quiet to do it.

Hayes lurched on, into the darkest part of the road: a stretch where some of the streetlamps were broken and the buildings had no outside lights. They were still in the open, but maybe this was his best shot.

He waited for a black cab to pass before crossing the street, losing some ground on his target, but ending up directly behind him. Hayes lumbered on without turning. Bull began closing the gap, careful not to make any noise, even though Hayes was probably too out of it to hear him anyway.

He was only ten yards back when it happened.

Hayes stopped without warning, took another swig. Bull slid out of sight between two cars. He gave it a few beats before leaning out, just enough to see past the bumper hiding him. Then he stood, looking around.

He moved from behind the car, checking up and down the street. He could see fifty yards in front and behind, but somehow Hayes wasn't there. Bull moved to where he'd last seen his target.

Where the fuck had he gone?

Then he realized. A small alleyway sat between two buildings on his right. He hadn't seen it before because the same lorry had been parked in front of it every night, hiding the entrance from anyone on the opposite side of the street, where Bull had been.

He moved into the black mouth of the passage,

freeing the hammer from his belt, feeling the adrenalin kick in. The walls were close but, as his eyes adjusted, he realized that enough light crept in from the far end to allow him to see. Bull kept his steps silent, alert for any signs that the other man was waiting for him. Could Hayes have faked being pissed?

Bull reached the back of the buildings, where the alley opened into a courtyard. A small car was parked on the left, just inside the large wooden gates in the rear wall. There was no security lighting, but the clouds had shifted, leaving the moon bright in a clear piece of sky, showing details on the peeling window frames, a stack of paving slabs against one wall. And, in the far corner, facing away, Matthew Hayes. Taking a leak.

Bull moved, gliding across the concrete towards his target, winding back the hammer, ready to strike. The gap between them closed: ten feet, six feet, four.

But just as Bull was about to swing, Hayes turned, and their eyes met.

The moment froze: two killers facing each other. Hayes was taller, leaner, maybe faster when alcohol wasn't involved. But Bull was armed.

Neither man spoke.

The hammer connected with Hayes' temple, punching its way through soft tissue, stopping only when the handle made contact with his eye socket.

Hayes dropped, jerking as his knees hit the ground, slumping forwards in the dirt at Bull's feet.

Bull used a few more heavy blows to cave in his skull, before levering the hammer free and walking back to the alley. He reached the street and headed for home, pleased that he'd been able to finish Hayes without wasting another day. He was making good progress.

Three down.

31

As usual, Hawkins was awake before the alarm.

For a moment she just lay, letting herself adjust to the new chapter of consciousness. Then she stretched and rolled on to her side, an arm out in search of the bed's other occupant, finding empty space. Mike must already be in the shower.

Hawkins rolled back and stared at the ceiling, pleasantly surprised at how rested she felt. She must have had a decent sleep, something she hadn't expected after the last couple of strenuous days at work. She'd been exhausted when she and Mike had arrived home the previous night. They'd eaten with her dad, who had managed to cook a surprisingly decent lamb hotpot without reducing the kitchen to a smoking ruin.

The other positive development was that she and Mike had successfully shared a bed, for the first time since her return home. Obviously, there had been no action after lights out; Hawkins still wasn't up to that, and neither had she broached the subject of her scars. Until now, Mike had remained on the sofa, mainly because there wasn't a huge amount of room in the bed for them both, and a collision in the night would have had Hawkins waking in agony.

As far as she recalled, though, that hadn't happened.

At that point, her professional brain assumed control, dragging their main case back on to the agenda. Hawkins had brought her work laptop home, and she and Mike had spent some time, post hotpot, reviewing Steve Tanner's shock news.

Just like Samantha Philips, Rosa Calano had done time. And, just like Samantha Philips, within weeks of her release someone had used a hammer to cave in her head.

The investigation team that had originally looked into Calano's murder was led by Sean Davies, another DCI with whom Hawkins had worked briefly on a couple of cases a few years before. He hadn't been exactly inspirational then, but his team's performance on the Calano case really stank.

Calano had been murdered just over four months ago, and Davies' team had swiftly labelled it an indiscriminate attack, connected to the victim's Portuguese roots. There had been a spate of race-hate crimes in north London around the time, using a variety of nasty methods. A few local gang members had gone down for the ones where evidence was found, and it had simply been assumed they were responsible for the others as well.

With Calano's young, easily appeased friends, and no family to placate, it had been simple for an overworked investigation team to lump the case in with the gangland murders, despite the lack of evidence to back them up. As a result, the investigative minimum had been done. So Hawkins had instructed her team, via emails they'd pick up that morning, to recheck every element of the original case.

The investigation in fact remained live, with Davies' team supposedly still looking into it, but they certainly wouldn't be disappointed when Hawkins applied to have it transferred into her name.

Already completing the handover form in her head, Hawkins eased herself into a sitting position, simultaneously deciding what to wear. She twisted, checking the quality of the light creeping around the edges of her blackout blind. It already looked like being an unusually bright day.

She turned back, realizing that she couldn't hear any of the banging her unsubtle American companion usually made in the bathroom.

She looked at the clock.

Oh fuck.

It was nearly 10 a.m.

Hawkins was off the bed and three steps towards the door before she felt the pain in her torso and realized what she had done. She froze, reassuring herself that the wardrobe was there if she needed support, trying to establish whether she should retreat to the edge of the bed or call for help. But the longer she stayed upright, the more confident she became. Her stomach wall wasn't impressed by this impromptu excursion, but she was standing straight nonetheless.

She challenged herself, stepping further into the no-man's-land behind the bed. She reached the door, heaving it open and edging out on to the landing, her hand skirting the rail, still cursing Maguire.

The bastard had left her. He'd got up, *chosen* to leave her sleeping and buggered off to work alone. No change of heart in the shower; no pang of conscience on the bog. Now it was late morning and by the time Hawkins reached the office Mike would have been there for three hours or more. She'd probably walk in to find him high-fiving Steve Tanner over some case-breaking event.

She rounded the corner and was almost at the bath-room door when she nearly collided with her dad, who came bowling out of the spare room in an indecently short dressing gown, a toothbrush poking out of his mouth.

'All right, love,' he mumbled through a mouthful of white foam. 'You've had a good sleep.'

She ignored his verve. 'Where's Mike?'

'At work, I expect. It's Monday, isn't it?' He walked to the sink.

'Exactly. Where I'm supposed to be.'

Her dad began rinsing his brush. 'He tried to wake you before he left, but apparently you weren't too happy about it.'

'I seriously doubt that.'

He shrugged. 'Mike also said you've been working too hard *in your condition*.' He glanced at his daughter's midriff. 'I hope he means the attack.'

186

Hawkins sighed. 'I'm not bloody pregnant, Dad.' She watched as he vacated the bathroom. 'Chance'd be a fine thing.'

'What?'

'Nothing.' She shuffled in; closing the door behind her. 'I'll just get ready and we can go.'

Her dad wasn't the sarcastic type, but Hawkins realized she'd pushed it too far when a curt knock preceded his response. 'I'll put some clothes on and drive you, then, shall I, madam?'

32

Hawkins walked slowly around her desk and turned to glare at Maguire. 'Why the hell didn't you wake me?'

'I tried, Toni.' He held up his hands. 'You told me to fuck off.'

'Rubbish.'

'You said we have Steve Tanner on the team now, so you might as well stay in bed.'

'My mistake, then.' She didn't remember a word of it. 'I should know better than to unleash the complexities of sarcasm near Americans.'

He ignored her scorn. 'You were obviously exhausted, so I let you sleep. You're doing too much too soon, Toni, and you swore not to.'

'Well,' she retorted, 'until they crowbar me out of this office, I'm still your boss. So mind your manners and button it.'

But Mike wasn't done. 'You want technicalities? How about the fact that I asked the DCS about you coming back? He says you're on contract hours only, quote "easing back in".'

'I'm fine.' She tried to wave the conversation closed. 'I've spent every day back sitting down, haven't I? Stop mollycoddling me.'

He shot her a sceptical glare. 'Where's your wheelchair?'

Silently, she cursed her negligence in raising the point. 'At home. I don't need it, and this morning I realized why everything's felt harder since I came back. It wasn't me; it was that *thing*. As soon as you're in a chair, people think you're an idiot.' She pictured Vaughn's secretary, Otis King and half a dozen others who'd patronized her, if they'd addressed her at all, in the last couple of days. 'You of all people should understand I won't put up with that.'

She elaborated no further, having decided she could handle a day without the chair, figuring that, if it wasn't even in the building, she couldn't resort to it in any moments of weakness or, more crucially, be forced back into it by Mike. The fact she'd had to take refuge in the quietest loos on the first floor of Becke House on her way in, simply to recharge before attempting the second leg to her office, wasn't something he needed to know.

Despite the fact her abdomen was now singing like a talent-show reject.

At least her office chair, now back in its rightful place behind her desk, was supportive, which was more than could be said presently of Maguire.

Fortunately, the DI pursed his lips, conceding the round, if not the entire fight.

'Anyway' – Hawkins moved on while she was ahead – 'the chair's not here, so we'll have to manage without. At least you don't need to ferry me around any more.' She left it there, hoping he wouldn't challenge her newfound independence, because, in truth, it was fragile at best.

'Whatever.' Mike rolled his eyes. 'But if you end up in ER, don't expect me to be there feeding you damn grapes all night.'

'I think we understand each other,' Hawkins closed. 'So now you've made me late, why don't you explain what I've missed?' She waited, omitting the fact that she had needed the lie-in.

She'd tottered into the operations room ten minutes ago, in foul humour thanks to her dad's geriatric driving style and his clucking about her disposal of the chair. It was eleven thirty when she arrived, having missed nearly three hours of research into Rosa Calano's death.

Discovering Maguire in conference with her competition hadn't improved things. Tanner was the archetypal man's man. He'd infiltrated the established male contingent straight away, but his arresting looks and implausibly white smile even seemed to have gained ground with Amala.

Mike had found himself summoned straight to Hawkins' desk.

'Okay,' he'd said at last, 'I'll tell you what's going on, but only if you swear to take things at a pace you can handle and get the rest you need in between. You're no good to any of us burned out.' He waited for Hawkins' sullen nod of agreement before taking a seat, sliding a photocopied Victim Profile Report across the desk. 'Rosa was nineteen at the time of her death, four months ago, October last. She finished work at the Masala Den, an Indian joint in Enfield, just before midnight, and caught the bus from the town centre to the end of her street, a mile or so to the south. She was on foot, a couple hundred yards from home, when someone took her out. Hammer to the temple, same as Philips. She had earphones in, so she didn't hear it coming, and the street was badly lit, so no one saw.'

'Only according to the original report,' Hawkins reminded him. 'I want all potential witnesses found and checked again. What about her background?'

'We're on it. Original investigation has some big-time holes, so we started from scratch, like you said. Nothing fresh yet.'

She rubbed her forehead. 'So what the hell have you been doing all day?'

Mike didn't say a word as he dug in the case file. Hawkins knew her DI well enough to know she'd riled him, but she was still too mad about being late to ease up.

He produced some papers and calmly began reeling off Calano's history. 'Rosa was a Portuguese immigrant. Dad went AWOL when she was eleven, current whereabouts unknown. Mom came to the UK the year after, looking for work; brought the girl along. She took a job in a hotel while the kid finished school, but she died of cancer right after her daughter graduated. Rosa wanted to stay here, though, and at sixteen she landed the au pair gig with a family in Camden.' He flipped a page. 'That didn't go so well. Kid had never worked with new-borns, managed to shake their six-month-old to death when he wouldn't quit screaming. She got five years, starting in a young offenders' institution, but they let her out after three. The court set her up in the shared condo and helped her get the restaurant job.'

'And two weeks later she was dead,' Hawkins added. 'Just like Sam Philips. They both killed, even though one meant to and the other clearly didn't, and they both did time. But dozens of prisoners are released every week. Why *these* two? Were they random selections chosen for their respective vulnerabilities, or are they linked some other way?'

Mike shrugged.

Hawkins was about to ask another question when someone knocked at the door. They both turned to see Steve Tanner enter. 'Sorry to interrupt. There's been a development.'

Hawkins eyed him. 'Go on.'

'Well' – Tanner's expression remained grave, but his eyes glinted – 'I rang a few contacts earlier on, asking them to look out for anything connected to these murders.'

Hawkins raised her eyebrows. 'And?'

'I just got a call . . .' He paused. 'We have a third body. Same MO.'

Hawkins felt herself lean forwards. 'What?'

Tanner repeated his statement, obviously unaware that she'd heard him perfectly the first time. Her query hadn't related to the fact itself, merely that he'd known before her.

At that moment her mobile rang. The two men waited while she salvaged it from her bag. 'Hello?'

Hawkins sat listening to the voice of Gerald Pritchard. She let the Home Office pathologist finish his sentence, trying not to let her frustration show as she stared at Steve Tanner before saying curtly:

'I know.'

33

Mike stopped the car as they entered the narrow street, pointing at the police cordon blocking the road ahead. 'Looks like the place.'

He parked up, slotting their VW pool car neatly between a Met-liveried Astra and a decaying Transit van that must have belonged to one of the locals. Hawkins watched Tanner climb eagerly out of the passenger side, reminding herself it would have been rude not to invite him. He was supposed to be shadowing her, after all, and he'd provided two breakthrough pieces of information in as many days.

They assembled on the narrow pavement, moisture-heavy winds blustering around them. Hawkins led off, with Mike and Tanner behind, matching her tentative pace. In the distance a large pair of black wooden gates stood ajar between grimy brick walls that ran the length of the street. Beyond that the road turned ninety degrees to skirt the worn buildings that towered above.

Their in-line formation made conversation hard, so for a moment nobody spoke, leaving Hawkins to her thoughts.

The journey from Hendon to Weybridge had taken just over forty minutes, London traffic failing to blunt

Maguire's whole-hearted approach to speed. Their excursion was the result of two phone calls. One an hour ago to Hawkins' mobile, made by Gerald Pritchard from a murder scene whose victim had been subjected to an increasingly familiar MO. The other call had been for Steve Tanner, informing him about the same homicide. Of greater concern, however, was the fact that Tanner's phone had rung before hers.

Even if there *had* been only moments in it, and Tanner had come straight in and told her, he'd still known about a major development first. Which grated. But both calls had given the same message: body count in the case that had looked until yesterday like an isolated murder inquiry had just reached three.

Serial homicide.

Again.

The fact that she still bore the scars of her previous encounter with a repeat killer didn't help. She just had to hope that, this time, the perpetrator didn't originate from quite so close to home.

Travel time from Becke House had been filled with discussion between the three detectives. Ten minutes' worth had involved potential fallout and courses of action should this latest corpse turn out to be connected with the others; something none of them was keen to bet against. The rest had been the Steve Tanner Show. Hawkins and Mike were already experts on how he'd cracked a multimillion-pound money-laundering ring operating through legal casinos in Birmingham.

Not to mention the three-year-old daughter he didn't see enough of. Things hadn't worked out with Kay's mum.

They reached the cordon, a double strand of crime scene tape strung between various posts and makeshift anchor points to form an exclusion zone that stretched out into the road. Manned by a couple of uniformed officers, its purpose was to hide from public view whatever unpleasantness was about to confront Hawkins and her two DIs.

One of the officers held up a hand, indicating there would be a few minutes' delay. Mike offered to find out what was going on and wandered across to the gates.

Hawkins watched him go before settling herself on a low wall to rest, also taking the opportunity to address Tanner. 'Sorry to throw you straight in like this.'

'Don't worry. I'm keen to get properly involved.'

'Great,' she pretended, already stuck for conversation. 'You're young for a DI. You must have impressed a few influential souls along the way.'

'It's all down to hard work.' He winked. 'Imagine where I'd be if I had looks as well.'

She nodded industriously, not wishing to stoke his ego. 'So what would you like to achieve while you're here?'

'I just want to learn. Tristan speaks highly of you, so when he suggested the chance to work together, I jumped. Plus, your team happens to be running the biggest case around.' He grinned.

Hawkins turned away from its glare. He was probably just biding his time, waiting for the next opportunity to upstage her. He might have appeared genuine, but he would definitely need to be watched.

Mike interrupted by waving them over to join him at the cordon, where they showed ID to the slimmer of the two uniforms and were ushered inside, allowing Hawkins to make a first appraisal of the scene.

Inside the threshold was a small courtyard, hemmed on three sides by the same high stone walls and on the fourth by even taller thirties buildings of charred-looking brick garnished with black iron railings and stairs. The ground was uneven; not quite cobbled, but not far off. Sodden leaves stuck to the tiles here and there. The entrance itself wasn't central; the area opened further out to one side than the other. In the resulting recess, Hawkins noted a dark-blue Toyota Aygo. And, beside it, a large male body with a deep-red halo, face down.

More crime scene tape sectioned off the area immediately around the body and the car, before stretching across to the far wall, while activity around the corpse confirmed its discovery as a recent event. Two scenes of crime officers in anti-contamination overalls squatted alongside, picking at various fibres, depositing them carefully in clear bags. Hawkins recognized Otis King buzzing around them. The wiry crime scene analyst kept lining his camera up, only to sag flamboyantly whenever one of the SOCOs shuffled in, ruining his shot.

Beside them, the driver's door of the city car stood open, a pair of white overshoes poking out, denoting a third officer kneeling inside on the seat. Otherwise, the area was deserted, until the glaring whiteness of a fifth overall emerged from an alleyway in the rear-left corner. Gerald Pritchard marched over to the inner cordon, greeting Hawkins and Maguire by name as the three Met officers joined him from the other side.

'This is all a bit exposed, isn't it?' Hawkins said once banalities had been exchanged, waving at the assorted windows above them. 'Shouldn't we tent up?'

'That's what I like about you, Detective,' Pritchard said, 'always procedure first.' He checked his watch. 'Normally, we'd be covered by now. Unfortunately, the forensics truck was being serviced this morning. Poor timing, of course, but they're on their way now. We'll have protection up soon enough.'

'Good.' Hawkins nodded at the corpse. 'Do we know who this guy is yet?'

'Matthew Hayes.' Pritchard handed her a black leather wallet. 'It doesn't look like anything's been taken; there's still twenty pounds inside.'

She flipped it open, pulling out the driving licence, staring at the face. Despite the grainy photo, and assuming it wasn't that old, Hayes looked good for the forty-two years of age his birthdate made him.

Hawkins checked the address. 'Chertsey. What's that from here – twenty minutes by car?' She handed the licence to Mike. 'See if you can get next of kin on the phone. Don't give them details, but make sure they're around when family liaison arrive to break the news.'

'Got it.' Maguire moved off.

Hawkins searched the rest of the wallet, finding the usual mixture of bank and travel cards, plus two ten-pound notes. Nothing of immediate concern.

At that moment, shouting and a scuffle of shoes on wet ground made them all turn towards the gates, where a young photographer had managed to evade the coppers manning the cordon and broken through into the yard. He saw the body and raised his camera, but he didn't get a shot off. Tanner had already blocked his view, and seconds later the two uniformed officers tackled him. He caught the camera just in time to stop it hitting the floor, before he was wrestled to his feet and marched back to the road.

Hawkins looked at the pathologist. 'How imminent is that tent?'

'Point taken.' Pritchard frowned.

'Well, that was worthwhile,' Mike said, re-joining them. 'Family aren't there, but I got the cleaner. She ain't exactly busting to talk about Matthew Hayes. Looks like he moved out of there a year back, but she gave me his forwarding address, right here in Weybridge. Anyone know where Mangrove Court is?'

None of them did, so Tanner looked it up on his phone. 'Not far. A minute or two west of here.'

'Good,' Hawkins said. 'We'll take a look when we're done.'

She turned back to Pritchard. 'Same MO as the others?'

'Almost,' the pathologist replied. 'There's no evidence of scratching or bruises on the body to indicate a struggle, so, again, the murderer appears to have given his victim minimal warning. Similarly, the fatal blow to the temple was inflicted with a large, hammer-like implement. But there's one crucial difference. You'll be able to get in closer once we've finished sweeping for fibres, at which point you'll notice that the initial strike mark is on the left side of the head, as opposed to the right. If we assume it's the same killer, still using his right hand, this indicates Mr Hayes was facing his assailant at the time of the attack. Which poses one interesting question . . .'

Tanner spoke first. 'Why didn't he defend himself?'

'Why, indeed?' Pritchard raised a questioning finger. 'Our murderer has already proven he can sneak up on a target, so why risk giving notice and opportunity for self-defence to somebody of Mr Hayes' size?' He stared at them, like a primary school teacher setting a riddle for his class.

Tanner just beat Hawkins to it. 'Hayes was drunk?'

'Correct.' Pritchard nodded approvingly at the DI. 'Toxicology will confirm it, but the odour becomes quite evident within a few yards of the body, thanks to the alcohol seeping out through the skin. Plus, there's the empty vodka bottle, of course. It's difficult to say how much he'd had. I'll know more precisely once we get him on a slab, but I'd say *steaming* just about covers it. If the killer had been following Mr Hayes prior to the attack, that level of inebriation would have been obvious enough in the victim's behaviour to reassure him.'

Tanner looked around the small courtyard. 'All he needed was somewhere quiet to strike.'

'So how'd Hayes wind up in here?' Mike asked. 'Wander in through these gates looking for somewhere to pee?'

'Half right, Detective,' Pritchard replied. 'The traces of ammonia-rich liquid on the floor in the far corner suggest our victim did indeed come in here to relieve himself. I suppose if nature makes an urgent call when you're that drunk, even a three-minute walk home is too far. But the gates were closed, as they are every night, according to the tenant who owns the car. He unlocked them for us earlier, after reporting the body he found when he came down this morning to leave for work. He lives in the top flat.'

Hawkins glanced up at the building. 'Is he still here?'

'Of course.' The pathologist smiled. 'I told him you'd require a statement.'

'Great, we'll catch him afterwards. Did he see anything?'

'Apparently not. Didn't even wake up, as far as he recalls, although I can't imagine there would have been much noise. The killer wouldn't have wanted to draw attention, and Mr Hayes probably missed his chance. I think they both came through there.' He waved towards the rear corner. 'The alleyway leads directly to the main road beyond these buildings.'

Hawkins nodded. 'Time of death?'

'Early indications are between midnight and 5 a.m.'

There were no further questions, so Pritchard promised to let them know when they could have access to the body and moved over to check on his colleagues. Tanner offered to collect anti-contamination overalls from the car and headed for the exit, leaving Hawkins and Maguire alone.

'Helpful guy,' Mike said when he'd gone. 'Quick, too. He'll be worth having around.'

'I was just thinking the same thing.'

'Really?' He grinned at her. 'Try telling your face.'

'What?'

'The disapproving pout. You don't even know you're doing it.'

Hawkins was about to deny his allegation when conscience clamped her mouth shut and forced her to think. On the surface, Steve Tanner's arrival was a good thing, adding competent reinforcement to the team exactly when it was required. He'd been eager and insightful from minute one, and although she didn't like the fact he'd already beaten her to a couple of key developments, Hawkins had to admit their relative conclusions each time were perfectly matched.

Maguire shrugged. 'I'm just saying, don't spend your life looking over your shoulder.'

'Fine,' she conceded. 'Maybe he has earned the benefit of the doubt, but can we discuss my personal shortcomings another time?'

She took Mike's muteness as accord and turned back to study their surroundings, silently working things through.

Rosa Calano, Sam Philips and now Matt Hayes; all murdered in public places by repeat hammer blows to the head. But Calano and Philips were convicted killers, too. If it turned out that Hayes had served time, a genuine pattern would emerge. Which changed things considerably. Three consecutive deaths would promote the case to major-investigation status, earning it a code name and higher profile inside the Met.

Thankfully, serial killers were rare, although that also made them big news when they appeared, which often led the public to panic and the media to stoke things up. If this case involved one, he'd be taking up where his murderous predecessor had left off, just a couple of months ago. The media would have a field day.

At least this time there might be something to tie the victims together, and pacify the masses as well. If the killer *was* targeting ex-cons, they still had a shot at convincing the rest of London there was no reason for alarm. What worried Hawkins, though, was the increasing pace of events.

After finding out about Rosa Calano, she'd accepted

the possibility of further attacks, just perhaps not quite so soon. The gap between the first and second victims had been four months, but Samantha Philips had barely been cold when Matthew Hayes joined her on the list of casualties. So why the variation?

And how long till he did it again?

Hawkins made a mental note to call Simon Hunter. The respected psychological profiler had provided valuable insight into the mind of Hawkins' last psychopath-shaped problem. If the three murders were linked, there was no harm in getting an early opinion. But first she needed to know if Hayes had done time.

Hawkins dug out her mobile and selected Frank Todd's desk number. It was approaching one thirty, so he'd likely be at his desk, tucking into the contents of his first Tupperware box. Monday was tuna salad day; part of a diet that everyone suspected was an effort to slim. Frank had been a bachelor for years, ever since the first Mrs Todd had packed his bags for him. A daily hint of Old Spice backed up Amala's recent suggestion that their Geordie detective was back on the romantic prowl. But, as the number started to ring, Steve Tanner reappeared through the gates, carrying three packaged crime scene overalls and nitrile gloves in one hand, his mobile in the other. He waved at them, suggesting that he had new information.

Hawkins sighed; ended her call.

Tanner arrived beside them. 'I just called a contact back at HQ . . .'

'And?' Hawkins asked, mentally kicking herself for being beaten to the next logical move yet again.

Tanner's mouth twitched, as if a satisfied grin was trying to break free. 'Matthew Hayes just got out of Pentonville Prison. He killed a kid.'

34

They pulled up at the crossroads, both of them leaning forwards to stare out through the Land Rover's dirty windscreen. Dark streets stretched away either side of the T-junction, disappearing into the blackness beyond the headlights.

'Which way?' Jim asked from the driver's seat.

Jim Wilson was a newbie. Barely eighteen and greener than a golf course, he had a lot to learn. For a start, he was too skinny, needed building up, but he got stuck in, which counted for a lot, and the kid was permanently smiling. That's why Trunks, who chose everyone's nicknames around here, had straight away started calling him Cheshire.

Like the cat.

'Hold on.' Bull struggled with the map in the narrow cabin. He tried to fold it over, bashing his elbow on the passenger door, dropping the torch. It hit the centre console and disappeared. 'Fuck.'

Bull shoved the map out of his way and bent forwards, digging under the seat. He could see the light leaking out from under him, but it wasn't full beam, so the torch must have jammed itself in a corner. He groped in the darkness, finding nothing but sharp edges, brackets, bolts.

'Don't worry, man,' Cheshire started. 'Take your time, yeah?'

'Screw this.' Bull slid off the seat and jammed himself into the foot well, grit crunching under his boots, going at the torch a new way.

The driver carried on. 'It's only 3 a.m., plenty of time.'

'Fuck you.'

'Yes, sir.' Cheshire gave a piss-take salute.

'Listen, dick brain.' Bull found the torch at last. He wrenched it free and shone it straight in the kid's face. 'I'm in charge of directions. You're in charge of shutting the fuck up.'

Cheshire squinted, stuck a hand over the beam. 'Whatever you say, boss man. Let's get going, though, yeah?'

They grinned at each other as Bull swung himself back into the seat. Backchat was sometimes all that kept them sane.

He grabbed the crumpled paper and smoothed it across his legs, griping at its lack of detail. This place wasn't like home at all. Not the scenery, not the people, and definitely not the directions.

Bull stared at the scrawled arrow pointing to where their targets had been seen the previous day, squinting up to see if he could find any of the landmarks circled on the map. But there were no markers outside.

He took a punt. 'Go right.'

Cheshire grinned, bashed the truck into gear and gunned the engine, bumping the heavy vehicle over the lip and on to the other street. 'Where next?'

'Stay on this road,' Bull told him. 'I'll tell you where to turn off.' He went back to the map, torchlight jumping as they picked up speed, still trying to find the junction they'd just left. He glanced over at the kid. But Cheshire didn't seem to be aware of any problems, which was good, considering that Bull had lost track of their position thirty minutes ago.

Bull checked the wing mirror, seeing the dark outline of a second Land Rover following them closely, headlights off. Tailgating, they called it: a tactic used to avoid unwanted attention.

Whenever vehicles travelled together at night, only the lead truck used its lights, taking responsibility for the others, which followed blindly behind. Up close it was obvious there were multiple trucks, but if anyone was watching from a distance all they saw was one set of headlights. In other words: less cause for alarm.

The trick worked even with large numbers of vehicles, although tonight there were only two in their train. There were five guys in total: Bull and Cheshire ahead; Trey, Collins and Ginger behind.

Bull stared out at the road as they rattled on, still seeing nothing that told him where they were. Low houses slogged past in the gloom, the gaps between them closing the further they drove into whatever fucking town this was. He'd pretty much given up on the map. Between the bumpy ride, the dim light and their makeshift directions, he'd have had trouble keeping them on the M25, let alone some half-arsed track, trampled into the dirt. He'd taken his best guess at the four-way junction that hadn't been marked on the map fifteen miles ago, but after that it had all been guesswork. And he had no idea how to get back.

He glanced over at Cheshire, realizing the kid hadn't said anything for about five minutes, whereas normally you couldn't shut the guy up. Which meant he was nervous. That was no surprise, though; they all were.

'What the hell is that?' Cheshire asked suddenly.

Bull clicked off the torch and leaned closer to the screen, staring up at the huge shape looming out of the darkness ahead.

Cheshire put the headlamps on full, lighting a set of spindly grey legs that rose out of the earth to a massive metal cylinder thirty feet above the road. His guess had paid off.

'Water tower.' He switched the torch back on, searching their map for the marker. After a few seconds, he found it.

Bang on the route to their goal.

'Keep going for a quarter-mile,' he instructed. 'Take a left when I say.'

They rode the rutted track until Bull saw the turning, then joined another street. The pavements were unlit, the windows dark.

When they got within two hundred yards of the point marked on the map, Bull told Cheshire to stop. The kid pulled over and shut the engine off. In the mirror, Bull saw the other truck parking up behind. He dumped the map and torch, reaching on top of the dash for his binoculars. He switched to night vision and brought them up. Forty yards ahead, three linked houses sat in darkness.

Just like the informant had said.

Bull checked their position. They were parked on the other side of the street, down a slight incline. The Land Rovers would be visible from any one of the three houses, although they were a fair distance away. But other vehicles were dotted here and there, giving them cover, and it was dark tonight, really fucking dark. Which meant whoever lived there was unlikely to notice them — unless they'd been tipped off.

Or if it was a trap.

That was the thing: you had to be smart. Things looked quiet one minute and turned to carnage the next. You never knew anyone's loyalties around here, until they tried to kill you.

But, for the moment, they had calm.

Bull switched the binoculars off and rested them in his lap. His eyes soon adjusted to the darkness, allowing him to see the front doors of the houses up ahead. Now it was just a case of waiting. It was nearly 3 a.m., and they were due back by eight, so they'd be here no more than four hours.

He pulled out his Marlboros and offered Cheshire the pack.

The kid took one. 'Cheers.'

They wound down the windows and sat, smoking in silence. They all knew the drill. No card games or dicking about; nothing that took their eyes off the street.

They waited for an hour, talking quietly about the usual stuff: old girlfriends, the craziness of this place, things they missed about home. By four o'clock, without having seen anyone on the street, Bull had given up the idea of action, and his eyelids had started to drop. He forced himself to concentrate. The slightest smudge had broken the horizon, lifting the deepest blackness from the sky. And still the houses up ahead remained still.

Then he caught sight of movement.

A group of men had appeared near the far end of the street, most in jeans and T-shirts. They walked in a pack, staying close to the walls.

'There.' He pointed, grabbing the binoculars from his lap and clicking them on, picking up detail in the green glow of night vision. There were six of them, all around Bull's age. Some of them looked up and down the street as they went, though none of them stared directly at the trucks. Either it was still too dark, or they weren't bothered about being seen. But was that because they had nothing to hide, or because they already knew Bull and the others were there?

The men crossed the road, heading for the house.

Bull kept the binoculars trained. He checked out the first five men one by one, seeing nothing of interest. But the sixth guy made him pause. The kid was skinny and small but he moved like he was in charge, and the others seemed to be matching his pace.

Shielding him.

The men stopped outside the house and started filing in through the door. The skinny guy went in last, disappearing from view. But Bull had already seen what he needed to see. The kid was missing a hand.

Their informant had been telling the truth.

Bull kept the binoculars pointed at the door as he picked up the radio, ignoring Cheshire's question about what was going on, and called in the alert.

35

Tanner's statement about Matthew Hayes having served time wasn't a surprise but, as she exchanged glances with Maguire in the windswept courtyard, Hawkins realized that Sod's Law was punishing her. Habitual impatience, combined with insecurity regarding her seconded post, had seen her trample right over everyone else's better judgement on her impulsive return to work.

She'd come back before she was ready, hoping for a simple common-or-garden murder investigation of the type they saw week after week, something that would allow her to start gradually rebuilding both her confidence and her recently blemished reputation.

Instead, here she was, still recovering from near-fatal wounds inflicted by one serial psychopath, only to sprawl on the tracks in front of another. The body lying ten feet away on the far side of the yard was the new killer's third, and the same media that had facilitated her previous brush with ignominy were about to become interested all over again. Now she had pressure from below, too, in the form of a zealous upstart with superintendent sponsorship, who was consistently beating her to every development in this case. Granted, her physical condition wasn't helping her concentration, and more often than not there had been just seconds in it, but the score was already three–nil.

Basic chivalry said he should have let her have one, at least.

She hid her anxiety, responding to Tanner's statement. 'What did Hayes go down for?'

'Hit and run,' he said. 'That's all I know, but my contact's digging the file up now. He'll send it to my smartphone in a bit.'

'Good work,' Hawkins accepted, beginning to wonder who was teaching whom.

But something inside her rallied, salvaging her flagging confidence, when she realized she was automatically taking charge again. 'Right, three bodies may not seem like a great start to our week, but at least it gives us something to work with. All the victims were released from prison shortly before they were killed, which means we're looking at two main possibilities. Either these three became connected in some way before or during their sentences, or they were targeted *because* they'd been inside, perhaps, more specifically, because they all did time for murder or manslaughter.' She looked at Tanner. 'So, in the interests of your development, what's our next move?'

'Well' – he paused, but only for a beat – 'I'd start by working up Hayes' past and cross-referencing it with the previous victims', looking for any historical links. Then I'd contact Pentonville to check his detention record; see if anything stands out.'

'Good,' Hawkins said. 'Do you want some support?'

Tanner shook his head. 'I'll be fine; I've got a few contacts stored away from my stint in organized crime. If I need a hand, I'll shout.'

She allowed herself to be impressed. 'In that case, Mike and I will start looking at whether these people were targeted purely for their type of crime. If we check out other recently released convicts and those due for parole, we might even be able to work out where this guy will strike next.'

'Shall I get started, then?' Tanner asked, waiting for Hawkins' nod before he retreated towards the far side of the courtyard, mobile pressed to his ear.

Hawkins watched him go, the word 'protégé' repeating itself in her mind, hoping she hadn't just unleashed the man destined to take her DCI badge on his first day in the job.

36

Five pairs of boots hit the dusty road as the men jumped down from the Land Rovers and gathered in the darkness.

Bull spoke first, his voice low. 'Okay, boys, we just got a fix on the target. Support's on its way, but they won't get here for an hour. Till then it's our job to secure the building and hold these guys till the others arrive.'

No more instructions were required. The others fanned out and began to close on the house, feet tramping quietly as they moved. Bull and Cheshire took the left side of the street, Trey, Collins and Ginger the right.

Bull watched his colleagues, all dressed in black clothing with body armour over the top. They were all armed, with guns that were more than a match for anything their targets would have. But still no guarantee of safety.

They moved within twenty yards of the house. Above them, the darkness was definitely lifting as the early signs of dawn began pushing above the horizon. Already Bull could feel the sweat running down between his shoulder blades. Part of that was nerves, although he was getting more and more used to situations like this.

He also kept an eye on the buildings around them. If this was a trap, any of those windows could be hiding gunmen. But no shots rang out as they reached the house.

Bull gave the signal for the other three to head round the back, then he and Cheshire lined up outside the front. A sliver of brightness bled out between the door and the frame, showing that the lights were on. They waited for the whistle to tell them the others were in place, then Cheshire shot the lock off the door and they charged inside.

The room opened into a lounge with dirty walls and low stools dotted about, mattresses stacked against one wall. The windows had been blacked out from inside, and the place stank. At a table in the centre of the room, their target was playing cards with his mates. They all looked round.

'Hands up!' Bull jerked his gun at them.

Everyone obeyed, raising their hands just as the others came in through the untidy kitchen at the back of the room. Trey signalled that the rest of the ground floor was clear.

Bull nodded, watching as the men were hauled to their feet one at a time and patted down before being lined up, sitting with their backs against the wall.

'Is anyone upstairs?'

No one spoke, so Bull asked again, louder this time.

One of the men looked up. 'Two women, three kids.'

Bull moved closer. 'How many rooms?'

'Err . . .' The man hesitated. ' . . . just one.'

Bull signalled for Trey, Collins and Ginger to cover their prisoners while he and Cheshire moved to the stairs and began to climb, sliding their backs along the stained plaster, every step creaking under their weight. There was no noise from the upstairs room, but that didn't mean they weren't being set up.

Cheshire was ahead as they reached the single door at the top. He looked at Bull, who nodded for him to go in. The kid's face was pale.

They both knew the door could be wired to blow.

37

The landlord's name was Joseph.

He slotted his beige Mini convertible into one of the visitor parking bays and joined Hawkins, Tanner and Maguire outside Mangrove Court, the former council block where Matthew Hayes had rented one of his flats.

Joseph was fortyish, short and well-groomed. He wore a khaki waistcoat over a white shirt and turned-up jeans, with a pair of bright-red plastic-framed glasses and meticulously tailored facial hair. Hawkins produced her warrant card and introduced the others, thanking him for coming at short notice. Joseph said it was no problem; better than paying for a new door, as he had last time the police *investigated* one of his tenants.

He opened the security lock and led them up two flights of functionally decorated stairs to an inner landing, where the three men waited as Hawkins struggled up behind, pretending to be engrossed by some facet of the building's architecture to explain her slow ascent.

Joseph fumbled with a large bunch of keys outside number twelve. 'What's all this about, anyway?'

'We can't discuss it just yet,' she told him, keen not to

taint any information he might provide. 'For now, we just need to check the flat.'

They'd come straight from the courtyard where Hayes' body had been found. Even the victim's wife wouldn't hear of his death until family liaison officers arrived there later that evening. Till then, information regarding his expiry was classified.

In contrast, Hawkins suspected the case itself would soon be common knowledge. The reporter ejected from the murder scene earlier that afternoon may not have managed to get photos, but the potential reward had obviously outweighed the prospective inconvenience of getting himself arrested. Which meant the media were gearing up for an exposé.

'I knew this would happen.' Joseph tried one of the keys. 'You've arrested him, haven't you?'

No one replied.

'He's done time, you know.' The landlord switched keys and struggled with the lock again. 'For drunk driving. But here's good old Joseph, never one to write somebody off. "Hello, Mr Waif," "Come in, Mr Stray, everyone's welcome here." And look where it gets me.'

He found the right key at last, pushing the door open and waving the three detectives by. Hawkins led the way into a compact hall that turned left immediately inside the door, past a grubby bathroom. Straight ahead she found the front room.

And stopped in the doorway.

The small lounge looked like it had been the venue for some sort of degenerate rave. Empty bottles and rubbish were strewn on the table, small sofa and floor, among half-eaten microwave meals and randomly discarded clothes. There were fist-sized dents in various walls and doors, while the television, picture frames and most pieces of furniture were damaged or smashed. The smell was on its way to overpowering.

'You're fucking *kidding* me!' Joseph squeezed past Maguire and Tanner into the room. 'He's only been in here two weeks. This place was immaculate. His deposit won't even *begin* to cover it. I'll drag that fucker through small-claims court.'

'Good luck with that,' Mike said quietly.

Hawkins flashed him a warning stare.

But Joseph hadn't heard. He was already in the kitchen, making further protest about the state of a flat that had obviously been a furnished let.

Hawkins glanced around at the dead man's room, strategizing in silence. Her first instinct had been to keep the murders from the public domain for as long as possible. After all, the capital had just emerged from the shadow of one serial killer, only now to find itself under another. But there were differences.

Now, a third victim, just like the first two, had been confirmed as an ex-con: the encouraging news was that this killer clearly had a target group. And the proportion of London's residents who had been indicted for murder or manslaughter was mercifully small. So at least this time they had a fighting chance of convincing the public not to freak out.

The downside was that the four-month gap between the first two victims had not been repeated prior to number three. In fact, the hiatus had closed to three days, which meant the killer might strike again at any time. Perhaps they could confidently predict the type of person he would target and the MO he'd use, but the pivotal question remained.

Why?

Hawkins turned back into the room, where Joseph was berating Tanner about how the Met consistently ignored the plight of the domestic landlord. She left them to it, wandering through to the bedroom, finding the same entropy. She looked at the cheap dressing table, its mirror cracked by some kind of impact, realizing just how inept the UK's penal system was when it came to reforming those in its keep. And she was willing to bet it wasn't just inebriation that had made Matthew Hayes such an angry man.

She turned to see Mike behind her in the doorway. 'When will the e-fit be ready?' she asked.

'Tomorrow afternoon.'

She frowned. 'Let's try to speed things up. Put the team on overtime if you have to. I may want that picture on the breakfast news.'

'Whatever you say, boss.' Maguire produced his phone and stepped back into the hall.

Hawkins turned back to Hayes' room, thinking about recent incidents. The e-fit team were already doing the rounds of the houses near where Matt Hayes was killed. The ex-estate agent had been seen by several residents as he wobbled along the main road to the nearest off-licence, where the shopkeeper remembered selling him cheap spirits, and not just on the night of his death. Since moving in, it seemed that Hayes' excursion to the local offy had been an almost nightly affair, often taking two or three bottles with him on the return leg. Which explained the rapid deterioration of his flat, if not the reason behind the drinking itself.

Fortunately, the locals overlooking the main road had proved to be a nosy lot; a disturbing number of them appeared to lead almost nocturnal lives. So far, they had given consistent descriptions not only of Matt Hayes en route to buy alcohol over the last few nights . . .

But also, on each occasion, of the man who'd clearly followed him there.

38

They stood together at the top of the narrow staircase.

From below, Bull heard one of the men asking to use the toilet. Collins told him to wait.

Bull turned back just as Cheshire finished checking the door surround for signs of wires. The kid nodded to show it was clear, before he eased the handle down and pushed.

The door grated against the frame, and Bull held his breath as the seal broke. Luckily, nothing happened as Cheshire shoved it open and they stepped inside.

The bedroom was almost pitch black, the only light leaking in from downstairs through the open door. In the dim glow Bull saw what looked like a jumble of duvets. Someone was snoring, but it was impossible to tell how many bodies there were. Cheshire switched on the light.

A bare bulb in the middle of the ceiling came on. It wasn't bright, but Bull still had to shield his eyes. The room was about three yards square, with cardboard boxes full of clothes in the far corner, opposite another door that must have been a bathroom. As the man said, there were five people: two women and three young kids, all on mattresses on the floor.

The younger of the two women and the children were just coming round, shielding their eyes against the sudden light. The youngest one started to cry. But the older woman was sitting bolt upright on a corner of her mattress. Her eyes were closed, her hands clasped in her lap, as if she'd been praying.

'Stay calm,' Bull told them. 'We won't hurt you.'

The younger woman sat up and pulled the crying child towards her. She held the girl, glaring at them.

'Downstairs.' Bull motioned with his gun.

Nobody moved.

Still the older woman didn't open her eyes.

Bull looked at Cheshire, who waved at his waist and pointed to the old lady, before spreading the fingers on one hand to mimic a bomb. Bull nodded.

They'd both seen the awkward bulges under her clothes.

'You' – Bull stamped his foot – 'look at me.'

At last the old lady's eyes opened, and she turned her head towards them.

'Stand up.'

Slowly, she stood.

'In there.' Bull jabbed the barrel towards the bathroom. She didn't move. There were tears in her eyes.

He glanced at Cheshire. 'Get the kids downstairs. Now.'

The kid stepped forwards, held out a hand to the nearest child. 'Come on.'

But, as he moved, the old lady let out a high-pitched scream.

And went for him.

In the split second that followed, Bull knew he should have pulled the trigger, put his target down. But, suddenly, Cheshire moved. He caught the old woman in a bear hug, herding her backwards into the bathroom. The pair tripped as they went through the door, falling further inside.

Bull grabbed the kids, pulling them up one by one and moving them towards Trey, who had appeared in the doorway. The younger woman hurried out of the room after them, as Bull arrived at the bathroom door.

He almost laughed.

Cheshire was kneeling between the old lady's legs on the bathroom floor. Her nightdress had ridden up, revealing her underwear. She was shouting and battering him with her fists.

She had some sort of corset on over her barrel-like belly. Its edges had stuck through the nightdress like a suicide vest, enough to convince them both she was a threat.

But Cheshire's bravery would have saved lives. If the old woman had blown at that range, they'd all have died, including the kids. Some belief systems would have encouraged that sacrifice. But Cheshire's decision to take her out of the room, putting a wall between them, smothering the possible explosion with his body, would have given the rest of them a chance. As it was, he'd still saved the old lady, not that she looked too happy about it. If he hadn't stopped her, she'd have got a bullet in the face.

If not for his friend, Bull would have been responsible for her death.

And that was something he'd never forget.

39

'Two serial killers in three months.' Simon Hunter turned back towards Hawkins from the window. 'Did you break a mirror, Detective?'

'I'm not superstitious,' she told him. 'It's why God hates me.'

She moved across to part the internal blinds, and peered into the operations room outside her office at Becke House. Since her previous check, Aaron Sharpe had joined Amala and Mike. It was 8.19 a.m.

She turned to face Hunter again, thankful that the psychological profiler was more eager than some of her team to address their latest killer's deeds. She'd left a message on his answerphone the previous afternoon. But Hunter hadn't responded directly, at least until Hawkins arrived at work early that morning to find him waiting in her office. The forty-three-year-old ex-counsellor was renowned within the Met, his insight having cut investigation times on dozens of cases over the years and, in Hawkins' first experience of working with him, helped them to bring down a psychopathic killer.

She regarded Hunter. He had something of Lieutenant Columbo about him, being as typically disinterested in sartorial affairs as your typical genius, but with a compelling manner that distracted from his crumpled attire. His gravelled tone and creviced physiognomy might have made another man seem older, but resolutely black hair and a youthful gait kept him looking young. As usual, under different circumstances, Hawkins would have welcomed his company. In reality, his appearance meant they were about to grapple with another potential nightmare of a case.

'So, to recap' – Hunter noticed his shirt was hanging out, and tucked some of it back in – 'we have three victims, the first two separated by four months, and the second pair by just three days. But all the targets had served time, and all three died during the early hours in public places, from head trauma inflicted with what appears to be a domestic hammer.'

'That's about the size of it.'

He looked down at the copy of the *Sun* on Hawkins' desk and gave an appreciative grunt, 'Great headline.'

She followed his eye line, never keen to credit the press, who would soon be sensationalizing every turn in the case. But she couldn't disagree: the nickname used by several of that morning's papers was appropriate for a man who liked to bring the hammer down on convicted killers:

THE JUDGE.

And, unfortunately, the media now knew that the deaths of Rosa Calano, Sam Philips and Matt Hayes were connected. One red top had already adorned its centre pages with the heading MURDER EPIDEMIC HITS LONDON. So strong was the symbolism of the pre-Christmas string of murders that it had taken very little effort from the press to reignite widespread alarm. Mercifully, in contrast to the one in Hawkins' previous investigation, this killer wasn't targeting apparently random members of the public, although, if the papers thought fresh panic would help boost sales, that's what they'd try to create.

Awareness of that fact had prompted Hawkins' decision to release overnight an official Met statement regarding the case, including the composite e-fit of the main suspect, appealing for any witnesses from the previous scenes to call in. That information had been looping on the news channels every fifteen minutes since, though even an optimist would have called the response tepid so far.

And yet, the stellar anxiety Hawkins had felt when her previous case began dominating the headlines was gone. It had been the largest serial-killer case in the UK for decades, as well as her first big murder investigation as acting DCI. Of course, this operation wasn't looking exactly routine, but her apprehension had been replaced, unexpectedly, by a calm determination to chip away at the case till something broke.

She'd already spent time that morning with Vaughn, discussing the third murder, having decided to extend him the same courtesy as she had Tanner. Mike was right: if she convinced herself they were enemies, she might end up making them both exactly that.

It still surprised her how much more comfortable such meetings were when your chief superintendent treated you like an intelligent adult instead of a petulant child, as had been the case with his predecessor – although her own, less fretful approach might also have helped lighten the tone. *There was nothing like a claustro-phobic brush with death to provide perspective once you returned to the daily grind.*

'Okay.' Hunter perched on the corner of Hawkins' desk. 'Let's look at this guy's motivation. He obviously has issues with people who've killed one way or another in their own right. But if the victims don't appear to be personally linked, the next possibility is that it involves their crimes.' He thought for a moment. 'How much remorse did each of his targets show?'

'During their trials?'

'At all.'

Hawkins thought for a moment. 'It's not something we've looked at specifically, although apparently Hayes was in pieces about the kid he ran down, even made appeals to the family for forgiveness – not that it was granted, of course. I don't really know about Calano, but Philips didn't show much of anything, by all accounts; she just shut the world out.'

'Odd.' Hunter's gaze drifted away.

'Why do you ask?'

He looked back at her. 'Well, my first guess would have been that our killer is castigating his targets for their actions. Had they all demonstrated a lack of remorse, for example, our self-empowered subject might feel justified in punishing them for that. However, as that doesn't seem to be the case, my next suggestion would be to look at how they might have benefited from the leniency of others.'

Hawkins frowned. 'You mean, did they get off lightly in terms of sentencing?'

'Exactly.' Hunter gave her an appreciative nod. 'Was there controversy regarding the length of each jail term?'

'Actually,' she thought back, 'you might be on to something there. Extenuating circumstances were cited by the legal teams in every case. Calano was under eighteen and not fully qualified, Philips had been raped by her victim, and Hayes was only doing twenty miles per hour at the time of the accident, the kid's bike had no lights and nobody could actually *prove* he was drunk.'

'And the length of each sentence was adjusted accordingly?'

She nodded.

Hunter's eyebrows twitched. 'Then, as unexciting as it sounds, I'd surmise that what we have here is a pretty straightforward case of vigilante justice. It's possible our killer believes these three people avoided fair sentences for causing the deaths of others. He thinks they still owe a debt to society, and he's taken it upon himself to redress the balance.'

'Ignoring the irony of his method, of course.' Hawkins shook her head. 'Don't you just love psychopath logic?'

'Actually, I'm glad you mention it, because that's our next problem.' Hunter's tone was grave. 'I'm afraid this killer's own rulebook creates a paradox for him. If he's dispensing what he sees as justice to those who kill without then serving sufficient penance, his actions place him in that very position. He's racking up quite a body count but, for the moment at least, *he* isn't being held to account.'

Hawkins felt a headache coming on. 'Which means?'

'That he, by his own estimation, is moving further and further beyond redemption. One way around this would have been to do it once or twice and hand himself in. Another would be suicide. Unfortunately, the longer he goes without doing either, the more likely the last possibility becomes.'

'Don't tell me.' Hawkins looked straight at Hunter. 'Unless we stop him, the Judge will just keep on killing.'

40

Heads turned and the clamour in the operations room at Becke House died down as Hawkins emerged from her office, with a copy of the *Sun* in hand and Simon Hunter in tow.

She creaked across to position herself front and centre, quickly checking she had a full team in attendance.

To her right, Mike perched on the edge of a desk. Directly ahead, Amala Yasir sat like a finishing-school prefect next to the cross-legged Frank Todd. On the floor in front of both were steaming coffees from the canteen. Lurking almost out of sight behind them was Aaron Sharpe. Nearby, Steve Tanner stood with arms crossed and his legs oddly wide, like an aspiring super-hero. Beside him, Hunter had pulled up a chair.

Hawkins cleared her throat. 'Good morning. Thanks for being on time.' She glanced around, catching a few eyes. 'As you know, developments in this case have been gathering speed. Our killer has provided us with a third irreparably dented skull, earning himself a bit of media branding.' She held up the paper. 'The press are calling him the Judge.'

She waited for her team to digest the implications of

that before going on. 'Of course, body number three also nets him a code name. And it seems our chief super has a sense of satire, because you will come to know this as Operation Appeal.'

Yasir raised a tentative hand. 'Does that mean we're about to have reporters back at the gates, ma'am, and fresh panic on the streets?'

Hawkins waved at the sergeant to lower her arm. 'I'm confident we can avert that sort of panic this time. That's why I chose to go public overnight; some of you may already have seen the TV coverage. A controlled release of information means that at least the public get the facts and not some hyped-up media fallacy designed to incite terror.'

She glanced around the group. 'I'd rather not be dealing with a third body, but at least its appearance allows us to establish a pattern for this killer.' She turned to the newly added photograph on the whiteboard behind her. 'This is Matthew Hayes. Forty-two-year-old ex-estate agent, killed, as you know, just after two o'clock yesterday morning, on his way home from the local off-licence, by the increasingly familiar hammer blow to the temple.'

Todd interrupted. 'Why *ex*-estate agent?'

'Good question. Ex because, just like the previous two victims, Hayes had just finished a stretch inside.'

There were slow nods as she went on. 'Which pretty much eradicates the possibility of coincidence. This guy is targeting ex-cons, so we should be able to convince the public they're not at risk.'

'Don't rate your chances there, like.' Todd laughed at his own comment and glanced around for support. Finding none, he looked back at Hawkins, resorting to a frown. 'So what was this one banged up for?'

'Steve's been looking at that.' She turned to their latest team member. 'Would you mind?'

'Of course.' Tanner straightened, uncrossing his arms and moving into everyone's view.

'Thanks, Antonia.' He positioned himself in front of the investigation board, turning back to face the group. 'I spent yesterday evening looking at the case file and doing the rounds of Hayes' family and friends.'

He reached for his briefcase, producing a handful of newspaper clippings, and began attaching them to the whiteboard as he spoke. 'Last December Matthew Hayes' life was going well. He'd just lined himself up for promotion by sealing a couple of big property deals, which he and his colleagues celebrated with a few drinks at a local pub. Hayes left early, taking his Mercedes from the car park and heading for home, just ten minutes' drive away.

'On his way he hit fifteen-year-old Mark Williams' – Tanner pointed to the photo of a teenage boy – 'who was riding his push bike without lights on a dark residential street two minutes up the road. Then came Hayes' moment of madness: he drove away instead of calling for help. Another driver found Mark within minutes, but it was too late. Coppers caught up with Hayes at home the next evening thanks to witnesses, but an eleven-month jail sentence was just the start of his problems. His wife, Jodie, threw him out before he'd even been sentenced and has stopped him seeing his kids, seven-year-old Tom and four-year-old Rebecca, since. Hayes had recently threatened legal proceedings for access.'

'But' – Aaron Sharpe's head emerged briefly from behind Frank Todd – 'how did he get off with just eleven months?'

Mike took over. 'I checked that out. Seems there's no charge in your screwy British law for killing some-one in a hit and run, or for turning tail afterwards. Hayes even kept his damn licence. Derisory sentence he *did* get was for causing death by dangerous driving, and for possibly being over the drink-drive limit at the time.'

Yasir raised her hand again. '*Possibly?*'

'Yeah,' Mike said. 'There were no witnesses at the scene, and nobody saw Hayes have more than two drinks at the pub. He drove away after hitting the kid, and the cops didn't catch up with him till the next night, so his test sample was clear.'

Headshakes and snorts of disbelief went round the room.

Tanner continued. 'Still, some say what goes around comes around, and he's definitely paid for it now. But even before that the man was sinking. He came out of prison to find his wife living with someone else, still refusing him access to his kids. His job was gone, too.

So maybe it's no surprise he turned to drink.' He explained the condition of Hayes' flat, and the statements from his neighbours suggesting that he was on a one-way ticket to alcoholism.

Hawkins held up the case file. 'Anyway, it's on the system, so you'd better familiarize yourselves with the report. It covers events on the night of Hayes' death, as well as the investigation into his own offence.'

'So' – Todd's Geordie burr went up an octave – 'what did this fella do to upset the Judge?'

'That's still up for debate,' Hawkins said. 'The victims don't appear to have been connected, but if we can establish a link we'll be a lot closer to taking this guy down. I've asked Steve to lead some research into potential connections between the victims' murders and their pasts, but it's also possible these attacks could be to do with the law itself.'

'Fortunately' – she motioned to the man sitting on her left – 'we're privileged once again to have some support.' She introduced Hunter, who shuffled across to explain his notion about a killer bent on addressing the inadequacies of a lame judicial system. Ominously, the killer's potential motive prompted dry but approving murmurs from Todd and Sharpe.

Frank's comment didn't help. 'Two kiddie-killers and a murderess? Sounds like he's done us a favour.'

'You may think so,' Hunter was quick to respond, 'but the Judge might not have intervened had his victims served full terms.' He explained each set of extenuating circumstances, and the relative shortening of each penalty.

When he'd finished, Hawkins pointed to the e-fit she'd attached to the investigation board earlier that day. 'This composite image was constructed from descriptions given by residents living near yesterday's murder scene. Unfortunately, no one, including the tenant whose building overlooks the courtyard where Hayes was murdered, saw anything on the night he died, but several neighbours noticed this man apparently following Hayes along the same route to and from his local off-licence the two previous nights. This picture has already appeared on the news channels, along with our statement, so hopefully someone out there will click.'

She went on: 'Frank and Amala, your first job is to show this e-fit to everyone we've already interviewed about Calano or Philips. Maybe one of them knows who he is; maybe one of them hired him and will give themselves away. Aaron, work with Steve on Hayes' past, especially any potential connections to the others, or common enemies they might have had. Frank, use your contacts to come up with a list of murder or manslaughter convicts due to be released in the next fortnight. Mike and I will look at similar parolees released in the last three weeks. If we can identify his next target in advance, we'll have a shot at protecting them, plus an opportunity to bag this killer in the process.'

'Don't forget' – Hawkins scanned the faces around her – 'all the victims were in London-based prisons, so restrict your efforts to the capital for now. Focus on anyone in for murder or manslaughter and, more specifically, anyone whose term was adjusted down at any stage.' Feet began to shuffle, so she raised her voice. 'One more thing. We have no idea *when* he'll strike again, so I want you all on this full time till it breaks. Drop whatever else you've got on. Let me know if there's anything urgent, and I'll clear it with the SIO on each case.'

There were nods and muted dialogue as the team rose.

Hawkins turned and headed for her office, followed by Maguire. Lines of inquiry flooded her mind, so many that she nearly lost track. She was out of practice and out of sorts, but she welcomed the fact that her instincts seemed to have returned at last, and intended to put them to full use. She was holding it together so far, and her confidence was rebuilding itself, both of which were good news.

Because, whatever she'd done to deserve it, Hawkins wasn't going to let her second chance at becoming permanent DCI slip.

41

The knock came later that morning.

'Come in.' Hawkins glanced up from some notes as Steve Tanner opened her office door.

'Antonia.' He stepped inside. 'Can we talk?'

She motioned to the chairs in front of her desk. 'Please.'

Tanner strode across and sat, resting an elbow on the desk between them. He wore the usual confident smirk, except this one seemed a little more forced. Briefly, Hawkins wondered if he'd timed his visit to catch her alone, having seen Maguire exit, chasing a file from the archives, moments ago.

'One second.' She finished her annotation. 'Sorry about that. What can I do for you?'

Tanner's smile widened. 'I was hoping we could spend some time together this afternoon.'

She hid a frown. 'How do you mean?'

'I've been watching you.' He leaned closer, his tone rich, almost musical. 'I have to say, I'm impressed.'

'Thanks, but you'll need to be a little more specific.'

'Well' – Tanner sat back, hands clasping in his lap – 'I've been around for a few days now. I'm getting to know the team, and I wouldn't be here unless I picked things up fast but, ultimately, I want to learn from *you*, having heard so many positive things about your work, and so far we haven't really been joined at the hip.'

'I see.' She nodded, giving herself a moment to think. In one respect he was right, they hadn't exactly been working *side by side*, but after Mike had convinced her to give him a fair chance, she *had* expected Tanner to earn his place on the fast track by doing a bit of legwork first. 'I thought you'd want to start with the basics – get involved with the mechanics of an investigation.'

Tanner sniffed. 'Of course, but I'd like to think I've done that now. You've been happy with my performance so far, haven't you?'

'Actually, yes, you've acquitted yourself well.' She was going to expand on her compliment, about how impressed she'd been with his insight and efficiency.

But he cut her off. 'Then let's move things up a notch. What I really need to see is the high-level stuff, like your chat this morning with the profiler.'

'I understand that,' Hawkins answered carefully. 'But the issue here isn't one of experience or enthusiasm. I'm sure you understand these meetings are high level for a reason: we minimize numbers to maintain confidentiality, especially in cases where media interest is high.' She drummed her fingers on the desk. 'But I'll make sure we get to work more closely in the next few days. Once we know each other a bit better, I'll talk to the DCS about involving you in some restricted meetings, okay?'

The corners of Tanner's smile dropped ever so slightly and the dark eyes above it narrowed. 'If I didn't know better, Antonia, I'd say you were fobbing me off.'

She shook her head. 'Not at all. Although perhaps I underestimated how quickly you'd settle in.'

'Apology accepted. So let's get started. What are you working on now?'

This time she let her frown show. 'That wasn't an apology, and I think you need to respect the chain of command.'

'Oh, come on, Antonia.' He leaned back, crossing his arms. 'I'm all for equality, but we both know what's going on here. Surely you recognize a handover when you're being asked to give one.'

She stared at him for a moment, determined not to shout. 'I'm afraid you've been misinformed.'

'Really?' He stood. 'Then perhaps you don't know Tristan or this organization as well as you think. General consensus among command is that you're on thin ice, so it won't take much for someone to extract that DCI badge from your delicate little grip, especially if they were to beat you to bringing this killer in.' He paused, letting his implication hang.

Hawkins stood, too, wincing internally, meeting his gaze. 'People have underestimated my grip before. And I think it's about time you left.'

He gave a terse nod before moving away, pausing at the door to look back. 'Consider yourself warned.'

42

Bull emptied the envelope and spread everything out on the table, carefully lining up the sheets of paper so nothing overlapped. His eyes moved over the different stories, catching words here and there among the text. 'Death'. 'Victim'.

'*Sentenced*'.

And, across the newspaper clippings, in all the photos taken from the web, the same face.

The same murderer.

He noticed the release date, but it had already passed. He had been at the gates when his next victim had first walked free. Since then he'd been watching, learning his target's habits. Soon it would be time to strike.

He sat back, reaching for his latest carving. He turned the lime-wood figure over in his hands, checking his work. The body was good, but the face needed more shape.

He picked up the scalpel and took a few slivers off the nose, used the knife edge to slim the cheeks. He nodded to himself. He *was* being critical, but this was the best likeness yet.

As he worked, his eyes flicked back and forth between the figure and the papers on the table. Each time he'd catch another word, memorize another part of his target's face. He imagined the hammer making contact, the soft jerk as its head dug in. Putting out the lights.

But, tonight, something felt wrong. He swallowed, trying to hold back the pressure building in his mind. It was dark outside, but the daytime confusion was still there, working away at the corners of his vision, trying to close him down. He rubbed his eyes with the back of his hand.

Don't let the past fuck you up.

He forced himself to relax, got his breathing under control and went back to carving. That's how he worked. Take in the target, their face, their *crime*. Let the anger build. But at the same time make something new, something *good*. It balanced his feelings, allowed him to think.

He moved on to the figure's jaw, trimming layers off the underside. Then he looked up, read another word.

'*Jail*'.

Suddenly, his hands were shaking, the ringing in his ears was getting loud, the blackness closing in. His fists clenched but he forced them open, dropping the knife and the figure on the table before bringing his hands to his head, trying to hold in what sanity was left.

The tears were building, so he shut his eyes, fighting them back. *Mistake*. There was Cheshire – smiling, happy. That stupid fucking grin.

242

Bull looked back at the table, reaching for the largest picture, bringing it close. Staring at a killer's face.

They *deserved* to die.

So why was he questioning himself? All his victims had caused someone else's death. While they were still around, the pain for everyone lived on. But the feeling remained, something in the back of his mind, telling him to stop. Was it right to end another life? Had the deaths so far changed anything?

It's just your mind making sure.

He kept on staring, reminding himself that the circle needed to be closed. These people hadn't paid for their crimes. The law wasn't going to punish them properly, so that job fell to someone else. They had unpaid debt, but if Bull didn't go after them, nobody would.

His penalty was to hand out justice.

Their penalty was death.

43

'Fuck, it's freezing.' Hawkins rubbed her palms together, watching her breath curl away into the rapidly darkening air. The charcoal clouds hanging above London's South Bank meant it was probably warmer than it should have been, but temperatures had still nosedived.

'How about we lay off the swearing?' Mike edged closer and put his arm around her. 'We're meant to be in love.'

'I'm in character.' She shrugged him off. '*Mrs M*aguire thought we were going to Barbados.'

He laughed. 'Maybe next year. My boss says I'm due a raise.'

Hawkins shoved him, watching as a couple who had been cuddling on one of the other benches stood and wandered past, heading for the garden area beyond, where manicured hedges framed concentric circular paths. They stopped a short distance away, this time for a mid-stroll clinch.

'Anyway,' Mike said quietly, 'who needs the Caribbean? We're due some quality time at home. Did you talk to your dad about moving out yet?'

'I . . . raised the subject.' She hadn't.

'And?'

'I think he was more interested in *I'm a Celebrity* . . .'

Mike frowned. 'Even on the commercial breaks? Come on, Toni, it's been nearly a week.' There was real concern in his eyes.

'He's an old man.' She fumbled. 'You have to approach these things with care.'

Mike's grimace deepened. 'That's all it is?'

'Of course.' She reached for his hand. 'Please don't think it's you.'

He seemed to accept that. 'I just hate to think we might not make it, especially after what happened. You feel the same way, right?'

'Yes.' She rested her forehead on his.

'And you'll talk to your dad again.'

'Yes.'

They kissed and embraced, Hawkins staring past Mike's shoulder along the Embankment, deep in thought. Up ahead, the Oxo Tower disappeared into the mist hanging over the promenade, and beyond it Blackfriars Bridge stretched out across a Thames that, after recent heavy rain, was higher than she'd seen it in a while. She could hear the dirty brown water lapping against the near bank, backed by the calls of London's resident seagulls. Three hundred yards away on the opposite side, a large grey warship edged into dock. And, in the distance, St Paul's Cathedral rose elegantly above the surrounding architecture. Lights were already beginning to dot some of the buildings. But there was still no sign of their man.

She asked, 'What time is it?'

'Nearly five.' Mike blew into cupped hands. 'How long are we giving this guy?'

Hawkins watched a businessman in a well-bred suit sashay past. 'As long as it takes. Stay alert.'

'You're the boss.' Mike buttoned his coat up to the neck. 'At least if he shows we won't miss him. Even you blue-blooded Brits are staying home today.'

Hawkins nodded. Thanks to the arctic weather that had superseded the capital's first white Christmas in decades, remarkably few people were braving the South Bank that afternoon. Which was good news, because, if their target made an appearance, he'd be easier to spot. Lucas Dean was on the list of murder and manslaughter convicts released from London prisons in the last two weeks. But he was also the only one they hadn't been able to find.

Since the previous morning, when Hawkins had instructed her team to round up every recent homicide parolee in the capital, fifteen ex-cons had been identified, traced and approached. Of those, the eight whose sentences had been subject to mitigation and were therefore most likely to be at risk, had been offered safe-house accommodation. Hawkins had enlisted Simon Hunter to help her pick out the cases with the highest chance of being targeted, based on the crimes of the Judge's previous victims. The resulting group included a religious extremist who had brutally murdered three followers of a rival faith, a football hooligan who had mown down a bus stop full of opposing fans, killing two, and a truck driver who had killed a young family of immigrants by trying to smuggle them through Customs in the back of his refrigerated truck.

In each case, the courts had ruled leniently. The extremist had been radicalized by a manipulative elder, the hooligan's brother had been disabled in a brutal attack perpetrated by the men he targeted and, however unsuccessful his attempt at smuggling might have been, the truck driver hadn't taken any form of payment from the refugees he had managed to kill.

After reading up on every case, Hawkins wasn't sure whether to be surprised that most of the former detainees had declined the Met's offer of protection. Granted, the former prisoners were more likely than she was to understand the finer points of staying anywhere courtesy of the UK's judicial system, and at no point was such a privilege likely to be luxurious. But surely it was better than being killed.

On the plus side, all but two had agreed to increased contact with the parole service, and the three who *had* ended up in protected accommodation left only the remaining twelve for the surveillance units to keep an eye on. Until the next batch of cons emerged, of course. That was likely to happen within days, which made their pursuit of the one missing convict even more pressing.

Lucas Dean was high risk.

Until his brush with the law, Dean had run two illicit careers. Primarily, he dealt drugs, but as a sideline he'd also managed the interests of a local pimp, which basically meant keeping various sex slaves in line with drugs – a precarious operation at best. Sure enough, in May 2010, Dean had inadvertently killed a sixteen-year-old Slovakian girl called Jana Macek by injecting her with enough ketamine to floor a small horse, to stop her complaining about being forced to have sex with up to twenty men a day. That had earned him nine years.

According to his record, it became clear during the trial that Dean had acted under duress. The pimp had obviously reached him, though, because he refused a deal to testify against his employer, who walked. Instead Lucas entered a guilty plea, despite probable advice from his barrister to do nothing of the sort. At the time, Dean was just a few years older than his victim and was clearly petrified by what his former boss would do to him if and when he got out. According to court archives, Dean had been offered bail but refused it. These factors, in tandem with his demonstration of genuine remorse, had prompted the judge to shorten the standard sentence by a third; a term which then shed a further twelve months by the time the kid had re-joined society.

Since his release, and now twenty-two, Dean had been placed in a halfway house. He'd also kept appointments like clockwork with his parole officer, whose notes depicted a defiant but basically misguided youngster with an honest desire to reform. Until two days ago, the consensus had been that Lucas' parole would soon be signed off.

Then he'd disappeared.

As per procedure, the parole service had rung the alarm bell after two missed appointments, sending out notifications to local forces, including the Met, that Dean had scarpered. But nothing had come back.

Within a month of conditional release, most criminals – even the *compulsive* ones – had enough sense to stay in touch with the parole service. So Dean's recent erratic conduct was definite cause for concern.

In fact, the kid's haggard-looking parole officer had seemed oddly ambivalent when Hawkins and Maguire turned up at the house that morning, asking after Dean and divulging that he might have become a target for London's latest serial psychopath. She'd taken it hard when Dean disappeared, having been convinced that, together, they'd progressed. But if the kid hadn't left of his own accord, at least her faith in him hadn't been misplaced.

She hadn't known where Lucas spent his hours of freedom between meetings, but she did point them towards Stacey Bingham, a reformed drug addict also staying at the halfway house, with whom Dean had been friends. After a round of Good Cop, Bad Cop, Stacey had given up some, hopefully, valuable information. She was adamant that Lucas hadn't confided in her about any plans to abscond, but she knew he used to do most of his dealing on this section of the river. So it was worth an afternoon in the cold.

Except it was already starting to look more like evening, as Hawkins noted the stream of distant headlights now moving back and forth across Blackfriars Bridge. It wasn't dark yet, but it wouldn't be long until their target, if he showed, would be a lot harder to pick out.

To compensate, Hawkins had tied up as many resources as she could reasonably justify, bringing Sharpe and Yasir along to book-end their surveillance of Dean's patch. She had positioned the two sergeants further along the river, just beyond the large viewing platform to her and Maguire's left, in the hope that a small-time drug dealer might be less sensitive to the more congruous presence of two plain-clothed couples, rather than lone visitors. The four of them represented Hawkins' full complement for now.

Todd had made some excuse when asked to join them about an unavoidable prior engagement, while Tanner hadn't been seen since Hawkins' confrontation with him. Of course, she'd had her suspicions, but the speed and arrogance with which he'd revealed his true intentions had still taken her by surprise. She'd been right about the coup; the only question mark was whether Vaughn was as heavily involved as Tanner said.

For the moment, however, Hawkins had decided to keep the DI's threat to herself, mostly because everyone on the team seemed seduced by Tanner's effervescence. He had been carefully ingratiating himself from day one and, however devious it was, it appeared to have worked. All the guys, including Maguire and Vaughn, were enamoured. Tanner was bold, hungry and self-assured and, while Hawkins had half expected it, she'd neglected to prepare for his subsequent broadsiding. If she kicked up now, it would look like simple, demoralized backlash, and alert a potentially complicit Vaughn. In contrast, ignoring Tanner's threat demonstrated a lack of intimidation on her part; plus, it gave her time to reassess the competition, a crucial benefit when his next move was difficult to predict. Patience felt like her best option for now.

But battle lines had definitely been drawn.

Steve Tanner wanted her job – now, if not sooner – and although she hoped he was bluffing about Vaughn's collusion, perhaps her initial instincts about the DCS wanting to marshal Tanner past her were correct.

As for her challenger's whereabouts, he was unlikely to be at home watching TV. He'd be out there working his own lines of inquiry, which, if his knack for revelation hadn't abandoned him, he'd leave till the last minute to disclose. As senior investigating officer, Hawkins was at the significant disadvantage of having to share new information with him, although, by storming off, Tanner had kept himself off the list of candidates for tonight's investigation. So if they did ensnare Lucas Dean, at least Hawkins would get first crack at him.

As if in response, her mobile rang.

She dug out the phone to see Yasir's number, and answered fast. 'What's up?'

'Chief, it's Amala.'

'Good.' Hawkins rolled her eyes at Mike, her head jigging to indicate that, as usual, the sergeant was taking time to state the obvious before saying anything of interest.

But her frustration dissipated with Yasir's next statement.

'I think Lucas Dean just turned up.'

They moved quickly out on to the main pathway, past skeletal trees, at a pace blending haste with touristy nonchalance.

Hawkins kept the line to Yasir open, plugging in her headphones as they moved. 'What's Dean's position?'

'There's a group of them.' Amala's voice was scratchy through the earpiece. 'Three girls and two guys, all IC3. They just passed us on their way towards the lookout point. Could definitely be him.'

'Stay with them, but keep your distance,' Hawkins instructed, mindful of Dean's fugitive status. 'If he realizes we're watching, he'll run.'

'Okay.' Yasir went on: 'They've joined the queue at a

doughnut stall. It looks like the girls want food.' There were a few seconds of silence before she spoke again. 'Now the two guys are moving away, leaving the girls, same direction as before.'

Hawkins could see the viewing area now, forty yards ahead: a large protrusion jutting out from the South Bank into the Thames. A few random people stood here and there at the railings, taking in the panoramic views. 'Where are they now?'

'At the lookout, sitting down on one of the seats. I think they're lighting up.'

Hawkins tried to pick up her pace. 'Don't approach them yet. We're almost there.'

They rounded the final corner on to the viewing point, which opened out into a wide hexagonal space with sculpted lamp posts at intervals along the railings and benches grouped in sets of four a short distance from the edge.

Scanning the area, Hawkins picked out the two kids, on the seat nearest the back, facing away from the water. Both were now smoking cigarettes. She also caught sight of Sharpe and Yasir, standing under one of the trees twenty yards to the left, and immediately regretted her decision to pair the two up. Neither was doing a particularly convincing job of looking like one half of a couple out for a casual stroll, which probably meant the rumours about Aaron making a pass at Amala before Christmas were true. Aside from having a boyfriend, Amala thought Aaron was even creepier than Hawkins did and had apparently said *no* in rather certain terms. Unfortunately, that tension was apparent in their body language, although perhaps it would come across as a lovers' tiff. Amala gave her a discreet wave.

Hawkins turned her attention back to the boys. They seemed at ease, leaning back on the bench, looking at their phones and chatting, clearly unaware they were being watched. But she also realized that, if you described them, the two would be interchangeable: black, early twenties, skinny, with fashionable dark jeans and white trainers. Both wore puffy black coats and sweatshirts with the hoods up which buried their faces in shadow. She'd seen detailed mug shots of Lucas in his file but, without getting close or removing their hoods, it was impossible to say which, if either, was Dean.

'Amala,' she said into the phone, 'which one of the hoodie brothers is Lucas? Red or Blue?'

'Sorry, chief, your guess is as good as mine.'

'Thought so.' She spoke loud enough that Mike could hear. 'Right, you two hang back for now. Let's see if we can do this without any drama. If I want you to come in, I'll put my hands in my pockets, okay?'

'Understood.'

Hawkins ended the call and looked up at Mike. 'Shall we go round and take in the view, dear?'

Maguire smiled, and they began moving along the outer edge of the area. As they went, Hawkins made another quick assessment of the scene. The three girls that had been with their targets were standing by the food cart, eating doughnuts from small white bags. Beside them, intermittent human traffic moved back and forth along the river bank. Members of the public were dotted here and there around the lookout point: an old couple on one of the other benches, a small family with two kids near the railings, and some Japanese tourists taking pictures across the water of St Paul's. The daylight was retreating faster now, and spits of rain were starting to fall.

Soon they were level with the bench where the two kids sat, and came to a halt near the tourists.

Maguire asked quietly, 'What's our play?'

Hawkins weighed her options. All four Met officers were plain-clothed, so the subtle method was an option: asking their suspects for a light, or for one of the men to take their picture, in the hope that a name might be casually drawn out. But if there were complications later on, something like that could easily come back to bite you in court. Neither could she see any useful way to employ Stop and Search. Even if this *was* Lucas Dean, she had no grounds to suspect him of terrorism or of carrying a concealed weapon, and any half-decent barrister would know that interrogating a member of the public without evidence of either contravened the police code of conduct. Technically, Dean had broken his parole conditions, but going in hard would put their subject off side immediately, and his cooperation may yet be critical. After all, they were here to *protect* Lucas Dean. Which meant the direct approach was best.

Even if she did plan to employ *minor* subterfuge.

She took a deep breath. 'Let's go and introduce ourselves.'

They began moving towards the bench, coming in from the side. As they got within six feet, Hawkins picked up the small glances both men made in her direction as their personal space came under threat. Seconds later, they were face to face, and the two boys looked up.

'Hi, Lucas.' Hawkins glanced from one to the other, trying simultaneously to recognize Dean from his mug shot and to mask the fact she was still none the wiser about which he was. Unfortunately, both subjects reacted in the same way, eyes narrowing in the gloom beneath each hood while two sets of stoic body language gave no clues.

At last Red responded; an authentic urban tone. 'What?'

Hawkins held up her badge, still addressing both. 'We're Met Police, but we aren't here about your breach of parole.'

Blue joined in, his voice quieter. 'Who you lookin' for?'

Hawkins' gaze flicked between the two boys as she struggled to maintain the façade. 'You're not in any trouble, Lucas. We're here to help.'

'Sorry, lady' – Red took a drag – 'you got your shit twisted. I'm Darren, this my boy Lester, so we can't help you. Come on, bruv.'

Both men stood.

Red flicked the half-finished cigarette away and put both hands in his coat pockets. Watching him, Hawkins copied his action, signalling for Yasir and Sharpe to join in. If this guy had a weapon, he'd be less likely to use it facing four officers rather than two.

Mike stood in their way. 'Look, fellas, we're here because you might be in danger, okay? Which one of you is Lucas?'

'I told you, *cuz*,' Red sneered, 'there ain't no *Lucas*.'

Both men looked around as Yasir and Sharpe joined the group, the four Met officers forming a semicircle around them. Hawkins saw Red's eyes flick past them, along the promenade. Looking for a way out.

Hawkins opened her mouth, ready to level with them about the recent murders, when Red bolted. He lunged at Sharpe, knocking the sergeant backwards, and before any of them had time to react he pelted along the promenade. The three girls, who had been watching from the edge of the area, cheered as he flew by.

Mike took off after him, followed a second later by Amala, leaving Hawkins and Sharpe with his friend. But Blue didn't move, just held up his hands and sat down.

Hawkins turned to see Sharpe regaining his composure. And, beyond him in the gathering dusk, her other two officers sprinting after Red.

She looked back at Blue. 'Is your mate Lucas Dean?'

For a few seconds he said nothing.

Then he nodded.

Maguire passed the three girls at a sprint, dodging the A-boards outside the doughnut cart. He hit the wide promenade that ran alongside the river, checking ahead for the kid who'd just taken off, making sure he hadn't doubled back or gone to ground.

At first he couldn't see the guy. Daylight was fading and the streetlamps along the waterfront had come on. Two rows of bare trees stretched into the distance, and there were folk standing here and there, blocking his view. But then he saw him, pounding along the outer pathway near the railings on the right.

The kid looked fast, too. Maguire was already thirty yards down. He tried to estimate whether he was closing but, if anything, the guy was getting away.

Suddenly, the kid broke stride and looked round, as if he didn't expect anyone still to be with him. Maguire cut back between the trees, but he was too late. The kid picked him out straight off and flipped, turning back to resume his crazy pace. Maguire sprinted on, trying to build on the free yards.

Something registered at the edge of his vision, and he heard someone pulling alongside. He glanced over to see Yasir drawing level.

'Geez, Amala, I didn't . . . know you could . . . run.'

'County athletics team.' She started easing ahead.

'Better get this guy quick . . . though. I only ever did . . . eight hundred metres.'

Maguire refreshed his efforts, trying to stay with her. At the same time, he angled across nearer the river, taking Amala with him, so they were in line with their target. The kid obviously had something to hide; nobody ran from the cops for the good of their health. But the answer came sooner than he expected.

The kid slewed around a wave of umbrella-toting day trippers, a move that forced him away from the water's edge. But then he headed straight back to the railings, digging in his jacket as he ran.

Maguire told Yasir, 'Watch out for . . . weapons.'

'I know.'

But the kid kept running; didn't turn. And a second later Maguire realized why, as the guy flung out an arm and launched a handful of small packets over the railings, into the river.

Drugs.

Hawkins stood, looking along the South Bank in the direction Maguire and Yasir had just gone after Lucas Dean, her hopes of a quick retrieval fading as fast as the light. Both detectives had disappeared beyond the doughnut stand a few minutes before, passing the three girls who'd arrived with the lads. The girls were now standing at the edge of the lookout area, obviously discussing the drama, intermittently checking the promenade and watching their other friend.

Hawkins' muscles weren't enjoying themselves, so she settled as elegantly as she could on to the bench beside Dean's mate. She glanced up at Sharpe, standing beside her with a pained expression on his face. She gave him a look intended to remind him quietly that at least Dean was alive, which made it likely the killer was yet to strike again. But the tall sergeant's scowl didn't lift.

Unimpressed, she turned back to Dean's friend. 'What's your name?'

There was a short pause. 'Lester Burnett.'

'What are you doing here today, Lester?'

He lit another cigarette. 'Enjoying the view.'

'Fair enough.' She took him at his word, hoping to generate some trust before moving on. 'Why do you think Lucas ran?'

The kid sniffed. 'Reckon he panicked. After missing them parole meetings, he never bothered going back; thought it'd just be slapped wrists or some shit like that. Didn't know it'd be such a big fuckin' deal.' He waved at her and Sharpe.

'It is' – Hawkins scanned the waterfront again, still seeing no sign of the others – 'but only because we think Lucas might be in danger.'

She heard the bench creak as the kid leaned forwards. 'From who?'

'I can't discuss details,' she told him, 'but when my officers bring him back, you'll be doing Lucas a favour if you encourage him to cooperate, okay?'

He shrugged. 'Whatever.'

She jerked her head at their audience. 'What about the girls? How well do you know them?'

'Just met 'em today.'

'Okay.' Hawkins turned to Sharpe. 'Wait here. I'm going to have a quick chat with them.'

Sharpe nodded. He looked nervous, but didn't protest.

Hawkins stood and walked casually towards the three onlookers. The girls noticed and exchanged glances, probably deciding whether to try and leave, except that two of them wore ridiculously high heels, preventing any kind of haste. They stayed put.

But, suddenly, Hawkins had a new issue.

From behind she heard a scuffle of feet and an alarmed yelp from Sharpe. She turned back to see the two men struggling. It looked like the kid had made a break for freedom, but Sharpe had managed to grab his coat as he passed and was hauling him back.

Hawkins turned, cursing her gullibility. *This* had to be Dean. His mate had bolted, knowing it would split their team. Then Lucas had been smart enough to wait until she and Sharpe had relaxed. But he knew the girls might give him away.

She set off towards them, as fast as her damaged body would allow, yelling at Sharpe to hold on.

Dean thrashed at the sergeant's wrist, managing to break free, stumbling as he was released. Hawkins swore, aware that her two fastest officers were long gone. She'd never seen Sharpe run before, but if it was anything like his handshake they'd have little chance of catching their quarry. If they let him escape, and he turned up in a day or two with his head bashed in like a boiled egg, there'd be hell to pay.

Sharpe lurched backwards, off balance, as Dean regained his feet and sprung away. But something was wrong; the kid had some sort of limp. It could have been permanent, or a recent injury sustained in jail. Either way, it was slowing him down, which gave them a chance, at least.

Hawkins swung right, trying to intercept Dean. But she was too slow. He staggered by, turning to head along the promenade, the way she and Mike had come. She laboured after him, rounding the corner, wishing she'd practised moving at higher speeds. *Fuck!* She was losing ground.

Seconds later, she heard someone stomping up from behind and Aaron Sharpe clumped his way past, flat feet pounding as he closed on Lucas Dean. He caught the kid after another twenty yards, calculatedly clipping his heel to send him sprawling near some steps leading down to the water. Sharpe dropped a knee in the kid's back and began fumbling with his Plasticuffs as Hawkins carried on closing the gap.

Dean lay still, breathing hard, his head resting on the ground. But as Hawkins got within yards he bucked, unsettling Sharpe enough to let him twist and land a kick in the sergeant's midriff. Sharpe slumped dramatically as the kid scrambled free.

'Lucas!' Hawkins shouted. 'Wait!'

Dean ignored her, lurching to his feet, looking winded from his fall. Hawkins was still too far away to stop him, but as he turned to run Sharpe lunged, grabbing his belt.

Hawkins reacted, driving her legs harder, despite the burning sensation in her abdomen and chest. She covered the last ten yards to arrive beside the struggling men, reaching out for Dean. They just needed to subdue him long enough to explain.

Sharpe had wrestled the kid back to the ground. Dean rolled on to his back, looking up to see Hawkins advance.

She extended a hand. 'Aaron, cuffs.'

Sharpe tried to pass them to her, but their hands collided and the cuffs dropped. Hawkins leaned forwards, reaching down, but the kid saw her and kicked out with his free leg, knocking her away. She righted herself, preparing to try again.

Then she saw the girl.

The youngest of Dean's female companions appeared out of the darkness, obviously having come to help her friend. Their eyes met as she bore down with anger in her eyes.

'Leave off, bitch,' she shouted, shoving Hawkins with force. Hawkins fought for balance, but her ankle turned and she stumbled backwards, reaching instinctively for support. She caught sight of the girl's expression, which changed suddenly from anger to surprise. And then she realized why.

As the ground beneath her disappeared.

The girl turned and ran as Hawkins tried to stop herself. She flung out an arm, her fingers finding anchor on some sort of rail. She glanced down to see an open gate, and a metal staircase descending into the hostile black water. She tried to pull herself up, but her muscles burned, and she lost her grip on the wet rail.

At first nothing happened, and for a split second Hawkins thought she had anchored herself. But then she fell to the side. There was an instant of weightlessness as her balance shifted, before her fingers released the rail, pitching her backwards.

Into the Thames.

'Met Police!' Maguire yelled at a group of shocked bystanders as he thundered past. 'In pursuit of . . . suspect.'

He swung past them, looking ahead. Yasir was further in front now, still closing on the kid. The gap between the two of them had closed to fifteen yards, but they were all getting tired. Slowing up.

He considered shouting at members of the public to stop the guy, but the kid still might have a weapon, and they couldn't risk putting lives in danger. Daylight was almost gone as they raced along the South Bank, the streetlamps dropping patches of yellow light on the glistening path.

Maguire swore over a ragged breath as he watched the kid throw more packets into the Thames. The guy had been dealing, so he was making damn sure he'd have no evidence on him in case they caught up. He was dumping a small fortune but, without proof of what was in those bags, they couldn't press charges at all. The chances of recovering any of them from the river were low. At this rate all they'd have to charge him with would be wearing indecently clean sneakers.

But their luck changed as the kid let fly with another bunch of packets. Three or four cleared the railings and scattered in the wind before dropping into the water, but one hit the base of a streetlamp, bouncing back to land on the ground.

Maguire veered towards it, telling Yasir to stay with Dean. He kept momentum as he bent and scooped up the packet, taking a quick look to make sure it was sealed. From what he could see in the poor light, there was white powder in the bag. Evidence, sure, but not enough for a conviction, and nothing compared to what the kid had already plunked.

He pocketed the bag, concentrated on regaining the ground he'd lost by retrieving it. He didn't want to be too far back if Amala caught up with the kid. She was trained to look after herself, but what if their target was armed?

Maguire renewed his efforts, driving his legs harder.

The others were a fair way ahead, but things changed again as the kid cut left, away from the front. Ahead of them, the reason for his move was clear. Waterloo Bridge loomed large, some kind of market beneath its archway providing the first big crowd they'd passed. The kid must have known it would slow him down, so he was heading for the widest passage to the far side.

He hit traffic right away, crashing into a couple of women as they stepped back from one of the tables. He spun, off balance, just missing a gang of teenagers coming the other way. He bounced off the wall and kept going, wrenching a box of books off a table into Amala's path. She hurdled the scattering contents, followed seconds later by Maguire.

They flew out of the market into some kind of fair, past some buskers playing guitars. Flickering stalls lined the front, and the smell of mulled wine and cooking meat reached Maguire as the three of them wove their way through the patchy crowds.

'Sorry, ma'am!' Maguire yelled as a woman yanked a stroller out of his way. He cleared the market beside a low concrete structure, hearing the crash and roll of skateboard wheels as he dodged another gang of pedestrians.

Ahead, he saw Yasir lunge for the kid. She missed, stumbling as he cut left down a ramp. Yasir glanced off the railings and went after him. Maguire let them go, veering right, past a yellow stairwell, sticking to the sidewalk's upper tier. If the kid came back up, maybe he could cut him off.

Mike rounded the steps and charged on to the next open stretch. He picked out the red hoodie around twenty yards in front, just as the kid disappeared below Hungerford Bridge. Maguire stayed on the high path, threading his way through tightly packed crowds, looking up to see the London Eye rising high above the trees. Steel drums filled the air as he skirted a brightly coloured merry-go-round, then the kid hauled over a large plastic bin and threw it in Amala's path. But it was a bad move. The container's weight spun him and he fell, just as the sergeant launched herself over the bin. She crashed into him, both of them sprawling aside. Yasir was first up, scrambling over and wrenching the kid's arm up his back.

Maguire covered the last dozen yards as fast as he could, pulling out his cuffs and helping tie the guy's wrists. They searched him, coming up with a few more packs of white powder, but no weapons. Amala held up her badge to a few alarmed witnesses as Mike hauled their catch to his feet and dragged him towards the entrance of Jubilee Gardens, where they all slumped on a low wall.

Maguire sat, staring across the Thames at the Houses of Parliament, catching enough breath to charge the kid with possession.

Then he reached up, pulled off the guy's hood, and stopped dead.

It wasn't Lucas Dean.

Which meant that, if the other kid *was* Dean, they'd left Antonia and Aaron with the real target. Unaware.

He found his phone, selected Antonia's number, watching a load of tourists crowding into a river taxi out on the water. But he growled in frustration when the call connected . . .

And her answerphone kicked in.

Hawkins fell.

For a split second, there was silence as the cloudy night sky wheeled above her. But suddenly the descent was over. Pain erupted in her shoulder as she smashed into the rail, twisting in the air.

She hit the water.

At first only her face felt the shock, a rush of icy cold. But then the liquid breached her clothes, shock emptying her lungs like an anvil on her chest. Blackness swallowed her, the mute blare of submergence engulfing her senses. She fought panic, reaching out for some kind of anchor, just as her feet hit the riverbed.

She pushed upwards, painfully launching herself back to the surface, emerging to see the streaked lights of the promenade. She grabbed the handrail rising out of the freezing gloom, pulling her mouth above the water to drag in a painful breath.

The seething black mass snapped at her chin, its current dragging her clothes, trying to sweep her away. Hawkins glanced up, fighting for a grip on the wet rail, gasping for air. Her shoulder screamed where she'd landed against the stairs, and her muscles contracted in the cold, further sapping her strength.

Above her, the steps stretched away, mere yards separating her from the sanctuary of the quay. But as her damaged body resisted attempts to drive upwards, Hawkins realized that, with every second she remained in the water, her chances of survival reduced.

She tried calling for help, but all that came out was a rasping wheeze. The shock of falling into arctic water had exhausted her. Yet somehow she managed to keep her head above the surface, renewing her grip on the rail, feet slipping on the submerged rungs.

She made another attempt at shouting Aaron's name, this time managing to get the words out. But her voice wasn't loud enough.

Still nobody came.

Perhaps that wasn't a surprise. The girl who'd pushed her in had turned immediately to run, Sharpe was probably still dealing with Lucas Dean, unaware she'd disappeared over the edge, and any other observers obviously weren't interested in risking their lives.

The blackness reared around her again and she took an involuntary mouthful of rancid water, almost choking in response. Her chest heaved and she lost her footing, gravity jerking her arms taut and dragging her face back into the water. Her lungs burned, and for a second she thought about letting go, but then her survival instinct kicked in. All feeling in her body had gone as she strained every muscle, managing to pull her head above the waves one last time, coughing up liquid.

Her eyes streamed, blurring her vision, but she couldn't risk letting go to wipe them clear. Vivid reds and blues danced before her, although she couldn't tell if they were lights on the water or figments of imagination in her cold, disordered brain.

She felt herself starting to lose consciousness.

But then there was noise. A man's voice, telling her to hold on.

Sharpe.

Hawkins tried to look up, call out to him. But no sound came, and all she could see was a shadow descending the stairs, a hazy limb extended in aid.

She tried to reach out.

As everything went black.

44

'There she i-is,' Kerry sang, pointing over the steering wheel as she turned the people carrier off the main street into Tremadoc Road. 'I had her valeted yesterday, so she'd be sparkling for your reunion cruise.'

Amanda Cain turned slowly to look at her best friend, the glum response taking a moment to reach her lips. 'What?'

'Your car, dopey . . .' Kerry pulled a face, still trying to humour Cain. 'Your pride and bloody joy. Remember?'

'Oh.' She followed her friend's gaze, seeing the corner of the Audi's sleek silver bumper just visible behind a Transit van fifty yards up on the left. 'Thanks.'

For the first time in almost a year, Cain remembered her car. The £46,000 A5 coupé she'd collected from the garage less than a year ago, brand new; the first desirable car she'd ever owned. Befitting transport for a successful – albeit single – doctor, she'd convinced herself at the time. For a short while the car had led a pampered existence, despite having to be parked on the road outside her London townhouse. But now, as they drove towards it, the thought of optional metallic paint and upgraded wheels served only to remind her how facetious life had been.

Before.

Kerry dug a set of keys out of the side pocket and waved them. 'I thought you'd want to take her straight out.'

'Maybe later.' Cain pinched the bridge of her nose.

'Oka-ay.' Kerry drew out the word, stuffed the keys in her coat pocket. 'I just thought you'd be excited, seeing as you only got her right before . . . well, you know.'

Cain stared at the dashboard. 'I guess I'm just not in the mood.'

'No problem.' Her friend swung into a gap, letting a car pass in the opposite direction, reaching out to paw her passenger's arm while they waited. 'Ple-e-ease cheer up. You're home, aren't you?'

'Yeah. I suppose.'

'Blimey.' Kerry pulled back into the single clear lane and drove on. 'Anyone would think I was taking you *back* to prison.'

Cain looked across at her, pausing for a second before she answered. 'Thanks for coming.'

'You're welcome. You know that.'

Cain forced a half-smile. Kerry had insisted on collecting her from Holloway, despite her attempts to use the travel warrant provided by the prison service. She watched her friend bring the car to a halt level with the house, waiting for her to make eye contact.

Kerry pulled on the handbrake. 'Jump out and get your bag. I'll park up and come in. We'll crack open some celebratory vino.'

'Oh, Kez, I really don't –'

'Coffee, then, or tea, if you're fragile.'

'It isn't that. I know it sounds stupid, but I just want to be alone; run a hot bath. You don't mind, do you?'

Kerry blinked a few times in quick succession, the way she did when she was disappointed but didn't want you to know. 'All right, but we're still on for tomorrow, aren't we?'

'Yes,' she lied, already reaching for the door handle. 'Thanks again for the lift.'

'Holy *shit*! Amanda.'

Cain looked at her startled friend. 'What?'

Kerry's mouth was open, hands cradling her face as she stared past Cain's shoulder towards the house. Slowly, Cain turned.

And saw her car.

Punctured tyres, smashed windows and scruffy red letters sprayed along the damaged bodywork, thin strands of overspray running down.

MURDERER.

'Holy shit, Mand,' Kerry breathed. 'It was fine yesterday, I promise. It must have been kids or something, it's been a fucking nightmare round here recently.'

Cain sighed. 'We both know it wasn't kids.'

The family of John Travis, her unintended victim, had publicly declared shortly after the incident that they held her *utterly* to blame. The exhaustion of regular eighty-hour weeks and double shifts might have garnered sympathy with campaign groups at the time,

273

leading to failed calls for her sentence to be reduced, but *they* would not forgive. Cain had returned home several times before the trial to find her front door covered in human faeces, and more pushed through the letterbox. Clearly, none of the perpetrators was in medicine, or they'd have known that anyone who works in a hospital is more than comfortable with bodily discharge. But the sentiment itself scared the hell out of her. She had dared to hope the intensity of their rage might diminish with time. But now, looking at her ruined Audi, Amanda Cain realized that certainly wasn't the case.

'There must be CCTV,' Kerry offered, peering through the windscreen for cameras. 'That's criminal damage, right? The police will follow it up.'

Cain shook her head. 'It doesn't matter.'

'But . . . you love that car.'

'It's going back to the garage.' Cain opened the door and began to step out. 'It's just an easy target now.'

Kerry grabbed her arm. 'I don't think you should stay here. What if they come back?'

'Please leave it, Kez.' Gently, Cain unpicked her friend's hand. 'No offence, but your menagerie is hardly peaceful. Really, the house is secure. I just need a quiet bath and my bed.'

It took another five minutes of reassurances that she'd be fine and a promise to call straight away if she wasn't, to convince her friend to leave, then Amanda

Cain stood on the pavement, waving slowly as Kerry drove away.

She watched the blue Citroën all the way to the junction at the end of the road, wondering what she'd have done over the years without Kerry to slap some sense into her from time to time. Part of her wished she'd accepted the offer of a bolt-hole, even for a couple of nights.

The people carrier turned on to the main road and disappeared, and her empty gaze fell on the damaged silver coupé in her parking space. The car had been fine until yesterday, Kerry had said that, which meant the Travis family had known the exact date she was being released and had waited nine months to do this the night before she returned home, so nobody would have the chance to clear it up. Which meant it was a message they wanted her to see.

We haven't forgotten.

And neither will you.

Amanda Cain closed the front door, distantly noting the absence of shit on her mat, and leaned against the wall. The knot in her stomach was familiar, but more vicious than usual. Of course, returning home for the first time since leaving Holloway was always going to be tough, but she genuinely hadn't expected past events to force themselves down her throat before she'd even made it through the door. After seeing the car, she felt more strongly than ever the sickening hatred of people left behind to suffer the consequences of her mistake.

Suddenly, her pulse was rapid and climbing, her breathing erratic, her skin damp. She closed her eyes. Inexplicably, the anxiety attacks she'd experienced in the weeks following her horrific error had stopped overnight when she'd arrived in jail.

Obviously, it had been too much to hope they'd stay away once she was out.

She swallowed, forcing herself to concentrate.

You're home.

Free.

Slowly, her eyes opened. Her heart still thumped, but the panic itself had reduced.

For a moment she stared into space, half wishing she hadn't made Kerry leave, half still glad that she had. Part of her craved company, but getting through the next few days would be hard enough without having to deal with the smothering concern of her closest friend. Kerry had been so supportive, visiting almost every week during her sentence, sometimes more than once, always chipping away at her friend's relentless insecurities. *You're a good person, Mand.*

It could have happened to anyone.

Cain always found herself nodding, telling Kerry she knew, carefully grading her responses to build in a few extra microns of positivity each time. *You're right, Kez, I know. I'm doing okay.*

Lying consistently to her friend about the horrors she faced on the far side of the visiting-room door still made her feel sick. It was hard work; unnatural somehow, but required.

That's why she needed space; time alone to think. To straighten things out.

But nothing was going to happen unless she *made* it happen.

She glanced around at the entrance hall, noticing detail for the first time since entering the house. Everything was just as she remembered: the high ceilings and narrow, elegant stairs. The ornate bannisters painted classic white to match the delicate picture rails, and the long hallway leading into the galley kitchen down the steps.

More pride and joy.

She pushed away from the wall and stood, trying to appreciate the stillness of the house. Thick walls meant she never heard the neighbours, and living alone ensured peace and quiet were never beyond reach once the front door closed. She shuddered, attempting not to think about months of atmosphere so vile that no one ever relaxed. For someone like Cain, so used to being in control, both of those around her and of her own time and space, Holloway had been true hell.

And yet, as she tuned into the silence, it became almost eerie. The floorboards had been resealed by the previous owner, so there were no creaks when she shifted her weight, and she'd had to rehouse Zhivago

277

the cat before her sentence began. A tiny, far-flung family, parents dead, no siblings, husband or kids. Aside from the small group of friends she made an effort to see, Amanda Cain was alone, splitting the majority of her time between her three refuges. The car. The house. The job.

Patently, the lack of constant commotion and slamming iron gates was a relief, but the absence of noise also freed her dissident thoughts. At that moment, she might have given anything for someone to appear on the void of the landing, slam a drawer or sneeze. But the silence remained, the far end of the hall stretching away, pulling the walls in as it went.

She shook off the feeling and drifted into the front room, past the wide leather settee facing the hearth. Everything was dustless, despite months of disuse. The only sign of recent activity was the small dent in the armchair cushion where Joan, the cleaner, sat every Wednesday to have a cup of tea.

Joan loved this place almost as much as Cain did, so much so that she'd refused to return her key even after letting all her other contracts go. She had cleaned the place for three different owners, and continued to service it for the very reasonable standing order she begrudgingly allowed her employer to increase every year.

Cain walked slowly to the antique bureau at the back of the room. It had been an impulse purchase shortly after she'd moved in, the dark wood and studded leather finish of the accompanying chair fitting the place so well she hadn't challenged its four-figure price. Plus, of course, there was no family board to mollify. For authenticity's sake, she had even stocked the classical writing desk with paper and pens, although it was rarely used.

She stood for a while, fingers resting lightly on its surface, staring at the embossed wallpaper on the wall behind it. The pattern was intricate: myriad swirls and spears curling outwards like the surface of stirred coffee, delicate branches spreading down and out, reducing each time like tiny Russian dolls. And, at the centre, holding everything together, the nucleus from which it all grew.

Just like her victim.

John Travis had been a family man. His wife, three daughters, two sons. Parents, cousins, friends; a dozen faces filling the court gallery, every day of Cain's trial. All staring at the negligent doctor who had taken him away, like the evil protagonist in a sick superhero tale. The fateful words echoed again.

Two mils of pethidine.

Cain sank on to the chair, the growing knot in her stomach making it too painful to stand. She sat forward, cradling her face, wishing she believed in some sort of God.

She pictured her former workplace, the hospital where she'd helped save so many lives. And where, single-handed, she'd cut one so tragically short. She remembered her colleagues' reactions, the mixture of pity, horror and doubt. But they were nothing compared to the eyes of her victim's family when she had tried to explain. They'd been close, that was evident, so Cain had been adamant that telling them herself was the right thing to do. But they hadn't been able to forgive, not with the enormity of events. The moment had been the worst of her life. A man's time ended; a family's trust gone.

She cried into her palms for a few minutes, letting the tears run down her forearms and soak from her elbows into her jeans, realizing that she was no freer now than she had been in Holloway. She would carry this burden for good.

Unless . . .

With that thought she became suddenly still, an unexpected calm spreading in her chest; the helplessness began to retreat. She *could* affect things; make them better, if never right. She opened the desk drawer, taking out the notepad and pen, still there ten months after she had last contemplated using them. The last time she had sat at the desk.

Trying to write a letter to them.

Her heart pounded, the faces of each Travis family member flashing one by one through her mind. The two that lingered were his sons, young men whose dad had been so cruelly ripped away. She'd never forget them. This thing would never be done; not without forgiveness from them.

Which meant there was only one course of action.

She picked up the pen, turned over the front of the pad.

And then, with sentiments flowing from her like spilled marbles, Amanda Cain started to write.

45

Sodding hospital.

Again.

Hawkins groaned, slumping against the insensitively firm mattress. She had recognized the smell as soon as her eyes had opened a moment ago. A few seconds of staring at the frosted light panel above her head, combined with the realization that she was lying down with no memory of having entered the room, made a glance at the passing nurse mere confirmation. And she was getting really fed up with hospital wards.

'Hey!' A familiar American accent came from her right. 'Someone's awake.'

Hawkins turned to face Maguire as he arrived at her bedside holding a can of Coke and a pre-packed sandwich. 'What kind of spectacular damage have I done myself now?'

'Actually, not much. Luckily, your wounds had sealed so, apart from a few antibiotics and having your stomach pumped, you just needed a damn good sleep.'

'So that's why my insides feel like they've been borrowed and put back upside down.'

'Probably.' Mike laughed. 'The doctors agree with me, though: you've been overdoing it.'

'Wait,' she interrupted. 'I've heard this one. The middle and the end are properly whiny, but maybe it's a grower. Do continue.'

She took his silence as a cue to move on. 'What hospital is this?'

'St Thomas',' Maguire reported from behind the scowl. 'Just a five-minute ambulance hop from your improvised pool.'

Unwelcome memories flared, and Hawkins tasted the foul water again, trying to focus on other things. 'What time is it?'

'Six a.m.' He reacted to the immediate look of horror in her eyes. 'Don't panic, you've only missed fifteen hours, but you're going nowhere for at least a few days. Doctor's orders.'

'We'll see about that.' She dragged herself more upright. 'Where's Tanner?'

'Not sure. I've been here, worrying about you. Why?'

'Because I'm in charge of his development. I just want to make sure he isn't being neglected.'

'Bullshit. You want to make sure his size elevens aren't under your desk.'

Hawkins almost told him about Tanner's threat, but the words caught in her throat. She still needed time to gauge her opponent before deciding on the best way to handle him. If she revealed her intentions without a cohesive plan, she'd end up giving further ground. And, once he was warned, who knew what the devious bastard might do?

'Look.' Mike reached for her hand. 'I know you worry about this stuff, but there's no need. Steve's a good guy; he just wants to help out, if you'll let him. He ain't after your job.'

'How do *you* know?'

He shrugged. 'I asked.'

'*What?*'

'We talked. I didn't tell you because I knew you'd be pissed.'

'Oh, fine.' She crossed her arms. 'Then I'll just rot quietly in here while you and Captain Altruism look after everything, shall I?'

She turned away in frustration. The silky-voiced arsehole even had Mike dancing to his cheating tune. Meanwhile, she was busy alienating her closest ally and she couldn't even tell him why. Now, with unadulterated access to the team, Tanner would soon wrestle her prized secondment from her unless she did something about it. But, wherever she looked, Hawkins couldn't escape the truth: in just four days she'd been out-manoeuvred, overshadowed. Undermined.

Mike leaned in. 'Come on, Toni, you gotta can this paranoia. Your job's safe, and you ain't even supposed to be working again yet. Have some faith in the rest of us, okay? We can cope.'

Hawkins chewed the inside of her lip, mumbled, 'Okay.'

'Good.' He held up his food. 'Want something to eat?'

'No, but you can call Aaron for me. I need to say thanks.'

Mike's head tilted. 'For what?'

'Well, he did sort of save my life.'

'No, he didn't.'

'Yes, he did. If you get swept away, unconscious in the Thames, you're done.'

'Oh, you were toast,' Mike agreed. 'No doubt about it. I didn't mean you weren't saved, just that Sharpe didn't save you.'

She frowned. 'Then who did?'

'Actually, he's here.' Maguire flicked his head towards the corridor. 'Has been all night. Wanted to make sure you were okay. Wanna say thanks?'

She nodded, confused.

Mike walked to the door and disappeared, only to re-enter a few seconds later.

With Lucas Dean.

The hoodie was down as the young black man approached the bed and for the first time Hawkins recognized the face she had previously seen only in his police record. He still looked like a street kid, but a lot of last night's bravado had gone.

They stared at each other as Hawkins silently pieced events together. Dean had been struggling with Sharpe when she'd fallen over the edge, but the two must then have realized she'd gone. She pictured Sharpe standing at the top of the steps, inept, as the supposed criminal waded in to save his drowning boss.

Dean broke the silence. 'Leisha's sorry, yeah?'

She regarded him. 'Who?'

'My girlfriend, the one who pushed you in. She didn't mean to. She's sorry.'

'Oh.' Hawkins remembered the look of horror on the girl's face as she'd stumbled towards the steps. 'Tell her, apology accepted.'

'Cheers.' The defensive scowl lifted slightly. 'You'll be okay, though, right?'

She shrugged. 'I've survived worse, but thanks for pulling me out. Anyway, why did you run?'

Dean scratched his ear, rattling a diamond stud. 'After what happened with Jana, and then spending that time banged up, I swore I'd never go back inside. I don't deal no more, I swear, but the kid I was with still does, a few wraps here and there, even though I've told him to stop. That's why he took off, to save me from getting yanked.'

'Well, I'm glad you were there.' Hawkins smiled. 'But you can't associate with these people if you're serious about staying out of trouble. Maybe make some new friends?'

'He ain't my friend.' Dean's eyes dropped.

'It's for the best,' she said, feeling oddly parental.

'He's my brother.'

'Right.' Hawkins nodded slowly, remembering why she usually kept such advice to herself. 'So what now?'

Dean jerked his head towards Maguire. 'Mike already talked to my parole officer about the sessions I missed.

The other guy's taking me back this afternoon to sort things out.'

Hawkins was about to ask which other guy when she noticed Aaron Sharpe hovering in the doorway.

Mike took over. 'I told them this kid risked his life to save a drowning woman, when he could easily have split.' He clapped Dean on the shoulder. 'They're impressed, Lucas. I don't think anyone will be recommending changes to your existing parole term.'

The kid thanked Maguire, said goodbye to Hawkins and headed for the door.

'Good.' She began lifting the covers. 'Let's get back to Hendon.'

'Sorry.' Maguire sat on the sheets, trapping her. 'You need rest. And, besides' – he pointed at her drip stand – 'you're wired.'

'What's Tanner doing today?'

'I told you already, I don't know.'

'My point exactly.' She tried to yank herself free. 'For all you know, he's out there right now arresting the killer, so I can't afford to spend *hours* in bed, let alone *days*. Not when he's after my job.'

'He isn't –'

'Of course he is.' She pushed him. 'Shift, you great lump.'

'No.' Mike's tone hardened. 'For once, you're gonna listen to me. You leave, the doctors say you risk permanent damage.'

'Nonsense.' Hawkins ignored the exhaustion sweeping her system. 'I'll be fine after some coffee and a burger.'

'Jesus, Toni.' Mike stood, his voice rising. 'This is so typical of you. Fuck the consequences, just get the job done, right? No wonder your life's so damn empty. Who the hell are you doing it for?'

'My life is not *empty*,' she retorted, lowering her volume in response to startled looks from the visitors around the adjacent bed. 'I've got family; I've got you.'

'Maybe, but for how much longer?'

'Blackmail?' She snorted. 'You wouldn't dare.'

'Oh, really?' An ironic grin crossed his face. 'So who do you think *requested* their transfer to Manchester last year?'

'I –' Hawkins froze mid-retort as her brain caught up. Until then she'd never questioned the fact that Mike's reassignment, three hundred miles north of London, had been an unwelcome surprise to them both. But if Mike had *asked* to be moved, he must have done it before Hawkins had even told her ex-fiancé, Paul, about their affair.

' . . . You *requested* it?'

'Damn straight I did. And you know why? Because of your crazy, self-destructive attitude. You might not even *be* in hospital if you'd gone to my place on New Year's Eve when you were meant to. I can't stand by and watch you flog yourself to death because the job's all you give a crap about.'

Hawkins' mouth hung open, but no words came.

She lowered herself into the pillow as Mike started talking again.

'If I mean a thing to you, Toni, listen, just this once.' He dug something out of his pocket and tossed it on to the bed. 'Your phone's in worse shape than you are after ending up in the river, so I'll keep you updated on the case using that. But don't you dare leave this bed, not even to pee, unless the doctor says it's okay. You got that?'

She stared at him for a second before nodding gently.

'Good.' He began backing away. 'And if you're right about Tanner, coming back before you can pass for someone fit to be at work will give him the perfect excuse to tell Vaughn you've been pushing it too far. And I don't need to tell you what will happen if he does that.'

He turned and headed for the door.

Hawkins just sat, staring at the Airwave unit in her lap, still thinking about his revelation. Leaving her hospital bed prematurely would damage their relationship for good.

And even *she* wasn't stupid enough to risk that.

PART TWO

46

Hawkins stood alone in the centre of the tiny metal room. It wasn't obvious when her stomach lurched whether it was in response to the corresponding change of motion or the anticipation of what was about to be revealed by her aptly theatrical exit.

There was a final jerk as the lift settled, then a distorted female voice announced that, however predictable such an outcome might be, the doors were about to open. Only one of the reasons she usually took the stairs.

Her frustration dropped away as the electronic woman was proved correct. The doors parted and a familiar scene began to appear in the widening gap: the serious incident suite at Hendon, headquarters for Metropolitan Police investigations into homicide and serious crime.

Hawkins watched the space opening out before her. Desks were scattered here and there, some lost beneath piles of unfiled paperwork from cases unexpectedly solved and discarded, while others held dirty cups and half-eaten packs of fossilized Belgian buns. As rooms went, there were few more soulless, but Hawkins wasn't interested in its character. Her focus was on the staff.

Fewer than six occupants were visible, less than average for this time of day, partly because, apart from Hawkins' own investigation, there were no large cases on. Plus, it was 7 a.m., well before most self-respecting detectives had rolled out of bed and looked in the mirror, wondering what possessed them to perform such thankless work. Doing a job where the public's *merest* expectation of you was to catch the bad guy every single time was inexorably skewed towards a perception of failure. Which was probably why the room contained a skeleton crew of those holding the proverbial short straws, designated by their respective teams to hand over to the oncoming shift; an event that would happen at some point in the next thirty minutes, and one that Hawkins had timed her arrival to avoid. If she was going to end up on her backside in modern policing's most gossip-ridden office, she was going to make sure there were as few witnesses as possible.

She edged out of the lift, focused on the door to the operations room on the far side of the area and set off, ignoring the tortured chorus from her abdominal muscles, visualizing elegant progress across the floor.

A few officers glanced up, exchanging pleasantries as she passed. She kept her head up, opting for grace over less majestic speed, trying to keep her mind off the strain on her stomach wall by thinking as she moved.

It was Sunday morning, and she had endured three days in St Thomas' Hospital, although her unease at being there had probably accelerated her recovery. The unplanned dip in the Thames had set her body back, re-straining part-recovered muscles and tearing some internal stitches. Mercifully, the doctors hadn't opened her up again, but they said she needed to go back in the chair, at least until fresh improvement was seen. She'd ignored them completely, of course, and had been lurching around on crutches by Friday afternoon, completely unaided by Saturday morning, determined not to resort to four wheels. Three fourteen-hour sleeps had paid dividends, too, doubtless expediting her return to upright mobility.

But there was only so far you could wander inside a hospital, and she had to admit the extra period of enforced recuperation had done wonders. The doctors recommended more rest, but they also needed the bed, and three days was all Hawkins could take.

No one in possession of their proverbial marbles pined for a messy room full of underpaid public servants, but as Hawkins ended her second sabbatical in as many months from just such a place, she couldn't have been more relieved.

More than that, she refused to give Tanner any more time to undermine her. Mike had kept his word on updating her on the case every few hours. There had been a few developments, but no further deaths, while the pressure from above to make inroads into other cases had already started to grow. Although that hadn't stopped Tanner from nurturing the gaps in her team. Maguire had tried again to reassure her that fretting was unjustified, but she could read between the lines. Tanner, the plotting weasel, had used his unexpected freedom to create a sub-team, not so coincidentally comprising the two members of Hawkins' team with whom she'd never gelled.

Frank Todd, the self-declared enemy of management flannel, was experienced and shrewd, and had probably jumped at the chance to assist Hawkins' nemesis, while Aaron Sharpe, limp-wristed underachiever that he'd shown himself to be, no doubt welcomed the opportunity for change.

According to Mike, Tanner's Angels had worked solidly for the last three days, obviously making the most of her forced absence. Perhaps it showed a degree of respect, but it would only take some overdue luck for Tanner's team to stumble across a breakthrough, possibly even a critical arrest. And, if that happened, Hawkins was going to have trouble convincing *herself* that he didn't deserve her job.

She walked on, still not confident that her body wouldn't crumple without notice under her. But it had to be this way. Returning to work in the chair was not an option she had entertained. Seeing off the challenge from her aspiring usurper would be possible only if she exuded strength. And, in the pugilistic world of homicide investigation, demonstrating your potency from a wheelchair with your head barely rising above your opponent's crotch was a big ask. She needed to face Tanner on equal terms: eye to eye.

Hence the heels.

She made good progress until she was halfway across the floor, still twenty feet from the operations room, when she caught herself trying not to wince, and slowing down. She spurred herself on, trying to maintain her pace, but her frayed muscles burned. She'd managed short distances on foot at hospital and last night at home without any trouble, although on those practice runs she'd paid scant attention to her appearance, often arriving at her destination uncomfortably hunched. But she'd made it every time, and her posture had improved dramatically, even in the short interim.

In contrast, driving her dad's Rover from Ealing to Hendon and then making it from car park to lift with a vertical demeanour had proved decidedly more difficult than she'd expected. Seven weeks of near-inactivity had left her physically weak, ill-equipped to deal with even the lightest exercise. The chair had been a pain. But, she now realized, a more bearable type of pain than this. Except it was too late for compunction.

Turning back would be worse.

An hour after getting to work, Hawkins eased back in her posture-supporting leather seat, frustration coursing through her. She tipped her plastic cup to find the remains of cold vending-machine coffee and pushed it away. It was a relief to be back in touch with the case, but she had also hoped that the intervening period of relaxation, sleep and contemplation would allow her to return with a fresh perspective on the case.

Not a chance.

Her laptop sat on the desk, displaying Samantha Philips' file. The surface around it was hidden under printouts of the case histories of the victims, but progress remained painfully slow. Hawkins rubbed her eyes, feeling the sting of excessive close work. She tried some eye exercises, switching her focus from near objects to far and back, a method suggested by the last health-related magazine she'd read with any semblance of attention. In 1996.

Her gaze drifted to the window separating her office from the main operations room, and to the view beyond, where two banks of cloverleaf desks were now populated by some of her team. By design, the operations room was at odds with twenty-first-century policing, because it provided a self-contained space for her people, rather than the more modern approach that favoured meetings in corridors and hot desks. Even Hawkins, as DCI, was lucky to have her own office these days, bucking the trend for 'accessible leadership'.

Through the half-open blinds, Hawkins watched Aaron Sharpe cleaning his keyboard and Amala Yasir on the phone, their contrasting approaches to the first hour of the working day a microcosm for similarly opposing attitudes to the remaining seven. Both were supposed to be working loose ends from recent cases, in the absence of fresh impetus in Operation Appeal. Developments had dropped off in the six and a bit days since Matthew Hayes had died, as the number of promising leads wore frustratingly away like the heels on your favourite shoes.

It was no surprise that the investigative fragments had been snapped up by Steve Tanner and his doe-eyed disciple, Frank Todd, who had it seemed pledged allegiance to a man he thought would soon be leading their team. According to a note left on her desk by Tanner the previous day, the two men were now researching the finer branches of the victims' family trees, still attempting to find some sort of connection beyond being bashed to death by the same assailant. Even so, Hawkins hadn't attempted to recall the pair, mostly because Tanner was doing as she'd asked. Ultimately, she had confidence that the answer to this case wouldn't come from mining minuscule gaps ignored for good reason first time around, but experience said they needed a new direction, something unconsidered as yet.

But, without fresh developments, there were no new leads to pursue. The e-fit picture of the man seen following Matt Hayes prior to his death had appeared in the local and national news, in print and on TV. The response, as so often was the case, had been flaccid at best.

Three deaths in such a short space of time had secured decent media coverage at first, but interest had waned when the chain of successive murders broke. And the fact that the victims were all ex-cons might have reignited the wider debate on capital punishment but it also meant that the public felt a lot safer than they had during Hawkins' previous investigation, less than two months ago, when every resident of London had been under potential threat. All of which meant the decisive question was still to be asked. They just needed to work out what that question should be.

She sat, turning things over in her mind, but suddenly her brain stuttered. She tried to hold her thoughts together, but it was like bailing water with a sieve, the old ideas spilling out as new ones came in.

Hawkins shook her head, finally accepting that a visit to the Met's counsellor was long overdue. She elbowed the memories of her attacker's face away and reached for the phone, but her hand froze when she realized catharsis would have to go on waiting for now. Because Mike had entered the operations room.

Her senses primed themselves as she noticed the stern expression on his face, and she bristled when he glanced in her direction through the glass. She looked away, unsure whether he could see her through the blinds, or if a reflection on the outside of her office windows would obscure his view.

The atmosphere between them had been strained since Mike's outburst at the hospital on Thursday morning. He'd still visited her daily, and driven her home the previous night, plus they'd continued to communicate, albeit in stoic tones. Conversation had been civil, but neither had forgiven the other sufficiently to attempt reconciliation, and the air between them crackled with weighty things left unsaid.

He was back on the settee.

She watched him cross the room, swap a few words with Sharpe and Yasir, and check his workstation for notes. He stood for a few seconds beside the desk, facing away. Hawkins could almost hear his decision-making process. Then he turned.

She took a deep breath as he moved towards her, resolving not to be the one to kick off. Mike knocked politely before opening the door. 'Okay to come in?'

She nodded. 'Of course.'

Mike stepped inside. He looked as tired as she felt, except *he* had the excuse of a poor night's sleep on a sofa three inches too short for him, having been kicked out of Hawkins' bed when she'd returned to it the previous night, although she hoped the reason for his lack of rest was the same as her own: lying awake, regretting their fight.

He attempted a smile. 'You shoulda said you were coming in early. I'd have driven you.'

'It's all right.' She smiled back. 'Dad didn't mind me using his car, and the doctors said I should get back to normal activities right away. So I don't go to seed.'

The doctors hadn't said anything of the sort, but he didn't know that.

'Great.' He made a decent stab at breeziness. 'So how do you feel?'

'Fine, actually.' She stood as quickly as she dared, demonstrating renewed mobility. 'The chair's in the car, but I don't think I'll need it.'

Conversation faltered briefly, and the unaddressed tension between them quickly turned into an awkward hush.

Mike broke it first. 'Maybe we should talk over what happened.'

'You're right. But can we do it later?' She waved dismissively at the laptop. 'I'm kind of preoccupied.'

'Sure.' He seemed happy to postpone. 'What's new?'

'Nothing, unfortunately. I'm going over the files, trying to Sherlock a new perspective on this bloody case, but so far I'm blanking.'

There was a pause, which Hawkins almost filled. Part of her wanted to tell him about her lack of sleep, her inability to focus, the flashbacks. But the rest of her said no. If Mike found out she was struggling she'd probably end up lashed to her sofa, pleading with her dad to throw the television away.

At last Mike took a step forward. 'Want some help?'

'Why not?'

He pulled up a chair and joined her at the desk, where they started working through previously explored avenues, ensuring that nothing obvious had been overlooked. Hawkins was relieved to find common purpose precluding any sustained negativity between them, but everything they discussed seemed like old ground. The same questions kept coming up.

First: how was the Judge establishing each convict's exact crime? It was possible he'd identified his targets before their sentences began, perhaps by following local news reports of each conviction and simply waiting for them to do their time. But that would have involved the kind of patience most serial killers didn't have in spades. It also led back to the original unanswered question: *why these particular three?*

And, second: how had he known when his targets were coming out? Mercifully, that answer seemed less obscure, because Yasir had managed to dig up myriad articles from the local media in each case. All three victims were sufficiently controversial to have received substantial coverage, both when they were incarcerated and again when they were released, while most reports included specific dates and photos of them leaving court. Unfortunately, the more outrage each case had sparked, the more prospective vigilantes there were likely to be.

More difficult to answer was how the Judge had tracked each target down once they were free. For example, Sam Philips and Matt Hayes wouldn't even have known their new addresses until shortly before being released, although that made the public services a good, albeit broad, starting point, comprising all the authorities that would have had a say in the specifics of each victim's return to civilian life.

Something told Hawkins this was the key to the case. In the modern era of lightly traded personal details, where supposedly private data was more available than ever before, it became almost impossible to ascertain a particular source for the killer's information . . . But now, with three separate instances to study, perhaps a process of elimination would help . . .

Suddenly, Hawkins was labouring her way out of the chair.

Mike stopped mid-sentence, intently watching her stand. 'Don't tell me you forgot your incontinence meds again.'

'Funny,' she fired back. 'I know where we should be.'

Mike's expression sharpened. 'Where?'

She made him wait a few seconds, inhaling theatrically, as if she might yet deny him the benefit of her acumen.

'Come on,' he urged. 'I won't yank your chain for the rest of the day.'

Hawkins let a smile break. 'Okay, we know Tanner's trying to establish a link between the victims, so perhaps we should balance things out by assuming there's no link at all.'

'All right.' Mike eyed her, probably wondering if she was more interested in making efficient use of resources or just in getting to the answer before Tanner did. 'So . . .'

Hawkins picked up her coat, fumbling in it for an armhole. 'Sometimes, if the reason things happen can't be defined, we need a more scientific approach.'

Mike raised his eyebrows.

'So,' she obliged, 'this killer's targeting ex-cons. But as we're having no luck working out *why* he's doing it, let's dig a bit deeper into *how*.'

47

'Bear with me.' Eileen Thomas gathered up the pile of thick folders and hoisted her ample behind off the chair with an uncomfortable groan. She shuffled across and returned the latest collection of paperwork to its respective drawers, while Hawkins and Maguire sat, politely appraising the medium-sized office where their host worked at one of two large wooden desks.

Eileen, as she insisted they call her, was chief administrative assistant of forty-odd years' service at Holloway Prison, and was clearly proud enough of her position not to mind having been summoned by the Met to attend her workplace on a Sunday afternoon. Her office occupied part of an uncomfortably cold attic conversion in the eaves of the main building, to which the detectives had been escorted forty minutes ago. They'd arrived a good half an hour prior to that, but for some reason the prison governor's approval had been laboriously sought before access was finally allowed. An excuse was mumbled at the time about newly tightened security procedures in the wake of recent inmate leakage from nearby open jails.

All of which was probably a good thing, given that the reason for their visit was to determine ways information such as release dates and post-discharge accommodation might escape from correctional facilities like this one. They had similar meetings set up with the institutions that had looked after Rosa Calano and Matthew Hayes.

The second workstation, diagonally opposite Eileen's, was unoccupied and contrastingly tidy, allegedly thanks to her subordinate's two-week holiday in Corfu. Aside from a few personal items, recycling bins and a coat stand, the room's centre space was filled to bursting with various boxes of documents, while every wall was lined with tall filing cabinets, where hard copies of every prisoner's case history lazed in mute denial of the increasingly digital world beyond the prison gates.

The office itself was tatty in a way that suggested constant heavy use, and even the most compulsive hoarder would have struggled to call the place organized, but their host had found every piece of information they'd asked for with swift, almost robotic ease. And their latest query, regarding correspondence between the prison and the address in Bethnal Green to which Sam Philips had been consigned, appeared to present no greater test, as the large Irish lady returned, file in hand, to her seat.

The admin assistant fished her plastic-framed glasses from the chain around her neck, wiped her nose on a crumpled tissue and adjusted her scarf. She opened the file and withdrew a couple of photocopied sheets, which she passed across the desk.

'Thanks.' Hawkins took them. 'If we leave you a list, could you send us electronic copies of all the documents we've looked at today?'

Eileen grimaced. 'I'll try if you like, but that's my colleague's department, really.' She nodded at the empty desk across the room. 'Leslie's younger than me, and a lot more au fait with this new-fangled computer lark. I prefer my documents to stay where I leave them, if you know what I mean.'

Mike eyed the stand-alone scanner-cum-printer in the corner. 'If everything's already scanned, what's with all the filing cabinets?'

'Well, I won't bore you with the legalities,' Eileen said, 'but we're still obliged to keep signed hard copies of all prisoner correspondence going back to dim and distant days, either here or in the archives. No doubt they'll change it eventually, but I'll thank them with a heart and a half to wait until I retire at least.'

Hawkins raised the letters. 'So, accounting only for departments that would have been privy to information regarding Samantha Philips, who sees sensitive documentation like this?'

'Now that depends. Usually, judicial matters are sent by secure post to the Ministry of Justice and the prisoner's legal team. Anything to do with accommodation or court-appointed work on the outside goes to those parties, plus the affected probation service and council office. Medically related bits go through NHS Central. As often as not, we copy in Media Liaison and Offender

Safety, in some cases the local police, and of course everything goes to the prison governor, Mr Fitch. Now let me think for a minute there, 'cause I'll have missed out loads.'

Hawkins watched Maguire noting down the extensive list, slowly realizing just how much work would be involved in unpicking the convoluted web of departments Eileen had managed to charm from memory alone. Once they added the ancillary staff involved in processing and distribution, and when you considered that three separate institutions were involved, dozens if not hundreds of people could conceivably have accessed the information necessary to trace all three targets post-release.

She was about to ask Eileen who else had access to the documentation subsequently held by each department when they were interrupted. Hawkins turned to see a short, bald man in an impeccable green suit enter from the corridor.

'Goodness.' Eileen shot to her feet. 'Mr Fitch. I . . . I didn't know –'

'Sit down, Ms Thomas,' he instructed. 'I'm not here to appraise.'

Hawkins rose, too. 'Mr Fitch. DCI Antonia Hawkins. And this is DI Mike Maguire.'

'I know who you are.' Fitch shook the hand she offered. 'I approved your impromptu visit, so it would have been remiss of me to let you pass through without introducing myself. And, given recent events, I'm sure you understand why we're more protective than ever, especially of our archive. I now personally greet all visitors to confidential areas of our institution, weekend or not.'

'Very wise,' Hawkins accepted.

Fitch retreated slightly. 'Still, don't let me interrupt. We can talk afterwards.'

'Actually, we're finished.' Hawkins stepped away from her chair. There was little point mining Eileen's kingdom any more. The list Mike had already made of services with access to parolee information would keep her research team busy for days, and even then she wasn't convinced it would lead anywhere.

She and Maguire left cards and thanked the administrator, who seemed more than happy for her visitors to depart, although Hawkins suspected that had more to do with the fact that they'd be taking her boss with them. Eileen offered to call a guard, but Fitch suggested they accompany him back to his office instead, which was on the way to the main gate, from where he'd provide further aid. They followed him out of the office and set off along the bluntly decorated corridor.

As they went, Fitch launched into unsolicited patter regarding his plans for Holloway. He'd been in his post for less than a month, but already disruption among inmates was down and fresh capital was being spent on renovating cells in older parts of the jail. He talked about the inscrutable standards he'd implemented and his forthcoming strategies to reduce drug use inside the prison, punctuating everything with swift, concise hand movements.

They reached a polished, dark wood door, fully at odds with the stark corridor in which it was set. Fitch used a fingerprint scanner to let them through into an opulent room where squeaky tiles gave way to plush carpets and homely shades. At the far end of the spacious reception area, a secretary glanced up from her desk.

'So, Detective,' Fitch asked as they moved on, 'was Ms Thomas able to provide the information you required?'

'Eileen was very efficient,' Hawkins told him. 'We actually came away with a bit more than we asked for.'

Without warning, Fitch stopped and turned to face them. 'And what *was* that, exactly?'

'Unfortunately, I can't discuss it.' She gave a penitent smile. 'I'm sure you understand the need to minimize awareness of our investigation. It saves potential complications at a later stage.'

The prison governor's brow tightened. 'And I'm sure *you* understand my duty to see this establishment's reputation preserved. Unnecessary association with an inquiry like yours can affect everything from average sentence length to prisoner conduct and staff morale. So if you come here unannounced and start questioning my employees about confidential detainee information, I have every right to know what's being discussed.'

'Fair enough,' Hawkins replied. Fitch was obviously

no soft touch, and he was correct about his entitlement to know. Legally, he could have sat in on their session with Eileen, had he wished; the reason Hawkins had tried to slip in under the radar in the first place. Their research into the various ways information left prisons like this one would be hard enough in itself to follow up, without the inevitable complication added by men like Fitch, whose motivation was to keep his house looking clean. So the less people like him knew about the Met's burgeoning interest in his establishment's affairs, the better.

Reluctantly, she gave him an overview, revealing a little more than she was obliged, in the hope that he might provide fresh insight on a line of inquiry that, for now at least, seemed to have stalled.

Fitch listened closely and, despite being unable to offer much in the way of help, he promised to assist where possible with the ongoing case, but only in return for Hawkins' guarantee that future inquiries regarding prison business would be directed through him. It wasn't a deal she had much faith in, but Hawkins took it, keen to escape his cynical stare.

His piece said, the prison governor led them the short remaining distance to his office, where he handed them over to a female prison officer he introduced as Jones, before disappearing inside, quietly closing the door.

Jones led them back the way they had come. She was a stern woman, slim, pushing fifty, in regulation navy trousers and white shirt. She had the apathetic-guard look down to a tee. Hawkins attributed that to experience, which made Jones a decent subject for her next question.

She moved alongside their escort as they walked. 'Do you mind if I ask you something?'

As she spoke, Hawkins felt Maguire bristle behind them.

Jones glanced across. 'If you want.'

'How much contact do you have with the inmates, day to day?'

Jones clearly wasn't eager to chat, her eyes narrowing in response to Hawkins' curiosity, but she answered. 'They like us to talk with the prisoners, build trust and that. But we have to keep it professional; you can't be mates with a convict.'

Hawkins nodded. 'What about inmate correspondence?'

The pause was slightly longer this time. 'Every warden has their own group of cons – sorry, prisoners. We have to read any emails or letters in or out, check for anything dodgy before we hand it over.'

Hawkins resisted a flippant urge to ask Jones if she'd seen any letters asking for quotes to murder fellow inmates. 'How much dodgy stuff do you see?'

'Nothing to speak of. Even the slower ones learn pretty fast that stuff like that gets picked up, so nobody does it. If they want to talk about anything secret in this place, someone comes in. Private stuff gets discussed in the visiting room, face to face.'

'Interesting.' Hawkins acted as if this was information she hadn't expected, stoking Jones' ego. 'So you must get to know them pretty well, over time. Where they're from, if they have family, stuff like that.'

'Some of 'em, maybe.' Jones paused at a gate, searching for the right key. 'A lot of the inmates ignore us.'

'I see.' Hawkins watched her open the lock. 'Did you know Sam Phi—'

'Chief?' Maguire's voice cut in loudly over her shoulder.

She glanced back. 'Yes?'

'Can I talk to you?'

She forced a smile. 'Can it wait?'

'Nope.'

They stopped. Hawkins apologized to Jones and moved aside with Maguire, fully aware of what was coming.

'What are you doing?' he hissed.

'Making conversation. Why?'

'You know damn well Fitch doesn't want you grilling his staff.'

'It's hardly the Spanish Inquisition.' Hawkins glanced over at the guard. 'I don't think she'll sue.'

Maguire's frown deepened.

'*Okay*.' She gave in. 'I'll stop.'

They re-joined their chaperone and walked on in silence, reaching the lobby, where the two detectives waited to reclaim their personal effects from the check-in desk as Jones lingered a short distance away.

The yelling became audible as Hawkins was handed her bag, and moments later a young woman in tight blue jeans was manhandled through a side door by two male guards, her stiletto heels screeching on the tiles.

'Leave off, wankers!' she shrieked. 'This is fucking abuse!'

The guards ignored her, obviously more intent on keeping their cargo under control without grabbing a handful of heavily augmented breast.

'Lara's done fuck-all, anyway,' the woman shouted as she was dragged past them and out into the car park, her voice fading as the door swung shut. 'Try banging up some real criminals for a change.'

'Normal day?' Hawkins asked the clerk, who had barely looked up.

They left the desk and walked out to the courtyard, as Jones closed the security door behind them. Hawkins watched her retreat into the gloom beyond the glass, turning back to see the young woman, who was now screaming about burning the prison down, being assisted towards the main gate.

They followed, quietly discussing other lines of inquiry, now that Hawkins' bright idea regarding prisoner information had put itself on hold.

'Maybe we should start retracing our steps,' Mike suggested. 'Go back to the scenes, talk to the relatives again.'

'Nice idea.' She looked over at him. 'But guess where Tanner is at this precise moment. He's already annexed half my team, and he's more intent than ever on solving this case before I do. I can't just follow his lead and hope to overtake. We need something he hasn't thought of; otherwise, he'll turn up in Vaughn's office with the answer, beaming like bloody butter wouldn't melt . . .'

She was about to address Mike's obvious confusion by filling him in on the full story about Tanner when they were both distracted by the noise from the recently ejected woman, who was now being propelled through the final gate on to the street.

'Arseholes!' she screamed. 'Lara's innocent! You'll be paying her compensation before long.'

Mike waited for her to stop shouting. 'What did you mean . . .'

But Hawkins was no longer listening. Maguire tailed off as she fell behind, and turned to watch her digging frantically in her bag. She found the papers she was looking for, pulling the sheets free and staring at them.

'Blimey,' she said. 'That's *it*.'

Mike came closer. 'What is?'

Hawkins didn't answer right away, turning to look back at the prison, letting realization course through her, the trickling progress of insight eke its way into her mind. She paused, mentally turning her suspicions over, testing them. All at once it felt fantastic to be back.

'Toni,' Mike said, agitated, 'I hate when you leave me hanging like this.'

She turned to face him, certain now of her insight. 'Hunter's theory is right, but it's only half the story. Yes, there were extenuating circumstances, but that isn't why these people were killed.'

Maguire just stared.

'Okay.' Hawkins handed him the printouts. 'What do you see?'

He looked at each sheet. 'The original victims.'

'Exactly, the baby Rosa Calano shook to death, the man Sam Philips murdered and the kid Matt Hayes ran down. So . . . ?'

Mike thought for a few seconds, shook his head.

Hawkins assisted. 'What if the connection isn't between Calano, Philips and Hayes? What if it's between the three victims?'

'So, link them.'

'Okay.' She pointed at the photos in turn. 'Six-month-old baby: innocent; teenage kid riding his bike; innocent.'

'Yeah,' Mike cut her off, 'but what about the rapist? We talked to the friend. Either Brendan Marsh was guilty or she's got her story all *kinds* of wrong.'

'Or she's lying.' Hawkins clicked her fingers. 'Did you consider *that*?'

She watched his assurance falter as he realized what she was suggesting.

'We've been looking at this upside down,' she told him. 'We assumed Philips was telling the truth about the rape, but what if Marsh didn't actually do it? If that's true, all three original victims were innocent, which definitely gives our vigilante something to avenge.'

'It's possible.' Mike ran a hand over his closely cropped hair. 'Geez.'

'So,' Hawkins waved the printouts, 'if I'm right, the Judge is targeting people who killed *innocent* victims. And, if that's the case, there are only three possibilities. Either someone other than Marsh raped Sam Philips, the rape didn't happen at all, or the killer doesn't know the full story. But whichever scenario's true, there's one person who knows a lot more than she's letting on.

'Which means,' she told him, 'it's high time we paid another visit to Sam Philips' best friend.'

48

Bull heard the other vehicles before he saw them. The sound of their engines grew from a distant hum into separate clatters that sounded like two control trucks and a tank.

He was right, too, watching through the open rear canvas of their truck as the three vehicles passed in the early morning light, kicking up the dust as they headed away at speed.

'Where the fuck are they going?' Cheshire asked from the opposite bench.

'Anyone?' Bull checked with the other lads in the truck. No one knew.

The kid was right to wonder, though. Control didn't usually send units out at this time, when the night shift was still coming in. That risked vehicles hitting each other in the dark on the narrow approach road and caused jams on the radio because everyone was talking at once. There were only a few reasons they'd be sending units out now. Either they were responding to an emergency, maybe picking up AWOLs, or rescuing a team whose transport had conked out.

Or there was a bigger problem.

Their truck didn't slow as they bumped towards home. The main drive in was nicknamed Ann Summers' Approach, because its surface was so fucking rough that by the time you got to the gate the vibration meant you couldn't see straight.

Bull shut his eyes, trying to ignore the headache he'd had since their shift began. It had been a tough night. They'd come under light-arms fire twice, and there had been more than a few close shaves. What made it worse was that they'd wasted their time. There had been no guns stashed in any of the houses they'd checked.

At last the truck stopped for a minute before driving on. Bull watched the south gate pass behind them, glad to be back. The next stop was the end of the road, and they all dropped out on to the dry, cracked ground before skirting the row of multi-coloured shipping containers to the equipment yard. Bull and Cheshire were first in, walking over to one of the tables to dump their kit.

Bull unclipped his pack and let it drop before rolling his shoulders. After eight hours in the field they all stank; all he wanted was a shower and his bunk. It was going to be a hot day, and forty-degree heat meant flies like you wouldn't believe, although, when he was this tired, Bull could sleep through anything. But suddenly everyone was called to attention.

He turned to see the section commander, Shaun Wilson.

'Sorry to do this to you, gentlemen. I know you just came in' — Wilson waved at a couple of the guys still removing their body armour — 'but you need to keep your gear on. Something's happened, and we need everybody back out. Follow me.'

He turned towards the gate, adding, 'Bring your guns.'

49

The door to the charity shop wasn't alarmed so much as booby-trapped. Hawkins dodged the wooden chime as it flapped out from behind the door, narrowly missing her face. It clanked against the glass.

A Welsh-accented cry came from the back of the shop as she and Mike stepped inside.

'Sorry! Let me get rid of that.' A dumpy woman in her fifties hurried out from behind the counter, carrying a small set of steps. She was dressed in a smart grey skirt and heavy red jumper that would only ever have matched if you set them on fire. 'The new girl put that up yesterday, while I wasn't here.'

'No problem.' Mike closed the door and untangled the chime from the low beam. He handed it to the woman as she arrived, panting, beside them. 'We're trained to handle these situations.'

The Welsh lady gave him a confused look.

'DCI Hawkins and DI Maguire,' Hawkins clarified, holding up her badge. 'We spoke on the phone.'

'Ah.' Realization broke on the woman's face. 'Now I get you. Yes, I'm Gwen Stevens, the proprietor. You're here to see Nicola.'

'Yes. You said she'd be here this afternoon.'

'She is, poor thing. Hasn't been herself since her friend died, you understand, but she insisted on doing her hours. Anyway, she just nipped out. We're rather low on milk, you see? She won't be long.'

'Good.' Hawkins glanced out through the window, hoping they hadn't underestimated the size of any secrets Nicola Watts might be hiding. 'Is it okay if we wait?'

''Course it is.' The shopkeeper winked at her. 'When Nicky gets back, we'll make you a nice cup of tea.' She waved at the shop. 'Feel free to look round, or you can take a seat out the back.'

Hawkins smiled. 'We'll browse.'

'Right you are.' Gwen picked up the steps. 'I've got some lovely jackets at the moment. Suit a pretty girl like you.'

'Thanks.' Hawkins watched her shuffle back to the desk.

She and Mike began looking around. Hawkins couldn't remember the last time she'd been in a charity shop, but this one certainly didn't look like any she'd visited before. Instead of dusty rugs, they stood on neat laminate, and where she'd pictured dead pensioners' cardies and chipped tea sets, there were modern coffee machines and designer shirts with prices to match. But her attention was mainly on the window, and on Bethnal Green Road beyond. Traffic was light, even for Sunday lunchtime, while the vicious winds battering the trees were keeping pedestrians at home. And as the minutes ticked by without sign of the woman they'd come to see, Hawkins' nerves only increased.

Before leaving the prison that morning, she'd purposely called the contact number Watts had given for afternoons, the charity shop where she helped out sometimes. Hawkins confirmed with the manager that Watts was due in and ensured that she and Maguire arrived at the start of her shift, trying to maintain the element of surprise. Unfortunately, it looked as if Watts had come in early and found out from Gwen that the Met were on their way. The subsequent mission for milk could have been genuine, of course, but it might also indicate that Nicola Watts was hiding even more than Hawkins had assumed.

But could it really be serious enough to make her run?

The answer came as Hawkins admired a pair of beautifully made leather boots. She bent to touch the supple hide, before glancing over when she heard the door open.

'Hello, Detective.' Nicola Watts stood in the doorway, holding a carton of milk. 'Sorry to keep you.'

'It's fine.' Hawkins straightened. 'Can we have a private word?'

'I was at home this morning.' Nicola Watts handed Mike a steaming cup of tea. 'You could have reached me on the mobile number I gave you.'

'I know.' Hawkins set her mug down to cool. 'Sorry to disturb you at work, but we were tied up until now.'

Watts looked unconvinced. 'I can't be long. Gwen needs to leave at two.'

'Don't worry, miss, we won't keep you.' Mike tried his most charming tone.

Unfortunately, their subject seemed immune, refusing to break eye contact with Hawkins. 'What's this about?'

Hawkins watched her retreat to a chair in the corner of the small kitchen, completing their small triangle of bodies between the close-set cupboards. Ironically, in contrast to the shop below, everything in this room matched Hawkins' preconceptions of a charity shop perfectly. But, while there wasn't much space, at least they wouldn't be overheard.

Watts looked a lot better than she had the week before. There was colour in her face, and her drained expression had been replaced with a warm and intelligent air. But Hawkins knew better than to judge interviewees on appearance alone.

She cleared her throat. 'We need to go back over the events that led to Sam killing Brendan Marsh.'

Watts frowned. 'Why?'

'We didn't cover the whole story before, and it may be a lot more important than we thought. I need to hear your version of what happened.'

'All right.' The woman's arms folded suddenly, and her shoulders hunched. 'Where do you want me to start?'

'How did they meet?'

Watts took a few seconds to think about it before

she replied. 'He was our English tutor at sixth-form college. He'd only joined the staff that year, so I guess they met in the first lesson. You'd have to check with the school when that was.'

Hawkins raised a hand. 'It's fine. Did they get on?'

'Yes.' Watts looked nervous now, eyes darting between her visitors. 'He was younger than the other teachers, so he was more of a laugh . . . you know, friendlier. Of course, at that stage we didn't know why.'

Her composure was already flagging, and Hawkins softened her tone. 'Did they see each other outside school?'

Watts looked at the ceiling. 'Yes, but not how that sounds; not . . . *socially*. Sam was struggling with her exams and he offered to help. He seemed nice, so they started meeting up, break times at first, then in the evenings as well.'

'Where did they meet?'

'At his house. He lived alone; it wasn't far.'

'Did you ever go there?'

'No.'

'So there was nothing between them, nothing unprofessional about his behaviour?'

Watts looked away. She had the appearance of someone being coaxed into breaking a friend's confidence. After a moment she turned back. 'He tried to kiss her a few times, but she never let him.'

'That wasn't in the court records. Why didn't Sam report it?'

Watts drew a deep breath and sighed heavily before answering. 'Because she did that to guys.'

Hawkins' eyes narrowed. 'She led him on?'

'Oh, maybe.' Watts stood, clearly frustrated. 'But she didn't consent to sex.'

'How can you be sure?'

Watts chewed at her bottom lip, her expression hardening suddenly. She turned to face them. 'What are you actually asking me here?'

Hawkins exchanged glances with Maguire before asking, 'Is it possible that Brendan Marsh didn't rape Sam?'

Watts' frown deepened. 'No.'

'You seem very certain. Last time, you said Sam lied about lots of things. How do you know she wasn't lying about this?'

'She just wasn't, okay? I knew Sam. I knew when she was telling the truth. She wouldn't have lied about that.' There were tears in her eyes.

'All right.' Hawkins paused, letting Watts recover, hiding her frustration. For her theory to work, Brendan Marsh needed to be innocent, too, although Watts' reaction said she really did believe he was guilty. Plus, the teacher's prior criminal record suggested she was right. But the theory still made enough sense that it was worth another try.

'Okay, Nicola,' she said, 'let's go over what happened after the rape. Can you do that?'

Watts wiped her face and sniffed. 'Yeah.'

Gently, Watts sat down, as Hawkins tried to block out the discomfort she felt after standing for the best part of thirty minutes. Despite three days of extra rest, her body still wasn't back to normal. Luckily, Watts was talking again, distracting her.

'Sam came straight to me after it happened. It was late on a school night, but she couldn't go home; her mum died a few years before, and she couldn't tell her dad. I tried to convince her to go to the cops, but she was too upset. She didn't come back to school for a long time after that, and I didn't see her much. The school contacted her dad, but he didn't do anything. He's a bit of a waster.'

'Neither of you told anyone else?'

'No. She swore me to secrecy, so I didn't say a word. And neither did she until the trial, though it all came out then.'

'*Everything?*'

There was a pause before Watts nodded.

'When did Sam start abusing drink and drugs?'

'Soon after the rape. She was never into any of that before.'

'And that's when she started sleeping around?'

'Yes.'

Hawkins chose her words carefully. 'So, if she slept around after the attack, and flirted with guys before it happened, how can you be sure she wasn't in a relationship with Marsh?'

She must have hit a nerve, because suddenly Watts

looked up. 'She wasn't – I'd have known. We were best friends. Best friends know.'

Hawkins pressed. 'Could Sam have *wanted* a relationship with him?'

Watts' face became still and she stared straight at Hawkins. She spoke quietly. 'What are you suggesting?'

It was all or nothing now. Hawkins went for it. 'Is it possible that he turned her down and she didn't like it?'

'How dare you?' Watts was back on her feet. 'Sam wasn't like that. All right, she flirted, but she didn't really understand what it meant. She was a virgin when he raped her.'

Hawkins knew she had Watts on the edge. 'But Sam didn't see a doctor afterwards. How do you know the rape even happened?'

'Because that bastard got her pregnant, okay?' Watts was shouting now. 'And if you're interested in how I know that, I was the one who held her hand while she had the fucking abortion.'

Hawkins thanked Gwen as she exited the charity shop with Maguire, as fast as protesting abdominal muscles would allow, keen not to engage the woman who would shortly be picking up the pieces of their heated exchange. The shopkeeper's subdued response suggested that she'd heard enough of her friend's shouting to know something was amiss.

A distraught Nicola Watts had just thrown them out. Under normal circumstances, Hawkins didn't take orders from interviewees, especially the ones that withheld vital evidence, but she had what she'd come for, and they were short on time.

They reached the pavement, squinting in response to a heavy gust of rain-infused wind, and headed for the car. Thanks to the weather, there were still few people about.

Mike left it until they were protected by a bus stand twenty yards from the shop before he grabbed Hawkins' arm, spinning her round. 'What the hell was that?'

'What the hell was *what*?' She pulled herself free, welcoming the opportunity to sit on one of the flip-down seats.

'Improper conduct. You bullied her.'

'Oh, come on, as if you've never pushed anyone into a confession before. It's practically the last decent tool we've got. And don't tell me it's an English thing; I've seen *Judge Judy*.'

Maguire looked about ready to shout, but instead he leaned closer, his tone hard. 'You are out of control. I'm not sure you even care about stopping this killer; you just don't want Tanner to get there first.'

Her own anger flared. 'That's not true.'

'You really upset that woman, Toni, and for what? What were you trying to prove?'

She raised her eyebrows. 'Well, perhaps you need to focus a bit less on me and a bit more on this case.'

'What's *that* supposed to mean?'

'Pushing her was the only way to get the full story.

She kept that abortion secret until now out of some misguided loyalty to her dead friend, and she'd never have volunteered it unless Sam's integrity was at stake. I did what I had to, and now we have a whole new line of inquiry to pursue, thanks to me and my risky but justifiable ways.'

Mike's brow contracted. 'What new line?'

She smiled. 'Samantha Philips had an abortion, right?'

'Yeah. So?'

'There's your innocent victim.'

50

Bull checked the position of the sun. It was getting high, which meant there were only a few hours of bearable temperature left. They needed to get this done before the day really kicked in.

He followed the convoy for another mile along the dusty road before their sergeant appeared at the tailgate of the truck in front, waving them off.

'Left here, boss,' Cheshire said from the passenger seat.

'I know where we're going,' Bull told him. 'Don't need you dicks to direct me.'

'Yeah, right.' Cheshire grinned. 'Keep this thing on the road for more than a mile and I might believe you.'

Bull told him to piss off, even though the kid was probably right. He hadn't felt this tired for ages. It might have been sunstroke. He hadn't said a word, of course; the boys would crucify him, but it was hard just staying awake and they'd almost ended up in a ditch several times. He blinked hard, trying to wake himself up. He needed to be alert for what they were going to do.

They bumped off the tarmac on to a stony track, and Bull watched the other three trucks disappear round the next bend, hoping it wouldn't be long before they re-joined their unit. In the last hour, Iraq had dropped even further into hell.

The briefing they'd been called to just after getting back from night shift had been packed: every soldier on the base was there, *and a few more besides. Some general nobody knew had told them what was going on.*

A series of coordinated bomb attacks had hit the previous evening, killing hundreds of people in two Yazidi Kurd villages near the northern city of Mosul. Command thought it might be the start of a major insurgent offensive, and that other soft targets like Basra might be at risk, too. They wanted everyone out on the streets as a peacekeeping force, and a show of military strength to see off other attacks.

And if you hadn't slept for twenty hours? Tough. You're a soldier; suck it up.

For now, British troops would stay in the south,but, depending on how things went, they might have to head north to help the Americans. That meant travelling on roads they didn't normally use, including one that hadn't been swept for mines in weeks.

It was a short, fifty-yard cut-through across some fields, but it would save them a fifteen-minute detour on main roads if they needed to move a lot of troops at short notice. The enemy probably wouldn't have bothered to mine anything that small, but it was best to be sure; Bull had seen what those things could do to a Snatch Land Rover.

He and Cheshire had been ordered to spend two hours sweeping the track, then to meet up with the others. Troops were spread pretty thin, so for now the two of them were on their own.

'That it?' Cheshire asked, pointing ahead at a stony dirt trail that split off the main track before leading up a slope towards what looked like another tarmac road.

'Yeah.'

Bull stopped at the junction where the track began, looking in his mirrors to make sure there were no other vehicles around. The roads were empty, pale earth stretching away to the horizon in every direction, and they hadn't passed another vehicle since leaving base.

He reached behind the seat for the mine detectors. 'Let's go.'

51

Mike stewed like a professional all the way to Hendon, staring ahead as he drove them back from Bethnal Green, shunning any half-hearted attempts Hawkins made at dialogue. She watched him pull into the car park at Becke House, still unsure what bothered him most, her mildly heavy-handed treatment of Nicola Watts or the fact he hadn't realized that Sam Philips' abortion made her responsible for the death of an innocent. He might have had a point about Hawkins' conduct, but he also hated being caught out, almost as much as she did.

In fact, she suspected his reticence was a mixture of both, although Maguire clearly wasn't in any mood to discuss it. He wore the default masculine expression that suggested men were easily understood at all times, and woe betide anyone who dared raise the issue.

He parked up, yanked the handbrake almost vertical and climbed out, banging the door closed. Hawkins watched with growing unease, only realizing when his midriff hovered outside the window that he was waiting to lock the car.

She counted to ten and followed, determined to stay calm, turning back to face him across the roof of their

Focus. But he'd already gone, blipping the alarm as he went.

'Hey.' Hawkins set off after him, determined now that this conversation was going to happen, wincing as she tried to match his pace. But she was ignored. She repeated the call, renewing her efforts, managing to catch him at the door.

'Don't you think you're over-reacting just a bit?' She grabbed his arm, making him turn. 'Stop, please.'

Mike met her eye for the first time in half an hour. 'Why, so I can be courtside for your next crazy stunt?'

Hawkins studied him, understanding his mood wasn't just about that afternoon; the problem was more deeply rooted than that. Which might explain why he was so worked up.

She softened her tone. 'What's this really about?'

'If I'm cramping your style, maybe I should ask for another transfer.'

'Hold on.' She lowered her voice as the door beside them opened and a couple of analysts came out. She ushered him away from the entrance. 'Where's this coming from?'

Mike waited for the two women to pass out of earshot. 'Seriously, Toni, what's the deal here? Because, right now, I'm no kind of partner, at work *or* at home.'

She frowned. 'Is this about *us*?'

'No, it's about *you*. You obviously want this job, even though you're still playing fast and loose with the rules. But you've side-lined me on every big call in this case and, for all the attention you pay me at home, I may as well not be there.'

'That isn't true,' she protested, desperately trying to come up with an example that didn't support his argument. 'I need you more than ever.'

'Exactly. Need, not *want*.' He made to leave.

She stopped him again. 'You know I didn't mean it like that.'

'Then why's your dad still talking in his sleep in *your* back room?'

'Ah.' She paused, realizing that, as usual where men were concerned, ultimately, it came down to sex. Not that she could blame him; since Mike's return they'd barely held hands.

'I know you're frustrated,' she soothed. 'I am, too. But you know me: I need to find my feet, properly make DCI; plus, the whole Tanner thing is stressing me out. I've been distracted, but I want us to work just as much as you do.'

She watched Maguire's scowl dissipate, capitalizing by moving in for a hug. 'We just need to reconnect.'

Mike made a confirmatory noise and pulled her close, as Hawkins wondered whether her scars would have faded in the few days since her last unsuccessful attempt to cover them with make-up.

She was busy composing further reassurance when Mike's pocket rang.

They parted as he found his phone and checked the screen. 'I'd better take this.'

She nodded. 'So we're okay?'

'Yeah.' He sighed. 'Guess the pressure's getting to us all. I'll catch you upstairs.' He moved away.

Hawkins held her pass to the scanner and entered the foyer of Becke House, thinking about the case, her footsteps echoing off the hard sixties floor tiles.

'Antonia?'

She stopped and looked round. She'd been so lost in her thoughts she hadn't even registered who she'd just passed in the corridor. 'Sorry, sir, miles away.'

'No problem.' Vaughn took a step back towards her. 'I was just looking for you. How's the case?'

'Good.' She realized they were beside the row of quiet rooms on the ground floor and gripped the handle of the nearest door. 'Let me update you.'

He checked his watch. 'If we're quick. I only came in to catch up on some paperwork, and I'm taking the wife out to dinner.'

They stepped inside the small office, which contained a circular table with two chairs, a phone and a data cable for visitors' laptops.

He watched her close the door. 'This must be worth hearing.'

She smiled. 'It's preliminary information at this stage, but it may turn out to be decisive. I was hoping to dig a little deeper before updating you, but since you asked . . .'

Of course, it would have made more sense to investigate how the killer could have found out about Sam

Philip's abortion before approaching Vaughn, as that was likely to be his first question, but at least this way Hawkins secured credit for the discovery, before she told the rest of her team and, more importantly, Tanner.

'Well,' she began buoyantly, 'as you know, initially we thought the Judge was targeting ex-cons whose sentences had been shortened due to mitigating circumstances. Unfortunately, that line of inquiry led nowhere, because I realized that Samantha Philips' case didn't tally with the rest, and we were at a loss till this morning. Anyway, cutting a long story short, I now believe that all three of our victims were responsible for the death of an innocent party.'

'Okay.' Vaughn nodded, but his face showed none of the surprise or delight Hawkins had expected.

She pressed on. 'You're probably wondering how I'm going to prove that Brendan Marsh was innocent. But I don't have to, because *he* wasn't Philips' innocent victim.'

'Right.' The DCS looked unimpressed. 'You're talking about the abortion.'

Hawkins felt her face sag. 'Yes. How did you . . . ?'

'Oh, you can't have seen each other.' Vaughn took a step towards the door, obviously aware that she'd exhausted her supply of pre-undermined revelations. 'Steve told me ten minutes ago in the ops room. Perhaps you should do a course in inter-team communications?'

He winked. 'Then you wouldn't have to worry about anyone stealing your thunder.'

'I'll look into it.' Hawkins crowbarred a smile on to her face as he squeezed past and left the room. She lowered herself carefully into the nearest chair and spent five minutes staring at the wall, trying to work out how a discovery she'd only just made could have found its way to Steve Tanner, and then on to Tristan Vaughn, in the time it had taken her and Mike to drive back from Bethnal Green. She came up with only one possibility.

She pulled the Airwave unit out of her bag, checking that all its various functions were turned off, cursing herself for resisting the new technology since it had been introduced almost a decade ago. Then she stood, resolving to organize a mobile for herself so she could bypass this new handset until she had mastered its treacherous ways.

But first she had a weasel to see.

52

Hawkins looked up from her email backlog in response to the staccato knock, but her office door was halfway open before she had the chance to invite entry.

'You wanted to see me?' Steve Tanner leaned in with a look of incredulity on his face, almost as if he thought the message she'd left with Frank, summoning him to her office on sight, had been some kind of joke.

'Yes.' She waved him in with the most convincing smile she could manage, conscious that this was the first contact between them since their unpleasant exchange on Tuesday morning, five days ago. For all its frustration, her seventy-two-hour incarceration at St Thomas' Hospital had allowed them both time to reflect on what had been said. Hawkins' temper had cooled – at least until she found out that Tanner had again beaten her to the DCS with a fresh revelation. But now she was more interested in *how*, rather than when, her adversary had come by the information. In truth, she'd rather not have spoken to him at all, but for now she was still his commanding officer, and ignoring this fact was only likely to assist him in changing it.

'Will this take long?' Tanner looked more self-assured than ever as he settled calmly in the chair opposite.

'Hopefully not.' She noted that, behind the cockiness, Tanner's expression was one of genuine curiosity. If she hadn't known better, she might even have convinced herself he had nothing to hide.

She opened with a nonchalant tone. 'Out of interest, do you use an Airwave handset?'

'Doesn't everyone these days?' Tanner patted his inner pocket. 'Why?'

'Oh, I just got one; haven't tamed it yet.'

'They're surprisingly useful once you learn how to handle them.' The grin intensified. 'I can show you, if it helps. Is that why you wanted to see me?'

'No.' Hawkins studied him. Did he know what she was about to ask, or had his comment been coincidence? She covered a scowl, opting to avoid direct accusation straight away. 'We need to discuss the case. Have you made any progress?'

Tanner shrugged. 'Plenty, thanks. You?'

'Likewise. I just wondered if there was anything you'd like to share.'

'I prefer to wait until I have something concrete.'

Hawkins fought rising irritation. 'Look, I appreciate we haven't exactly hit it off so far, but we still need to communicate. Otherwise, we're giving this guy even greater scope to kill.'

'Is that a bad thing?' Tanner snorted. 'No one would blame you for thinking this killer's got a point. Maybe it wouldn't be so terrible if he took out a couple more before we tackle him.'

She frowned. 'Why would I think that?'

'Well, his victims were hardly paragons of virtue.'

'Perhaps not, but they all did their time.'

'Come on, Antonia, you know as well as I do that jail isn't the deterrent it used to be. Anyone who rattles a baby to death or mows someone down with their car and fucks off without calling for help should get a lot more than a few months inside. Not to mention your murderess.'

'Are you saying they deserved to die?'

'I'm saying it was still a life for a life in this country until 1965, and since they banned the death penalty the murder rate has doubled. There are plenty of people out there saying it's time for a rethink. Maybe this guy's just ahead of the curve.'

'So we should all take to the streets with pitchforks?'

'Hardly, but maybe we shouldn't be surprised when people take matters into their own hands.'

'It's still vigilante justice.'

'It's natural law. If the powers that be don't act, things balance themselves in the end.'

Hawkins turned away, realizing she wasn't making any headway. The scary thing wasn't just that someone with these views had already made it to such an influential rank but also that he had the momentum and drive to go higher, potentially into a position from which such opinions could filter back down.

'Anyway' – she changed tack, hoping to catch him off

guard – 'I just spoke to the chief super. Apparently, you have new information regarding Operation Appeal.'

'News travels fast.'

'Yes, it does . . . So?'

'Actually, I don't feel like discussing it.'

'Interesting.' She leaned back in the chair, folding her arms. 'I can understand why, having made your intentions so clear last week, you consider me the enemy. But, if and until you match or surpass my rank, I can make reasonable requests for you to explain your methods, especially when there are grounds for suspicion of misconduct.' She paused to let the implication breathe. 'And if you do have the DCS on side, even *he'll* have trouble evading procedure if I write you up for insubordination. Whatever happens after that, the original black mark will stay on your record for good, and your sources will have to be revealed during the inquiry, so I'll find out either way. It might be easier just to tell me, don't you think?'

For the briefest moment, uncertainty entered Tanner's expression, and then it was gone. But Hawkins had already seen it: the first tiny tremor in a hitherto unshakeable poise.

They sat in silence for a long moment, eyes locked, before Tanner caved. He explained slowly what she, and everybody else, it seemed, already knew about innocent victims and secret abortions.

'And how did you come to discover this?' she asked

when he'd finished, watching his face for signs of untruth.

He frowned. 'Does it matter?'

'That depends.' Hawkins leaned forwards, linking her hands on the desk. 'For now, I'm simply intrigued to know how you know.'

Tanner shifted in his chair. 'I flexed a few rules. Don't tell me you never do.'

'Which rules, exactly?'

She had him cornered. He'd have to admit whatever trick he'd pulled with the Airwave unit to listen in to a senior officer's conversation, and then that he'd tried to impress Vaughn by revealing her discovery before she had the chance. *Rookie mistake.*

'The guidelines governing requisition of hospital records.'

She blinked. 'What?'

'You wanted me to connect the three victims, so I asked a contact in the NHS to dig up their medical histories. I'm aware we're supposed to submit request forms through official channels, but that can take days, and there are lives at stake.'

Hawkins felt her rage flip straight to embarrassment and muttered, more to herself, 'That's how you knew about the abortion.'

'Yes. It meant all the victims had been responsible for killing innocent people. Frank tried to ring, but your mobile was off.'

'It's broken.' She breathed. 'And then you saw Vaughn.'

'Right.' Tanner had obviously watched her crest fall. His bravado was back as he stood. 'Maybe you should send out your Airwave number. You know, just in case.'

'Yes,' she said, hoping she wasn't as red as she felt. 'Maybe I should.'

53

Bull released the detector's trigger and called up to Cheshire, a few feet in front. 'Stop a minute.'

'What?' The kid turned, his boots crunching on the gritty track.

'Stay still, man.' Bull pointed at him, trying to tune into the sound. But as they stood there in silence, all he could make out were the swirling winds bouncing back and forth across the plain.

He breathed again, waving at Cheshire to carry on. 'It's nothing. Keep going.'

The kid smirked. 'Ears playing tricks again, gramps?'

'Fuck off.'

Cheshire turned back, carried on moving his detector from side to side, slow step after slow step, heading for the far end of the uphill track.

Bull watched him, checking he was doing it right. He shouldn't have let the kid lead; the slow role up front was a lot more dangerous than the sweeper's role behind. But he didn't trust himself. His head was pounding, and the rising desert heat was only making things worse. He squinted up, checking the position of the sun through his UV shades. It was climbing fast and, although the temperature was probably still below thirty, in the coming hours it would hit forty-five.

Bull went back to sweeping, trying to estimate how much

longer they'd need. They were about halfway between the Land Rover at the lower end of the field and the break in the Armco barriers on the road at the top of the slope. It had taken about thirty minutes to check half of one side, so another ninety to finish was about right, although they'd have to keep up their pace.

Suddenly his finger clicked off the trigger again, and he hissed at Cheshire. 'Hey.'

The kid stopped and turned. 'I hear it now.'

Bull nodded, listening hard, as the noise he thought he'd heard a moment before became unmistakable.

The distant sound of an engine.

He spun slowly, trying to work out which direction it was coming from, but it kept moving around in the wind. It was rare to see the enemy out on these roads, but then it was rare to see anyone at all. And there was no point lying down, trying to avoid being seen, because nobody would miss the Land Rover parked at the end of the track.

He was about to suggest they head back to the truck, but it was already too late. A black Toyota Hilux appeared around the bend to the south. For a second the sun reflected off its windscreen, stopping Bull seeing how many people were inside. If it was just one, they'd be okay. But as the truck turned down the slope towards them, he saw two figures in the cab and four more in the flatbed at the back.

He thought quickly, telling Cheshire, 'Get on the verge.'

'Eh?'

'Move to the side of the track. Now.'

They both stepped carefully on to the scruffy edge of the trail, *where the flattened earth of the makeshift road began to break up and become part of the field.*

Bull rested the detector against his hip, freeing up both hands, one for the radio, the other for his gun. 'Sierra three one to Charlie two one, come in.'

He released the button, dropping his arm to hide the handset, waiting for a response. But nothing came. Bad signal, out of range – who knew? He was about to try again when the Hilux turned across their position, allowing him to see that all the passengers were looking their way. The faces were Iraqi; now it was just a question of how friendly they were.

He held his breath as the vehicle got closer to the end of the track, willing it to move on. But the Hilux slowed and pulled on to the verge, next to their Land Rover. He watched the two guys in the cab check there was nobody in the other truck. Then the doors opened and all six men dropped on to the dusty ground between the vehicles. They all had guns.

'Fuck.' Cheshire said from behind.

'Yeah.' Bull didn't turn.

They both knew who they were facing, which meant this situation had just gone properly sour.

54

The expensive-looking Audi was wrecked.

Hawkins watched the bashed-up coupé emerge, as the truck driver yanked its fitted car-cover away. The reason for the owner's discretion became clearer still as the nearside flank was revealed. Hawkins read the word scrawled along the pale-silver panels of the dented passenger side, noting that, aside from the physical damage, writing 'MURDERER' along the side of this car would have taken a good few minutes. Admittedly, matching the handwriting was improbable, but they might still be able to identify the culprit.

She turned, checking the likely mounting points for cameras. Given any sense, a well-funded council like Clapham would have invested in CCTV, even on residential streets like this, especially so near the high street. They'd soon find out, anyway, because Hawkins had already requested continuous footage from every CCTV camera in a half-mile radius of each new potential target's home.

If the killer was watching any of them, hopefully he'd have been caught on film.

She finished her sweep, relieved to find an electronic eye watching her from the top of a lamp post further along the road. Beyond it, Amala Yasir was entering the far end of the street, returning from wherever she'd parked their car. Hawkins had jumped out when they'd arrived a few moments before, to save her having to walk. She hadn't expected Amala to take quite so long to find a space, but neither had she anticipated such theatre outside the house they were visiting.

Having discussed the latest developments with Simon Hunter, Hawkins had agreed their strongest chance of success seemed to be keeping an eye on potential future victims, the logic being that the killer probably spent time observing each target before making his move. He was also likely to repeat this pattern, so if they could identify a smaller group of probable marks and wait for his next attack, they might just get lucky.

Beside her, the driver attached his pulley system to the Audi's towing eye, and began winching the despoiled car on to the back of his low-loader, which was parked in the next space.

Hawkins looked up at the house, seeing a woman's face retreat into the shadows of the front room inside the window. Evidently, the owner was curious about the person standing outside her home, watching her vandalized car being removed, but not so eager to chat.

Amanda Cain, a senior doctor from the local NHS hospital, was on their newly extended list of possible targets. Of the original fifteen recently released murder or manslaughter convicts, six had killed arguably innocent victims, and of those, two were already in protective custody. That left four as yet unapproached potential targets, including Cain.

There had been no adjustments to the doctor's sentence for extenuating circumstances, so she hadn't been approached in the first wave, but now the team's focus had shifted on to killers of innocent victims, she was at the top. John Travis, the man Cain had killed just over a year before by prescribing drugs to which her patient had been allergic, was about as innocent as victims came.

Hawkins agreed with the court's judgement that the doctor hadn't intended to cause harm, although, judging by the state of her car, it looked as though the effects of the woman's mistake would continue haunting her for a while yet.

Aside from Cain, there were three other potential marks that hadn't been on the previous list. Mike had gone to see a man in Brixton who had just finished a stretch for mistakenly bottling an intervening bystander to death in a drunken pub brawl, and then he was due to visit the fitness coach who had pushed a client too far in training, causing a fatal heart attack.

Yet, somehow, Hawkins had managed to lumber herself with the worst call of the day. She definitely wasn't looking forward to her next appointment, with the woman who had attempted to kill herself, and her one-year-old child, in her car with a hose pipe through the window from the exhaust. The mother had been rescued just in time, after concerned relatives contacted the police, but it had been too late for the child's tiny lungs. Mum had been under suicide watch ever since.

But all four visits still qualified as groping in the proverbial dark. There were still big, unanswered questions.

Previously, Hawkins had assumed the perpetrator's information must have been limited to details of the victims' convictions, the addresses to which they'd been relocated and release dates, but now it seemed the Judge had links that allowed him to uncover the most arcane details of each victim's life – secrets that only a privileged few would have known. Apart from her best friend, the only people who had knowledge of Sam Philips' abortion were likely to be the medical professionals who arranged and carried it out. Okay, so it was difficult to say how many hospital staff might have had access to any record of the procedure, but if they could establish how the killer had known about Sam's abortion, as well as the address to which she had moved following her release, a pattern of sorts should become clear. The cross section of individuals with access to such information in *every* case, potentially via council or medical files, had to be smaller still. And once they had that list, a suspect just might emerge.

She knew Tanner, Todd and Sharpe were now working hard to establish every potential route by which supposedly classified information could leak from government departments into the public domain. Gaining access to their findings might involve a delay, but the stand-off couldn't continue long term; eventually, both teams would have to reveal all at some sort of conciliatory confab. But while there was still a possibility of progress on her part, Hawkins was prepared for the two factions to operate autonomously, because she had more to lose than her competition did. And the outcome of this case would define immediate futures on both sides.

The rivalry itself seemed to be escalating; a situation only intensified the previous afternoon by what Tanner undoubtedly saw as his victory in their most recent clash, when Hawkins had played the authority card before being forced into ignominious retreat. Humiliating as it was, however, the result might still work in her favour, because the boost to Tanner's already titanic confidence had led him to exclude himself, and his sub-team of Frank Todd and Aaron Sharpe, from that morning's eight-thirty brief. Ostensibly, they were chasing an important lead that required all three of them all day. Hawkins knew an attempt to avoid disclosing progress when she saw one, but she hadn't complained, because it meant she didn't have to reveal tactics of her own. Now, she just had to hope that, if their investigative paths crossed, she'd pass through first. And, if they didn't, that hers bore better results.

A loud scraping sound dragged her back to the present. She looked round to see the Audi's low rear bumper grinding along the tarmac as the damaged car was winched on to the ramp.

'Wow.' Yasir arrived beside her. 'Is this Amanda Cain's car?'

'Looks that way,' Hawkins said, checking the digits painted on the tarmac as the Audi was dragged fully out of its space. 'Number twenty-six.'

'Somebody's still upset with her, then,' Yasir said quietly. 'Who'd be a doctor these days?'

'I don't know.' Hawkins turned towards the house. 'Let's find out.'

Hawkins rang the bell again.

The house was well insulated, so the classic double chime from inside was distant. But this time she was certain she'd heard it ring. Just like before, though, there was no response.

She gave it another few seconds, turning to watch the truck driver crank another retaining strap into place around one of the Audi's front wheels.

Yasir stood beside her on the step, wringing her hands, shifting her weight from foot to foot. 'Maybe she's out.'

'Someone's here.' Hawkins told her about the face at the window.

Amala pointed to the letterbox. 'I could tell her who we are.'

Hawkins nodded. 'I suppose we should identify ourselves, though I don't suppose it'll help.'

The sergeant crouched, easing open the spring-loaded cover with upturned thumbs before calling through it into the property. 'Dr Cain? DS Amala Yasir, Metropolitan Police. Please answer the door.'

She looked up at Hawkins as they waited again, then glanced back to monitor the hallway for any sign of capitulation. But her eventual frown said there was none.

Yasir stood and shrugged. 'You were right, chief. What now?'

For a moment Hawkins said nothing, just stood watching the low-loader, engine running in the parking space at the bottom of the steps, the driver busily completing paperwork in his cab.

'Come with me.' She grabbed Amala's arm, ignoring her colleague's confused glances as she was ushered back on to the street. Hawkins turned them both right out of the gate and moved them off along the pavement. She waited until they reached a safe distance before glancing back, just in time to see the truck driver heading for Cain's house, forms in hand.

She stopped Amala, half using the sergeant for support as they turned back to face the house. They waited as the driver creaked his way slowly up the steps. He was the archetypal tow-truck cabbie, tall and thickset, wearing a scruffy white T-shirt and dungarees under a puffy winter coat. He reached the door, using his clipboard to scratch his chin through a healthy-looking beard as he ignored the bell and banged the heel of an oversized fist on the door. 'All loaded up, love.'

He stepped back, as Hawkins pictured the same

timid face at the window, checking to make sure her previous visitors had gone. She gave it a few seconds before easing Amala forward. 'Now.'

They began walking back towards the house, reaching the gate and turning left up the steps. The truck driver looked around as they approached, giving a bemused nod when Hawkins stopped Yasir in line with him, two steps from the top.

Hawkins smiled, and the three of them stood in silence until a shadow arrived on the opposite side of the glass, before a lock was released and the door swung inwards.

In the gap stood Amanda Cain.

55

The eight men waited twenty yards apart, watching each other across the plain.

Six Iraqi insurgents facing two British soldiers, the wind swirling between them, blowing dust into their eyes. Everyone was armed, but no one had raised a weapon yet and, for a moment, nobody moved.

Bull knew they were in trouble. Their SA80 weapons were superior to the AK47s carried by the insurgents, more powerful and a lot more accurate, but it was six against two, and where the Iraqis had the trucks for cover, he and Cheshire were in the middle of a field, exposed. If they stood their ground, they'd make easy meat.

At last one of the insurgents stepped forward, showing himself to be in command. He pointed at his weapon, then at the floor, telling them to drop their rifles. Slowly they lowered their guns. The leader nodded, raising a hand and waving for him and the kid to go over.

Bull heard Cheshire's boots grind the dirt. He raised a hand. 'Don't move.'

'What?'

'We'd be fucking crazy to go over there.'

'No crazier than if we run. We'll get shot to shit.'

'Shut up, man. Let me think.'

Cheshire might have been right. If they surrendered, there was a small chance they'd survive; there had been a few reports of the enemy taking more hostages recently, rather than leaving soldiers' bodies lying around to demoralize the troops. But Bull didn't like those odds.

So what the fuck were they going to do?

Bull was in charge, so it was his call. He'd bought time by moving them both on to the verge; that's why the insurgents hadn't followed them along the track. They could see from the detectors that the soldiers had been sweeping for mines, but it wasn't obvious from where they were standing which parts of the trail they'd checked, or if they'd already found a device somewhere between the two groups. Which was why the Iraqis wanted him and Cheshire to go to them.

Plus, the insurgents' guns were inaccurate at this range. They were designed to spray bullets all over, to pin an enemy down. At twenty yards they could miss a building.

Which gave them a fighting chance.

'Listen up.' Bull spoke quietly over his shoulder. 'When I say, turn and run like hell for the far end of this track.'

'You sure, man? That's twenty-five yards, uphill.'

'We go over there we're dead, so we might as well run. They won't come after us.'

The kid blew out his cheeks. 'Okay.'

'When we go, drop your detector but take your rifle.' Bull waved at the insurgent who had stepped forward, as if they were about to head over. 'Ready . . .' He took a breath, felt the adrenalin kick in.

'Now!'

He reached out, grabbing the shoulder strap of his gun, dumping his detector, hearing Cheshire's feet grinding the dirt as he took off. The Iraqi shout went up as they turned and sprinted away, and a second later the first shot cracked the air.

'Run!' he shouted at the kid, who was already a few yards ahead, as the bullets began hitting the track around them, tiny thuds going off as they slammed into the soil.

He kept going, skidding on the loose surface, not daring to look round.

Then he felt the punch on the back of his thigh, so hard that it took the leg out from under him. He stuck his hands out, but as he fell there was a flash. Suddenly, he was on his back, ears ringing, vision blurred.

And all he heard before passing out was the patter of dirt landing all around.

56

Hawkins watched the low-loader pull out of the parking space and edge off down the congested street, carrying the mangled Audi like wounded offspring. She turned back from the window to find their host staring at her from the far side of the room.

A decade ago, such behaviour might have unsettled Hawkins, but these days she'd seen it too many times. Prison had a way of changing anyone who spent a while inside, the pressurized environment driving inmates towards the extremes of confrontation or retreat, often without them being aware. Back in the fluffy outside world, ex-cons often ended up fearlessly aggressive or .eternally scared.

She decided Cain was in the former camp. The doctor was in her mid-forties, a few inches shorter than Hawkins, attractive despite the apparent lack of make-up or sleep. She wore a dressing gown and her hair was pulled back in a frayed ponytail.

Cain hadn't paid even lip-service to hospitality, for them or the truck driver, since appearing at the door. She'd signed the driver's collection form and offered scant thanks, before turning to the people waiting behind him, addressing them in a tone the detached side of stern.

You'd better come in.

She'd shown them into a large front room with high ceilings and tasteful decor. Yet there was an oddly vacant feel to the place, despite the well-coordinated furniture. The house was tidy, almost spookily so, possibly because there had been no one around to mess it up, but it was also unnervingly clean. Hawkins guessed at an overzealous housekeeper, because Cain herself wasn't much of a host.

Amala nervously occupied the single armchair at an angle to a large, empty sofa. She was also first to break the silence.

'The Audi,' she asked Cain, 'is it owned or hired?'

Their host turned to look at her. 'Neither any more.'

'But it was . . .' The tremor in Amala's voice might not have been detectable to Cain, but it told Hawkins she now regretted her attempt at small talk.

Cain sighed. ' . . . owned.'

Amala looked as if she was trying not to wince. 'It's insured, though?'

Cain ignored her, re-engaging with Hawkins instead. 'Why are you here?'

'We'll come to that,' she said lightly. 'Staying with the car for a moment, do you have any idea who might have vandalized it?'

The doctor paused. 'You look like an intelligent

woman, Detective, so I'll assume you're familiar with my past. Notoriety means that people don't need to know me to wish me ill.'

'What about John Travis' family?' Hawkins kept her tone approachable but firm, carefully watching Cain's response.

A flicker that could have been a painful memory ghosted across the woman's expression. 'What about them?'

'Have they contacted you since the court case?'

'No.'

'You understand we have to ask,' Hawkins said. 'We'll be speaking to them about the car.'

Cain nodded.

There was a pause, into which Amala jumped as if to avenge her previous rebuff. 'Is there anyone else who might have had reason to damage your vehicle?'

'Like I said,' Cain answered flatly, 'the court case made everything public in the most damaging way. There are plenty of strangers out there who hate me, although it all becomes normal remarkably fast.' She shrugged. 'What's another death threat when you've already had three?'

Hawkins eyed her. 'Since the accident, have you been physically attacked, either in prison or outside?'

'No.' Cain's expression clouded again, her eyes bouncing suspiciously between her two visitors.

'And have you left the house after dark in the four nights since you've been home?'

Another pause. 'No. Your colleagues were pretty indifferent about my case at the time; why the sudden interest?'

'The situation has changed,' Hawkins acknowledged. 'I take it you haven't seen the news since leaving prison.'

The doctor frowned; shook her head.

'Okay.' Hawkins phrased her next statements with care. 'We're investigating a string of murders, all apparently by the same killer. We believe he's targeting newly released convicts, specifically those who caused the deaths of *innocent* victims, a category into which you undoubtedly fall.'

Amanda Cain didn't react straight away but, after a few seconds, she sat down on the arm of the sofa, her gaze drifting down towards the floor. 'And you think –'

'It's possible,' Hawkins conceded. 'The papers are calling him the Judge.'

Their host continued to stare at her feet, blinking as if trying to wake herself from a daze. Her voice was quiet when she asked, 'How many?'

'Three so far, all within weeks of release. The first attack was four months ago; the most recent in the last few days.'

'What happened to them?' Cain whispered, her breath catching. 'Actually, I don't want to know.' She stared into space for a moment longer before looking up, suddenly with steel in her eyes. 'What are you proposing?'

'We can place you in protective custody, at a safe house not far from here. Just until the killer is caught.'

Cain recoiled. 'I don't want . . .' She paused, breathing harder now. 'I'm not leaving.'

'Fair enough.' Hawkins had expected some resistance. It was understandable, considering where this previously respectable woman had spent the last nine months. She met her halfway. 'At least let us provide you some protection here.'

There was an almost imperceptible shake of the head. 'I won't have people in my house.'

'I think you should consider it,' Hawkins urged. 'A safety net, just in case. You won't even know they're here.'

'You're right,' the doctor stood, emotion flaring in her voice for the first time, 'because they *won't* be.'

There was a moment's silence, as Hawkins hoped their subject would change her mind. She'd seen this reaction in recently released prisoners before. In newly granted liberty, privacy often became paramount, although if anything might challenge that it was the threat of death.

But no retraction came.

Hawkins took a step forwards. 'Look, I know the last few days have been hard. Leaving prison is traumatic in itself, but returning home to find your property damaged, that others reject your right to freedom . . . well, I can understand why you didn't want to answer the door.'

Cain looked confused.

'I'm just saying,' Hawkins made to clarify, 'it's natural to be scared.'

The doctor shook her head, tears forming. 'I just got out of one cage, Detective. I don't intend to let you turn my home into another.' She raised a hand towards the front door. 'Please leave.'

Hawkins followed Yasir down the steps, turning to watch Amanda Cain's front door close behind them with a bang. She told Amala to wait as they arrived on the pavement, hoping the doctor might change her mind about their offer of in-home protection. But the door stayed shut.

It wasn't really a surprise. Hawkins was glad she'd taken the opportunity on the way out to suggest that Cain keep an eye on the news for updates about whether the Judge had been detained. And that, until it happened, she didn't leave the house after dark.

At least Cain had agreed to that.

They began walking back towards the car, in silence. Hawkins glanced up at the front window as they passed, but no face was visible this time.

Amala's comment didn't help. 'That didn't go so well.'

'I can see her point, if I'm honest. But . . .' She stopped and turned to face the way they had just come.

'Ma'am?'

Hawkins didn't answer straight away. She stood,

scanning the street. The road was lined on both sides by parked cars, despite it being well after 10 a.m. Some were in designated spaces; the overspill lined the pavement on the opposite side, reducing the entire street to a single lane. Other cars threaded their way back and forth, diving into gaps to let one another pass.

She looked at the DS. 'Do you think this road is always so busy?'

'I suppose so.' Amala studied the melee. 'We are in the middle of London.'

'Good.' Hawkins went with her instinct. 'Organize some round-the-clock surveillance on the good doctor's house, will you? One car out here to cover the front, another in the next street watching the back. I'll authorize overtime if needs be.'

'Unmarked?'

'Definitely. With instructions to notify me if Cain leaves the house after dark, and to be close enough to step in if she gets a visit from anyone that could be you-know-who.'

'And if she leaves, you want her followed?'

'Yes. It's our job to protect her, whether she appreciates it or not.'

'Are you sure, ma'am? She was pretty clear about not wanting us around.'

'Exactly,' Hawkins replied. 'Which is why we aren't going to tell her they're here.'

57

He woke with a start.

Brightness. Heat. Dry air.

He lay for a moment . . . Where was he?

Then the agony arrived.

The pain in his leg was fierce, ripping through him like barbed wire grating on the bone. He tried to sit up, check his wounds. But his body wasn't working, and he slumped back against the lumpy ground, turning his head to the side.

The truck was about fifty yards away on the dirt-track road.

Nobody near it.

The land around him was open and flat, the road they'd come in on snaking away towards some low hills far in the distance. He could feel shrapnel in his neck.

But his mind was blank.

He turned to look the other way, but the wind blew sand in his eyes. He screwed them shut, bringing his fists up to rub the grit away.

Where the fuck was he, and how long had he been lying here?

It was afternoon; he could tell that much, at least. The sun was beating down, the skin on his face cracked and dry.

Then it came back to him.

Cheshire.

'Jim?' he screamed. 'You there, man?'

He waited, breathing hard, hearing nothing except tiny bits of dirt rolling around in the wind.

But he knew no answer would come.

58

Hawkins leaned back, pinching the bridge of her nose, blinking to relieve the strain of looking at a computer screen from close range for too long. She couldn't remember when she'd last been for an eye test. Perhaps it was time to get herself checked.

She looked up at her office ceiling. Polystyrene tiles filled square holes in the latticework of supports, clean apart from those that housed smoke detectors or sprinkler heads and were therefore more awkward to change. She tutted.

She also noted there were a couple of dead strip bulbs, which probably wasn't helping her eyes, especially now daylight was gone. She glanced at the clock, surprised to find she'd been in front of her laptop for an hour and a half. More depressing was the fact that she'd completed less than a third of her task.

She leaned forwards and switched on the lamp, lighting her desk. Beside her, the e-fit of the man seen following Matthew Hayes sat beside two KitKat wrappers and three empty vending-machine cups. In the centre, her laptop showed paused images from four of the ten CCTV cameras nearest to Amanda Cain's home. The footage from the different sites ran in parallel, synchronized to give an overview of the scene.

But the set-up was hardly ideal. First, the only camera situated within the doctor's road was mounted at the far end of the street, putting Cain's house sixty yards from the lens. Plus, the technology wasn't exactly cutting edge. The low-res black-and-white images refreshed themselves once every second, so the action jerked along cartoon-style, making it difficult to follow a specific person, especially when you were watching at twice normal speed. It was also tricky to scan multiple images at once, but with so much footage to check it was the only logical way. At least the software helped, picking out pedestrians by highlighting each with a coloured box.

So far, Hawkins had watched all that was available of Monday, on the four cameras nearest the doctor's home, from midnight just gone till the file had been saved at four o'clock that afternoon. She'd watched a few pedestrians meander this way and that during the night, seen herself and Amala visit at around 10 a.m. and sat through the mid-afternoon school run, as parents shepherded kids back and forth on the pavements while their SUV-owning compatriots clogged the roads. But none had yet resembled their man.

The other annoying factor was that none of the cameras in Cain's vicinity offered sufficient resolution for number plates to be read. From this footage it was difficult even to determine the make of each car. As a result, Hawkins was hoping their killer would turn up on foot, or at least leave whichever vehicle he had used.

Last time she'd checked, the rest of her team weren't having much better luck. She had a contingent of four in the media suite, all watching similar tapes, with a night shift primed to take over at ten. But even then there was too much work to get the job done by morning, so the task would run into the next day. Everyone needed to be sharp, because even a fleeting glimpse of the killer was potentially vital, so they couldn't afford to overlook a thing. Progress was necessarily slow.

Only one of the four new potential targets' homes had no CCTV within a quarter-mile, the radius Hawkins had set for initial scrutiny. The guy from the pub brawl lived in a run-down part of Brixton where the council had given up repairing cameras that were vandalized again within days. But the other three homes were covered by between six and fourteen cameras each, and the parolees in question had been out of prison for up to three weeks. That meant hundreds of hours' worth of footage, all of which had to be carefully scrutinized for the slightest glimpse of the Judge.

As soon as each CCTV record had become available earlier in the day, it had been scanned by video content analysis software, which carried out a high-speed check for any movement indicating violence or unusual activity. Unfortunately, the only incident it picked up was Amanda Cain's car being vandalized on Wednesday night – hours before she returned home for the first time in nine months. The two perpetrators weren't identifiable from the low-res footage, but they bore a striking resemblance to John Travis' two teenage kids. Hawkins had already despatched someone to question the pair.

The fact that nothing else had been found left them no choice but to carry out a painstaking manual search in case anyone of note had wandered into shot, their presence insufficient to trigger the VCA software's alarms, but enough for the human eye.

Okay, so it was a long shot, but it was worth a go. Hawkins' hope was that, if they *had* accurately identified the killer's target demographic, it wasn't beyond the realms of possibility for him to be watching any one of these four already. All they needed was for him to appear on one of the cameras. Then it would be a case of setting a trap, maybe getting the target involved to draw him out, and picking him up before he killed again.

She'd allocated two detectives to analyse each set of available footage, having coerced Amala and Mike into staying late, along with two DCs unlucky enough to have been around at the time. Those four officers currently occupied the entire row of large-screen PCs in the media suite, leaving Hawkins on her laptop as the fifth pair of eyes.

She and Amala had the cameras outside Amanda Cain's home, purely because they'd both been there, which made it easier to decode what was going on in the grainy images. Amala had started with the Wednesday night before Cain's release, while Hawkins was working her way back from today. But they were behind, mainly because Lambeth Council had been slowest in sending over their CCTV footage. The digital copies had finally arrived on the Becke House server just after 7 p.m., which at least meant somebody at the council offices had breached office hours to pull out footage from the relevant dates.

Relaying her method to the others, she and Amala had started with the four cameras closest to Cain's home, covering each day since the doctor's release. If nothing showed up, they'd move on to the next nearest set of cameras for the same period, the theory being that the killer would likely avoid the cameras in the immediate vicinity of each target but perhaps be less wary in surrounding roads. Therefore, the odds of finding their man were pretty well balanced. Statistically, he was more likely to be present near each home, but with a higher probability of being caught on camera the further out they looked.

So far, though, everyone had drawn a blank. It seemed the killer, if he *was* watching any of the newly identified four, was adept at keeping himself out of shot.

Hawkins looked at the printed list of ten cameras supplied by Lambeth Council, reassessing her task. It had taken her ninety minutes to check sixteen hours' worth of images from four cameras. Assuming that she and Amala made similar progress, accounting for breaks and fatigue, checking these ten cameras over almost six days would take the two of them the rest of the night. The next shift weren't due in for another ninety minutes, and considering there was plenty more footage to check from other locations, the dilemma would then be whether the current team stayed on to help. She sighed; it was going to be a long night.

She settled down for another session at the laptop, clicking Sunday's file. After a few seconds the software organized itself and the same four camera angles appeared, except that each scene was back in darkness, the time signature showing midnight had just passed. Activity was minimal, and Hawkins tried to focus on the mostly deserted pavements as cars passed through the images at varying rates, their headlights creating patches of washed-out whiteness in the gloom. Three of the cameras were positioned close together, one on Amanda Cain's street itself and two out on the main road, which allowed Hawkins to track most vehicles from one scene to the next as they moved down the high street and either kept going or turned to pass along Cain's street. The fourth camera was in one of the roads away from the main thoroughfare, although the far end of the doctor's street was visible in the back of the shot.

At one point Hawkins caught her eyes starting to close, just as a red box popped up in Cain's road. She shook herself awake, staring at the screen, waiting for the figure to move further into view. The person was male, just stocky enough to fit the witness description, coming towards the camera from the far end of the street. The camera in the adjoining road hadn't picked him up, but as she watched the figure jolting along, daring to let her hopes climb, she saw he was being followed by four others, emerging from the shadows behind. Her excitement stalled as she watched the men gather outside another house a few doors along from Cain's before filing inside.

She renewed her concentration and pressed on. What remained of the darkness passed without further event, and within moments daylight broke across her screen, headlights clicking off on some of the cars as they jerked by, flows of foot and road traffic picking up as morning arrived. Intermittently, residents began leaving the various houses in Cain's street, getting into cars and driving away. Pedestrians started passing the house. Hawkins followed them all, blinking back tiredness, reminding herself to be thankful that, despite the cold, the weather had been dry throughout. Her task would have been almost impossible had everyone been hidden beneath umbrellas or hoods.

But still there was no sign of the Judge.

Ten minutes later, Hawkins paused the footage again and leaned back in her chair to stretch, just as someone knocked from outside.

Mike pushed the door open and leaned in. 'There you are, you big fibber.'

Hawkins stopped mid-yawn. 'What?'

'You said you were coming to join us. An hour ago.'

'Sorry, got caught up.' She clicked to restart the film. 'Anyway, don't distract me, I'm concentrating.'

Mike stepped inside. 'Why don't you bring the laptop upstairs and sit with the rest of us?'

'In the media suite?' she mocked. 'We'd be like sardines.'

She maintained her smile but, silently, Hawkins was kicking herself. She'd intended to contact the others by now, get an update, if nothing else, even though she'd already have heard if someone had spotted their man. But the continued absence of Tanner and his two musketeers would become obvious to the others pretty soon, and she didn't want to be answering awkward questions she didn't have to. Plus, space to think was becoming increasingly valuable, especially because she still hadn't decided how to handle the ever-widening rift in her team.

Mike laughed. 'We'll budge up. Come on, we're ordering pizza.'

'I've eaten.'

'You mean *those*?' He was obviously referring to the chocolate wrappers, although she didn't look up to check. 'That's it. Dead or alive, you're coming with me.'

'I'm fine.'

'You might be *fine*.' He moved nearer. 'But if you don't eat, your concentration won't be worth a damn.

You're already finding it hard to focus. Tell me I'm wrong.'

'Bloody hell.' She kept her eyes on the screen. 'Order me a Full House, then. I'll eat it in here.'

Mike joined her at the desk, knocking her hand off the track pad. He paused the footage and gave her a stern look. 'Okay, what's with the solitude? Did someone upset you, or do you have embarrassing wind?'

She smiled, immediately restarting the film. 'Piss off.'

'Is this about our fight?'

'No.' She glanced at him. 'I thought we sorted that out.'

'We did. So it's Tanner, then?'

Hawkins hesitated, taking just too long to muster a denial.

Mike sat on the corner of the desk. 'What's he done now?'

'Apart from using this case solely to advance his career? Nothing. We just . . . don't get on. It's a personality thing.'

'Yours or his?'

She ignored him, kept her eyes on the screen, willing him not to inquire why Tanner, Sharpe and Todd hadn't been around for the past twenty-four hours. Fortunately, he didn't.

In Clapham on screen, it was already mid-Sunday afternoon; people and cars jolting away. She watched vehicles to and fro past Amanda Cain's door, queuing either end of the street as opposing streams of 4x4s jostled in the overloaded road, black-and-white brake lights flickering as they negotiated the T-junction in the distance.

Mike mumbled something about being invisible.

'Shhh,' Hawkins urged, shifting forward in her chair, clicking to rewind the film.

She tapped the screen. 'Look at this.'

Mike moved in next to her, suddenly alert, recognizing that her focus had changed.

Hawkins restarted the footage, running it slowly this time, watching again as the dark saloon edged on to the bottom of the screen and approached the line of other cars waiting at the far end of the street. It joined the back of the queue, and again Hawkins' recall sparked.

'Gonna need a clue over here,' Maguire said.

She murmured. 'Only one brake light.'

'What's that, some kind of British omen? Are we due a sunny day?'

She ignored him. 'What type of car is that?'

'Oh yeah, ask a Yank.' Mike turned the laptop towards him and squinted at the image. 'All these damned Euro-boxes look the same.' He moved closer. 'Zoom in.'

She did, rewinding until the car was front of shot, before accessing the software's menu to make it fill the screen, still frustrated that the resolution was too low to read the number plate.

Mike considered it, rubbing his chin. 'Looks like . . . an old Vectra. Why?'

Hawkins realized that her discovery still wasn't obvious to Maguire, and turned to face him. 'I've seen it before.'

He frowned. 'Where?'

'CCTV. Outside the home of one of the other victims. If I can just remember . . .'

She drew the laptop towards her, minimizing the current screen. Then she accessed the server, clicking through various files until she found the records from the scenes of the previous murders. Instinct said Calano.

Hawkins opened one of the files, skipping through the footage as fast as she dared. The film had already been assessed, of course, but not in the context they now had.

The camera angle was high, showing part of the main road in Enfield adjacent to the street where Calano had lived. The area wasn't in the same social bracket as Clapham, so this was the nearest camera to the victim's home, but it had been installed more recently, so its image was better, both colour and higher res. Hawkins tempered her positivity; she could still be wrong.

Traffic was predictably heavier on this thoroughfare than on Cain's smaller, shorter street. Pedestrians and vehicles pinged through the image in both directions. The sheer volume of movement made it hard to follow everything, but Hawkins was interested only in cars that took a specific route: the left turn, mid-shot, into Calano's road. She and Maguire viewed the whole file.

She tried another, fast forwarding again, watching night-time turn quickly to day. Mike stayed beside her, his hand on the back of her neck, comfortable and warm. Still nothing.

Hawkins was about to curse her memory when it delivered.

Time on screen passed 3 p.m., as a dark saloon entered from the lower right corner, jumped to the centre of the screen and disappeared. But Hawkins' senses had already fired. She hit pause, wound the footage back to bring it into view and, at quarter speed, played the sequence again.

They both leaned in, watched the vehicle approaching the turn.

'Vectra?' she asked.

'Yeah.'

The car came within yards of its turn, the point it needed to slow. For a nasty second Hawkins thought she'd made a mistake; perhaps it had no lights at all. But then the driver braked, and Hawkins let herself grin.

Only one brake light.

'There.' She paused the file, turning triumphantly to Maguire. 'This car was present at two scenes of interest, including the street of one of the victims within days of her death. I'm guessing that's our killer. He needs to get a feel for the area around each target's home without being caught on camera wandering about. So he drives casually by during daylight when it's busy, using what would normally be an inconspicuous vehicle, obviously unaware of his faulty light.'

Mike shook his head. 'How in *hell* did you remember that car?'

She smiled. 'Well, partly because I'm a great detective, but mostly because I'm a woman. In case you hadn't noticed, we memorize small details that aren't necessarily important at the time. So I can tell you where I've seen cars with broken tail lights and list every time you've been wrong since we met.'

'Impressive. If only we could teach you to cook.'

Hawkins punched him playfully, but her mood stayed high as she turned back to the screen.

Because every character on the Vectra's number plate was clear.

59

Bull felt the jolt as the brakes released, then there were grinding sounds as the huge aircraft moved. He couldn't tell how fast, because there were no windows, so he just sat in the dim light, trying to ignore the smell of burnt rubber and aviation fuel. The whole cabin reminded him of the mechanic's workshop back at base, the place he'd never see again, which had just started feeling like home.

The plane rolled on, heavy equipment clanking whenever they went over a bump. Bull flinched as lightning stabbed at the bullet wound in his thigh. The pain didn't bother him; he could block out the physical stuff. What made him wince were the images the pain brought back. The two of them running, the gunshots, the road. The blast that ended it all.

Get a grip.

Bull threw the thoughts out. He wasn't ready to deal with that shit. Not yet.

In a couple of days he'd be home, away from this hell. At first he hadn't wanted to leave, thinking the pain would fade. No one had forced the kid to sign up; war was a dangerous place. But a week later, after the nightmares and cold sweats, home became Bull's only hope. He'd never get Cheshire's face out of his mind here, where they'd worked together, become friends. But if he went somewhere from before they'd known each other, perhaps he could forget.

For now, he just had to hold on.

He was already booked in with some sort of head doctor. They said it might be post-traumatic stress, that he needed checking out.

But he wasn't the only one. Beside him on the flip-down seats that ran along one side of the hull were other soldiers; all hitching on the FUBAR express.

Nobody talked.

He glanced at the faces around him in the dark. He didn't know any of them; they were from other units. Some were injured; some dishonourably discharged; others messed up in the head. A lot, like Bull, would have more than one sick note. But everyone wore the same empty look.

The boys said he was lucky: one of the guys who survived. But that depended on whether breathing in and out meant you had a life worth saving. What about the memories you couldn't hand back? No one warned you on the way out how hard any of that was going to be. You learned that shit for yourself.

That's why most of the soldiers killed were just kids, teenagers who thought it was a big fucking game. Some expected to get hurt, but none of them knew what it would do to their heads. And to cap it all, as soon as you were too messed up to fight, they loaded you into a big catapult and fired you home.

See ya.

The flight would take fifteen hours, then they could all head back to whatever they'd left behind and try to make it work again. None of those lives could have been that fucking great, or they wouldn't have left in the first place. But, however bad they'd been, they weren't going to be any better now.

There was another jolt as the aircraft stopped and the cargo nets swayed. Then the strip lights dimmed and the roar from the engines built. They'd soon be in the air.

Bull held on to his pack. Inside was the deck of cards he and Cheshire used to play Blackjack on slow afternoons at the base; his only reminder of the nearest thing he had to a brother.

Outside, the scream from the jets went up and the plane began to roll. His leg ached like hell. He'd refused drugs for the pain, even though the bullet had shattered the bone. He wanted to feel his wounds.

Parts of his shins were missing and there was shrapnel in his neck and thighs. If not for the body armour, he wouldn't have lived.

Just like the kid.

Suddenly, he was back on the dirt track, telling Cheshire to run. He'd known at the time how risky it was, sprinting across land that was probably mined. But there had been no better option, so he'd taken a shot at saving them both.

The kid had been his best friend, at home or in Iraq. All he could see when he closed his eyes was that stupid grin. Over the months, they'd laughed together, kept each other sane, saved each other's lives. But not this time.

The kid had stepped full bore on a mine: a big one, although perhaps that was for the best. There was nothing left of him when the other soldiers came back to find Bull on his back in the dirt, an hour from bleeding out.

The kid had taken the full force of the blast, partly protecting

Bull, who had been far enough behind that his injuries weren't fatal. The insurgents must have decided it wasn't worth risking their lives crossing a minefield to make sure Bull was dead.

That had been ten days ago.

Since then he'd been in the field hospital, being assessed twice a day. He thought he was doing all right, until his section commander came to tell him they were sending him home.

Within hours he was packed and ready to fly, even though it made no difference to the question still going round and round in his head.

Was he to blame?

For the death of an innocent man.

60

Headlights entered the terraced street from the south end, scything through the darkness, dipped beams highlighting patches of the rain that continued to fall in delicate sheets.

Hawkins watched them approach in the wing mirror of their unmarked Volkswagen Golf, trying to work out whether they belonged to a Vectra. Seconds later, light from the vehicle's headlamps crept through their car, flicking watery shadows left to right across the dashboard. Hawkins and Yasir sank low in their seats, watching it pass.

It wasn't their man.

They both straightened as the car, a red Citroën, eased into a space further along the road, from where the driver unloaded two kids and herded them into one of the houses. Darkness returned to the poorly lit street, drawing in like evil closing them down.

'Everyone relax,' Hawkins said into her Airwave handset. 'It isn't him.'

The speaker buzzed. 'Roger. Standing by.'

The voice was Maguire's. Along with Aaron Sharpe, whom Hawkins had bumped into at Becke House and managed to segregate from Tanner's herd, he occupied an equally inconspicuous Ford Focus parked in the next road over, in case their suspect chose to cut between the houses and enter through his own back yard. Granted it was unlikely, but she wanted all the angles covered. Mike's reply was followed by an acknowledgement from the other members of their impromptu squad.

'Understood.' That was DI Pete Bishop, in command of a team from SCO19, the Met's armed-response unit. The four firearms officers were in the black BMW X5 parked diagonally opposite, also unmarked.

They'd arrived half an hour ago, just as daylight had gone, after Mike's phone call to the DVLA had confirmed that the Vauxhall Vectra with the broken brake light was registered to this address. If Hawkins' theory about its owner being the killer was correct, the case might be closed before bedtime, with the Judge behind bars, various parolees out of danger, and Hawkins' reputation restored.

She also knew better than to count on any of that, at least until the last few elements dropped into place, especially considering recent news from enemy camp. She'd managed to isolate Aaron Sharpe and enlist him in their hopeful acquisition of a suspect, but Steve Tanner and Frank Todd were still making determined headway of their own. When pressed, Sharpe revealed that Tanner had hauled in another member of the family of Amanda Cain's victim for questioning. Apparently an in-law on John Travis' father's side, the woman now being interrogated by the rogue DI tag-team worked as a GP's assistant in Ealing. Her job warranted subsidiary access to classified information on the medical records, release dates and forwarding addresses of just about every high-stakes prisoner in London.

The theory was obviously that, whereas families afflicted by loss through the negligence of others often ended up campaigning peacefully to prevent such a thing happening again, the Travis dynasty may have taken the more direct preventive approach. According to Simon Hunter, it was plausible that a family racked by grief would find it hard to wait nine months in order to exact their own style of justice on a relative's killer. So it was also possible that the interim period might be utilized to 'help' others in similar situations, almost certainly uninvited to do so, effectively staying their hunger for reprisal in the round. In effect, Calano, Philips and Hayes became precursors to the main event, when Cain would pay for her past indiscretion with her life.

Unlike Hawkins' contender, the fifty-year-old woman wasn't a direct suspect, but at least Tanner had been able to *find* her. In contrast, it could conceivably take days' worth of resource-hungry chasing around the country for Hawkins to apprehend her target, after which he could still be unconnected to the case, perhaps proving to be no more than a delivery driver unlucky enough to pass the homes of two of the victims in recent days. Such diversion would give Tanner scope to investigate at will, potentially delivering the killer while she wasted precious man hours on an extensive but ultimately wild-goose chase. If that happened, he and Hawkins were likely to swap ranks pretty fast.

She quickly reassured herself she could also be right. Though a clue either way would have been welcome hours ago.

Since the police team's arrival, filtering into the road one vehicle at a time with five-minute gaps to avoid announcing their affiliation, there had been no sign of the Vectra. It wasn't parked anywhere in this road or those bordering it; Mike had driven round to check. Neither had it passed through this street.

It was still possible the owner had parked elsewhere, or that someone else was using the car. They had already logged it with the number-plate-recognition network, which would flag the vehicle at any of their cameras if it passed. Neither had it been reported stolen, although it might have been borrowed or sold in recent weeks. But the fastest way to answer any of those questions was to ask the person who lived at number thirty-nine.

Except that, for now at least, it looked like there was nobody home. The shabby terraced house slumped between two better kept residences, as if it might collapse without their support. Paint peeled from the window frames, mucky glass betraying no signs of life from inside. That, and the absence of the only vehicle registered to the address, had prompted Hawkins' decision to wait. The only risk involved was that the longer they paused, the more opportunity they gave the killer to strike again. But all the potential targets were under observation, whether they knew it or not, and all the previous attacks had been well after midnight, which gave them a good few hours to play with yet.

She had opted not to approach the property. Apart from the fact that the place looked deserted, and considering their target's potential for violent behaviour, it would be wise to take at least one armed officer with them if and when they went to the door. But that also meant revealing their intentions to anyone who happened to be watching. Should their suspect be elsewhere, it only took one of the neighbours to tip him off and the element of surprise might conceivably be turned into a head start for a fleeing killer – even though, if he had a mobile phone, it wasn't registered via contract to this address. So, for now, it made sense to wait.

Hawkins turned her attention back to the file in her lap, switching on the small reading light clipped to the top of the folder, reacquainting herself with the face of the man she hoped would soon be identified as the Judge.

A young, angular face stared back at her from the page. Marlon Wells had blue eyes, a shaved head and a thick neck suggesting a build stocky enough to agree with his modest height and generous weight statistics. The file wasn't a criminal record, because Wells had never been arrested or charged with an offence, but enough of his history was available to give Hawkins hope that he was their man.

Responding to Mike's inquiry earlier in the day, the DVLA said they had no record of Wells' current occupation, although he'd registered the Vectra as 'off the road' for an apparent tour of duty in late 2006. That information led them straight to the national archives, where twenty-nine-year-old Wells was registered as an ex-army lance corporal who had returned from his second stint in Iraq in 2007. They were still waiting for the Ministry of Defence to provide information on the classified parts of Wells' file, such as why he'd been released from his contract twelve months early, and what he'd been doing since then. But Wells' appearance, which fitted the description of the man seen following Matt Hayes, the combat training he would have received in the forces, plus the fact his car had recently been at two separate addresses pertinent to the case, were enough for them to legally question him, at least.

Her thoughts were interrupted by a delicate groan from the driver's seat. She looked across to see Amala staring down at her mobile.

'Trouble in paradise?' she asked without thinking, rebuking herself for opening a conversation her colleague probably wouldn't welcome, as well as subject matter that could potentially distract them both.

'Not really,' Yasir replied, although the pursed lips through which her answer came suggested otherwise. 'It's probably my imagination playing tricks.'

Hawkins felt a pang of concern. It was unusual for

Amala to express anxiety about anything private at all, let alone the intimacies of her relationship. Things must be serious. But she'd already shown too much interest simply to withdraw.

She spoke softly. 'Try me. I'm better with advice than people think.'

There were a few seconds of silence before Amala drew a long breath. 'It's Christian.'

'Go on.' Hawkins watched in the wing mirror as two cars skimmed past the end of the road before turning back to her sergeant.

'He's fed up with the hours I work, says he never sees me. He has a point, obviously; you know what it's been like since November. I've tried spending more time with him, but he's never been one to wait around. He just texted to say he's out with friends, ones he never used to see that much, which is fine, but now I'm petrified there's somebody else.'

'I see.' Hawkins tried to picture Yasir's boyfriend, whom she'd met only once at a drinks evening organized for the whole of Becke House by an exiting chief constable. As far as she remembered, Christian was good-looking and fit, courtesy of his job as a martial arts instructor. But he was also self-assured and had flirted too forcefully for Hawkins' liking throughout their brief chat.

She watched another car enter the road ahead, failing to conjure consolatory words. All she managed as the old Mercedes passed was, 'I'm sure he appreciates you.'

But her thoughts were already focused elsewhere. Something about Christian's latent infidelity offered fresh perspective on their current situation, changing her mind. Murder represented the ultimate compulsion, and those who succeeded in perpetrating it repeatedly had to be both resourceful and cold. Ruthless efficiency was a prerequisite, which mostly led murderers to kill as soon as circumstances allowed.

Which meant Hawkins' improvised team weren't biding their time here; they were wasting it.

Every minute they spent outside Wells' house was one he could be using to line up future prey. And if there was evidence inside that could help to track him down, it was her duty to find it and put it to use.

'Sorry, Amala.' She reached for the Airwave handset. 'Can we finish this chat another day?' She caught Yasir's questioning glance, adding:

'We're going in.'

61

Hawkins eased the car door closed, scanning the windows of the houses around her for curtains being disturbed. Seeing no sign that she was being watched, she turned and casually began crossing the street, thankful that the poor light from widely spaced streetlamps helped to mask her approach.

She glanced back, catching sight of Yasir in the driver's seat of their unmarked Volkswagen, where she'd been instructed to wait. Whether their target was home or not, Hawkins wanted to keep their arrival discreet, thereby minimizing the potential of anyone nursing sympathy for the local murderer to warn Wells. Their first wave comprised the two armed officers currently approaching the rear of Wells' house and two more, plus Hawkins, now approaching the front.

Yasir was on lookout duty this side, while the other car, containing Maguire and Sharpe, was in the road behind, in case Wells returned and parked up at the back. The plan was to get into the house regardless of whether their target was home. If he was out, they'd look inside for something to help locate him. Or, better still, he'd return while they were still there, at which point they'd arrest him and be done. That was the theory, at least.

Hawkins passed between two parallel parked cars to reach the pavement, watching the pair of armed SCO19 officers approaching Wells' house from the opposite direction, their black bodysuits and headgear hard to pick out in the darkness among the deluge of slow, heavy raindrops that continued to fall.

They met outside the house.

Just as Hawkins had specified, nobody spoke. Bishop nodded: a gesture that simultaneously conveyed a greeting and a request for consent. *Good to go?*

She nodded back, and the three of them crossed the tiny garden area to the front door. The two gunmen took up positions either side of the entrance with handguns raised, as Bishop pressed a button on a remote device that told his other colleagues to stand by.

He waited for whatever confirmation it gave and nodded at Hawkins again, who knocked firmly on the door and moved aside. If Wells was there, he was keeping the place in darkness for a reason, so any reaction was likely to be sudden, maybe violent.

Seconds passed, but all she heard was the patter of raindrops and the sluggish trickle of water running down the inclining street into a nearby drain. The potential horror of this being the wrong place crossed her mind, but she shook off the thought, dropping to one knee and easing open the letterbox in the tatty wooden door, keeping her body to one side.

'Mr Wells?' she called through the gap, trying to mediate her volume so as not to alert the entire street. 'Met Police. I need you to open this door.'

She waited, peering into the blackness of the hallway, watching for signs of movement that might betray an attack from a trained killer. She repeated her instruction.

No response.

She gave it thirty seconds before allowing the letter-box to creak shut, then stood and turned to Bishop, jerking her head back towards the house.

More nods were exchanged between the armed officers, before the second man holstered his gun and shrugged off a shoulder strap to produce a compact battering ram. He stepped forward, put one foot on the step to steady himself and aligned the ram with the solitary lock visible from the outside. Then he swung the cylinder back and forth once, crashing it into the door, where it met the frame.

The wood must have been older than it looked, because the resulting thud was accompanied by the unmistakable sound of splintering timber as the lock burst. Hawkins glanced around at the road, but still their activities seemed to have gone unnoticed. She turned back as another strike punched the door inwards. The officer shouldered the ram and redrew his gun, as Bishop moved past him into a small sitting room.

'Armed police!' he shouted. 'Stay where you are!'

Hawkins followed the two armed men inside, watching them edge forward with guns raised, their torches like searchlights, probing the darkened room. She hung back as they moved further in, their uniforms emblazoned across the shoulders with bold white letters: ARMED OFFICER.

She closed the damaged door behind them, restoring the appearance of normality from outside, hearing another crunch from the rear of the house as the other gunmen gained entry.

'Lounge clear,' somebody reported as Bishop and his partner edged slowly up the staircase along the right-hand wall, while the other two checked what must have been a kitchen, through a side door at the back of the room.

Hawkins waited in the dark, listening to the search being conducted upstairs. Within a couple of minutes the two marksmen returned from the upper floor, declaring the property clear.

She flicked on her torch, taking her first opportunity to scan the restricted space. At best the room was ten feet square, with a single armchair and small folding table taking up most of the floor. Everything appeared to be in good condition, adequately set up for a single occupant, and the air smelled fresh enough for someone to have been here in the recent past. But then it struck her why the place felt odd. She swept the torch around, remembering to keep the beam away from the windows, and confirmed her suspicion. The basics were there: carpet, curtains, TV. But there was nothing coincidental, no clutter.

No soul.

The house looked vacant, as if nobody had lived there for some time, even though Wells' driving licence had been registered here for the last six years. There were no pictures on the walls, no piles of unread mail; none of the obligatory clutter found in a regular home. Either Wells was compulsive about tidiness, or his life involved no complication at all, which gave Hawkins even greater hope he was their man. She'd studied this type of behaviour and the people likely to exhibit it. Such myopia had many degrees, but it tended to arise in those with distended concern for their future welfare, as the necessary distractions of everyday life began to shrink and fade in response to whatever psychological malfunction was in control.

A common trait of the insane.

Thirty minutes after first entering Marlon Wells' home, Hawkins stood defiantly in the darkness of his small front bedroom, resisting the urge to move on. Her anti-contamination suit and gloves weren't doing much to fend off the cold in a house that appeared to have no heating at all. And common sense said that, after a difficult torch-lit examination, the house was bereft of clues as to where its occupant might be found.

She had grudgingly accepted Mike's cheerful observation that the cramped property, with its bare surfaces and almost empty rooms, was at least an easy search. But that also led to an irritating lack of progress in their attempt to confirm whether or not Marlon Wells was the Judge.

Currently, Maguire was across the landing, checking every aspect of Wells' bedroom for less obvious hints. They had already scoured the lounge and kitchen downstairs, while Sharpe and Yasir still occupied their respective vehicles in front and behind the house, to give them warning in case Wells returned. The armed officers from SCO19 had retreated to their response vehicle, to avoid further contaminating a house that might yet require forensic scrutiny. Hawkins and Maguire had suited up and re-entered the house to look for clues but, as the minutes ticked by without evidence being found, Hawkins had become increasingly tense.

They could place Wells' vehicle at the address of one of the potential targets, and outside that of one of the previous victims, but not on the day of the attack and without proof he'd been driving at the time. And while he also fitted the description of the man seen following Matt Hayes, using SCO19 to bash their way into his home so they could rifle through his sock drawer now seemed a little extreme.

Having found precisely nothing, her next option was to get SOC in to take DNA samples and conduct a more detailed search, but all the while Steve Tanner was chipping away at his own suspect, potentially opening the fissure through which confession would pour.

Hawkins swallowed her frustration, realigning her torch with what seemed to be the only feature worthy of interest in the place. Admittedly, searching an unfamiliar building in the dark, in case the owner returned to find the lights on and scarpered without being seen, was awkward. Having to keep her torch away from the windows didn't help, but her main problem was the lack of overview. Every feature had to be examined in near-isolation; within the torch's narrow beam, which made it possible to miss things that might have been obvious in the light. But if there were answers here, Hawkins' intuition contended that this room was where they'd be found.

Just like the rest of the somewhat rickety house, this area clearly had a specific purpose. Except, where the rear upstairs room held a bed, plus storage for some rudimentary clothes, and the kitchen had food and equipment to sustain a basic existence for one, this room contained something that constituted expression. Not in the cheap desk and chair near the window, nor in the plain rug in the middle of the floor, nor even in the shelves attached to the back wall.

But in what they held.

Of the four medium-sized planks fixed to the tatty plasterboard, only the highest was empty. The remaining three were filled with small figures carved from some kind of dense, light wood. The level of craftsmanship varied, the sculptor's apparent dexterity having improved with the practice of creating each one, but they were meticulously arranged. Fifteen effigies occupied each of the bottom two shelves, with a further nine on the next level up; evidently a growing collection, judging by the half-finished nature of the last one.

Hawkins picked up the delicate figure, turning it over in gloved hands. It was no more than four inches tall and only the section above the waist was complete; its legs were still misshapen and outsize. But it obviously depicted a soldier, from the carefully sculpted clothing to the weapon it held, just like every other figure on the shelves. Their significance was anyone's guess ... perhaps they represented people Wells had known or fought alongside. But something about the arrangement held Hawkins fast, and she stared at the wooden army, trying to fathom its maker's mind.

Yet, leading a meagre existence and making wooden effigies still didn't make the man a psychopath.

The abrupt sound of the Airwave handset made Hawkins jump. She flicked off the torch and unzipped her suit to drag the jangling unit out of her pocket. She'd primed herself to see Yasir's name on the display, expecting to hear that Wells had returned. But the number was unknown, and Amala would have used the radio function, as agreed.

She answered. 'Hawkins.'

'Ma'am?' The Brummie accent belonged to Bill Ames, a young DC at Becke House whom she'd requisitioned to look into Wells' past. The kid sounded permanently irate, due more to his burr than actual discontent, but he was trustworthy and precise.

'Billy. Have you got his military file?'

'Yes, ma'am, no thanks to bloody out-of-hours MOD. They won't breathe without clearance, so it took ages for them to track down –'

'Tell me later,' Hawkins interrupted. 'What does Wells' record say?'

'Right you are.' Ames gathered himself, clearing his throat. 'Marlon Wells, nickname Bull, joined the army in 2005. His first tour of Iraq, running supply trucks between two bases near the green zone, was cut short because of a kidney infection. But ten months later he was back in Basra. That went okay for a year, but then a close mate of his called Jim Wilson got killed by a landmine, taking a few non-essential chunks out of Wells in the process. Wells pulled through, but it looks like he blamed himself for his friend's death. That's when the army quack diagnosed post-traumatic-stress disorder and packed him off home for counselling.'

'What happened then?'

'Sorry, ma'am, record's empty after that.'

'There's stuff missing?'

'No, the pages for counsellors' notes are here, but only the first one's filled in. Nothing dramatic, just preliminary chat and confirmation of suspected PTSD. After that, the only thing written on them is "non-attend". Looks like Wells didn't bother going back.'

'And what the hell does *that* signify?' Hawkins' frustration flared. 'Did you find Simon Hunter?'

Ames didn't reply directly, but a few seconds of clanking on the other end of the line preceded another man's voice. 'Hello, Detective. How can I be of aid?'

'Hunter.' Hawkins breathed a sigh of relief. Quickly, she told him about their discovery of the ex-soldier's house and the collection of carved figures, before switching the conversation back to his file. 'Why would they let Wells get away without seeing a therapist? Isn't it a requirement for repatriated veterans?'

'Nowadays, yes, but it wasn't back then. And the counselling practice would have been paid regardless, so they'd have no incentive to complain.'

'Is it possible he got help from elsewhere?'

'Perhaps, but if he didn't show up at the arranged sessions, it's unlikely he'd seek out support for himself. PTSD manifests itself on many levels, Antonia, I'm sure you of all people understand that. Often, sufferers will do anything to convince everyone, including themselves, that they're fine.'

Something in his voice made Hawkins pause, as she realized her free hand was scratching at the scars on her chest. She stopped herself, ignoring his apparent inference. 'So what can we expect from someone with PTSD, who hasn't received treatment for years?'

Hunter was silent for a few seconds. 'In some cases, symptoms lie dormant, so the time gap itself isn't necessarily a factor. However, if a subject receives no assistance once the effects begin to take hold, it becomes a far more dangerous beast. PTSD tends to feed off the incident that caused it, although I accept that in your soldier's case there was potential for a lot more than one. A sufferer's problems can start with feelings of isolation and guilt. They may also have trouble sleeping or concentrating on even the simplest tasks, which will significantly impact on daily life. But the most common indicator is re-experiencing – reliving the trauma through nightmares, although in extreme cases flash-backs can occur while the sufferer is awake, blurring the lines between present and past.'

'So how would you expect that to play out for Wells?'

'Unfortunately, Detective, that's where the bounda-ries distort. If I had to guess, I'd say the carvings represent fallen comrades, while the elementary lifestyle demonstrates obsessive behaviour, as you say. After that, the manifestations become more personal, and much harder to predict. Considering the potentially unfettered nature of his PTSD, Marlon Wells may no longer be able to distinguish between reality and dreams, which makes it possible for him to think he's still at war, except there's no longer a defined enemy for him to attack. It's pure speculation, but if Wells feels guilty, either for surviving his colleague or for letting him die, he may be attempting to absolve himself by fighting other evils or correcting other wrongs. Basically, select-ing enemies for himself.'

Hawkins took over. 'I suppose it fits. The nearest things a peaceful country has to domestic enemies are the criminals it sends to jail.'

She moved across to the window and eased the curtain aside, peering through the gap. A car slid past in the road below, but it was the wrong colour and make to be Wells'. She glanced at the VW parked on the far side of the darkened street, noting Yasir's presence in the driver's seat, and the fact that she appeared alert. The sergeant would let them know if Wells returned.

She addressed Hunter again. 'So when we do finally catch up with this guy, what can we expect?'

'Now you're asking.' The profiler thought for a moment. 'You have to bear in mind that the army made Wells a killer before any of this, but now he may have no sense of restraint. He's likely to be suffering advanced and increasing delusions, which means he's going to crash at some point, although it's impossible to say when that will occur. For now, he still appears to be in control, in which case he's highly dangerous. I'm afraid your only option may be lethal force.'

Hawkins thanked him and hung up, feeling like she now had at least a basic understanding of their man. A soldier emotionally damaged by war and the traumatic loss of a friend, sent home with severe psychological issues then allowed to develop unchecked. The result was a demented vigilante, confused by the lack of a definite foe, now selecting arbitrary targets in line with his own chaotic agenda. All of which was great in theory, but it moved them precisely no closer to tracking him down.

She began crossing the room towards the door, but halfway there her foot caught something hard. She lurched forward, reaching for support, her foot stamping against the floor, making her wince.

'Antonia?' Mike called from the other room. She heard him move across the creaky landing to the doorway, shining his torch at her. 'You okay?'

'Yeah.' She switched on her torch, aiming it where she had stumbled. 'Tripped over something.'

But as she scoured the floor, Hawkins realized there was nothing there. She used the beam to search the far corner, in case she'd kicked whatever it was out of the way.

Mike pointed his torch at the rug. 'Carpet must have been rucked.'

'No,' she continued, checking the corners, 'it was too hard for that.'

Unless.

She turned suddenly, bending to grab the mat, moving it aside. Then she stepped back and shone her torch at the floorboards underneath, testing them one at a time with her foot. The first couple creaked; didn't move. But as she placed her weight on the third plank it dipped, raising the far end above the floor.

'There,' she announced. 'That's what I fell over.'

'Great.' Mike started to turn. 'At least if he ain't the killer, we got him for wilful neglect.'

Hawkins didn't follow. 'Hold on. This place might be old, but it's hardly falling down.'

She crouched, grabbing the raised end of the plank, trying to pull the unsecured section free. Mike joined her, producing a pocket knife, using it to prise the tight-fitting board away from the ones on either side. After a short struggle, it came loose.

Mike dumped the plank as Hawkins picked up her torch and shone it in the gap. At first she thought it was nothing: just a cavity holding spider webs and dust, but as she angled the torch further in, something else became visible, hidden right at the back.

She adjusted her position and fed a hand down into the recess, reaching for the item. She had to use the rubberized fingertips of her gloves to drag it closer before she could grip it and pull it free. Hawkins placed her discovery in the beam of Maguire's torch: it was a thin plastic sleeve. She glanced at Mike, his face barely visible in the reflected torchlight.

He returned her gaze. 'Come on, the suspense is killing me.'

Hawkins nodded, turning her attention back to the file. She took a deep breath and undid the clasp, hoping its lack of weight didn't mean it was empty. Then she reached inside, easing out the contents. Envelopes – but as they came out something else fell, back through the gap in the floor.

Mike followed up with the torch and retrieved it, turning it round so he could see what it was.

'Holy shit.' His face registered shock. 'I think we found our man.'

Hawkins scrambled around beside him, craning her neck to see what he held, her heart pounding as she registered what she was looking at in the wavering light.

A photograph of Matthew Hayes.

Suddenly, she was reaching for the nearest envelope, noting Wells' address on the front, removing the paper from inside, unfolding it with trembling hands. But nothing could have prepared her for the shocking handwritten words she read, slowly, aloud:

Hello

My name is Samantha Philips. You probably heard about me in the news six years ago when I went down for murder. My tutor raped me when I was eighteen, so I cut his throat with a bread knife. I don't care about that. I did it and I'm not sorry.

The reason for this letter is that I got pregnant from the rape. At first I tried to forget what he did, to convince myself I'd love the baby no matter what. But it didn't work. It felt like evil growing inside me, poisoning my soul. I couldn't bear it, so I had an abortion. I knew I'd made a mistake as soon as it was done.

I murdered my child.

I tried to forget that, too. I took drugs, went off the rails, but none of it worked. I even tried to kill myself, though I messed that up as well. That's when I snapped, and murdered the tutor who raped me. He didn't deserve to live.

So they locked me up. And every day for six years I sat in my cell, wondering if I had any more right to life than he did. Now I realize I don't.

I regret my actions more every day. I used to have faith, but not any more. So God can't help me, but maybe you can.

As you request, there will be no suicide note. I don't want to know when or how it will happen. All I ask is that it's quick, merciful, soon.

My address is 28 Gladstone House, Chambord Street, Bethnal Green, London E2. I include a recent photo of myself.

Thank you
Samantha Philips

Hawkins finished reading and grabbed the next envelope. She removed the letter and read a few similar lines, checking the signature at the end:

Matthew Hayes.

The next note was from Calano. Broken English, but the same thing again.

She and Maguire stared at each other as the truth about the Judge's victims slowly came to them both.

They had all *wanted* to die.

Hawkins and Maguire sat in the gloom of Marlon Wells' front bedroom, reeling from the discovery they'd just made. It took Hawkins a moment to find her voice, but even then she whispered the words.

'They wanted to die.'

Maguire nodded slowly. 'Yeah, and this guy was just . . . helping out.'

Sam Philips' suicide attempt reared in Hawkins' mind. Had the others tried and failed, too? Either way, all three had come to Wells because of what he offered. A *service* for those who needed release but couldn't bring themselves to take the final step. He'd known when each target left jail, and where to find them afterwards, precisely because they'd *wanted* him to.

'Suicides that looked like murders,' she breathed. She lowered the torch, her gaze drifting away into the darkness.

'Wait.' Maguire picked up the folder. 'There's another envelope.'

Suddenly, Hawkins' focus was back. She watched him open the final letter and read.

Familiar emotions began to unfold – self-hatred, torment, guilt – and as Maguire talked, Hawkins realized what the letter meant. Either there was a fourth body still to be found, or there was another victim out there somewhere, waiting to die. But the biggest shock came as Mike read on, because the story was one she already knew.

She reached out, taking the paper from him, turning it over, seeing the signature she already knew would be there.

Amanda Cain.

'Shit.' She stood. 'This makes Cain his prime target.' She picked up the Airwave handset, fumbling with the keys, thankful that she'd worked out how to store contacts. She scrolled down, selecting the number for one of the officers they'd posted outside Cain's home.

He answered fast. 'Edwards.'

'Neil,' she said, 'has anything happened there?'

'No, ma'am, nothing to report. Doctor lady hasn't left the house, and there's been no one hanging around.'

'Good. Listen, Cain's in danger. I want her moved into protective custody right now, the nearest high-security location we have. She won't like it, but *don't* take no for an answer. Arrest her if you have to, for conspiracy to murder.' She told him that Wells might be on his way there, and that she'd ring back to explain once they were inside.

'Understood,' Edwards confirmed. 'Anything else?'

'She's a flight and suicide risk, so watch her, okay?'

'Got it.'

Hawkins hung up and turned to Maguire. 'I want full undercover teams set up on this place and at Amanda Cain's, and get an all-ports warning out on Wells' car. We need to –' She trailed off as Maguire pointed his torch at himself so she could see he was already on his phone.

He shook his head. 'Don't need an APW.'

She frowned. 'Why not?'

'It's Amala, for you.' He held out the phone. 'Wells is here.'

62

The room was dark. Not too dark to see, but dark enough. It was warm and comfortable, with a heavy green carpet and leather chairs. But it was all another trick, to keep fucked-up patients calm.

Fucked-up patients like Bull.

'Would you like some water?' The army shrink sat back in his chair.

Bull ignored him, carried on looking around. The room had no wallpaper, just panels of wood. There was silence for a while.

'So, Marlon,' the shrink said at last, 'what would you like to talk about?'

'Do I have to be here?'

'No, you can leave, but these sessions are to help you.'

'To help me what?'

'. . . deal with things that trouble you.'

Bull watched him scribble something. 'Why, so you can make notes about why I'm fucked up?'

'I don't have to take notes.' He put the pen down. 'Is that how you feel?'

'Fucked up? Yeah.'

'Why?'

'I went to war. Now I'm fucked up.'

'How do you know?'

'I get nightmares.'

'What about?'

'Death.'

'Is that why you were prescribed anti-depressants?'

'Yeah. I don't take them.'

'What's war like?'

'War's the worst fucking day of your life, every day you're there.'

The shrink moved his hands from the armrests of his chair into his lap. 'Tell me about Jim.'

He looked away. 'Jim's dead.'

'How did he die?'

Anger flared. 'He stepped on a fucking landmine. That shit happens.' Bull crossed his arms. 'I don't want to talk about it.' He was quiet for a few seconds. But suddenly he was talking again, about the day Cheshire died.

The shrink listened without interrupting. Then he said, 'Why do you have nightmares about that?'

Bull realized he was shaking. 'It's my fault he died.'

'Why?'

'I told him to run.'

'I thought you had no choice.'

'That's not the point. I was in charge. It was my call.'

The shrink paused. 'Did you kill anyone else?'

'Only insurgents.'

'Is that different?'

'They're the enemy. You're meant to kill them.'

'So it's about killing a friend?'

'No, it's about killing someone who didn't deserve to die.'

'Even if you were trying to save him.'

'Yeah, people should pay for their mistakes.'

'And what should the penalty be?'

'Death.'

'An eye for an eye.'

'I guess.'

'Do you *deserve* to die?'

Bull thought for a moment. 'Yes.'

'Is that what you want?'

'Maybe. But not yet.'

'Why not?'

'I want to put things right before I go.'

63

Hawkins' heart leapt as she clicked off her torch, plunging the small bedroom back into darkness, expecting at any second to hear the front door opening downstairs.

She took the phone from Maguire. 'Amala, where's Wells?'

'He just drove past me.' Yasir's voice was hushed, and Hawkins imagined her crouching in the driver's seat of their VW. 'He's parking now.'

She let out the breath she'd been holding. 'Did he see you?'

'I don't think so.'

'Good.' She moved away from the door. 'Will he notice if I look out of the upstairs window?'

'No, he's still in the car to your left, facing away from the house.'

'Okay, hold on.' Hawkins reached the outer wall, eased the curtain aside. She swore at the condensation that had formed since her previous visit to the window, now blocking her view through the lower panes. She stood on tiptoes, not wanting to leave marks by wiping the water away, still hoping their target would approach the house unaware.

She could see most of the street in one direction,

although the misted glass meant her view wasn't clear. But she made out Wells' dark-coloured Vauxhall backing into a space about thirty yards away. He'd gone a fair distance past the house to find a gap, but at least that would give them a few more seconds to track his approach and organize themselves.

Hawkins also noted SCO19's unmarked BMW, still parked on the same side of the road, a few spaces nearer the house, although from her current position Amala's Golf was out of view to the right.

She handed the Airwave unit to Mike. 'Use the radio channel to let everyone know what's going on. The plan is to stay hidden until Wells leaves his car and heads this way. Tell Bishop to wait till he passes their vehicle, then I want him pinned down and arrested before he gets to the door.'

'On it.' Maguire switched to the radio channel and began talking to the others. Hawkins turned back to the window, watching the blurred outline of Wells' Vectra making its final adjustments in the restricted space. The car stopped and its lights went out.

'Stand by,' she said to Mike and Amala at the same time. 'Everyone keep their heads down till he moves.'

Mike confirmed her instructions to the others and joined her at the window, his extra height allowing him to look over Hawkins so she didn't have to move. They watched the car, waiting for the driver's door to open. But the seconds stretched, and the door stayed shut.

'What's he doing?' Hawkins asked. 'Amala, why isn't he getting out?'

Yasir's voice came through the speaker. 'It's difficult to say from this angle; he might be using his phone.'

'I need to know,' she flared. 'Is he using it or not?'

Yasir's voice remained calm. 'Sorry, ma'am, I can't see. Do you want me to pop over and ask?'

Hawkins hid her satisfaction at Yasir's fortitude. 'Just keep watching.'

She stared at the roof of Wells' car, annoyed that she hadn't considered this scenario beforehand. She'd concentrated on keeping their presence concealed, expecting their target to approach the house, but she'd neglected to consider what would happen if Wells realized they were there before leaving his car. And his vehicle was parked beyond both of theirs, making it impossible for them to block his exit.

She tapped Mike's arm. 'Get Sharpe to bring the other car round to the far end of this street and start heading this way. If Wells scarpers, Aaron can block him in. Make sure the guys from SCO19 know what's happening.'

Maguire nodded and began relaying instructions as Hawkins turned back to the window, cursing the fact that the armed-response car was facing in the wrong direction to go after Wells if he left. They'd have to turn the vehicle round in order to follow him, a tricky, time-consuming manoeuvre in such a narrow road. Amala's Golf was further back, but at least it was pointing the right way. And still there was no movement from Wells. Was he simply sitting in the car while he finished a call, or did he know something was wrong?

Hawkins listened to Mike's conversation with Sharpe, who confirmed he was on the way. Then she gave Wells a few more seconds, painfully aware that the longer he stayed in his car, the more likely it was that he knew they were there. Still no movement.

It was time to gamble.

'Amala,' Hawkins said into the phone, 'Wells won't be able to see from there that you didn't just get into the car. I want you to start the engine, put your lights on and move away as if you're a local heading out. Just drive alongside and block him in. The armed guys will back you up.'

'No problem, chief. Here goes.'

On the line, Hawkins heard the distant sound of the Golf's engine kicking over and, beside her, Mike quietly passing everything on. She still couldn't see Yasir's car, but suddenly its headlights illuminated the street below. No reaction from Wells.

Yasir's lights swept left and right as she pulled out of the space, then the car came into view, steadily closing the gap to the Vectra.

'Keep to a normal speed,' Hawkins reminded her. 'Stop alongside and get your head down just in case. SCO19 will be there in a few seconds.' She glanced at Maguire, who gave her a thumbs-up.

Yasir was only fifteen yards from Wells, then ten,

then five. She slowed as she reached the other car and, for a split second, Hawkins thought it was going to work.

But as Yasir got level, the Vauxhall's rear lights flickered as it started up, and its engine began to race.

'Amala!' Hawkins shouted.

Too late.

The Vectra lurched out of the space, clipping the car in front, and smashed into the Golf. Both cars skidded across the road, the VW slamming sideways into a Volvo parked on the far side.

'Shit!' Mike pressed the button on the Airwave set. 'Bishop, get in there.'

Down in the street, Wells reversed away from the Golf, prising the damaged cars apart with a crunching sound. He backed up into the space as the left-hand doors of the BMW opened and two armed officers emerged on to the street, advancing with weapons raised.

The Vectra's engine revved again and it rammed back into the side of the stricken VW, punching it further into the parked car as it scraped past and slewed away.

The SCO19 officers opened fire, blowing out one of the Vauxhall's back tyres and smashing its rear screen. The car slowed and pitched on its deflated rubber but kept moving.

'Go!' Hawkins shouted, sprinting for the stairs with Maguire right behind her, gritting her teeth as still-weak muscles screamed. She flew downstairs into the road, catching sight of the armed officers beside the Golf, pulling a dazed Yasir from the driver's seat as their colleague turned the BMW round. Ahead, the damaged Vectra retreated towards the far end of the street.

Maguire passed her, heading for the crash scene. Hawkins launched herself after him, realizing there wasn't room for the larger X5 to pass the back of the Golf without risking their currently undamaged pursuit vehicle. If, as she hoped, Sharpe managed to stop Wells, she didn't want to delay the armed officers getting there.

She neared the Golf, feeling the rain on her skin as it fell from the blackness above. They reached the car as Yasir was lifted clear. Maguire lunged through the open passenger door as Hawkins checked her, relieved to see she was conscious, despite a glazed expression and a nasty cut on her head.

'She's okay,' one of the armed officers said. 'I'll wait with her for the ambulance.'

Hawkins thanked him as Mike started the Golf and reversed away from the other car.

'Hey!' he shouted, pulling forward. 'This bucket still runs. Get in.'

Hawkins didn't hesitate, throwing herself into the passenger seat and slamming the door. Maguire gunned the engine and they skidded away, to the sounds of tortured tyres and a loud scraping noise as they accelerated after Wells, a solitary headlamp beam lighting their way.

She dragged on her seat belt, shouting, 'You sure about this?'

'It's just the fender running on the road,' he yelled back. 'It should hold.'

'Great.' She twisted in her seat, seeing the third armed officer climbing back into the BMW, which took off after them. She turned back, alert to every tortured sound from the battered Golf, any of which could signal imminent failure. But it was worth the risk to have two vehicles in pursuit. Her attention moved ahead as a single brake light flared. Wells had reached the end of the street, but he seemed to have stopped, which meant one of two things. Either his car had given up, or Sharpe had blocked him in.

She glanced at Maguire. 'Can't this thing go any faster?'

'You wanna drive?' He jerked the wheel to stop the wounded Golf from swerving off line. 'Steering's a hoot.'

'I'm sure you're doing your best.'

She watched his brow crease in response to her taunt, feeling the surge as he pressed the throttle to the floor. The scraping noise increased.

They closed to within a hundred yards of the Vectra. Hawkins leaned forward as the wipers cleared the screen, seeing Wells get out of his car, advancing on the Focus now visible behind. Aaron Sharpe was inside, but he wasn't looking at the ex-soldier. Instead, he seemed to be searching for something in the cabin and, a second later, Hawkins realized why.

He was trying to lock himself in.

Wells wrenched the door open and pulled the sergeant from his seat. Sharpe offered mild resistance as he was flung aside by the stockier man. He crumpled at the roadside as Wells took his place in the Ford and sped off.

But the delay had allowed them to close the gap. Maguire braked hard, skidding around the abandoned Vauxhall and on to the adjoining road, with Wells a short distance ahead. Hawkins reached forward and switched on the siren before checking behind to see the X5 easing through the gap to follow them, its own grille-mounted lights and siren coming on in response to their lead.

She turned back and grabbed the Airwave handset Mike had dumped in the console, switching it to open frequency. 'Come in, Control, DCI Antonia Hawkins and DI Mike Maguire, in pursuit of IC1 male believed to be Marlon Wells, requesting air support. Suspect's vehicle is a black Ford Focus, currently approaching Brixton town centre from the east side, sixty miles per hour, traffic moderate.'

The operator confirmed, and Hawkins maintained dialogue, detailing the pursuit as she and Maguire approached the end of the road. The noise inside the VW was getting worse but, mechanically, the car seemed to be holding up. For now.

With any luck, one of the Met's three permanent surveillance helicopters would be near enough to pick up their chase. And, once they had Wells in their sights, his chances of escape fell off a cliff. The Eurocopter EC145s were all fitted with video cameras and thermal imaging systems, capable of tracking their target till he gave up or ran out of fuel. They just had to keep him in view until the chopper caught up.

Wells reached the turn and threw his car right, sweeping on to a one-way system against the traffic flow. Mike followed, the damaged Golf screaming its dissatisfaction as they rounded the sharp corner at speed. Wells swerved to avoid an oncoming bus, mounting the wide pavement, scattering pedestrians. Maguire was forced to follow, crashing up the low kerb, but ahead the Focus was cutting through a busy intersection to re-join the road.

'An upside to traffic lights at last,' he shouted, fighting the wheel, threading the Golf between cars swerving left and right, horns blaring as the chase barged its unexpected way through.

Hawkins gritted her teeth as they missed the final car by inches, and Mike floored the throttle again, dragging the raucous Golf into line with their target. They swung on to the high street, shops closing in on both sides as Wells began weaving in and out of the late-evening traffic on the main road through the centre of Brixton.

Clearly, their target wasn't familiar with the area, or he wouldn't have chosen this route. There were only two lanes, separated from the oncoming traffic by a raised central pavement, hemming him in. For a second it looked like he was lining up to veer off into a side street, but instead he ploughed straight on. Hawkins checked the turn as they passed, noting red-and-white barriers just inside. She leaned across to see the speedometer reaching seventy miles per hour. Fortunately, the noise coming from the two police vehicles was warning passers-by, though it only took one oblivious teenager plugged into an iPod to wander out in front of them in the restricted space . . .

She had to trust Mike's skill.

'How's the car?' she yelled.

'Holding up,' he came back. 'Feels okay.'

Wells wasn't pulling away. They swept under a couple of small bridges, past Brixton tube station, drawing startled looks from swathes of pedestrians either side, their attention being pulled in by the sirens and the worsening racket from their lagging bumper.

Hawkins had just finished another radio update when she straightened in her seat. Three hundred yards ahead, every lane was blocked, backed up with queuing traffic both sides.

'Mike,' she warned.

'I know.'

Wells had obviously seen it, too, and the Focus braked as it approached the next turn. Maguire did the same, changing down through the gears as Wells took his only option, screeching into a side street, clipping a post as he went. The Ford skidded but stayed on track, racing away as Maguire hauled the VW round after him, into a narrow road lined with bollards and parked cars. Hawkins noted the street name, reporting to the operator that they had entered Ferndale Road.

People on the pavements recoiled as the cars screamed through, but suddenly there were brake lights ahead. Hawkins craned her neck, seeing the slower car that Wells had caught and couldn't pass.

They closed on him fast but, before she could think of how they might stop him in the restricted street, the distance between them widened again. Wells surged around the other car, mounting the kerb, drawing a blast from the horn of a driver coming the opposite way. Maguire threaded the Golf through the same gap and swung them back into the killer's wake. Wells accelerated around a gradual bend with high walls either side, then took a left at a fork in the road, brake lights burning, almost losing the rear. Mike followed him through a narrow tunnel, shouting at the oncoming cars to wait as their convoy swept through.

'Antonia.' Bishop's voice came through the Airwave unit in her hand. 'We've taken the other fork. I think these roads join up again, west of here. Keep us updated on his position and we'll try to get ahead.'

'Affirmative.' Hawkins breathed again as the road opened out, revealing a long residential street. Cars were parked either side, though there was room for traffic to pass in both directions, while small but regular speed bumps took the edge off their pace. The adrenalin in her system retreated slightly in response, giving her opportunity to think.

Hopefully, Bishop's unilateral decision wouldn't cost them. If he'd given her the choice, she'd have told him to stay close behind, in case the maltreated Golf let them down.

She checked on Mike. 'You okay?'

'Swell.' He grimaced as they jarred over another tarmac ridge.

Hawkins shared his frustration. The restricted back-streets gave them no chance of stopping Wells. Unless Bishop found a way to overtake and cut him off, their only chance was to hope they'd reach more open areas, where Mike could use their vehicle to ram him off the road. As things stood, they needed to stay with him long enough for a chopper to arrive.

Hawkins didn't know this part of London, so she carried on relaying information about their trajectory via the Airwave unit, hoping Bishop or the support crews would come through. According to the operator, back-up was less than ten minutes away. But if their vehicle let them down, they could lose Wells in a fraction of that.

For now, her priority had to be trying to work out where Wells would go. Was he simply running away, or did he have a destination in mind? Either way, his flight definitely had an air of desperation about it. As if he had nothing to lose.

Her thoughts were interrupted as the car reached the

end of the street. Wells hardly braked, slewing right at a four-way junction, scattering traffic as he went. Hawkins tensed as Mike followed, causing a truck to brake and swerve, its tyres screaming in unison with theirs. He spun the wheel, somehow keeping them on track behind the fleeing Ford. Hawkins swallowed hard, twisting in her seat, looking for road names to update Control. But there were none, and within seconds they had left the junction behind.

Instead, she searched for other signs. To the left, modern flats flanked the pavement and, opposite, a retail outlet advertised tiles. But no street name presented itself, and Hawkins was forced to give up as they built speed, scenery blurring to the sides.

The gap to Wells had increased, and Hawkins sensed Mike's frustration as he swore and changed down a gear, forcing more power from the Golf. The Focus flew under a bridge, visibly stretching its lead. But, suddenly, as Wells moved out of his lane to pass a slower car, their luck changed.

Up ahead, a large black shape appeared from an adjacent street. It took Hawkins a second to identify the lowered suspension and blacked-out windows, but then it registered as the BMW X5 from SCO19.

Bishop.

The X5 pulled straight into Wells' path, far enough ahead to build sufficient speed to prevent their target from overtaking. Within seconds, Wells was on the BMW's bumper, weaving from side to side, looking for a way past. But Bishop moved with him, expertly slowing at the same time, forcing Wells to brake.

Hawkins scanned the road ahead. Bishop's tactic might work, but only if Mike could get alongside and box the Focus in. If they lost too much speed before then, he might be able to accelerate past. Or, worse, if they passed a turn, Wells could simply change course.

It had to be now.

Mike had seen the problem, too. Hawkins glanced across as he tried to counter Wells' movements in order to draw level, but as he lined up to make the critical move, two cars and a truck flashed towards them in the opposite lane, no doubt having pulled aside in response to the sirens.

'Shit!' Maguire swerved back into line.

Up ahead, the BMW decelerated further, dropping below fifty, although Mike still couldn't get alongside, due to cars blocking their way. But this time Wells didn't brake, and Hawkins heard the crunch as the bumpers met. The Ford's engine raced, bouncing off the limiter as it pushed the BMW, edging their speed back up.

Abruptly, Wells steered left, angling his vehicle, easing the front of the X5 into the oncoming lane. Maguire had just pulled out when the BMW snapped across in front of them, tyres screeching as friction took hold. Bishop had to release the brakes and bolt for the far pavement to avoid a head-on collision with the truck bearing down on them from ahead.

Released, Wells sped away. Maguire went with him as Hawkins watched the X5 mount the wide pathway and skid to a halt.

'Pete' – she spoke into the Airwave – 'is everyone all right?'

'One piece, just about. Think the car's okay. Keep going; we'll catch up.'

'Understood.' Hawkins turned to Maguire. 'Be careful. I think we just had our warning shot.'

'Sure thing, boss. Though you might wanna shut your eyes for this part.'

Hawkins followed his gaze ahead, where more cars were backed up at some lights, blocking their path.

Wells didn't slow down.

Mike said, 'He's going round.'

The Ford swung out. There was no way to tell if they'd meet other traffic head on, and the gap was small enough now for them to share Wells' fate, whatever happened. But they were lucky, making it past the lights and on to the junction just as a stream of cars was unleashed their way.

Wells reacted, slamming on the brakes, turning hard. Maguire followed, narrowly missing the front of an SUV that swerved violently out of their path. Horns sounded as they cut left, joining the adjacent road, although suddenly Hawkins' attention wasn't on the chase. Instead, she stared at the squat building flashing past her window as realization sparked in her mind.

'Clapham North underground,' she said, half to herself.

'What?' Maguire steadied the car, keeping them in line with Wells, the noise from their ruined bumper increasing as the speed climbed again.

'I know where he's going,' she told him, fumbling with the Airwave set. 'All units be advised, suspect may be heading for Tremadoc Road, Clapham. He was caught on camera there a few days ago, outside the home of a potential target. He may be planning a final attack.'

Mike glanced across, an ominous frown etched on his face.

Hawkins nodded, answering his silent question. 'Amanda Cain.'

Hawkins braced herself as Mike ploughed on after Wells, reselecting the mobile number for Neil Edwards. By now, the constable and his colleagues should have taken Amanda Cain into custody so, if that was Wells' intended destination, he'd be disappointed. But if there had been any kind of delay, and Cain was still there, Hawkins needed to warn the guys on the scene. Not only did they have a target who wanted to die but, judging by his reckless behaviour in this chase, they were dealing with a killer in similar mood.

The call connected and started to ring, but Hawkins

didn't get the quick answer she was hoping for. She checked ahead, trying to recognize the scenery flashing past, to estimate how far they were from Cain's road. Shops rushed by, a restaurant, a bike shop, but nothing she recalled. Last time, they must have come in from the far end of town.

Suddenly her attention was back on the phone as Edwards picked up. 'Ma'am?'

'Neil,' she blurted, 'is Cain with you?'

There was a pause. 'Not exactly.'

Something in the pit of her stomach fell. 'Why not?'

'Sorry, ma'am. She didn't answer the door, so I thought something had happened to her. We had to break in, but we've searched the house and she's not here.'

Hawkins' heart rate leapt as she watched Tremadoc Road fly past the window. Wells had driven straight on, which meant one of two things. Either he'd missed the turn, or that wasn't where he was . . .

'Fuck!' Hawkins said, to Edwards and Mike at the same time as the most likely scenario came to her. 'Wells has contacted Cain; told her it's now or never. She must have known we were watching, so she's sneaked out while he tries to shake us off. They're going to meet up.'

Edwards apologized again.

'Listen to me.' Hawkins closed her eyes, trying not to swear. 'We're chasing Wells now. As long as we don't lose him, he'll lead us to Cain, so get your team together and follow us, west on the main road. Cain must be on foot, so she can't have gone far.'

Edwards answered with renewed purpose. 'Copy that. We're on our way.'

'And if you see the doctor, pick her up.' She ended the call.

'Geez.' Maguire swung out to pass a slow truck. 'You're a damn magnet for anarchy. I need a transfer.'

'Oh, right.' She watched him saw at the wheel. 'Because you hate an excuse to drive fast.'

He glanced across, clearly suppressing a smile. 'So where's he going?'

'I don't know. What's around here?'

'Coffee shops and rain?'

Hawkins ignored him, trying to assume the mind-sets of a defeated ex-soldier and a desperate ex-con. *Where would they go?*

They were on a busy main road in the centre of London, just after rush hour on a week night. The conspirators would probably have opted for somewhere quiet, away from public eyes, although Wells had obviously hoped not to have a police escort with him at the time.

Of course, guessing where they'd meet only became relevant if they lost him, but as the burning smell in the VW seemed to increase, Hawkins couldn't ignore the risk. It could be the bumper rubbing on the road, but the engine was a possibility, too. And as the road opened out to twin lanes, their speed climbed in response and she watched with dismay as the distance between the cars began to stretch.

'Control,' she barked into the Airwave, 'where's our air support?'

The operator's voice was mostly drowned out, but the last word sounded like 'minutes'.

Ahead of them, the Focus was weaving past other cars, still increasing its lead. But then the situation changed again as Wells' brake lights flared. Mike responded, slowing their pace, and Hawkins glanced around, trying to predict his next move. The street was wide: four lanes separated by islands here and there, houses lining both sides and no adjoining roads.

Nowhere for him to go.

The answer came as Hawkins scanned the pavement to their left. Up ahead, beyond railings that protected pedestrians from the fast-moving traffic flow, was a female figure, walking away.

Hawkins pointed. 'That's Cain.'

As she spoke, Wells' car passed the woman. The horn sounded and the vehicle slowed, diving into a layby just beyond. Hawkins reiterated their location, asking again about back-up, glancing across at the walking figure as they flashed past. Amanda Cain started to run.

She looked back at Wells, out of his car, now moving towards the doctor.

Hammer in hand.

Wells obviously didn't want to escape. He knew the

police were right behind him, that in seconds he'd be caught. The focus on his face was absolute: a man intent on fulfilling his grim promise. They had just one chance.

'There.' Hawkins pointed at the end of the railings. 'Get between them.'

Mike swerved, mounting the kerb with a bang, skidding to a halt, separating the two advancing figures. Wells stopped, covering his ears, apparently confused, but Cain kept moving. She skirted the front of their car as the two detectives opened their doors.

'Amanda! Stop!' Hawkins shouted, but Cain ignored her, continuing to move towards Wells, away to their right. Mike wrestled his way out of the driver's seat, also calling the doctor's name, when tyres screeched out in the road. Hawkins turned to see the BMW pulling up behind them. The doors flew open as Bishop and his two armed colleagues jumped out with firearms raised, just as Cain reached Wells. The officers fanned out, weapons trained on the pair, but their red laser sights hovered on the doctor's torso as she turned to face them, shielding the ex-soldier. Forcing them to stay back.

'Both of you on the floor!' Bishop yelled. 'Now!'

Neither complied.

'Leave us alone,' Cain screamed, edging backwards. 'This is what I want.'

Hawkins joined in. 'You know we can't do that, Amanda.'

But her words had no effect. She watched Cain take a breath and shut her eyes, obviously expecting her accomplice to complete his gruesome role. Behind her in the darkness Wells' arm rose, lifting the hammer, ready to strike. Still the officers had no clear shot.

'We *will* fire!' Bishop shouted. 'Put it down.'

'Do it,' Cain countered, addressing Wells.

Hawkins looked at the ex-soldier. The hammer was raised, but there was uncertainty on his face. Cain must have sensed it, too, because she glanced at him, still protecting her ally, repeating her command.

But still no strike came.

Wells looked up, his eyes searching the sky. Hawkins followed his gaze. She saw nothing, but then she realized what had drawn his attention, as her ears picked up a noise that grew swiftly from whisper to roar.

Seconds later, the surveillance helicopter swept into view, rising from behind the trees to their left, passing over the traffic rushing by on the road beneath. The aircraft rounded on them, rotor blades churning the air, their downdraught lifting dust and leaves in its thunderous wake. Hawkins' eyelids flickered in the turbulence as the pilot swung round to face Wells, bringing the helicopter's searchlight to bear.

The killer cowed as the powerful beam hit, saturating its target in blaring white. He took a step backwards, away from Cain, using his free arm to shield his eyes.

'No!' the doctor screamed, going with him, keeping her body between Wells and the guns. 'Finish this!'

'Wait!' Hawkins yelled. The hammer was still raised, but Wells was clearly in turmoil, distressed by the amplified fury of events. He seemed confused, as if woken abruptly. Then she realized that perhaps he wasn't struggling with his situation as it stood, but with the memories it stirred. Maybe the effects of PTSD were playing themselves out. Hunter's words came back to her: 'Flashbacks can occur while the sufferer is awake; blurring the lines between present and past.'

Suddenly, the situation made sense. Wells' beleaguered state came from an inability to separate current events from their traumatic predecessors, specifically the death of his innocent friend, a horrific incident for which he blamed himself. His coping strategy, it seemed, was to assist others in extricating themselves from similarly haunted despair. This whole series of murders wasn't just about helping the disaffected to die; it was borne of a need to atone for what he saw as *his* mistake. Until now, he'd been able to operate in hermetic conditions, one-on-one with each willing victim, but here, in this maelstrom of confusion and noise, he was falling apart.

Which meant the weak point here wasn't Cain's resolve.

It was Wells'.

Hawkins refocused on the killer, shouting his name above the piercing clatter of the helicopter blades. He didn't seem to hear. She turned to wave her arms at the helicopter, trying to signal to the pilot to back off. If they could communicate with Wells, they might have a chance of saving Cain, but the aircraft's blaring presence muted everything, preventing negotiation, increasing the chance that Wells would strike. But the pilot either ignored her or didn't see, as the aircraft held its place.

She turned back to Wells.

'Last chance!' Bishop roared.

Hawkins glanced around at the armed officers. They were edging apart, opening the angles. Cain wouldn't be able to shield Wells for much longer and, unless the killer surrendered, they'd take him out as soon as they had a clear shot. She needed to tell them he wasn't a sadistic killer, merely a plagued war veteran that hadn't received the help he so badly required.

Not evil; just sick.

She had to intervene, but Bishop's team were zoned in, running a drilled procedure that culminated in one of two outcomes: comply or die. Hawkins forced herself to think over the din from the helicopter and the busy road. If Wells was tuned into his army past, maybe she could broadcast on that frequency instead.

She moved around the front of the car, yelling the only word that might have a chance of reaching him. Still there was no response.

She waved her arms, shouted louder. 'Bull!'

At last Wells responded, the hammer dropping slightly as he looked towards her, squinting into the searchlight's glare.

'Hold your fire!' Hawkins yelled at Bishop's men,

turning back to Wells, forming her words carefully to breach the overriding din. 'You are not at war, Marlon. There's no enemy here. You're home.'

Now Cain was looking at Hawkins, too, obviously sensing that her accessory's attention had been drawn, aware that her window of opportunity was going to close. Tears hung on her cheeks as she turned towards him, begging for death.

Hawkins moved closer, watching the ex-soldier's face in the light, seeing emotion running riot within. 'I know what happened to Jim,' she shouted, 'but this won't help either of you.'

Wells blinked once, hard, as if he were being woken up. He took a small step away from Cain.

Hawkins saw it; pressed harder. 'You're sick, Marlon, because you were ignored when you needed help. Now you're trying to help others. I understand, but this isn't the way. Amanda's sick, too; she doesn't deserve to die.'

She stopped shouting, watching the two people in the spotlight. Cain's expression was a mixture of shock and confusion, but Wells' was of pure remorse. He half crumpled, stepping back as the hammer dropped from his wavering hand.

'No!' Cain screamed, as the three armed officers descended on Wells, kicking his legs out from under him, pinning him down. The doctor stumbled backwards, stunned, clearly not having expected to walk away from her grim pact.

'Amanda.' Hawkins moved forwards, still having to

shout over the helicopter's noise, aware of Mike coming in beside her. They closed to within a few feet. The doctor was still staring at Wells, now being handcuffed by Bishop's men.

'It's okay.' Hawkins reached for her arm. 'Let us help –'

But she didn't finish the sentence. Cain spun, avoiding her.

'Wait.' Hawkins tried to grab her coat. Maguire lunged, too, but the doctor moved with surprising speed, dropping out of range, turning away.

They both followed as Cain ran towards the layby. The woman was fast but clearly distraught. Her cry had changed into more of a desperate wail, audible even above the helicopter's roar. She stumbled, scrambling back into her stride as the two detectives closed in. For a second Hawkins felt relief, expecting the disorientated doctor to try taking one of the abandoned cars, a futile strategy they could easily curb. But as Cain passed between the vehicles, Hawkins realized with horror that she wasn't heading for either of them.

She was going for the road.

'Stop her!' she yelled at Maguire, who had pulled ahead, but he was too late. Cain didn't hesitate as she passed the X5 and burst into the near carriageway, causing a car to veer into the Armco barrier on the far side, a shower of sparks exploding upwards as contact was made.

But the next car didn't swerve.

It barely braked before ploughing into Cain, smashing her legs away and flicking her sideways on to the bonnet. Hawkins heard the crack as the doctor's head hit the windscreen, before she was thrown up and over the car's roof in a graceful arc, torpid limbs flailing as her body dropped back on to the road.

64

Hawkins eased the interview room door shut, releasing the handle, hearing the mechanism crank into place. Outside, Lavender Hill police station was fortified with security airlocks, coded access panels and endemic CCTV. Some criminals were intimidated by that sort of thing. But others definitely weren't. Modern legislation meant that if a prisoner didn't want to talk, there was pretty much bugger all you could do about it, and Hawkins had the distinct feeling her latest subject would be tougher than most.

She turned to see Mike settling into one of the plastic chairs behind the desk set against the right-hand wall.

And, opposite him, the daunting figure of Marlon Wells.

The ex-soldier's shaved head was bowed, but he looked even stockier in this confined space: not tall, but powerfully set. Hawkins wondered whether the single pair of plastic cuffs currently binding his wrists would be sufficient, should he decide to test their strength.

Twelve hours ago she'd arrested Wells on suspicion of murdering three people – almost four. At the time he'd been forcibly restrained by three armed officers, which made it tricky to judge anyone's underlying mood, before being bundled into a meat wagon and brought here to spend a pacifying night in the cells. She didn't expect him to have slept, especially after last night's traumatic events, perhaps having now realized the true gravity of his deeds. Unsurprisingly, he looked drained, slouching in the chair with hands clasped in his lap, a vacant stare resting somewhere between his knees and the floor.

Hawkins' mind alighted briefly on the less serious casualties of their chase: Aaron Sharpe had walked away with nothing more dramatic than bruising to ego and limbs, while Amala Yasir had suffered mild concussion and was still under observation in a hospital bed. Both had been fortunate to escape further injury, considering the expired state Wells' other recent acquaintances now shared.

Hawkins took her seat, assessing their detainee. The small window set high in the far wall was closed, although, even fully open, it would have had trouble expelling the pungent tang of sweat coming from Wells, suggesting his mind hadn't been on the present for a while. It could all have been an elaborate front, of course, driving towards a soft mental-health-facility stay rather than a throw-away-the-key jail term, but Hawkins' instinct said not. Despite killing three people, he'd received substantial help from his complicit victims. The chase, once established, had been over quickly, and he'd made several big mistakes, such as the repeated use of both weapon and MO.

There was no criminal mastermind here.

Which made the outcome of this interview even more critical. It was unlikely that Wells and the ex-convicts could have known about each other without assistance from a third party, so if the ex-soldier hadn't operated alone, then what would any former accessory do next?

Now it was all about finding any partners in crime. Knowledge of the ex-soldier's identity made that less of a challenge, but it would still take time. And the public nature of last night's action meant news of an arrest – and speculation about the reason for it – was already starting to break, which gave any potential accomplices time and warning to fabricate alibis or take off. Soon, anyone with an interest in making themselves scarce would be far, far away. So their best option was to convince Wells to give them a name.

But his apparently ingenuous demeanour was a worry in itself.

Often, the police were the first point of contact for someone in psychological crisis, so Home Office legislation was predictably tight. Thankfully, due to his hammer-wielding antics, Hawkins hadn't needed to have Wells sectioned under the Mental Health Act in order to bring him in, but if his behaviour proved irrational here she'd be forced to curtail the interview and have him professionally assessed by a mental-health practitioner. In such cases, supposing unfavourable results, the proverbial woodwork immediately began haemorrhaging social workers, all sorts of time restrictions came into play, and everyone started getting touchy about potential mistreatment of the infirm. And, if they were really unlucky, given Wells' documented history of PTSD, a forensic medical examiner might declare him unfit for interview.

Typically, it took less than ten minutes to establish if a prisoner was emotionally stable, so unless Wells stayed silent or decided he was in the mood for disclosure, their initial line of questioning was key.

Hawkins nodded at Maguire, who started the recording equipment. She introduced the session and its occupants before directing her first question to Wells, opening cautiously: 'Can I call you Marlon?'

The ex-soldier's head lifted slightly in response to his name, but his gaze remained vacant.

She adjusted her approach. 'Lance Corporal?'

Nothing.

Hawkins drove on, conscious of time. 'I appreciate you're military, so I won't bore you with civilian fluff. You're here because you murdered Rosa Calano, Samantha Philips and Matthew Hayes. And we narrowly stopped you doing the same to Amanda Cain.'

No response.

'We found the letters.'

Wells looked at her, the empty stare turning to sharp focus, his head tilting like a dog trying to understand its owner. Or a predator assessing game.

Hawkins maintained eye contact. 'We know they wanted to die.'

The ex-soldier looked away, his gaze dropping back into space, his expression now approximating remorse. But there was no room for pity yet.

'What I would like to know,' Hawkins said, 'is how they found you . . . how they knew where to send the letters.'

Silence.

'Who put you in touch?' Hawkins pressed, glancing at the clock. They'd already had five minutes. This stand-off couldn't go on long, but Wells' first response might be decisive. If he displayed even the smallest sign of feeling under duress or imbalanced it was mental-assessment time, while a request for legal representation would introduce a similar choking complication. So, when they came, his quiet, muttered words were a surprise.

'Is she okay?'

It took Hawkins a moment to work out he was talking about Cain. Everything had happened so fast once Wells had surrendered that she hadn't considered the possibility he didn't know what happened to the doctor afterwards. Obviously, he'd been there when she was hit by the car, but being held face down by three armed officers and then dragged into the back of a van was a fair distraction, evidently sufficient to ensure he had no knowledge of subsequent events.

She paused, watching the minute tremors now

chipping away at his expression. Perhaps the realization that appeared to wash over him the previous night had stuck. His interest wasn't just curiosity, it was *concern*.

Hawkins spoke gently, aware that his reaction might be detrimental to their investigation. But it could also be the breakthrough she craved. 'Cain's dead.'

His brow tightened, and ever so slightly he shook his head. 'How?'

She explained.

Wells listened until she was finished before looking down at the desk. He closed his eyes. 'Did she suffer?'

'Maybe for a second. Our pathologist thinks the impact of her head on the windscreen was instantly fatal. She wouldn't have felt anything after that.'

Wells exhaled slowly, raising his head again to look at them. 'What happens now?'

'Prison. Your case is unusual, but the law says assisted suicide is still murder. You killed three people.'

He nodded. 'They didn't feel it. I made sure.'

'Fair enough' – Hawkins saw her chance – 'but how do you know your associate won't carry on? What if the next person they find to do your job isn't so humane?'

She didn't mention that she'd already arranged for Wells' future mail to be redirected to a psychiatric char-ity. At least that way any outstanding would-be victims would receive help instead of a fatal blow to the head.

'Come on, Marlon,' Maguire joined in. 'An ex-military

444

colleague with links to the parole board? A friend in the CPS? Who is it?'

They both shut up, watching Wells wrestle with his conscience, his concern clearly not for himself. The stress-induced detachment that had allowed him to assassinate three people had gone for now, a change emphasized by his capitulation the previous night, but now they were testing his loyalty: a requisite trait in someone drilled to rely absolutely on his peers, and be relied absolutely upon.

Hawkins saw the panic build as the ex-soldier's head dropped again; his chest began to heave. She glanced at Maguire, checking he was ready for any explosive response. They were rattling a man on the edge. He might clam up, fall apart or attack, none of which helped their cause. But, just maybe, he'd give up his source.

The tension grew as Hawkins watched the clock edge past ten minutes, into the critical zone. She was so focused on what could go wrong that she jumped when Wells spoke two simple words. But when her brain decoded what he'd said, she almost fell off the chair.

Because she recognized the name.

65

'Wait there, please.' The secretary stood, her tone rising as Hawkins strode past with Maguire and two uniforms in tow. 'You can't just –'

She danced awkwardly around her desk and caught up as the two detectives reached the inner door. But Mike blocked her advance as Hawkins entered, without knocking.

They burst one by one into a large office with thick grey carpet and floor-to-ceiling shelves lined with ornaments and books. Subtle down-lighting bathed two leather armchairs and a glass coffee table in its delicate glow. Beyond them, several open folders and an ornamental lamp adorned a heavy wooden desk.

From behind which Pierce Reid looked up.

'I'm sorry, Mr Reid,' the secretary announced, 'I tried to stop them.'

'It's all right, Lynn.' The counsellor rose, pushing his glasses up his nose, calmly closing his laptop. 'I'm sure the interruption is necessary. Please tell Mrs Williams I'll be with her as soon as possible.'

The secretary complied, scowling at Hawkins as she backed out of the room. There was silence until the door closed.

'DCI Hawkins,' Reid said pensively. 'And . . . ?'

Maguire nodded. 'DI Maguire, Constables Grayling and Weir.'

'Okay.' The counsellor retook his seat. 'So what can I do for you?'

Hawkins moved closer, not in the mood for pleasantries. 'Tell us about Marlon Wells.'

Reid frowned, shook his head. 'Sorry, I'm not familiar.'

'Really?' She produced a photograph of Wells from her bag and slid it across the desk. 'He remembers you.'

'Hmm.' He studied the picture. 'I don't know him, but it's possible he was a client. Generally, my patients arrive at pivotal times in their lives, which often means they come to regard me as more of a friend than a professional acquaintance. An awkward side effect of my work, I'm afraid. I'll check my records. Why do you ask?'

'We arrested him last night,' Hawkins said evenly, 'for murdering three people.' She laid down more photos, pointing to each one in turn. 'Rosa Calano, Samantha Philips, Matthew Hayes.'

'That's tragic.' Reid's tone remained typically calm. 'I hope you aren't suggesting my failure to rehabilitate an alleged client makes me accountable for his or her future conduct.'

'Not exactly.' She waved a hand at the new pictures. 'How many of these people do you recognize?'

The counsellor returned her gaze for a second before looking down at them.

'Samantha.' He placed a finger on Philips' image. 'You know very well that I carried out her pre-release assessment a few weeks ago.'

'How about the others?'

Reid sighed. 'Again, it isn't beyond the realms of possibility. As you're aware, I conduct similar sessions for a dozen correctional facilities – hundreds of cases a year. Call it professional detachment, but I don't commit every harrowing interaction to memory, Detective. Do you?'

She ignored him. 'Actually, we checked with the centres in question. Matthew Hayes' assessment was carried out by a Richard Ellison, while Rosa Calano saw a consultant called Jameson Mane.'

The counsellor frowned. 'Surely that answers your question.'

'I thought so, too.' She looked at Maguire, who added a copy of Matthew Hayes' letter to the growing pile on Reid's desk. 'Until we realized they all wanted to die. Although, for whatever reason, they were unwilling or unable to end their lives themselves. So they contacted Marlon Wells, who was prepared to help out. Obviously, you can't advertise a service like that, which means somebody put them in touch. He says that was you.'

Their subject straightened. 'That's quite an allegation.'

'Yes, it is. But I also find it hard to believe the victims would have taken up such a virulent offer without encouragement, especially when you had both the opportunity and the expertise to recognize their suicidal tendencies and steer them off that path.' She watched the counsellor's eyes narrow. 'Which is why I think you played an active part in convincing them that they wanted to die.'

Reid gave a disbelieving laugh. 'Are you suggesting I'm in league with these other counsellors?'

'Not at all.' Hawkins made her final play. 'The signature logs may show three different therapists, but there had to be a link somewhere, so I had the CCTV footage checked; it's amazing how much storage these modern systems have, isn't it? Oddly, the three counsellors share a strikingly similar appearance – yours, in fact. So, no, I'm not suggesting you're in league with Ellison and Mane, I'm suggesting you *are* Ellison and Mane.'

She stopped, watching his face. The truth was that since Wells' revelation about Reid earlier in the day they'd only been able to obtain footage of Matthew Hayes' visitor, showing the man who signed in as Richard Ellison at a distance from behind. His build and hair matched Reid's, but it was hardly conclusive. For now, the rest was conjecture.

Reid said nothing, so she pressed harder. 'You must have planned it in advance; otherwise, you wouldn't have used a false name the first time, for Calano's assessment.'

She let the claim hang, radiating confidence, holding her breath. The counsellor stared through her and

Maguire for a few seconds, as if deciding whether to drag his heels or come clean. If he chose to fight, they'd have to rely on the testimony of Wells – someone with a clear incentive to transfer as much blame as possible on to others, guilty or not – plus any more evidence they could find between now and an eventual trial. Even if it came down to statements from prison staff, it should be possible to prove that Reid had seen all three victims pre-release, but she was willing to bet there were no transcripts or recordings of the sessions, and none of the subjects would be much good as witnesses now. They had the letters, of course, but there was no proof that Reid had told the victims where to send them. The air seemed to thicken as time passed.

At last the counsellor moved, taking off his glasses and placing them gently on the desk. He rubbed his eyes with thumb and forefinger for a long moment. Then he looked up at his visitors, taking a deep breath that came out in a protracted sigh.

'Fine,' he said quietly. 'You're right.'

Hawkins blinked. *Was that a confession?*

She shook her head. 'Why?'

Reid's gaze dropped, and there was another pause as he appeared to order his thoughts. Eventually, he spoke, with the decorous air of a man resigned to his fate, but also of someone justifying his faith, in a soft, almost poetic tone.

'All parties consented, Detective. Malice was never involved. Grief and remorse are a potent blend; they override logic and cause, but they don't always lead to recklessness. Sometimes they provide clarity where, previously, hope was lost. Those people were already dead; they merely lacked the strength to complete the physical transition. But if somebody craves release, ultimately, they will find a way. Marlon and I simply offered painless means.'

Hawkins nodded, remembering the events of the previous night: Amanda Cain running into the traffic, twisting through the air, hitting the ground. An ambulance had arrived within minutes, but the paramedic's doleful headshake told everyone that was that.

They will find a way.

She stowed the thought. 'You're suggesting that Wells played a part in organizing all of this?'

The counsellor paused, looking towards the window and the drab Southwark skyline beyond. Hawkins waited, picturing the ex-soldier in his cell at Lavender Hill: sullen, withdrawn. After giving them Reid's name, he'd clammed up, apparently overwhelmed by his own actions since having been offered a renewed glimpse of sanity. Ironically, he seemed more shocked than anyone about what he'd done to his victims, and what he'd almost done to Amanda Cain. But it was the doctor's suicide that appeared to affect him most, as if his failure had forced her down the very path he'd sworn to help her avoid.

Reid sighed. 'It was Marlon's idea.'

'So let's get this straight.' Hawkins felt the anger rise.

'A war veteran comes in with post-traumatic stress, seeking professional help. He tells you he wants to rect-ify a personal tragedy by killing the depressed, and your way of helping is to provide a list of *nominees*?'

He glared at her, and when he spoke it was with an edge in his voice. 'Oh, come on, Detective, it's little more than euthanasia.'

'Bullshit. You exploited them. What was it: bore-dom? You're sick of appeasing the deranged?'

'*Deranged?*' Reid stood suddenly, making Maguire straighten. 'Don't give me that conformist nonsense, Detective. I know you see these people in your line of work, individuals so damaged by the world's brutality that they become totally unable to deal with everyday life. Some resort to crime, hurting others to redress the balance for themselves, but there are also those who just want a way out. Legal fights are in progress all over the world to allow the sick to decide when enough's enough.' His voice continued rising. 'No one should have to endure the torture of unwanted life. Locked-in syndrome, paralysis, disease – these things are tangible, so it's easy to argue about whether it's right to let the sufferer die if they like. But I deal with the unseen trauma caused by mental distress, invisible purgatory borne by more people than most of us like to admit. Where are *their* rights? How do *they* find release? And what if they don't have the will to take their own lives? Where do they go? Marlon was a hero to them, and he was proud to be.'

'You're wrong.' Hawkins shook her head. 'Marlon's curled up in one of our cells, distraught. He thought he was doing the right thing till last night, when he watched Amanda Cain kill herself because you convinced her she was beyond reprieve. Marlon never would have chosen to kill others suffering like himself if you hadn't told him it was justified. But now he recognizes the truth: that you masterminded the whole thing, using him to keep the blood off your suit.'

Reid held her stare for a moment. Then he sat, crossing his arms, visibly calming himself. 'Not at all. Marlon saw it as penance: a way to compensate for the wretched event that won't let him be. He understands the agonizing paradox of survival instinct and death wish caused by inadvertently taking innocent life. All he wants is to atone for his mistake, and I've treated countless patients over the years who would gladly have accepted his offer. So, yes, I played my part, but the so-called victims did, too. They wrote the letters, left their homes alone after dark. *They* gave him the opportunity to strike.'

Hawkins fought to keep her voice steady. 'Yes, they did, but *you* led them to it. You were their last hope, a trusted practitioner with a duty of care. But instead you nurtured their misery, validated their distress and then offered them an easy way out.'

'No, Detective,' Reid hissed. 'I offered *mercy*, that's all. Most of my clients aren't hopeless; I rehabilitate where I can. But there are those beyond redemption, even in their own eyes. Can you *begin* to imagine what it's like, stalling at the final threshold, beaten by weakness, being forced to live on in pain?'

'The problem,' Hawkins said, signalling for the constables to cuff him, 'is that you conducted it all. You steered Wells to murder when you could have turned him away. You fuelled the victims' desperation, and then you put them in touch. *You* made the critical decisions – judgements that were never yours to make.'

Reid started to say something else, but Hawkins had heard enough. She turned away as the two uniforms pulled the counsellor upright and marched him towards the door. He was already protesting about being seen by his patients, but the officers' expressions said they felt no more sympathetic about that than Hawkins did. It was only as he disappeared through the door that she allowed herself to wonder what Steve Tanner was doing at that moment, having been forced to release his prized suspect, following Wells' categorical statement that no one else except Reid was involved.

She turned to Mike. 'Is there some sort of lesson here about life being too short to let your future be controlled by your past?'

A wry smile skirted his lips. 'Isn't there always?'

'Then let's get home and have that talk with my dad.' She leaned in for a kiss. 'I think it's about time he moved out.'